UNLOCK

# Kingoom

*The Battle for Walt Disney's Magic Kingdom*

# Jeff Dixon

Deep River
B O O K S

Jeff Dixon
www.jeffdixon.org
www.unlockingthekingdombook.com
jdixon@touchandchange.com

*Unlocking the Kingdom: The Battle for Walt Disney's Magic Kingdom*
© 2012 Jeff Dixon

Published by
Deep River Books
Sisters, Oregon
www.deepriverbooks.com

ISBN 13: 9781937756512
ISBN 10: 1937756513

Library of Congress: 2012951259

Printed in the USA

Cover design by Joe Bailen, Contajus Designs

## For My Mom

I have watched you face a changing world with bravery, dignity, and style.
Your strength and faith have given me a glimpse of the Savior in you.
You are an inspiration, and I love you.

## Author's note

This book is built upon the following facts:

**November 15, 1965**—The Disney brothers, Walt and Roy, met at the Cherry Plaza Hotel in Orlando, Florida for a press conference. Seated with Florida Governor Haydon Burns, they announced to the public their plans to build a new Disney theme park in Central Florida.

**December 15, 1966**—Walter Elias Disney passed away at the age of 65 in St. Joseph's Hospital in Burbank, California.

**December 16, 1966**—A private memorial ceremony was held at the Little Church of the Flowers at Forest Lawn Cemetery in Glendale, California. No announcement of the funeral was made until after it had taken place. Only members of the immediate family were in attendance. Forest Lawn officials refused to disclose any details of the funeral or disposition of the body, stating only that "Mr. Disney's wishes were very specific and had been spelled out in great detail."

**January 1967**—Disney department heads were invited to a screening room at the Disney Studios. Sitting in assigned seats, they viewed a film featuring Walt Disney sitting behind his desk and addressing them as individuals, gesturing toward them as he spoke, and laying out future plans. Roy Disney postponed his retirement to complete the Florida project.

**February 2, 1967**—Roy Disney is the host at Wometco's Park Theatre in Central Florida for Project Florida. This invitation-only event screens the film *Walt Disney World Resort: Phase 1* followed by a press conference. The film included portions of the documentary EPCOT featuring Walt Disney filmed just months before his death.

**October 1, 1971**—The Walt Disney World Resort opened the gates to the Magic Kingdom theme park.

**October 23, 1971**—Roy Disney dedicated the Magic Kingdom theme park based upon the philosophies and vision of his brother, Walt Disney. Roy passed away less than two months later.

**October, 1973**—The Western River Expedition is forever lost as a great Disney attraction that would never be built as planned.

**November, 2010**—A novel, *The Key to the Kingdom*, a work of factual fiction is released for the first time.

**Today**—The lives and legacy of Walt and Roy Disney continue to touch the lives of people around the world.

 *Day One*
*Morning*

"MOVE!" THE BOOMING VOICE of Reginald Cambridge echoed in Hawk's ears.

"Keep up," Hawk called back over his shoulder as the two men raced around and through the crowds of people leisurely walking across the bridge into Adventureland.

Heart hammering and driven by dread, he ran, in stark contrast to the others around him. The Magic Kingdom of Walt Disney World was brimming with guests beginning their day in the bright Florida sun. Startled tourists scampered to get out of the path of the two men charging through their midst. Hawk sidestepped between people, trying to find open areas where he could pick up his pace without running over and hurting anyone.

Suddenly a child broke loose from his parent's hand and darted into Hawk's path. Planting his foot, Hawk veered to his left, putting him on a collision course with Bwana Bob's souvenir stand and a Disney cast member tending the cash register. Having avoided the child, Hawk now was confronted with a wide-eyed young lady who didn't have time to move out of his way. He grabbed her in a bear hug and spun around, wildly out of control and trying to regain enough balance to keep both of them from falling. Lifting the girl off the ground and using her as a human counterweight, he slowed his momentum and regained his footing. Gently he lowered her back to the ground.

The young cast member looked up into the face of her unexpected dance partner. She caught his sleeve before he could move away. "Grayson Hawkes." She gingerly placed weight on her right foot and grimaced.

"Hawk." He smiled with concern. "Call me Hawk. Are you alright?"

"Fine . . . I'm great." She steadied herself, using his arm for support. "I just twisted my ankle a bit, but I'm fine."

Dr. Grayson Hawkes exhaled with relief, realizing she wasn't seriously hurt. Her reaction at seeing him almost amused him. It had been nearly eighteen months since he'd become the chief creative architect for the Walt Disney Company. Like most people, he hadn't known what the CCA position entailed when he was introduced to the organization, but it had quickly become apparent it meant he was now the boss. Right now, being the boss meant he had to keep moving, but he could spare a second to apologize for almost trampling one of his cast members. "You're sure you're not hurt?"

"Yes, I think I'm fine."

"Sorry about bumping into you like this." Hawk freed himself from her grip while reading her name badge. "It was nice to meet you, Barbie."

In an instant Hawk was moving again. He accelerated through the crowd of onlookers who had stopped to see the collision at Bwana Bob's. Some of the gawkers realized they had just seen the new leader of the Walt Disney Company—cameras clicked and peopled shouted his name as he disappeared from view under the tribal masks on the gates of Adventureland.

Hawk raced past the Magic Carpets of Aladdin and caught up with Reginald at Caribbean Plaza. Now running side by side, the two ran past the entrance to Pirates of the Caribbean and into the shopping area beyond it. The congestion of people slowed their pace, and the buzz of the crowd crackled with a higher energy level than normal. Hawk slid in behind Reginald, as he cleared a path in the thickening ocean of people.

"You should let me handle this situation, boss." Reginald tossed the suggestion over his shoulder.

"Just keep on moving." Hawk raised his voice to be heard over the crowd.

"Keep up," Reginald answered, with just the hint of a smile cracking his lips.

He placed his hand on his guide's back and pushed firmly as they plowed a path through the people. Stepping out of the traffic flow, they entered an unmarked doorway leading them out of the public area of the Plaza. When they emerged into an alley of drab walls dotted with unmarked doors, a panicked cast member named Bill scurried over to them and gave a radio to Reginald.

"What do we have?" Hawk looked past Bill to the door propped ajar behind him.

"We're currently evacuating Pirates of the Caribbean."

"The entire attraction?" Hawk felt tensing muscles crawl up his neck.

"Yes, sir . . . everyone," Bill responded, joining the two men resolutely heading toward the doorway.

"Why?"

"It's gotten a little bit manic in there," Bill said, his eyes darting between them.

Reginald's head snapped back toward Bill as he paused with his hand on the doorknob.

JEFF DIXON

"Explain."

"We found a body floating face down in the water." In a glance, Hawk and Reginald registered their concern as they moved through the portal into the Pirates of the Caribbean. Blinking while his eyes adjusted to the darkness, Hawk heard Reginald call for additional security.

Reginald Cambridge served as the chief security officer for the Walt Disney Company. His job was far more complicated than Hawk completely understood, but Reginald was excellent at what he did. He was fair and fearless, perhaps intimidating to most, and always in close proximity to wherever Hawk happened to be. Over the past year and a half, the two had become friends and had forged a close bond.

Bill, Reginald, and Hawk moved through the dimly lit offstage corridors that wound behind the sets of the water-filled attraction. While Reginald barked commands into the radio, Hawk pressed Bill for more details.

"Tell me what happened." Hawk pushed forward along the corridor.

"Everything was going fine. The attraction was operating properly. The guest flow through the attraction was steady." Hawk's raised eyebrow prompted Bill to provide the information Hawk was really looking for. "Even though our crowds are extremely high, the wait time was not exceptionally long. We had a guest in a boat start screaming in the burning-city section of the attraction. Then more started screaming, and then the belts in the unload area stopped . . ."

Hawk inhaled sharply. "Stopped?"

"Yes, they just stopped, so we couldn't get anybody off the ride in the unloading area."

"So the attraction shut down?" Hawk tried to process what he was walking into.

"Well, sort of, but something strange happened."

"Tell me," Hawk said as he craned his neck, battling the stiffening muscles.

"The unload area shut down, but the belts in the loading area didn't shut off; they just kept running, sending boats into the attraction."

"Did anyone get hurt?"

"Oh, no," Bill assured him. "It was frightening for the guests in the queue line waiting to board. They saw boat after boat go racing past. But no one was hurt."

"So the attraction is full of boats?"

"Yes, most of them empty, but they're jammed up in there. And the body is just floating dead in the water."

Hawk's head snapped toward Bill. His eyes narrowed.

"Uh . . . sorry," Bill stammered. "Poor choice of words. We're having problems in there."

Hawk hustled past Reginald, as the security chief coordinated his team in and around the attraction. Bill gestured toward a nondescript door to their right, and Hawk swallowed hard.

Bill hesitated. "This entrance will put you closest to the problem."

"You mean the body."

"Yes, sir."

Placing a hand on the door and giving it a shove, Grayson Hawkes bounded into the burning city.

 *Day One*
Morning

PIRATES OF THE CARIBBEAN WEAVES through looted and pillaged towns, a dark boat voyage that takes guests into the heart of a pirate adventure. Due to the huge popularity of the Pirates of the Caribbean film series, additional characters have been added to the ride, and a whole new generation of guests flock to enjoy the attraction.

Hawk stepped into the "set" of the attraction and saw an endless line of boats now backed up on the waterway. Walking out onto a bridge over the water gave him a better view of the chaos below as he searched for what to do next. He stepped around a pirate and a parrot that normally the guests would look up at as the ride passed underneath. Glancing to his left and right, he saw guests being evacuated from their boats onto the set area itself and led behind the scenes and out of the attraction. The boats directly in front of Hawk were empty. Bill stepped up beside him and pointed out into the water, where a chilling shape floated. Quickly Hawk jumped down off the bridge onto the front of the empty boat beneath him. He high-stepped over each row of seats until he reached the back, then he jumped onto the front of the next boat in line. Again and again, he leaped from seat to seat until he got closer to the body drifting along the waterway.

Reginald, having appeared behind the animatronic pirate on the bridge, bellowed something unintelligible to Hawk.

"What?" Hawk paused in the boat. He leaned back toward Reginald, trying to hear him over the singing pirates and the driving theme song from the Pirates of the Caribbean films.

"Why hasn't anybody cut the soundtrack yet?" Reginald roared into his radio. "Do it now!" Turning back to Hawk, he shouted, "Paramedics are on their way inside now." The *now* echoed in the building as the soundtrack suddenly cut off.

"Good." Hawk turned away and jumped off the boat into the dark chilly water.

His feet found the bottom and slipped slightly as he took his first step. Over his shoulder he heard Bill anxiously shout, "Shouldn't we wait until the paramedics get here?"

"It is very rare that Grayson Hawkes waits to do anything," Cambridge answered in a loud voice, as he jumped down onto the front of the boat in front of him. Hawk glanced back and saw his friend following the same path he had taken over the boats.

Hawk sloshed through the waist-deep water as the reflection of the fire effects danced across the surface. The body in front of him was rocking back and forth, face down. Getting closer, he could see it was a woman wearing a billowing dress that rippled over the swells in the water. The dress wasn't the typical attire of the theme park's guests. Surging forward, he grabbed her by both shoulders. In one motion, he flipped her over in the water and positioned his hand behind her head. When he bent to begin CPR, he saw the woman's face and paused.

Cambridge leaned over the side of the boat. "What's wrong?"

Hawk shoved the body toward the boat like a raft in a swimming pool. Reginald watched as she drifted toward him and with an unceremonious clunk hit the side of the boat he was standing in.

"She's animatronic!" Hawk shook water off his arms with an exaggerated motion.

"Well, isn't that interesting?" Reginald reached down and hoisted the body into the boat.

The audio-animatronic figure was life sized, but as with many of the figures used in attractions throughout the theme parks, only the parts that were seen by the public looked lifelike. This woman was really just a plastic-and-metal mesh structure with a realistic head, arms, and legs. The hollow body gave the figure a surprising buoyancy similar to that of a raft. Lifting her and laying her on the seat in front of him, the security chief turned back toward the water to look down at his boss.

Hawk had now arrived back at the boat. His arms were crossed along the edge of the vessel, and he was resting his head. He grinned. "You can tell the paramedics not to hurry."

"I'm not so sure I'm satisfied with their response time." Reginald turned back as he heard them enter. "They should have been here sooner."

"You can yell at them after you help me get out of the water." Hawk extended an arm, and Reginald grasped his hand and lifted him up. Hawk placed a foot on the side of the boat and effortlessly landed in the boat next to him. The hands-on work of a chief creative architect had drastically transformed Hawk, who used to be sadly out of shape. As water dripped into the bottom of the boat, they peered over at the animatronic victim stretched out on the seat.

"Are you thinking what I'm thinking?" Hawk continued to stare at the soggy female scrap-pile in the boat.

"That you're relieved that she's not real, and that no harm has come to any of our guests?"

"I'm relieved and thrilled that no one is hurt, that's true. But that's not what I'm thinking."

"You are thinking," Reginald calculated, "how did this audio-anima-tronic creation end up floating face down in the water?"

"Nope."

"Hmmm." Reginald pursed his lips. "You're thinking that this is a very unlikely accident and that our female friend here did not just jump in the canal by herself."

"Not that either, although I'm sure I will think about all of those things later."

"Very well, it's apparent that I don't know what you're thinking."

"I'm thinking about how cold that water was and how much I could use a towel right now." Hawk now turned his head toward Reginald and winked. "And I really am glad no one is hurt."

The boat they were standing in lurched in the water, causing them to wobble. Looking forward, Hawk could see the boats in front of them were empty and had started to move. As the boat floated along the river, it would momentarily pause as boats further up the line were caught by the belt and pulled up and out of the water. On shore, Bill started walking alongside their boat.

"So, the body is a piece of the attraction?"

"I guess." Hawk took a seat and plowed through the scenarios that would have taken place for the body to end up in the water. The grim reality he couldn't think past was that no sequence of events allowed him to conclude it might have happened by accident. Pondering why someone would have done this deed caused him to plop into the seat, to stay on the boat for the rest of the ride. "Did we get everyone out?"

"Yes, sir, and no one was hurt."

"Were they taken care of?"

"Yes sir, we have been trying to make sure that every guest is satisfied as always." Bill responded.

"Give them each a pass, please." Hawk instructed Bill.

"They all are receiving Fastpasses."

"No, bypassing a line isn't enough this time. I mean a one-day pass." Hawk noticed the surprise on Bill's face. Normally a Fastpass was given to visitors who needed compensation for unsatisfactory experiences. "I want each of our inconvenienced guests to get a free admission ticket to come back to the Magic Kingdom. Got it?"

"I'll take care of it." Bill, still on foot, had reached a break in the set piece. The boat traveled under a bridge, which kept him from walking along with it any farther.

"You're very generous," Reginald said as he took a seat next to Hawk, content to ride the rest of the way out of the attraction.

"Why thank you, I try to be." Hawk turned, his face growing serious. "I want to know what happened here, Reginald. I want to know why there's an audio-animatronic figure floating beside our boats, I want to know why no one pulled the body out of the water until we arrived, and I want to know how it got there."

"You want me to close the attraction for the rest of the day?"

"Yes." He glanced over at the prisoners behind bars trying to convince the dog holding the key to come over to them so they could snatch it. He inhaled slowly and deeply, held his breath momentarily, and then exhaled, trying to blow away the tension clawing at him. "What I really want to know is how we lost control of the attraction. That can't happen. It's impossible. Yet this morning, for some reason, it did happen. Reginald, I want to know why."

"I seek to know things as well. I'm on it."

"Thanks. Get everyone that needs to be there in my office later to debrief this."

Their boat jerked for a few seconds as the belt drive system of the Pirates of the Caribbean ride lifted them into the unloading area of the attraction. The boat squeaked to a stop as they got up to exit. Hawk stepped out, water still dripping from his soaked clothing. Reginald stepped out of the boat then went around the exit barrier and stepped back in a row, gesturing for the ride attendant to make sure the boat stayed in place. Reaching down, he gripped the artificial woman by her arms and lifted her up. "I'll also try to figure out where she came from." He nodded toward Hawk. "Perhaps you should stop at the gift shop at the top of the ramp. Maybe you can purchase a beach towel with a pirate on it."

"I might just do that." Hawk turned to head up the ramp. He hesitated and then turned back toward the boats. "Reginald, this little mess here doesn't feel right. What do you think happened?"

"What I think and what I know are very different right now, boss." Reginald shook the animatronic figure slightly. "Let me see what I can find, then what I know will help us both think more clearly."

 *Day One*
Morning

HAWK TOOK CAMBRIDGE'S ADVICE and picked up a towel in Caribbean Plaza. Walking past the black sail emblazoned with the Pirates of the Caribbean logo, he escaped from the crowded street into a deserted backstage area.

His face had become more recognizable over the past few months, and it was getting extremely difficult for him to walk through a theme park unnoticed. In the last eighteen months, his influence had rippled throughout the company. In some circles it was believed that his leadership was second only to that of Walt Disney himself. Most days he didn't mind and took the notoriety in stride. Right now was not one of those times. Drying off after taking his dip in the Caribbean waters, he decided to walk back to his apartment. Winding through the backstage area, he arrived on Caribbean Way and turned left. This road, unseen by guests, would take him behind the scenes and allow him to walk behind the Jungle Cruise and eventually behind the buildings in the Town Square. This maintenance road was traveled by work trucks, golf carts, and any other motorized vehicle needed to keep the Magic Kingdom operating efficiently.

The pounding Florida sun was quickly drying his clothes with each step, while his mind was still saturated by what he had just seen. The image of the floating body both puzzled and troubled him as he walked. A white truck drove past, then slowed and came to a stop. Its backup lights warned him it was now coming in his direction again.

The driver pulled back next to him and greeted him with a cheerful smile. "You're Grayson Hawkes, right?"

"Yes, I am." Hawk stopped walking and turned to face the driver.

"Great to meet you." A hand reached out of the vehicle toward Hawk. "My name is Zeke Reitz, I work maintenance. Been here nearly twenty-five years now."

"Nice to meet you too." Hawk accepted the hand offered and shook it. "Call me Hawk. I've been here about eighteen months."

"Oh, I know who you are, everybody knows who you are." Zeke laughed. "You're our new boss."

"Sorry I haven't had the chance to meet you yet—it's been pretty busy—but it's good to get the chance to meet you now."

"You look like you've been swimming. You need a ride?"

Hawk glanced down at his dripping clothes. "We had a little event happen in Pirates. I was checking it out and got wet."

"An event, huh?" Zeke scratched his chin and looked into the distance. "I guess you could say we had an event this morning in Tomorrowland that I helped clean up."

"What kind of an event?" Hawk leaned in but was interrupted by a low humming noise coming from his left.

"Hawk!" Albert Shepherd waved as he erratically navigated a golf cart toward them. He was driving way too fast and didn't leave enough room to stop. Hawk pressed up against the truck as the cart skidded to a stop less than a foot away. "I'm glad I found you. Why aren't you answering your phone?"

"My phone?" Hawk turned slightly, wedged in the narrow space between the truck and the cart. Fishing his phone out of his pocket, he saw the screen was dark, and he realized why. "I had it in my pocket when I jumped into the water."

"Well, that explains why you look the way you do." Shep nodded apologetically to Zeke, then gestured for Hawk to get into the cart. "Sorry to interrupt you, but we have to go."

"Sure." Hawk turned again in the tight space back to Zeke. "Zeke, this is Albert Shepherd. Shep, this is Zeke." Hawk's curiosity consumed him—why was Shep here looking for him?

Both men nodded at each other as Hawk slipped out from between the two vehicles and strode around the front of the golf cart to the passenger seat. Stepping up on the edge of the cart, Hawk grabbed a hold of the top and looked over the roof toward Zeke.

"You mentioned you had to clean up an event in Tomorrowland. What was it?" Hawk refocused on the conversation they'd had earlier. The morning had already thrown him one surprise; his fear was that he was about to hear another.

"Yeah, well, you reminded me of it when you mentioned your event this morning." Zeke's hand again moved to stroke his chin. He stopped abruptly when Hawk impatiently starting drumming his fingers on the top of the cart. "It was odd, really, harmless but odd . . . When they started running the Carousel of Progress this morning, they found someone."

"What?" Hawk's stomach dropped like he was riding a roller coaster.

"Not someone. I guess some*thing* would be a better description." Zeke shook his head. "I'm not sure the best way to describe it, but there was a pirate sitting in one of the empty theaters of the attraction."

Shep turned his head toward Zeke. "Did you say a pirate?"

"Yep, just sitting there, pretty as you please." He shook his head. "Weren't real, you know, one of our audio-animatronic figures, I guess . . . kinda scared the cast members working, though. I was on a crew to make sure nothing else was wrong. We got the pirate out of there so they could open for the day. Weird, huh?"

"Yeah, weird . . ." Hawk felt Shep tap him on the arm from inside the cart.

"We need to go, Hawk." His voice had grown more urgent. Hawk noticed the change in tone and swallowed, only to find his throat had grown dry and tight.

"Good to finally meet you, Zeke. Thanks for all you do." Hawk's voice was now tense too. He stepped down and slid into the cart, as Shep pressed the accelerator.

Tires spinning briefly on asphalt, the golf cart lurched forward, pressing Hawk momentarily back into his seat. Leaving the maintenance truck behind, the two raced down Caribbean Way back toward Adventureland.

Albert "Shep" Shepherd had indeed been a friend to Grayson Hawkes for a while. Shep filled a role for the Walt Disney Company created especially for him by Hawk himself. He was an Imagineer who worked on a variety of special projects, usually assigned by the CCA, which meant that Hawk saw his friend almost daily.

"What's going on?" Hawk reached up and grabbed the front bar for support as the cart skidded to a stop.

"I've got something you need to see. Follow me." Shep jumped from the cart and headed back toward the door that would carry them into Caribbean Plaza.

For the second time today, Hawk found himself on a mad dash through the Magic Kingdom as he dodged strollers, guests, and scenery in Adventureland. Coming to a wide set of steps, the two men descended toward the entrance to the Jungle Cruise. Hawk noticed the wait time was fifty minutes, according to the sign, and people were jammed tightly into the queue area for the attraction. Bypassing the waiting lines by going through the exit, Hawk and Shep stepped onto an awaiting boat. The *Bomokandi Bertha*, one of the canopied launches usually packed with guests taking the jungle adventure, motored away from the dock with just Hawk, Shep, and the skipper on board.

"Welcome aboard, Hawk." The skipper nodded as he took the boat around the first bend of the attraction. "I'm Skipper Bobby, but when I'm not working, I'm Bobby Pike. It's nice to meet you. I've heard a great deal about you."

"Nice to meet you as well. Where are we going, Bobby?" Hawk tucked away yet another name in his mental file. Even after eighteen months, he'd met only a small fraction of the cast members; he intended to know them all by name, no matter how long it took. He stepped up next to the skipper as he spun the wheel on the boat.

The Jungle Cruise propels guests down four different rivers on three different continents: the Amazon in South America, the Congo and the Nile in Africa, and the Mekong River in Southeast Asia. Each bend in the river offers a variety of audio-animatronic animals and jungle residents. The skipper provides the narrative and bombards the passengers with silly jokes and bad puns. The result is a classic attraction loved by guests of all ages. It was one of Hawk's favorites, and he had ridden it many times. This private cruise through the winding rivers was different.

Entering the Mekong River area of the attraction, Skipper Bobby slowed down and cut on a spotlight as he navigated into the ruins of an ancient Cambodian temple. Never taking his eyes off the water, Bobby began unpacking why they were there.

"This morning, we were running a trip through the attraction like we always do, just to make sure everything was working and getting ready to bring our first tour of guests through. I found this." Bobby pointed his light onto the water ahead of them, just past the Bengal tiger with the glowing green eyes.

"Then I will assume this is not normal?" Hawk leaned forward as they grew closer and watched as the light traced the outline of something floating in the water.

"Right, this makes no sense." Bobby reduced the boat's speed as they approached the object, which was blocking their path.

*Amazon Annie*, another canopied launch, floated in the water in front of them. The spotlight illuminated the name on the top of the boat, and Hawk could see it was nearly identical to the one they were riding in. Bobby let the light drift to the back of the boat and held it in place so Hawk could see clearly, as the *Bomokandi Bertha* drifted to a stop right up next to the *Amazon Annie*. On the backseat of the boat sat a solitary pirate.

"No way." Hawk lunged to the side of the boat and jumped on board the *Amazon Annie*.

"Careful sir," Bobby cautioned, after Hawk had already made the transfer.

Hawk stepped to the back of the boat and picked up the pirate figure. It was an audio-animatronic form, fully detailed, minus the electronics used to bring it to life. Hawk lifted it, spun it around, and studied it closely.

"Now there's something you don't see every day." Shep stepped to the side of his boat and looked across at Hawk.

Hawk kept studying the pirate. "Bobby, is there any reason this boat should have been here?"

"No, sir. We account for each boat every night, and we never leave one adrift. Even if we did, it would never have a pirate on board. This is the Jungle Cruise—pirates belong next door."

"Right." Hawk glanced toward Shep with a look that told him to remain quiet. "Will this boat run?"

"It should." Skipper Bobby moved the light toward the bow of the boat. "The keys are in it. Do you want to try to crank it up?"

Hawk lowered the pirate back into the seat, stepped to the wheel, and turned the key. The *Amazon Annie* fired to life, and following a quick set of instructions from Bobby, Hawk had the boat in gear and moving. In just a few minutes, guests waiting in line to ride the Jungle Cruise craned their necks as the two boats come floating around the river bend toward the dock. The first was the *Bomokandi Bertha*, with Skipper Bobby and one passenger on board. The second was the *Amazon Annie*, with Skipper Grayson Hawkes and a pirate seated at the stern. Both launches pulled up to the dock, where cast members helped secure them. As Hawk stepped out of the boat, he carried the pirate figure and handed it to Shep.

"Is there any reason we can't go ahead and open the attraction?" Hawk looked toward the bulging line of guests waiting to board. Many of them were watching the activity in the disembarking area, taking pictures, and pointing to the unusual sight of staff manhandling an audio-animatronic pirate.

"No, Hawk, everything else seemed to be fine and in working order." Bobby followed Hawk's gaze to the crowds staring at them.

"Then let's get the attraction open." Hawk smiled and patted Bobby on the back. "Good call, letting me get a look at this. Thanks."

Hawk spun and motioned to Shep it was time to leave. The two friends began making their way out of the area. Hearing a rustling noise behind him, Hawk turned in time to see Shep hoisting the pirate figure over his shoulder in a fireman's carry position. They ignored the stares of the curious onlookers and moved back toward the Pirates attraction so they could retrieve their golf cart. Hawk saw the large frame of Reginald moving toward them. Halting in front of the pirate's ship sail, Cambridge raised an eyebrow as he inspected what Shep had slung over his shoulder.

"Interesting." Cambridge nodded toward the pirate figure.

"You don't know the half of it." Hawk shook his head. "Are we still inspecting the Pirates attraction?"

"Of course." The security chief paused. "There is something I believe you will want to examine."

"Alright, show me." Hawk moved back toward the entrance of Pirates of the Caribbean.

"No." Cambridge placed a firm hand on Hawk's arm, stopping him. "Not here."

The Disney CCA tilted his head slightly as he waited for Cambridge to continue. Following the gaze of the security officer, Hawk turned to Shep.

The pirate-toting Imagineer grinned and tilted his head toward his passenger. "If I'm going with you, I should probably do something with our friend here."

"That is probably the prudent thing to do," Cambridge agreed.

"Stash him in the golf cart." Hawk pointed to the gate that hid the vehicle from the public area. Shep moved off through the gate to deposit the figure on the seat of the cart. As they waited, Hawk studied Cambridge's face, trying to read what he wasn't telling him. Hawk opened his mouth to ask what was going on, but paused when several men wearing Disney security uniforms joined them.

"I asked them to help us get through the park with less distraction." Cambridge spoke before Hawk could. "It would be better if you were not stopped by guests. We need to get there without being sidetracked."

"Where are we going?" Hawk asked, as Shep rejoined the group. He knew curiosity had Shep on the brink of blurting out some observation, but with a quick glance he once again silenced him.

"Let me show you." Cambridge moved to the front of their troupe and motioned for them to follow.

 *Day One*
Morning

HAWK WALKED WITH THE SECURITY DETAIL through the passageway from Adventureland into Frontierland. Capturing the look of the Old
West, it was heavily influenced by Walt Disney's love for exploration and the
quest to find new frontiers. Stepping off the raised wooden sidewalk and into
the street, they pushed toward Liberty Square.

Hawk was always amazed and fascinated by the detail inside the Disney
theme parks. That attention to detail and the ability to notice things that
others missed had proven to be an invaluable skill less than two years ago.

After forming a close friendship with one of Walt Disney's most trusted
friends, Grayson Hawkes had been given a key with the challenge to take the
key and "do what Walt had done." It propelled him into a mystery full of
clues, hidden treasures to find, and puzzles to unravel, that ultimately had
led him to being named the chief creative architect of the entire company.
He had used his knowledge and love of all things related to Disney and had
been entrusted with the key to the kingdom. His role now was to guide and
lead the company in ways that would not only honor Walt but also secure the
direction that Walt envisioned for his creation to take. In many ways, Hawk's
rise to the highest position in the Walt Disney Company was one of the greatest Disney stories ever, created and designed by Walt and his brother Roy to
ensure that their dreams would always stay on track.

Hawk smiled, distracted by the memory of his quest to discover the key to
the kingdom; he had found some of the clues he needed on the streets of Frontierland and Liberty Square. Like an early American explorer, he had made some
great discoveries in these places. Upon entering Liberty Square, the ensemble
moved off to the left toward the Haunted Mansion. Rounding the corner, Hawk
noticed a sign indicating the attraction was closed and braced himself for the
sight of another unplanned addition to the display. The security detail dropped
off and went another direction, while Cambridge, Shep, and Hawk entered the

queue line and made their way along the ominous waiting area for the attraction. The stony eyes belonging to statues of the dearly departed watched them as they wove their way through the waiting line. Dodging monuments and twisting past the interactive tombs, they turned toward the entrance of the house.

"There." Cambridge stopped and pointed beyond a wrought-iron fence into a faux cemetery where guests could amuse themselves reading the witty tombstones set up into the tree line.

Hawk moved past him, closely followed by Shep. He gripped two of the bars of the fence and peered into the graveyard, following the imaginary line from the tip of Reginald's finger. A shadowy shape protruded from behind a tombstone near the top of the hill. Hawk looked more intently and noticed that the body was dressed in pirate garb.

"There's a dead pirate lying in the cemetery?" Shep asked the obvious.

"It is neither dead nor a real pirate," Cambridge stated dryly.

"Another audio-animatronic figure . . ." Hawk's stomach sank at the observation.

"Precisely."

"How did it get here, Uncle Reggie?" Shep turned toward Cambridge, calling him by a nickname he alone used for the security chief. A nickname that Reginald Cambridge usually ignored. This time he made an exception.

"That is what we must find out."

The security detail now emerged from behind the trees and trudged through the cemetery toward the body. Working his way down the hill, one of the men slipped, causing another to lose his balance; both slid across the ground until they were right on the pirate figure. Regaining their footing, they looked down through the iron bars toward the three men who were watching their descent.

"Careful," Hawk said with concern.

"Go ahead and move the pirate out of the area," Cambridge instructed.

"Reginald, there was another pirate figure found this morning in the Carousel of Progress," Hawk said, as he watched the men hoist the pirate up and cautiously retrace their steps back up the slippery slope, through tombstones and trees, with the animatronic figure in tow.

"Really?" Cambridge paused. "That is very interesting. We seem to be having an outbreak of displaced pirates this morning."

"Shep." Hawk addressed the Imagineer. "Make sure there's nothing else wrong with the Haunted Mansion, and let's get the attraction open. This is the fourth attraction today that has been down."

"Got it!" Shep headed toward the front doors of the mansion and disappeared inside the darkened entrance.

Hawk turned and leaned back against the cool metal bars in the queue line. Placing a hand on his chin, he drummed his fingers slowly along his jawline.

As he tried to process and assemble the events of the morning, he became aware of Cambridge standing quietly, staring at him. Hawk cut his eyes toward him and knew that Reginald was giving him time to connect the events so he could give some decisive direction. He appreciated that Cambridge respected his ability to discern and to find creative solutions under pressure. Often Cambridge would wait in silence for him to formulate the next step of whatever plan they needed.

"Reginald," Hawk began with a smile. "This is not what I expected when I started the day. How about you?"

"No, sir, it has been a day of surprises."

"What do you say we make sure the rest of the surprises today are ones that we create for our guests?"

"I think that is what our guests would expect."

"Will you get your teams to do another check of the Carousel of Progress, the Jungle Cruise, and the Haunted Mansion just to make sure we haven't missed anything?" Hawk paused.

"Consider it done." Reginald looked back over his shoulder toward the cemetery and then turned back to Hawk. "We have not finished checking on what happened to the ride system in Pirates yet."

"I understand. Take as long as you need to there. I don't want to open the attraction until we know all is well. Reginald, I also want you to double-check and make sure we have enough security in place today. Up the number if you need to—I don't want to find any more pirates making special appearances in the Magic Kingdom."

"I'll do my best." Cambridge tilted his head slightly. "May I inquire as to what you are getting ready to do?"

"Right now?" Hawk laughed, as he lifted his arms out from his sides. His shirt and pants were still clammy and cold from his swim in the Caribbean. "I'm going to change into some dry clothes."

"And then?"

"I don't know." Hawk rolled his eyes. "I'm sure I missed something I was supposed to do while I was running around with you all morning."

The one part of his new role that he didn't enjoy was the number of appointments and meetings he had to attend. Although over the past few months he had gotten a better handle on controlling the maddening pace of his life as CCA, there were times he was still amazed at the number of people and things that would try to get a piece of his time. Cambridge was very aware of this, as they had discussed it seriously and even joked about it many times. To emphasize the point, Hawk pulled out his cell phone and held it up.

"Normally, someone would have called to tell me what I was missing, but since I baptized my phone this morning, it appears to be dead."

"Perhaps I should get someone to accompany you back through the park." Cambridge opened his cell phone to get someone there.

"No, I'll be fine." Hawk waved off his friend. "I can make it back to my apartment."

"I know, but I would feel better—with the strange events of the morning and your not having a phone—if I could get you an escort back down Main Street."

"Are you afraid I might go wandering off the grid?" Hawk raised his chin slightly with a quizzical look.

"Not at all." Cambridge spoke slowly. "But there are times that you tend to go . . . how shall I say this? Off the marked roads."

"Really?" Hawk feigned surprise. "Me? I'll be fine."

Reginald looked doubtful, so Hawk gave him a reassuring pat on the back as he walked away. He started to step over a chain to exit the attraction but stopped mid-step. Instead, he turned and very slowly began to retrace the winding path they had entered the attraction through. Being very careful to stay in the center of the queue line, he stopped and turned back toward Reginald.

"See?" Hawk furrowed his brow in mock seriousness. "I am quite at home on the marked pathways." He waved his arm along the queue line. "I won't get lost on my way home."

 *Day One*
*Morning*

**MOVING AWAY FROM THE HAUNTED MANSION,** Grayson Hawkes mentally plotted the course he would take back to his apartment in the Town Square on Main Street USA. Angling to his right would take him through Liberty Square, where he could cut around Ye Olde Christmas Shoppe, then use the lightly traveled guest bridge past the edge of Adventureland onto Main Street.

Things had been going well for the Disney theme parks since he had taken the helm of the company. While many gave credit to the leadership and vision he had brought to the entertainment empire, Hawk disagreed. His strong moral compass and leadership skills were important, to be certain, but he believed the Walt Disney Company's success came from the fact that it was offering guests exactly what they desired—the best possible entertainment experience. Whether they were watching a motion picture, purchasing a toy, or staying at a themed resort, for Hawk the message was simple common sense: create magic, and show all guests and all cast members they are important.

His frustration over the last eighteen months came when people seemed to forget the message. Slowly but surely, his influence was rippling through the company, and he was growing more confident in his new role. As he moved toward the Liberty Bell, his mind went back to a childhood trip to Walt Disney World he'd made with his parents. A ceremony used to take place in front of the bell each day. It had been called "The Sons and Daughters of Liberty" and featured a fife-and-drum corps that would march through the crowd. A child was chosen to be an honorary member and was presented with a copy of the Declaration of Independence. On one particular visit, he had been chosen from the crowd, and he had kept the Declaration displayed on the wall of his bedroom for years.

A guest interrupted his trip down memory lane, offering him a camera. "Would you mind taking a picture of me and my family in front of the Liberty Bell?"

"It would be my pleasure." Hawk gave them a second to position themselves just where they wanted to be. "Did you know that this bell is the only one in the world made from the same authentic cast used for the original in Philadelphia? Once this replica was completed, the mold from the original was destroyed. Is everyone ready? Smile . . ."

Taking the picture and returning the camera, he noticed that the young boy in the family seemed to be fascinated by something behind him. As the father thanked him, Hawk turned and looked back toward the Hall of Presidents attraction. Blinking in surprise, he saw a man standing in a dress suit with a mask over his head. With its famous overblown smile, the mask resembled former president Jimmy Carter. The smiling face was standing right in front of the entrance to the attraction and staring directly at Hawk.

"He looks weird," the son in the family stated, breaking Hawk's attention for a moment.

"You're right, he does." Hawk gave the boy a reassuring smile and then looked back toward the suited figure, who, still staring at the CCA, slid into a side entrance door of the attraction and disappeared inside.

Hawk strode toward the entrance and noticed the attraction was not scheduled to have its first show for another hour. Masks were not allowed to be worn into the park, and nothing like this full mask of a former president was sold anywhere on Disney property. It was against policy to have an entrance door unlocked prior to guests filling the attraction. Gripping the handle on the door and pulling it toward him, he discovered it was still unlocked. He stepped inside the darkened lobby of the Hall of Presidents.

The door silently sealed him inside, and he gave his eyes a moment to adjust to the reduced level of light. Sunlight streamed dimly through the glass on the doors and windows, creating a disconnected pattern of muted sun squares on the floor. Listening closely for any sound of the masked intruder, Hawk glided quietly toward the center of the lobby; his steps were muted in the plush carpet. He stopped next to the presidential seal embedded in the carpet. It was the only one allowed to be displayed outside of the Oval Office in Washington.

This attraction was a classic; it was in place when Walt Disney World had opened and still created waves of patriotism in the crowds that viewed it each day. But as a rule, they did not have presidents wandering in and out of the building. Hawk placed a hand on the cool rail that surrounded the seal so guests would not walk across it, and slowly began to circle the railing with his head slightly cocked, listening for any noise or movement. He heard the faint click of a door closing to his left.

In the stillness of the lobby, the soft sound seemed much louder than it might have, and Hawk gripped the rail tightly and spun toward the noise. Pushing away, he crept toward the door as he freed his cell phone to call Cambridge for assistance. He recalled that it was useless to him at the moment, so he put it back into his pocket. Reaching the doorway, he inhaled and swung the door toward him, stepping inside the massive theater. Even in the darkness, the empty seven-hundred-seat theater was cavernous. Trying to blink back the blackness, he cautiously moved toward the massive stage, which was a curtained barrier between the theater seats and the audio-animatronic presidents of the United States. He walked along the front of the stage and still saw nothing. A soft shuffling sound brought him to a startled stop. The noise had come from behind the curtain and dissolved into the stillness of the theater.

Hawk moved with less caution toward a corner of the stage. Lifting himself off the ground, he jumped up to catch the edge and pulled himself forward. His mind replayed Reginald Cambridge's statement from not too long ago. *There are times that you tend to go, how shall I say this? Off the marked roads.* This might qualify as one of those times. He probably should stop and go get security to join him in checking out the attraction. The morning had been a strange one, and this masked character did not belong in the park. Yet he was here, so he might as well see what was going on and find out who the masked president might be. There was surely some explanation. Standing up, he joined the collection of individuals who had served America as president of the United States.

During a normal presentation of the Hall of Presidents, each president is introduced as a spotlight illuminates him. They move, lean, twitch, and interact with the other presidents sitting around them. Eventually, George Washington stands and recites the oath of office, and the current president addresses the audience. This allows the attraction to be updated and revamped at least every eight years. Bill Clinton was the first president ever to record a specific message for the attraction, and the tradition has continued with every president since.

Hawk walked carefully past the figures. Even in the dark, they seemed incredibly lifelike and more than a bit eerie. He thought he noticed movement from the line of presidents in front of him. Pausing, he strained to see through the darkness. He wasn't sure if it was a shadow in his own mind or if there really was movement ahead. Hawk stepped back between two of the commanders in chief and stoically waited. Through slow and even breaths, he again tried to determine whether he was really there alone or there was someone else on the stage with him. Standing ramrod straight, he gently leaned his head forward and looked down the line of figures toward the other end of the stage. Carefully, he began to weave between the presidents as he navigated toward the center of the stage.

The back tier of presidents featured figures that predominately were standing. On the lower section of the stage, closest to the audience, many were seated so all could be viewed easily. Reaching the center of the presidents, Hawk turned and looked around. He saw no movement behind him in the shadows, but his eyes were now adjusting to the minimal amount of light that kept the stage from being completely opaque. Abraham Lincoln and George Washington, who would dramatically rise and speak to the crowd during the show, sat next to one another, silent, their backs to him.

He sensed movement next to him and turned toward President Thomas Jefferson. There was an explosion of movement from behind Jefferson, as someone lurched out and grabbed Hawk. A second set of hands grabbed him as well and threw him backward into a chair on the stage. Out of the darkness, still another set of hands emerged and pulled Hawk backward by his neck.

With an attacker behind and on either side of him, he struggled to break free from their grasp. A tearing sound heightened his fighting instinct as he felt a thick band of material wrap across his chest, pinning his arms at his sides and hopelessly securing him to the chair he had been thrust into. Once the strap was in place, the hands released him.

The attackers remained behind him. He craned his neck to see them, but they had moved just beyond his sight line. He twisted his shoulders, trying to break free, but he was firmly fastened to the chair. He tried to stand and lift himself to his feet along with the chair, only to discover the chair was bolted to the floor. Frustration overwhelmed him.

Then he saw the suited figure step out from the line of presidents and loom toward him.

 *Day One*
Morning

JULIETTE KEATON PLANTED BOTH HANDS firmly on the desk of Dr. Grayson Hawkes's administrative assistant and leaned forward over it. "Where is he?"

"I don't know." The expression on Nancy Alport's face made Juliette's palms sweat. "He's somewhere with Reginald Cambridge."

Juliette stood straight and stalked around the office of Grayson Hawkes. She had known asking Nancy where he might be was a shot in the dark. But there was always a slim possibility she would know. It was so like Hawk not to tell her. Nancy had been with the Disney Company for many years. Her previous role as a cast member had been as the administrative assistant to Farren Rales, a legendary Disney Imagineer and the man responsible for her current boss's meteoric rise to the top of the Disney empire. When Rales became an ambassador for the company and Hawk offered her a position to work with him, she eagerly accepted. During the past year, Juliette had spoken with her many times and had vented about how infuriating her friend, boss, and the CCA of the company could be. They had laughed about it on occasion; the current conversation was not one of those occasions.

Today, Juliette paced briskly across the main floor of the offices created for Hawk in the Bay Lake Towers at Disney's Contemporary Resort, with an intensity that grew with each stride. This was prime Disney real estate. Hawk felt the office was overkill and tried to avoid going there as often as possible. He preferred being out in the resort. Although built as a part of the Disney Vacation Club, one of the multi-floor suites on the top floor of the resort had been converted for the new leader of the Disney Company at Juliette's insistence. She had worked with him long enough to know he hated to be trapped in an office and did his best to avoid meetings. She had tried to help him understand that he would need to have a place to work besides his apartment in the Magic Kingdom. Eventually she had gotten her way.

When business needed to be done, he got there . . . usually. But right now he was late, and she was starting to boil. Nancy worked in the massive downstairs portion of the office which included a waiting room, a dining area, balcony, and a spectacular view of the Magic Kingdom. The actual private office Hawk used was upstairs, and that portion of the suite featured a huge conference room which had the same view of the theme park as downstairs. Juliette stormed across the waiting area that featured art created by Disney Imagineers, some models of familiar sites within the Walt Disney World Resort, and a wall featuring some of the pictures, magazine covers, and articles written about the new CCA at Disney.

She could feel herself growing tenser by the moment, so she slowed her pace and began reading some of the displays on the wall. The cover of *Time* featured the headline THERE IS A NEW KING IN THE KINGDOM with a picture of Hawk, clad in his usual faded jeans and sporting a slightly too long mop of tousled hair, grinning in front of Cinderella Castle. *People* magazine featured a picture with the headline WHEN YOU WISH UPON A RISING STAR. *Entertainment Weekly* placed Hawk in a picture next to Mickey Mouse on a cover that read, WHERE DID HE COME FROM . . . AND WHERE WILL HE TAKE THEM? *Money* magazine showed a smiling Grayson Hawkes dressed in a tuxedo, which he had resisted wearing, with the phrase A HAWK TAKES FLIGHT AND THE MOUSE SOARS, and *Leadership Journal* showed a split cover of Walt Disney and Grayson Hawkes with the words WORK WILL WIN WHEN WISHING WON'T! Each of these features had been carefully set up to help create the image of Grayson Hawkes that had become known to the world.

She had made sure that each investigative article had been able to dig only to a certain level and Hawk's secrets were always preserved. Sometimes the demands of protecting him were overwhelming.

Juliette pointed to his picture on the cover of *Leadership Journal*, Hawk's personal favorite, and spoke to Nancy.

"I'll bet he doesn't even remember who is going to be here this afternoon." She shook her head. "He's probably out somewhere on some great adventure and has no clue how important this week is."

"You're probably right," Nancy softly responded. "I'm so sorry I didn't get the chance to remind him of the appointment. I haven't seen him yet today."

"It's not your fault, Nancy." Juliette smiled. "This is just a big deal, and I'm a little nervous for him." The truth was, she was so anxious she could barely eat. She had told him how crucial this was going to be. "And for some reason, he's not even answering his cell phone."

"I know you're nervous, dear." Nancy responded back in the hushed tone of a kindly grandmother. "Are Tim and the kids doing well?"

"They're great!" Juliette bubbled, realizing that Nancy was shifting the subject to a non-stressful topic. "Tim is loving his work in Imagineering, and the kids are fantastic."

Juliette Keaton had known Grayson Hawkes for a number of years. She had served alongside him as a minister on staff of the Celebration Community Church. Months ago, when Hawk had been given the key to the kingdom, it not only changed his life, but it also changed the lives of his closest friends. Tim and Juliette Keaton were some of those friends. Tim had worked in Disney animation years before, but after Hawk became the head of the company, he went to work for Imagineering and was working on one of the most ambitious projects ever within the company. Juliette had been offered a role in Imagineering but had turned it down and instead accepted the role of Executive Press Relations. Officially, she had been in charge of working alongside Farren Rales as the company began introducing its new chief creative architect to the world. She now made sure the brand, the spin, and the corporate working of the company not only stayed on message, but that the message was heard. Unofficially, she would explain to most that her job hadn't changed since her days on the church staff; she still had to take care of Hawk, Shep, and Jonathan—which, some days, was like raising children.

She spun on her heel and walked toward the window overlooking the Magic Kingdom. The phone was constantly ringing in the background, and she listened as Nancy answered questions, relayed information, and took care of business for Hawk. Juliette wondered if the risk they were about to take was going to be worth it. The eyes of the world had been watching as Hawk took the leadership reins of the company, and there were questions about where he had come from, how he had managed to get the job, and whether he was qualified to do it. She had not anticipated how difficult it would be to provide enough information to keep the hunger of the media world satisfied. The event she'd planned next, destined to begin with a meeting this afternoon, was either brilliant or would become a cataclysmic disaster. No matter the result, it was her responsibility. She felt nauseated. Finally she turned, as the phone fell momentarily silent, and she looked back toward the smiling face behind the desk.

"Nancy, how long ago did Hawk go to meet Reginald?"

"It was before I got here. I got a call from security telling me where they were."

"That was hours ago." Juliette glanced at her watch. "He should have at least checked in by now."

"He usually does." Nancy nodded.

"I'm going to call Reginald." Juliette punched her phone and paced back and forth as she waited for the call to connect. "Reginald, hi, this is Juliette

. . . Fine, thanks. Sorry to bother you, but I'm trying to track down Hawk, and I understand he is with you . . ." She narrowed her eyes and cut them back toward Nancy, who got up from behind her desk and headed toward her. "Please do that and call me back."

Juliette hit the end button on her phone and slowly shook her head.

"What is it? Is something wrong?" Nancy asked.

"Hawk left Reginald an hour ago. He was going back to his apartment to change. He doesn't have a cell phone—it got trashed this morning in the water at Pirates."

"What was he doing in the water at Pirates of the Caribbean?"

"I'm not sure." She raised an eyebrow. "This is Hawk we're talking about. He was with Reginald at the Haunted Mansion, and that's where they parted ways. He should have been here by now."

Her head began to hammer, as stress pounded a beat just above her eyes. Dueling instincts formed the source of her pain. Her instinct to worry battled her instinct that Hawk was simply making up a new agenda, one he hadn't bothered to tell anyone about. Normally that wouldn't have been a big deal, but today, it was a deal breaker.

"Maybe something happened. He could still be at his apartment."

"Maybe." Juliette looked toward the door. "Perhaps he's just running late. I'll head that way to take a look. Call me if you hear from him, please."

"Of course I will."

Juliette rechecked her watch. They had a crucial meeting scheduled a few hours from now. She and Hawk had to go over what they had agreed to. He had to sign off on it, and she had to make sure he understood exactly what they were getting into. If he didn't, it would escalate into a disaster that would impact his influence, the company's stockholders, and the public's view of him as a leader.

Placing her hand on the door, she paused before opening it. Inhaling deeply, she looked back over her shoulder toward Nancy. "And tell him I'm going to wring his neck if he misses his appointment."

 *Day One*
Morning

**GRAYSON HAWKES STARED INTO** the smiling rubber face of President Jimmy Carter. The suited man wearing the mask leaned in, until their faces were inches apart. Hawk squinted, peering into the mask's eye holes. In the darkness, his captor's eyes were emotionless black orbs.

"Who are you?" Hawk kept his eyes riveted on the expressionless face.

"I'm surprised you don't recognize me," the muffled voice behind the mask answered. Straightening up, the figure moved around the chair, and with the wave of a hand, dismissed his three assistants. They disappeared among the presidents. Slowly circling, he returned to face Hawk. "I am President Jimmy Carter, of course. Whom else would you expect in the Hall of Presidents?"

"OK." Hawk sighed deeply. "I'll play along. What do you want, Mr. President?"

"I just wanted to speak to the chief creative architect of the Disney Company."

"You could have made an appointment."

"Really?" The muffled voice raised its tone. "Somehow I don't think I would have been given a place in your busy schedule. Between your posing for magazine covers, appearing on television, and playing in the theme parks, you don't have much time for anything else."

"Is that what this is about? You wanted an appointment to see me and you didn't get one?" Hawk had been trying to recognize the voice behind the mask, but because it was muted, it did not sound familiar.

"No, this is not about an appointment to see you." Again the president leaned in. "Your ego really does know no limits, doesn't it? This is about what you have been doing to this company, to the Disney brand, and about your trying to be something you are not."

"I appreciate your concern, but I think the company is doing pretty well, and I am learning how to do my new job." Hawk leaned closer to the rubberized face. Straining against his restraints and lowering his voice, he continued. "So why don't you take off your mask so I can thank you face-to-face for your concern?"

The suited president straightened up, creating space between himself and his captive. Tilting his head as if measuring what to say, he suddenly unleashed a backhanded slap against Hawk's face. The blow came out of the darkness and surprised Hawk. The sting of the slap danced across his cheek like needles marching over his skin. Recovering from the strike, he again locked eyes with the dark orbs behind the mask and then slowly smiled.

"Is that what you really wanted to do?" Hawk calmly spoke through his smile. "If that made you feel better, you can let me loose, and we can move on with our day. If you have something else you want to say, then you better go on and say it. I'm listening."

"Ah, that sense of humor you have. It was one of the things that made you a good preacher." Pointing a finger at Hawk, he continued, "That is what you need to go back to doing. Go back to your pulpit, crack jokes, tell people about God, and get out of this company."

Hawk tried to process where this encounter was going. His captor knew enough about his background to know of his preaching at Celebration Community Church. He believed in using humor to illustrate the truths he would try to share. But that didn't help narrow down the man's identity. Hawk's shift from pastor to chief creative architect had been well documented. The attention the church had received on this journey had been beneficial, and the ministry had exploded with all the media attention.

Hawk's friend Jonathan Carlson had taken over the day-to-day administration of the church itself. Hawk still managed to preach in at least one service each weekend but was free from the everyday responsibilities at the church. Jonathan also was on the payroll of the company, where he served as a project consultant in Imagineering. People who followed Jesus had full-time occupations in being followers. The way they paid for those occupations was by working in various vocations. In the case of his staff at the church in Celebration, he had made sure they all had jobs within the Disney Company. This helped the church financially, to be sure, but it also allowed Hawk to surround himself with a set of Warriors of the Kingdom, a term that Farren Rales had introduced him to. Jonathan Carlson, Shep Albert, and Juliette Keaton were like his family, and they served as friends, counselors, and consultants to the chief creative architect.

"Look, if you just want to hear me preach, then you can hear me this weekend . . ."

"I don't care about your preaching." The suited figure paced. "I care that you don't ruin this organization. Your fifteen minutes of fame are over. I want you to step down and turn over control to someone else."

"Who would that be? You?"

"No, not me." The figure stopped pacing. "But there are others better equipped to lead and understand what needs to be done so much more than you do . . . preacher."

"Well, it isn't that easy." Hawk kept the smile on his face. "I didn't just decide to start doing what I am doing now. I was . . . selected to do this."

"I know how you were selected. You were given a key." Once again, the masked figure drew closer to Hawk as he growled. "That key is what gave you the authority, the power, and the control of Disney. Whoever has the key has the key to the kingdom."

Hawk's mind raced, replaying the last eighteen months. This person, whoever he was, knew about the key from Farren Rales. But how much did he really know? The key was not merely a key to open locks; it had been a key to unlock a mystery with many layers. When Hawk unraveled that mystery months before, there were those who tried to stop him. They had also wanted the key, although they didn't understand what it was or meant. He had always known there was a network of conspirators who wanted this key. He had been warned about them. Now they were resurfacing, and one of them was behind the mask.

"If you just want a key, then let me loose, and I'll go get it for you."

"Somehow I don't believe you. That would be the right thing to do, the best thing to do, but you are too stubborn for that. I am hoping you will understand why it is important to give up the key." The man circled the chair. "You probably have noticed a few problems in the Magic Kingdom today. The unexpected pirate attack was just a little warning for you. Four different attractions were shut down today because pirates took over. You may have the key, but I can control the kingdom."

Whoever Hawk was dealing with had been able to get access to attractions and areas that were accessible only by those who knew their way around the resort and had freedom to move behind the scenes. He knew that Reginald would figure out how the pirate audio-animatronics had been repositioned eventually; but if this person was able to create the pirate attack, what else might he be capable of doing?

"Like I said . . ." Hawk laced his voice with diplomacy. "I will give you a key if you let me loose."

"Now a preacher should not lie like that." The masked president leaned in, and the musty smell of the mask wafted past Hawk's nose. "I know you won't just give up the key so easily. You will have to be convinced that it is the only alternative you have."

His captor had done exactly what Hawk had hoped he would do. Earlier, as Hawk had strained to lean forward, he had measured how far he could actually move.

In a thunderous rush of motion, Hawk threw himself forward against the restraints. His forehead connected with the forehead of the mask in a thudding head-butt that sent the suited figure tumbling backward. Falling between Presidents Lincoln and Washington, the man crashed on his back and did not move for a moment.

Hawk twisted violently, trying to free himself, but the bonds were too tight and he could not find any give. Slowly the masked figure rose. Reaching up to adjust the presidential mask, the suited man groggily began making his way back toward his captive. He wobbled but did not get close enough for Hawk to unleash another assault.

"I should have known you would be unreasonable." The man spoke as he struggled to adjust the mask Hawk had knocked askew. "Since you are so good at solving puzzles and mysteries, here is the way we are going to do this. In this building there are two lanterns hung in the window in tribute to Paul Revere. Remember this little poem . . . 'One if by land, two if by sea, put out the lights and give us the key. . . .' When you are ready to give up the key, turn out the lights in the window and wait right here. Until then, whatever happens . . . whatever happens . . . is your fault!"

Again, Hawk felt a backhanded strike against his face. The blow splattered a wave of numbness across his jaw. When he swung his head back to where the masked president had stood, he was gone. Twisting his head side to side, he saw no one. He was now alone, strapped to a chair, sitting in the dark, surrounded by animatronic presidents.

*One if by land, two if by sea, put out the lights and give us the key.*

When you stand in Liberty Square, you can look at the second-floor window of the Hall of Presidents building and see two glowing lanterns. It is a detail many would miss except those familiar with and fascinated by the detail the designers placed in theme parks. The masked man knew Hawk was not only familiar with those details but had used that knowledge to solve a mystery. That concerned Hawk more than he wanted to admit.

This adversary knew much more about him and the key than Hawk liked. The man had threatened Hawk, and the events of the morning had created havoc in the park. With growing concern, Hawk wondered how far these enemies—and they were a group, because the man had said *give us the key*—would go to accomplish their goal.

 *Day One*
Afternoon

**HELEN REED AND MARCUS HOLMES MOVED** their group of students across Liberty Square toward the Hall of Presidents. The American Story was one of the Disney Youth Education Service offerings, as it shared the rich history of the United States of America by highlighting the sights and attractions of Liberty Square. Excellent teachers and historians, Helen and Marcus kept the students on this field-trip program enthralled, as they brought the heritage of the past into the present. Leaving the Liberty Bell, they usually concluded their day with a special onstage visit at the Hall of Presidents with the students, before they allowed the group to view the entire presentation during the first show of the day with the rest of the theme park guests.

After Helen pointed out some of the unique sights in the lobby of the attraction, the group moved into the theater. Marcus spoke of the conflicts that had to be overcome for a nation to survive. As he spoke with his back to the stage, the curtain rose and the spotlights hit the presidents. Marcus noticed one of his students lean and speak to another. He saw the next student widen his eyes in surprise. One of the female students screamed. The others stared or pointed. Helen had made her way to the stage and was now running across it, weaving in and out of presidents. In stunned disbelief, Marcus watched as she made her way to a man who was bound to a chair onstage. A very non-presidential Grayson Hawkes waited as she began to loosen the straps that held him in place. The students gawked in silence as he was released and stood to his feet.

Grayson Hawkes had taken an aggressive leadership in expanding Y.E.S., and both Helen and Marcus had met him in their final interviews. In his opinion, they were the best guides in the program and his personal favorites.

Helen whispered, "Are you alright, sir?"

"Fine." Hawk handed her the remaining strap as he freed it from around his arm. He reached up and rubbed his cheek, which was now sensitive to the touch. He flexed his jaw to make sure everything was working correctly. "Thanks for letting me loose."

"Yes, sir."

"Great." Hawk gazed out on the still-silent students studying him. Stepping between Lincoln and Washington, he knelt at the edge of the stage and motioned for the students to come to the edge of the platform. "Hi, there," he began. "I didn't mean to startle you. Obviously, I'm not one of the presidents of the United States. As a matter of fact, I'm not the president of anything at all. My name is Grayson Hawkes—my friends call me Hawk—and I'm the chief creative architect of the Walt Disney Company. You're probably wondering why I was tied to a chair on the stage in the middle of all the presidents."

He smiled and glanced back to where he had been seated. "That's a good question. As you have been studying about history today, you have been reliving the stories of the past and hopefully learning some lessons that might help you in the future. That's the fun of history. When we learn it, we get the chance to look back, and because time has passed, we have the luxury of deciding whether someone made the right decision or did the right thing, because we know how things turned out. Someone said if we are not willing to learn from our past, we are destined to make the same mistakes in the future. That applies to all areas of your life.

"But what sometimes we forget about history is that the men and women who made decisions, like all of these presidents on the stage, not only had to know about history, but they had to make decisions in real time, in the middle of a crisis, and they didn't have the luxury of knowing how it would turn out. So they faced moments of great importance by holding on to what they believed, what they had faith in, and what values made them the people they were. They had to draw from the experiences of the past, and then make a choice right then that would impact the future. Usually, the unexpected and the unplanned is what forced them to make a decision. History becomes vitally important because what you learn from it, how you grow from it, and what you discover about yourself, help  prepare you for the unexpected. Today, seeing me sitting up there was unexpected. Maybe it will help you to remember what I just told you.

"History helps prepare you for right now and for the future. Especially when something surprising happens . . . like an unexpected visitor showing up with all the presidents."

Hawk leaped off the stage and again glanced back to where he had been held captive. He glanced toward Helen, who stood there with her mouth slightly opened. He turned toward the students and began making his way through the group. Reaching out, he patted Marcus on the shoulder as he passed.

"Great job, Marcus." He smiled again at the students. "Thanks for letting me interrupt you and surprise you. Bye."

As he walked through the theater, it dawned on him that the lessons he had learned in the past once again were going to be very valuable. He was now facing an enemy that was going to try to use the unexpected to wrestle away control of Disney from him. Things were starting to happen that he did not have time to plan for. The decisions he would make would be the difference in protecting the kingdom or perhaps losing it forever. Grayson Hawkes stepped through the exit doors of the attraction as the excited voices of students saying good-bye and talking among themselves echoed down the hallway.

## CHAPTER NINE

## *Day One*
## Afternoon

GRAYSON HAWKES SWUNG OPEN the door to his office in the Bay Lake Towers at exactly 3:48 p.m. Nancy Alport immediately pushed the Do Not Disturb button on her phone and stood up behind her desk as Hawk entered.

After leaving the Hall of Presidents, he had stopped by his apartment above the Fire Station in Town Square, changed his clothes, and then exited the Magic Kingdom and walked over to the office at the Contemporary Resort. His cheek felt a little swollen, but there was no serious damage. Apparently, his captors were more intent on getting his attention than on harming him. They had succeeded, and his brain was swamped with ideas of what to do next.

"Hi, Nancy," Hawk said, as she handed him a stack of papers. "How has your day been?"

"Fine," she replied, but she kept her grip on the paper. He noticed her glance toward the side of his face. "Yours?"

"Busy . . ." He turned his cheek away from her as she stared.

"Everything going OK today?" Nancy tilted her head to try to get another look at his jaw.

"Yep, all good." He knew she was fishing for more, as he tugged on the papers, finally freeing them from her hands.

"Did you remember your three o'clock meeting with *Total Access*?"

"Are they here?"

"Upstairs." She pointed to the second story of the office. "In the conference room, meeting with Juliette."

"Yikes." He turned to head toward the stairs.

Bounding up the steps two at a time, he reached the second floor in moments. He rushed directly toward the conference room. The door was closed, and with a quick tap on it, he pushed inside. Seated around the table were two men and one woman. At the head of the table, with her back to the window and its magnificent view of the Magic Kingdom, was Juliette. All the attention in the room turned toward the door as Hawk walked in. Glancing at Juliette, he registered her this-better-be-good-or-I'm-gonna-kill-you stare.

"So sorry I'm late," Hawk said convincingly. "I trust all is set up for this week?"

"Yes, it is." Juliette slowly crossed her arms. "Let me make some introductions. This is Pete Brady. He is the executive producer for *Total Access*. This is Allie Crossman, the executive assistant to Kate Young. And this is Punky Zane, director of *Total Access*. I'd like for you all to meet Grayson Hawkes."

"Great to meet all of you." Hawk enthusiastically shook hands with each. "Sorry I was delayed. I look forward to spending time with all of you this week."

Sliding into a chair, he nodded toward Juliette to keep the meeting going. He was actually hoping she was wrapping the meeting up. He genuinely felt bad that he was late. He had forgotten completely about the gathering, which had been set up for weeks. The events of the morning had derailed any plans he might originally have remembered for the day.

"Hawk." Juliette directly addressed him, fixating on his cheek. "As you know, *Total Access* is producing a prime-time special about you, and the crew will begin work tomorrow."

"Dr. Hawkes." Pete Brady leaned forward. Placing his elbows on the table, he slowly intertwined his fingers. "You are aware that *Total Access* means just that? You have agreed to give us complete access to do a behind-the-scenes, in-depth look—at you, your life, and the world you work in. We are the top-rated prime-time news series in the country, and we look forward to having you on the show."

"I look forward to it as well." Hawk shifted uncomfortably in his chair.

"We will begin filming some of our background footage tomorrow, in and around various sites of the resort. We are coordinating with Juliette's office for all the clearance and permission we need.

"Of course. I don't see any problem."

"We will be here for a week to ten days, depending on how it all goes. On two of those days, we have blocks of time scheduled for you to actually do two sit-down interviews with Kate Young. Those interviews will be woven around other footage, informal interviews, and material we collect while we are here."

"That is what I've been told." Hawk looked toward Juliette, who nodded that all was as it should be.

"Dr. Hawkes?" Punky Zane's rich voice reminded Hawk of a radio announcer. "We're very good at what we do. That's why we're rated number one. But our desire here is not to do the standard fluff interview or documentary specials that others do. You're agreeing to let us follow you with cameras, and for Kate Young to sit in on meetings and tag along with you through your normal agenda for the week. You don't anticipate that being a problem, do you?"

"I think it's important to restate something at this point," Juliette said, before Hawk could answer. "We reserve the right under extreme circumstances to amend the agreement or limit the access as it involves company secrets and other issues expressed in the contract."

"As per our agreement, if the circumstances are deemed extreme." Zane nodded slightly.

"I don't think there will be a problem," Hawk reassured them. He hoped he sounded convincing. He rolled his shoulders to loosen them as he again shifted in his seat. The events of the morning were not only distracting him, but he felt a tidal wave of issues racing toward him. This was an extremely bad week for him to be dogged by a camera crew and a reporter.

"Kate will arrive tomorrow," Allie Crossman said. "She is our award-winning host: six Emmy Awards, nominated eleven times, Journalist of the Year eight different times, and one of the most powerful and influential women in America. Even though she is not scheduled to be with you until the following day, she would like a chance to meet you once she arrives. Just a chance to stick her head in the door to say hi."

"I'm sure we can work that into our schedule." Hawk tried to sound reassuring and forced a smile, which causing a twinge of pain in his jaw.

Juliette noticed activity across the hall from the conference room at Hawk's office. She could see Nancy escorting a handful of people into the room. There was another meeting getting ready to happen. Seeing that as her opportunity to wrap this one up, she cleared her throat.

"Pete, you know how to get in touch with my office. They will provide whatever help and people you need. I again emphasize our desire to be most helpful in giving you total access, yet to do that, you will comply with the security codes and standards we have already discussed and negotiated." Juliette paused as she saw each person nod in agreement. "Then I look forward to seeing you all tomorrow." She motioned for everyone to get up, signaling the meeting was over.

After everyone was out of the conference room, Juliette stood in the doorway with Hawk.

"Well?" She waited for the explanation as to where he had been.

"It has been an unusual day . . . to say the least."

"I can hardly wait to hear it." She feigned frustration. Juliette trusted

Hawk enough to know he would not have forgotten if there wasn't a good reason. "Hawk, you realize this special with *Total Access* is a big deal, right?"

"Sure."

"Seriously, we have never given any media group this much access to you before, and Kate Young is tough. She hasn't won all those awards because she does cotton-candy interviews. She is the real deal, an investigative journalist and reporter."

"I know, I know, I know . . ." He raised his eyebrows. "I am taking this seriously, I promise."

"I will help all I can and hopefully keep the whole experience from being too crazy or keep it from getting out of control." Juliette paused with a smile. "So, where have you been all day?"

"Come on into my office for this next meeting." He guided her by the arm from one doorway to the next. "You will not believe the morning we have had around here."

Juliette didn't budge as Hawk tried to nudge her across the hall. He turned back toward her to see why she wasn't moving. She tilted her head slightly and nodded toward the side of his face.

"Did you have an accident?"

"Oh, my face?" Hawk rubbed his cheek lightly. "Does it look bad?"

"Just a little puffy." She had no intention of letting him off the hook. "Looks like you've been in a fight."

"Really?" He rolled his eyes and once again tried to get her to follow him across the hall.

"Really." She stood her ground.

Juliette felt queasy when Hawk turned back toward her. She had seen the intense stare he got when things were more serious than he wanted to admit. That was the look she saw on his face now. She looked from his eyes back to his cheek, which was slightly swollen, and then back to his eyes again. His expression relaxed when he noticed the concern on her face.

"It's going to be OK. It's just been a strange morning."

"I don't believe you." She shook her head.

"Seriously?" He smiled and winced slightly. "It has been a very strange morning."

"Oh, I believe it has been strange." She decided she was going to have to wait to hear the rest when he was ready to tell her. "But just because you say it's going to be OK doesn't make me feel any less nervous."

This time, when he guided her arm toward the office, she went. As she took the few steps across the hallway, she felt danger creeping in from the edges of her mind. She had worked with Hawk long enough to know that everything was not fine. If something was going to go wrong, it was bound to happen now. After all, she had invited the most powerful investigative journalist in the world to be their guest.

 *Day One*
Late Afternoon

THE MEETING WAS HELD IN THE OFFICE of the Disney Chief Creative Architect. Prior to his inheriting that title and task, Grayson Hawkes had been a Disney junkie. A collector of various Disney items that ranged from books, DVDs, figurines and pins, to items from the theme parks themselves. Once he became the head of the company, he moved his entire collection into this new office and then added to it, acquiring more than he had ever dreamed possible. The executive office was nearly a museum with all of the Disney items arranged neatly in lighted display cabinets. The room featured a small desk, which Hawk rarely used, and a circle of six chairs for meetings like this one.

Each person in attendance had been invited by Reginald Cambridge as the day unfolded. The original problem, the event at the Pirates of the Caribbean, had been troublesome. Evacuating an attraction with guests on board was never taken lightly. Throughout the day there had been various meetings, security briefings, and evaluations. The discoveries of additional pirate audio-animatronic figures had let them know it was not an accident. Hawk's experience in the Hall of Presidents, which no one else knew about yet, had cemented the fact there was a purposeful effort to disrupt the park operations.

Cambridge looked up as Juliette and Hawk entered from the conference room across the hallway. Already seated and waiting for Hawk to arrive was Bill, who had been in charge of the evacuation of the attraction earlier, Shep, Clint Wayman, and Chuck Conrad. Clint and Chuck were two of Reginald's most trusted leads in security, and Hawk was sure they had been actively involved in the investigation. Quickly greeting everyone, Hawk offered Juliette a seat and then eased into the only remaining chair, which was his, behind the desk.

"Thanks for coming everyone," he began. "It is safe to say it has been an interesting day. I can't wait to hear what you have found."

Reginald leaned forward in his chair. "Pirates of the Caribbean has been closed since the incident this morning. As Bill explained to us, a variety of things happened, which included a body floating in the water, losing control of the ride-operating system—"

"Momentarily!" Bill interrupted, as his gaze darted between the others in the room. "And it wasn't really a body . . . it was an audio-animatronic figure."

Cambridge cleared his throat. "—*momentarily* losing control of the ride operating system and then involving a complete evac of the attraction itself."

"You had to take people out of the boats along the waterway?" Juliette's mouth slightly opened as she looked for verification. "And how did an audio-animatronic figure . . . ?"

"Yes, as I said," Cambridge continued. Pausing, he closed his eyes and rubbed the center of his forehead with his fingertips. "The attraction was evacuated without incident."

"You alright, Reginald?" Hawk asked.

"Fine, just a slight headache." He twisted his neck and repositioned himself in his seat.

"Um . . . as we looked into this further," Chuck Conrad spoke in a thick northeastern accent, "we concluded that all was done according to procedure and within acceptable protocols and guidelines."

"Acceptable protocols and guidelines?" Bill wiped his palms along the arms of the chair. "What does that mean?"

"It means you did a good job." Hawk gently smiled.

"Did we do anything for our guests?" Juliette looked toward Cambridge and then toward Hawk.

"Yes." Cambridge nodded. "Each guest received a complimentary pass good for admission at any of our parks. This was a decision made by Grayson Hawkes."

"Wow." Juliette sat back in her chair. "You sure are generous."

"Yes, I am a great guy." Hawk grinned. "Tell your friends—"

"They wouldn't believe me." She shook her head side to side.

"May I continue please, sir?"

"Sorry, Reginald." Hawk allowed his grin to evaporate. "Continue."

"However, we do not know why we lost control—momentarily—of the operation of the attraction. There seems to be no mechanical reason. We will have to assume it was an operator error. Later in the morning, we were notified another pirate figure had been found in a boat on the Jungle Cruise attraction."

"Yeah, that was weird," Shep chimed in.

JEFF DIXON

Earlier in the day, Hawk had done his best to keep Shep quiet. Hawk respected the honesty and the ability Shep had to say what everyone seemed to be thinking. He was quick to chime in with an opinion or a thought that usually was on the mark. His ability to communicate exactly what he was thinking and feeling amused Hawk. However, Hawk knew that for Cambridge it could be more than mildly irritating.

"Yes, that would be a good way to summarize the entire morning," Cambridge dryly continued. "Then another pirate was discovered in the Carousel of Progress and one more at the Haunted Mansion."

"You've got to be kidding." Juliette wrinkled her brow. "We were attacked by pirates, and I didn't even know it."

"Bothersome to be sure. Clint spent some time doing inventory and discovered that one of our warehouses where we store some non-functioning figures had ten that are unaccounted for." Cambridge looked toward Clint Wayman.

"According to inventory, they should have been there. They are not." Clint frowned. "Don't know why, we don't know where they are, can't find any one person who missed them, so we aren't really sure when they might have disappeared."

"Or jumped ship?" Shep couldn't resist.

"Let's circle back to the operator error you mentioned on the pirates attraction. Who did it?" Hawk directed the question to Bill and Reginald.

"No one, sir. I have checked, and no one accidently kept sending boats into the attraction after we shut it down." Bill slid to the edge of his seat.

"If it *is* an operator error, then that means an operator had to have been involved . . . correct?" Hawk had every eye in the room riveted on him.

"That is correct, sir." Cambridge inhaled deeply. "However, we have been able to find no individual who will admit to making an error, and all security evidence available gives us no indication as to what happened . . . yet."

"What does that mean?" Hawk folded his hands and placed his elbows on the desk.

Suddenly the door to the office clicked open. Every person in the room turned toward the entrance. Hawk's eyes widened when he saw who was coming inside.

"I know what it means," the newcomer said. "Pardon me, but I couldn't help but overhear. If you don't mind my saying so, it means that you have a problem . . . a serious problem."

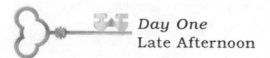

## CHAPTER ELEVEN

## Day One
## Late Afternoon

**HAWK IMMEDIATELY STOOD AND MOVED** around his desk to embrace his old friend Farren Rales. Rales had been hired by Walt Disney himself as an animator at the Walt Disney Studios on Rales's thirtieth birthday. In the years that followed, he had worked on animated features, been involved in projects at Disneyland, and eventually become a part of that exclusive group of creative designers known as Imagineers. The Imagineers are the design-and-development arm of the Walt Disney Company. Walt created the name of this group by combining the words *imagination* and *engineering*.

After Walt died, Farren moved from California to be one of the lead Imagineers as Walt Disney World was developed in Orlando. Rales was part Disney historian, part Disney philosopher, and a modern-day keeper of the dream that Walt had begun. It had been Farren Rales that had given Hawk the key that started him on this rocket ride of his own dream. Farren was the one man who knew that he'd given Hawk more than just a key, and he was a living reminder of how important it was to protect the things he had been entrusted with.

Cambridge, Shep, and Juliette all knew Farren. Hawk wasn't sure about the security men. "Let me introduce Mr. Farren Rales, the official Imagineering ambassador of the Walt Disney Company."

A somber Rales shook hands with both Clint and Chuck. Hawk ushered Rales to his seat behind the desk and stood next to the old man and waited for him to get settled into the comfortable leather. It seemed to swallow his frame as he rocked backward and faced the group.

"You do have a problem, a serious problem." Rales looked frailer than Hawk remembered since he had seen him last. But his eyes sparkled as he spoke. "This company is under attack. Today it was a pirate attack. It closed down an attraction, caused an evacuation, caused you to lose control of the attraction . . . You have no idea why or how this was done. Which means that tomorrow, whoever has decided to launch this attack upon you can do it again. And right now, you can do nothing about it."

---

"So you think it's going to happen again?" Clint asked the obvious question.

"Why wouldn't it?" Rales raised an eyebrow. "People are trying to get your attention for some reason. Of course they will do something else . . . until they get what they want. So you have to figure out who did this, what they want, and how to prevent them from doing it again."

The office grew deathly quiet. Rales locked eyes with Hawk, who cracked the slightest smile at his friend. Although unnoticed by most in the meeting, it signaled to Rales that Hawk already had more information than he had shared. Cambridge, however, had not missed the glance and came to the same conclusion as Rales. Standing, he addressed his two security chiefs.

"Gentlemen, I trust you will continue to investigate the events of today and heighten security throughout the resort." As they nodded affirmatively, Cambridge turned toward Bill. "We will need to continue to test the attraction throughout the evening and strive to open it uneventfully tomorrow."

"Yes, we will." Bill rose to his feet.

The official meeting was over. Chuck, Clint, and Bill shook hands with everyone, said their good-byes, and left the office. Juliette closed the door behind them, and then turned and leaned back against the door as if someone might come bursting in. Tilting her head, she broke the silence.

"Now, what is going on?"

"Indeed, tell me what I do not know," Cambridge injected.

"I'm not sure what you know and don't know." Rales leaned back in the comfortable chair. "You will recall that when Hawk became the possessor of the key I gave him, I told him it was the key to the kingdom. He used it wisely, figured out the mystery, and ended up sitting on top of the world . . ." Rales let his gaze drift toward the window with the view of the Magic Kingdom. Turning back to the group, he completed his thought. "Literally . . . on top of the world."

"So you believe this is an attempt by an individual or group to remove Hawk from his position here at the company?" Cambridge ran a hand across his forehead.

"Yes, but it's more complicated than that." Rales pulled himself forward toward the desk. "This is not about taking Hawk's job, it's about taking what Hawk has. It's about getting the key. The keeper of the key has the power, has the control, and has the kingdom."

The old key Rales had given Hawk was very special indeed. It had opened a variety of things that surprised Hawk along the way. Yet each time the key had opened something, it had helped him to find a clue, a puzzle piece, and eventually helped him unravel the mystery that had given him the real prize. The real key was far more than just a key. It was information, it was insight, and it was a secret. Now, as the keeper of that secret, he had the authority from Walt Disney himself to guide the destiny of the company.

"If I understand completely . . . " Shep pursed his lips. " . . . the key is not the big deal, it is just a piece of a far bigger prize. The only two people who know what the key really is are the two of you." He pointed toward Hawk and Rales.

"I would venture to guess that others don't know that," Cambridge stated. "They believe that if they can get the key, then they can have whatever they believe Hawk has discovered."

"Correct." Rales nodded. "They don't know what the key really means or really does. But they believe if they can have it, then they will have control and power . . . and all those entail."

"So . . ." Juliette pushed away from the door and made her way across the room. Relaxing in a chair, she exhaled. "There's a group of thugs somewhere trying to get your attention so you will give them the key."

"And since no one else knows what the key is or really does, they have to convince you to give it up." Shep smiled at his summary.

"Pretty much," Hawk shrugged. "But I'm not giving up anything."

"That does not mean they, whoever they are, are not going to coerce you into giving them what they want." Cambridge spoke slowly and softly.

"It would be foolhardy to think they would stop. But there is some more information that you don't have that might be helpful." Rales looked to Hawk, who nodded for him to continue. "As Hawk has entrusted you with as much of the story of the key as he could, you need to understand that the key was a plan that Walt and Roy Disney put into place years ago to make sure that there would always be someone guiding the company into the future. I was one of three Imagineers who helped design this elaborate and well-orchestrated plan to secure the future of Disney. It took years for us to find someone like Hawk who had the skill set to do what he has been entrusted to do."

"Whoa." Juliette leaned forward. "So if you are just one of three Imagineers who helped design the mystery of the key . . . who are the other two?" Turning toward Hawk, she asked another question. "Do you know who the other two are?"

"No." Hawk shrugged. "I don't know who they are."

"He doesn't." Rales stood behind the desk. "My role was to give Hawk the key and see if he could prove himself worthy to be entrusted as the keeper of the key. All of you got involved in that process and discovered that the details and clues he needed were to be found in the resort itself. Each one of us Imagineers has a different task, a different job, and a different responsibility. When the time is right, Hawk will be given more details."

"But you guys are getting pretty old," Shep said without harshness. "If Hawk needs to know more, shouldn't the other two be giving up some details while they still can?"

Rales smiled brilliantly and moved to look out the window at the theme park. "You would be correct. Time and common sense would dictate that very soon Hawk should be given the rest of the information he might need to be successful in guiding the Disney Company."

The four others stood in the office, waiting for the old Imagineer to turn back from gazing out the window. Shep got up out his chair and paced around it. When he finished circling it, he opened his mouth to speak; but Hawk waved him off, telling him to wait.

Slowly, Farren Rales turned back from the window. His brow furrowed as he looked toward the ground and spoke softly.

"When Hawk unraveled the mystery of the key, there were those that tried to stop him. Apparently another attempt to take the key from him is just beginning. What we have to figure out is how we stop them."

"Farren." Cambridge narrowed his eyes toward the old Imagineer. "Do you think this latest attempt to take the key is related to either of the other two Imagineers whom Hawk has yet to meet?"

"I believe so." Farren looked up toward the group. "Why wouldn't it be? When I gave Hawk the key originally, I was being watched. So was Hawk, and they mobilized to do everything they could to stop him then. I have to assume that the timing is not by accident. There is a reason they are attempting to disrupt things now. As I said, I fear this is only the beginning."

"Farren is right." Hawk spoke, drawing the attention of all in the room. "Something else happened today. I haven't had a chance to tell you yet."

The sound of a cell phone startled the group and stole the attention. Cambridge grabbed his phone, activated it, and placed it to his ear. A knock on the door occurred at the same time, and as it silently swung open, Nancy popped her head inside.

"Hawk," she said apologetically, "I'm sorry to interrupt, but we have a situation."

"A what?" Cambridge raised his voice to the person on the other end of his call. "On my way." He abruptly ended the call.

Hawk turned back to the doorway and nodded for Nancy Alport to continue.

"I've been asked to see if you would go back to Pirates of the Caribbean. There is . . ."

"A problem at Pirates . . . again."

Cambridge was on his feet, moving toward the exit. "That is what my call was about. We need to go."

Shep, Juliette, and Cambridge hustled past Nancy and headed toward the stairs. Hawk paused in the doorway and turned back to Farren, who was watching as they left.

"Farren, are you coming?" Hawk asked.

"No, I think I will sit this trip out."

"Everything OK?"

"Yes, except for the fact that I am afraid you are getting into a very dangerous situation."

"I'll be fine. I can take care of myself," Hawk reassured him.

"Of that I have no doubt. You are one of the most resilient individuals I have ever met." Farren smiled. "Have time to meet me for breakfast in the morning? I feel the need for us to meet with our very old friend."

"Sure, what time?"

"Grayson Hawkes." The echoing voice of Reginald Cambridge lofted up from the first floor.

"Coming!" Hawk yelled back. Refocusing his attention to Rales, he asked, "What time?"

"Seven?"

"Sounds great, can't wait."

Hawk raced out of the office and down the stairs.

As Farren's young friend left, the Imagineer turned back toward the window overlooking the Magic Kingdom. He smiled as he thought back over the incredible journey that had brought them to this moment. It had been many years since the original plan for the future had been put into place by Walt and Roy Disney. The friendship he had developed with the preacher, Grayson Hawkes, who wanted to become a better storyteller, had changed both of their lives forever. Now that he had entrusted Hawk with the key to the kingdom, he knew he had made the right choice. Hawk would do everything within his power to keep the kingdom and drive it into the future. But it was not going to be easy, and it would not be without a shadow of risk.

"Is there anything I can get for you, Farren?" Nancy asked, still standing beside the doorway.

"No, I am just leaving." He placed his hand against the window and looked into the distance.

"Take your time, sir." Nancy had known Farren a long time. As she moved away from the door to head back down the stairs, she heard him speak softly.

"Be very careful, Hawk . . . be very careful."

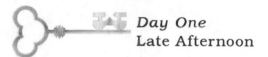 *Day One*
Late Afternoon

**PUNKY ZANE LISTENED AS ALLIE CROSSMAN** talked to their *Total Access* star, Kate Young, on her cell phone. He had worked with them for a couple of years and was used to the flurry of phone calls whenever a new project began. Pete Brady was ahead of them, also talking on his cell phone, trying to mobilize and coordinate the production staff about to descend on the Walt Disney World Resort. The three were moving across the covered bridge that connected the Bay Lake Towers, where Grayson Hawkes's office was located, back to the Contemporary Resort, where they all had rooms. The Contemporary was where they had taken a block of rooms for their staff over the next week.

Midway across the bridge, Pete had stopped and was referencing his electronic tablet for some morsel of information he needed to relay to their staff. His stop had brought the entire group to a halt and they separated, giving enough space for the dueling conversations to take place. Punky absently listened in to Allie's half of the conversation with Kate, because Kate was their boss. *Total Access* had made her one of the most powerful women in the media, and the four of them had forged a powerful and highly respected team, in an industry where sometimes credibility and integrity were suspect.

"Of course everything is set," Allie spoke. "I also conveyed to Dr. Hawkes your request to meet him informally after you arrive tomorrow . . ." Allie listened to Kate as she replied, then glanced toward Pete as he continued to fumble with the tablet. "Pete is working on the final details right now. I believe we're in good shape."

Punky turned and leaned against the rail and gazed across the Contemporary's parking lot toward the entrance of the resort. In the distance, he could see the Magic Kingdom. His mind wandered to a visit he had made as a child with his parents to this place. Noticing movement below him, he glanced down and then immediately narrowed his focus on what he was seeing. With a wave of his hands, he attempted to get the attention of Allie and Pete, but kept his eyes fixed on the ground below. Noticing the hand motions, they both turned to see what he was doing and moved toward where he was standing. They paused mid-conversation on both calls.

Below them, running across the parking lot, were two men, whom Punky did not recognize, with one woman he did know. Juliette Keaton jogged alongside these two men toward an SUV parked in a reserved spot in a small parking area off the main lot. As the three looked down, as if on cue, Grayson Hawkes emerged from the building and raced across the parking lot, attempting to catch them. Punky turned and exchanged a puzzled look with both Allie and Pete. Pete punched the end button on his touchscreen without saying good-bye.

"Kate, we are watching Hawkes, Juliette Keaton, and a couple of other people run out of the Towers and pile into a vehicle."

Allie explained the action to Kate Young, whose instructions to the team had been interrupted by this unexpected sight.

"And now they are tearing out the parking lot exceptionally fast."

The white SUV had woven through the parking area, taken a cut-through road, passed a security gate, and taken a right-hand turn that sent the vehicle speeding along a roadway between the theme park and the resort. Pete raised his eyebrows and shoulders simultaneously, gesturing what the other two were thinking.

"I wonder what that was all about." Punky scratched his chin and leaned against the railing. "Hmm . . . this week might be more entertaining than I first thought."

"They're gone . . . but it was odd," Allie continued her narrative for Kate. "They're heading somewhere in a hurry . . . yes, like an emergency kind of hurry."

 *Day One*
Late Afternoon

THE WHITE SUV BOUNCED OUT of the parking lot and turned sharply onto North World Drive, then raced past Space Mountain, heading toward the far side of the Magic Kingdom. Still accelerating, Cambridge navigated a jagged series of quick turns that put the vehicle on Floridian Way, which would carry them around the back of the theme park. The herky-jerky journey got smoother on this stretch of road that was free of any winding turns.

"Uncle Reggie, you about flipped us over back there." From the backseat, a wide-eyed Shep looked at the driver in the rearview mirror.

"I am an excellent driver," snorted Cambridge. "Perhaps you should be a silent passenger."

Hawk, riding in the shotgun seat, glanced back at Shep and smiled. Although the road had straightened out, Cambridge was still pushing the limits of how fast he could drive and keep them safe. Seeing how quickly things were moving past them out of the window, Hawk turned toward the driver. "What's the hurry? What's going on?"

"It would appear there is another situation at the Pirates of the Caribbean." Cambridge steered the vehicle to the left around a lazy turn.

"A situation?" Juliette leaned up so she could see Cambridge's face.

"Yes, a situation." Cambridge gave the steering wheel a hard left turn, causing the passengers to rock awkwardly in their seats.

"Whoa!" Shep yelped.

Hawk said nothing but found himself gripping the handle of the door tightly to stabilize himself. They tilted as the vehicle cornered. Cambridge concentrated intently on the road, his jaw set in a rock-solid bite.

He had been around Cambridge enough to have seen that look of controlled intensity before. Under pressure or a potential crisis, Reginald had an uncanny knack for remaining engaged on the problem at hand. The vehicle began to slow as they made their way down Caribbean Way and approached a security station.

Cambridge rolled down his window and pointed toward the guard, who recognized the security chief and the passenger in the front seat. Rushing back into the structure, he raised the gate and energetically waved them through. They were approaching the back of the Pirates attraction, where they had been earlier in the day. The SUV screeched to a halt and Reginald had his door open before he turned the engine off.

Now Hawk followed his lead and yelled as they got out, "What are we heading into Reginald?"

"We need to get inside quickly!" Cambridge called back.

"Why?" Hawk fell in behind him as Juliette and Shep did the same.

"Because we don't want to miss it." Cambridge grabbed the door and swung it open.

"Miss what?"

"The ghost." Cambridge's expression was intense, and his eyes showed no signs of kidding or playing.

"Did he say a ghost?" Shep looked back over his shoulder to see if Juliette had heard the same thing he had.

As the group paused at the door, everyone looked at Cambridge, waiting for him to give them more information. Holding the door, Reginald realized they were not going to enter until he said something else. "Yes, they have seen a ghost in the attraction." He raised his arm to invite them in. "I suggest if we are going to find it, we need to get inside."

"This day just keeps getting better and better." Hawk cracked a smile as he spoke.

"That's why you get the big bucks." Juliette shoved him toward the door. "If there's a ghost in there, you go in first."

For the second time today, Grayson Hawkes made the pupil-blowing transition from daylight into the darkness of the attraction. Unlike the first time, this time there was no chaos or confusion. The attraction was silent, with no soundtrack blaring in the background. The small band navigated the backstage area and made its way into the main loading area of the ride.

Normally there would be a line of people being sent into short lines to climb aboard the boats. Now there were two empty boats, no guests, and a few cast members milling about. Chuck Conrad made his way over to meet them. Hawk looked across the boat loading area to the observation area that monitored the ride while it was in operation. Bill was there, waving for them to join him.

Chuck addressed them all. "I am sorry, I know you were still in a meeting."

"Tell us what happened," Reginald said curtly.

"We had just gotten back, continuing to run the attraction through all the system checks. A cast member up there—" Chuck pointed up to where Bill was still looking at them through the observation window. "—said he saw something on one of the security cameras."

"What did he see?" Hawk positioned himself in the queue line.

"He called it a ghost." Chuck shrugged. "It was a pale grayish figure, and it moved across the screen and then disappeared."

"Did we manage to capture this . . . ghost . . . on a tape that we can review?" Reginald asked skeptically.

"Bill is reviewing the system now."

"Where did this happen?" Hawk folded his arms and leaned back against the railing.

"Here, actually." Chuck swept his arm past them.

"In the load area?" Juliette moved in just a little bit closer to Shep as she asked the question.

"You know this place is supposed to be haunted." Shep lowered his voice and closed the distance between him and the rest of the group. "There have been stories about this attraction for years."

"Haunted? Seriously?" Reginald rolled his eyes.

"Seriously." Shep turned his hands palms up. "Cast members have been telling stories about this attraction forever."

"I doubt seriously that it's haunted." Hawk straightened up. "Tell me where the ghost was seen."

"Right here on Moonlight Bay."

They all turned to look.

Over the years, Moonlight Bay has reflected a ship at sea that guests barely notice as they wait to board the boats in the load area. It is a work of art, a beautiful and massive display, yet often missed in the anticipation of the pirate adventure that awaits each guest at this point.

"I don't see anything there now." Hawk studied it closely. "It just appeared and then disappeared?"

"The way he described it is that it kind of walked through it."

"To where?"

"Out the door, according to what he said."

"A door." Hawk strode over to the edge of Moonlight Bay. The dark expanse of water rippled at his feet. "What door?"

"It's there, just out of your line of sight." Chuck stepped up next to him and pointed. "It's a door that has been rarely used. As a matter of fact, it is not used at all anymore. It used to be called . . . well, it isn't important."

"Used to be called what?" Reginald now stood next to them.

"I would rather not say." Chuck apologetically nodded toward Hawk. "Out of respect for Hawk."

"You know, Chuck, I have no idea what you're talking about." Hawk looked at him, puzzled.

"It was called the Jesus door." Chuck sighed. "No offense, I know you are also a pastor, sir."

"None taken."

Shep leaned out to see if he could see it. "Why the Jesus door?"

"Because this is Moonlight Bay, to get to the door you have to walk across the water . . . right?" Hawk looked back toward the diorama.

"Exactly," Chuck replied.

"Actually, that is a creative name for it." Hawk now stepped out gingerly onto the Moonlight Bay set. "Will it hold me?" He was surprised to find that although it looked like water from a distance; it was merely a painted solid floor. Standing on it, he looked like he was standing on the surface of the bay.

"It should," Chuck moved to the edge of the diorama. "The door is still there but not used. It takes you to a backstage area."

"Fine, I'll go see if I can find any signs of our ghost." Hawk paused and turned back to the group. "Go find us something on the footage."

"Do you want anyone to go with you?" Shep moved to the edge of the painted water as if to join him.

"Would you like to come?" Hawk smiled, knowing the answer.

"Well, actually, no . . . since you're going ghost hunting and all . . . and you know, I have a sense about these kinds of things."

"I'll see you in a few minutes." Hawk walked across the bay. He found himself stepping softly across the solid floor as if he expected to sink at any moment. When he spotted the door that was now visible as he navigated across the set, his disorientation abated.

The Jesus door opened easily after the miracle walk across the water had been accomplished. Hawk faced an overly large step down to the concrete foundation of the attraction. The hallway was extremely narrow and claustrophobically closed in on him as he made his way through the dark hallway.

The interior of the attraction had not seen the light of the outside world since the day it was opened. Added to the constant darkness was the overwhelming amount of water in the ride. The result was in essence a dark, damp, and musty cave system. Hawk moved down this corridor, and it widened slightly as he rounded a darkened corner. Safety lights dimly illuminated various set pieces and props that had been unceremoniously stashed offstage.

This labyrinth echoed dully with each step Hawk took. Creeping slowly and cautiously, he thought he heard footsteps in the hallway along with his. Stopping and listening closely, he heard nothing except water dripping somewhere near him. Again he inched forward, allowing his hand to lightly touch the wall to his right to keep him oriented in the dim light. A stairwell descended downward, and Hawk grabbed the handrail. Two legs, slumped on the ground, blocked his path.

He jumped back with a start, nearly stumbling and taking a seat on the stairs. A pair of wading pants, much like a fisherman might use, had been absently flung over the handrail. He had managed to knock them off when he placed his hand on it. A few feet ahead he spotted another pair in the low light. They looked like limbs jutting out of the blackness. He smiled at his skittishness. *Hold it together, you great ghost hunter.* He could sense that the bottom of the stairs was near as the stairs got wider and less steep.

As his descent leveled out, a gray shape swooped out of the darkness toward him.

 *Early Evening*
Day One

Huddled in the low light of the control room, the small group anxiously studied the images rapidly passing across the monitor. Reginald and Chuck were seated, operating the video system, scouring the tapes for a glimpse of the ghost that had been reported in the attraction. Shep, Juliette, and Bill stood looking over their shoulders toward the screen. Occasionally, Juliette would look back out the window toward Moonlight Bay for any sign of the ghost or the return of Grayson Hawkes. Growing restless with the waiting, she leaned toward Shep.

"You said this place is haunted?"

"That's what I've heard." Shep whispered, so as not to disturb the men searching for video evidence. "Supposedly a lot of weird things happen here."

"He's right," Bill said. "When you've worked here as long as I have, you get used to the stories. But then every so often, something happens that really shakes you . . . like someone actually seeing a ghost."

"That sounds crazy." Juliette closed her eyes for a moment. "I seriously doubt this attraction is haunted."

"That's what skeptics think," Bill continued. "If you work here long enough, you start believing it. George and his friends do not like to be messed with."

"George?" Shep asked. "Who is George?"

"One of the ghosts."

"George . . ." Juliette shook her head. "The ghost is named George . . ."

"Seriously!" Bill said. "The story goes that back when they were first building the attraction, there was a welder named George who fell to his death while he was working in the upper portion of the building. From the day Pirates opened, George has haunted the attraction. Most of the cast members at one time or another have had to deal with George and his mischief."

"Seriously?" Juliette rolled her eyes.

Shep's gaze remained fixed on Bill. "What kind of stuff happens?"

"Breakdown for no apparent reason, people getting touched, footsteps heard in hallways when no one was there, and even an occasional appearance or someone hearing his voice. In the center of the attraction—you've all seen it before—the waterway winds through the city. Most people don't realize it winds back around, and there's a huge support pole that provides stability for the roof. It's decorated to look like a tower. It's known as George's Tower."

"Named after a ghost?" Juliette was trying to ignore Bill but found the story strangely compelling.

"Named after or in honor of someone who had an accident." Bill glanced away from Juliette to Shep, who was a better audience for his story. "The top of this pillar is decorated as a set piece. It looks like a tower with a number of windows in it. It is to the right of the famous well scene. If you look up toward the roof, you'll see it. Most guests never even notice, because there is so much to see, and it's designed so that it blends into the background seamlessly." Bill leaned forward. "Rumor has it this is the very tower George fell from."

"No." Shep's eyes widened and he blinked nervously.

"Yes, really. At the bottom of the tower, you can find the initials *G.C.* carved into the set piece. I've been told that when you paint over them and try to cover them up . . . the initials bleed back through the paint."

"That is nuts!" Juliette turned away from Bill and looked back toward the video monitor.

"No, what is really crazy, though, is what happens if you're riding the ride and look up at the tower and see a light burning at the top of it . . . it means that George is home. If you round the curve through the burning city scene and look up at the tower and the light is still on—usually it's out—it means that something bad is likely to happen."

"Bad?" A bead of sweat ran down Shep's jaw.

"The ride is going to shut down, something strange will happen during the day, things like that. The cast members get all freaked out by it. That's why when the day begins and ends, they say good morning and good night to George. They just don't want to make him mad."

"I'll bet. Why would they?" Juliette said.

"Back in the day, when the attraction first opened, occasionally a woman would request to ride a boat alone. She would have to wait a long time, but she always waited. Usually at the end of the day she would go through, and on the security cameras the cast members could see her talking to someone and crying."

"Weird," Shep whispered.

"Let me guess," Juliette said. "It was George's mom, and she was coming in to talk to her son."

"Yes, how'd you know? Have you ever seen the door by the jail scene?" Bill looked back and forth at them.

"Where they're trying to call the dog?"

"Yes, there is a door there, and it's called George's door."

"Does he go in and out of it?" Shep looked at Juliette for a moment and then back to Bill.

"Yes, if the door is closed, everything goes well . . . but then all of a sudden, the door will just open. When it does, the ride is going to shut down or something weird is going to take place."

"It couldn't be that some cast member accidently left the door open or didn't make sure it closed completely?" Juliette looked for a reasonable explanation.

"I'm sure that happens sometimes, but everyone is so alert about keeping George happy, they're careful. They wouldn't just leave it open."

"Wow, so this place is really haunted." Shep nodded toward Bill, who nodded back.

"Please . . ." Juliette waved her hand, dismissing the story.

"There." Reginald's deep voice echoed in the small room.

"I see it," Chuck added.

Now the other three were crowding in to get a look. Cambridge slowly manipulated the controls and played back the footage. The camera had caught a partial view of the Moonlight Bay set. Because the attraction was dark, the footage was not a high definition capture, but instead had that night-vision look that ghost-hunting shows on cable channels often use. The end result was a very spooky, dark, distorted view.

"Look closely." Cambridge eased the footage forward.

Suddenly a gray shape jumped into the frame at the extreme corner. It was clearly the shape of a person. As the next few frames advanced, this shape moved across the bay in the same direction that Hawk had gone as he went out the door. All eyes were riveted to the screen, and then the shape moved out of the shot.

"And that is all that is there." Cambridge rewound the footage to view it again.

"You found the ghost." Bill sounded impressed.

"I found something." Reginald looked back over his shoulder correctively. "There is nothing to indicate that we just saw a ghost. It could easily have been a cast member."

"That didn't look like a cast member to me," Shep said in a higher-than-usual pitch.

"Shep, you aren't helping here," Juliette scolded. "So what does this mean?"

"It means that someone is moving around in the attraction." Cambridge played the footage again and paused with the image, although distorted, in the clearest view they had on the screen. "And whatever or whoever it is . . . is not supposed to be here."

"It's a ghost," Bill restated.

## CHAPTER FIFTEEN

*Early Evening*
Day One

GRAYSON HAWKES STOPPED AND STOOD his ground, as the shadowy figure eased into the partially lit passageway. Dressed in what Hawk guessed were gray polyester trousers and gray rumpled shirt, the man also came to a halt before getting too close. Stringy, brilliant-white hair was splayed across the top of the man's head. His skin was pale, almost translucent, as if he had not seen the light of day for many years, much like the interior of the attraction. The man appeared old but surveyed Hawk with clear blue eyes that almost glowed in the dim light.

"So I finally get to meet you." A smooth voice emerged from the translucent-skinned figure.

"I'm Hawk." He stepped forward with a hand extended to shake.

"I know who you are, my boy." The man waved the hand away.

"I'm at a disadvantage. You know me, but I don't know you." Hawk pulled back his hand.

"Why don't you call me . . . George." The old man snorted and took a seat on an old crate that Hawk had not noticed until that moment.

"OK, George . . ." Hawk allowed his eyes to dart around the area to make sure there was nothing else or no one else he had missed. "What are you doing down here in these damp old passageways?"

"Waiting to meet you, of course." George smiled. "I've been waiting to meet you for years."

"Years?"

"Yes, years. Are you really as good as I've heard?"

"Again, I'm sorry . . . I don't know what you mean." Hawk took another step forward.

"You know the history of Walt Disney, you understand the work of the Imagineers, you are a walking encyclopedia of Disney trivia, you enjoy the art of storytelling, and you are the visionary who is the keeper of the key to the kingdom . . . that is what I have heard about you."

"Where have you heard all of that?"

"Oh, I have my sources . . . but everyone knows those things about you. What I want to know is what I asked you before—are you really as good as I have heard?"

"I don't know how to answer that." Hawk tilted his head.

"I hope you are . . . because if you aren't, then the kingdom is at risk."

"Who are you?" One possibility loomed before all others. Hawk felt his heartbeat quicken as he realized who this might be.

"I told you, call me George." The old man raised his chin and smiled again. "Tell me, how difficult was it for you to discover the true meaning of the key?"

Hawk did not know for sure how much this old man knew about the key, what the key really meant, and what being the keeper of the key really involved. In just a few moments he'd given Hawk the impression that he knew a great deal. But with the events of the day, the pirates, and his threatening encounter in the Hall of Presidents, Hawk knew better than to divulge any detail about the key beyond what the man offered and already knew.

Hawk stepped over beside the man and spotted another wooden crate. He slid it across the floor, and it scraped liked metal running over a chalkboard. Hawk winced at the noise and felt the hair on the back of his neck tense. The pale man watched, expressionless, and Hawk sat down and then answered the question.

"It's just a key. You find the things it opens, and that's about it." Hawk smiled.

"Very good." The translucent man laughed loudly. "Very good indeed. You are wise not to tell me anything. You don't know me. Right now you're afraid that I might be your enemy, that I might be the one trying to take the kingdom from you, that I might be the one who caused all the disruptions in the park today."

"The thought had crossed my mind."

"As well it should have. But I assure you I am not your problem. . . . But how can you be sure of that? How do you know who I am? The man again leaned toward Hawk with a mischievous grin on his face. "Figure it out, Dr. Hawkes. Who am I?"

"You are someone who knows your way around the Pirates of the Caribbean. You are someone who is aware of who I am and what my job is. You are someone who knows about a particular key I possess. You also know there were a few incidents in the theme park today . . ."

"Good, good . . . keep going . . ."

"You meet me here, in an attraction that has been shut down all day, away from anyone else in the building, and you tell me to call you George. Conveniently, you choose the same name of the legendary ghost that many cast members think haunts this attraction."

"And you don't think I'm a ghost?" laughed the old man.

"No, I don't . . . and I don't think the attraction is haunted. But you are someone who said a moment ago that you have been waiting to meet me for years . . . and that intrigues me."

"Very good, you didn't miss a thing." George smiled a warm, genuine smile that seemed to chase away some of the dampness from the hallway. "I have been waiting to meet you since the day Walt Disney died."

"That is because you were a friend of Walt's, and he and Roy chose you to help design the mystery of the key." Hawk smiled too, as the pieces started to fall into place in his mind.

"Yes . . . and you managed to tell me all of that without mentioning any detail about what the key really is, what the key means, and what Farren Rales told you when he gave it to you," George offered, as if they were playing a game of verbal chess.

"That is because each of you has a different part, a different piece of the puzzle. You don't know the details about what Farren Rales did or didn't tell me . . . just like he has no idea that you are talking with me right now . . . correct?" Hawk advanced the rook in their cerebral chess match.

"You are correct. But after observing you over these past months, I think you are ready for the next piece of the puzzle, as you called it." He paused and sighed deeply. "Sadly, there are others who seem to be intent on trying to take away what you have been given. My friends Walt and Roy always knew there would come a day when someone who saw the world, the culture, and the industry with the clarity they did would need to be leading this company. Farren Rales was tasked with finding that individual . . . you. He was to follow the guidelines and criteria that Walt himself designed. He chose you, and from what I have seen, it was a good choice."

"Thank you," Hawk was genuinely touched that this stranger approved of the choice. Hawk understood that this was an Imagineer, one of a very select few that knew Walt and Roy Disney well enough to be entrusted with the future of what they had built over their lifetime.

"You've been given the key to the kingdom . . . but how will you unlock the kingdom?"

Hawk sat in silence. The question had placed him in checkmate. If there was something to unlock, something to know, something to do, he didn't have any idea what it was or where to find the answer. His instincts told him he needed to trust George. Although he had just met him, he was a part of an elite group in history. He was also a part of Hawk's history now. And what happened next would impact the lives of many people for years to come.

"So, how do I unlock the kingdom?" Hawk asked.

"Aw, you know it is not that easy." George slowly rose to his feet. "I can't just tell you." He gestured around them. "These walls have ears. There is a group of people who want to take the kingdom from you. Information, time, and discovery are the most valuable commodities any one person can possess. You have to figure it out, my friend . . . and if people want to take it from you, then they will have to figure it out for themselves."

George took a step toward Hawk and embraced him. As he gave him a hug, he whispered in Hawk's ear, "Unlock what never was, to protect what is yet to be."

He let him loose and stepped away. As George stopped just on the edge of disappearing into the shadows, Hawk once again extended his hand toward the old man.

"It has been an honor to meet you, George. Will I get the chance to talk with you again?"

This time George reached out and took his hand, shook it, and said, "Start in my tower." And with a wink and a nod, the translucent man slipped away into the darkness.

The sounds of the passageway once again echoed around Hawk, the dripping of water from some unseen source. The hushed sound of air breezing through the catacombs and the words that George had left with Hawk, *Unlock what never was, to protect what is yet to be . . . Start in my tower*, echoing in his head. Reaching down to grab his phone, Hawk once again remembered that he had ruined it in this very building earlier in the day. Snapping his fingers in frustration, he turned and began retracing his steps back through the backstage hallways. Each step he found himself moving a little bit quicker until he broke into a run trying to unravel himself from the twisting tunnels.

 *Evening*
Day One

HAWK BURST THROUGH THE JESUS DOOR, startling the people standing in the load area just beyond the Moonlight Bay diorama. In three strides he had managed to join the group who was still stunned at his unexpected entrance.

"Hawk, is everything alright?" Juliette asked, as he stepped next to her.

"What are you running from?" Shep asked, and then smiled an impish grin. "Did you just see a ghost?"

"Not funny," Juliette fired back. "I told you that story is just—"

"Where is George's Tower?" Hawk asked. Juliette's jaw dropped slightly, Shep stared at him in disbelief, and Bill looked both startled and confused at the same time. Hawk impatiently continued. "George's Tower . . . have you heard of it? Do you know where it is?"

"It's between the well scene and the burning city scene." Juliette stared at Hawk. Hawk pivoted his head toward her, a bit taken back that she knew so quickly. He turned toward Bill, who had not yet spoken. "How do I get there?"

"Follow me." Bill turned and stepped through the boat in the loading area and hopped out on the other side.

Hawk, Shep, and Juliette followed their guide over the boat, along a pathway on the other side of the loading area, through a door, and into a set of corridors. Single file, they walked behind Bill as he quickly navigated through the backstage area. Hawk had seen this backstage area earlier in the day when he had entered Pirates, but it still was unfamiliar to him; without a guide, he would only be guessing how to get where he was trying to go.

Over Hawk's shoulder, Juliette said softly, "Why do you need to get to George's Tower?"

"Because George told me to go there," Hawk tossed back.

Shep leaned in next to her. "I knew the ghost was real. Hawk has seen and talked to a ghost."

"Stop it," she retorted. "You know better than that."

"I'm just a little spooked out, that's all," Shep replied.

Hawk became aware that nobody was following him. Turning back, he noticed that Juliette and Shep had stopped and were in an intense conversation. He glanced back to make sure Bill wasn't going to get too far away and then stopped and spun back toward the pair.

"What are you doing?" He asked, loudly enough for them to stop talking. "Are you coming with me or not?"

They stopped their argument and rushed to catch up to their boss and friend. When they got closer, Juliette spoke up first, "Sorry."

"We were just discussing that you had talked to a ghost," Shep blurted out.

"*We* were not discussing that, Shep was the one saying that." Juliette raised her hands in frustration.

"What is wrong with you two?" Hawk again made sure he could see where Bill went. Keeping his voice in a controlled whisper, he continued, "I didn't see a ghost, I didn't talk to a ghost, there is no such thing as ghosts. This attraction is not haunted, that is just an urban legend passed along from cast member to cast member . . . so get a grip!"

"Told you." Juliette gloated at Shep.

"Juliette . . ." Hawk scolded as he turned to catch up with Bill.

Their trip through the attraction slowed, and they found themselves on the set standing next to the well. While Hawk studied the tower, Juliette and Shep noticed the audio-animatronic figures all around them. The attraction was shut down, the lights were on, and the soundtrack was silent, but there was still movement around them.

"I never knew these things twitched when they weren't running." Shep watched as the audio-animatronic pirate seemed to have a slight muscle spasm in front of him. "Weird."

"It does give you the creeps, doesn't it?" Bill asked. "Being in this attraction after it's closed down can make your mind start playing tricks on you."

Hawk turned toward Bill. "How do I get to the top of the tower?"

"You're going to climb it?"

"That is probably the only way to get to the top."

Bill motioned for them to follow and guided them to the base of the tower. Out of the view of guests, a vertical ladder ran to the top of the structure. Standing at the base of it and looking up, Hawk hesitated. It looked much higher than he had originally thought. He glanced back down toward the base of the tower. Something on the wall caught his eye, and he moved to inspect it more closely.

Looking back at Shep, he tapped the place with his finger. Shep stepped

JEFF DIXON

over to take a closer look, as did Juliette and Bill. They all leaned in to see what Hawk was pointing at. There was graffiti written randomly on the base of the tower, but Hawk was directing them to look at two initials—not written, but carved into the tower itself.

G.C.

"Whew, look at that." Hawk widened his eyes in feigned terror. "A ghost who carves his initials . . ." He pretended to shiver as he smiled at his friend. "There is nothing to be afraid of."

Shep laughed and retorted, "Except climbing up that very high ladder."

Hawk looked back up toward the top of the tower, inhaled sharply, grabbed the first rung of the metal ladder, and pulled himself up. The ladder stretched straight up, and he kept his body close to it as he made his ascent. Hand up, step up, hand up, step up . . . he kept focused on where he was going, being very careful not to look down.

When he reached the top of the ladder, he looked into the alcove at the peak. He reminded himself this was a decorative set, not really a tower, a facade to hide a support pillar. Because of that he wasn't sure what he should assume would support his weight. He clung to the ladder, hoping he wouldn't have to move too far away from it.

His eyes searched inside the tower from his new vantage point, and he noticed it—an envelope. Nothing fancy, just an envelope with something written on the front. He stretched while holding onto the ladder, and with the tip of his fingers, he caught the edge of the paper. With a flick, he pulled the envelope back toward him, and it slid just enough for him to be able to pick it up with his fingers.

As he drew it toward his face, he saw the handwritten name on the front of the envelope, one word scrawled in oversized letters. Hawk. With one hand still on the ladder, he shoved the discovery into his back pocket and took another glance around the alcove. Seeing nothing of import, he took in another deep breath and began his descent. He exhaled slowly, while carefully making his way to the bottom. When he was close enough, he jumped to the ground with a flourish.

"Well?" Juliette tilted her head to one side and raised her hands, palms up.

"I found what I was looking for." He smiled.

"What were you looking for?" Bill wrinkled his forehead.

"What I found, of course." Hawk began retracing their path to get to the base of the tower. "And what did you all find as you were looking at the security tapes?"

"We found an image on film." Bill narrowed his eyes. "It is strange, it looks like it could be a ghost." He paused. "I mean . . . if you believe in such things."

"I don't and it's not," Hawk said kindly. "Finish up your work here and get the attraction ready to reopen tomorrow, please." He turned toward Shep and Juliette. "See if you can round up Jonathan and find Reginald, and let's meet at my place as soon as you can get there."

"Sure thing, boss." Shep nodded. "Should we order dinner?"

"Maybe Jonathan can bring pizza," Juliette suggested, then turned to Hawk and raised her eyebrow. "And exactly why are we all meeting?"

"So I can show you what I found today." He fingered the envelope. Raising it in front of his face, he twisted the package, trying to peek at what was hidden inside. "And because I think a ghost might be trying to tell me something."

## CHAPTER SEVENTEEN

## Day One
## Evening

THE CALL OF CURIOSITY HAD COMPELLED them to come. The unexpected invitation to visit the home of Grayson Hawkes was one that couldn't be ignored. Hawk's place was also known as the Hawk's Nest. It was on the second floor of the Fire Station in the Town Square on Main Street USA. As the only permanent resident of the Magic Kingdom, Hawk had the freedom to move about the park in the evening when preparations for the new day were always being made.

Most people never realize how busy the Disney World Resort is after it is closed to guests, but each park is a beehive of activity, taking care of details that can't be addressed with guests present. The members of this third-shift crew had grown used to seeing Hawk move about the park; they enjoyed his visits, and on occasion, he would treat everyone in the area to ice cream from the ice cream parlor at the end of Main Street.

This evening, the Hawk's Nest was full of people who had entered a bit more discreetly. The Magic Kingdom was still open. Directly below the apartment was a shop with a constant flow of people moving in and out. The parade was moving past the apartment window, and guests were jammed together up and down Main Street USA. Juliette, Shep, Reginald, and Hawk had been joined by Jonathan Carlson.

Jonathan had worked with Hawk for years on the staff of Celebration Community Church. When Hawk had shifted responsibilities and become the CCA of Disney, Jonathan had accepted a cast role in consulting much like Shep had. In addition, Jonathan had kept an active ministerial staff role at the church, working alongside the new administrator the church had hired and leading in the worship events. He had been the last to arrive, and he bore an armload of pizzas.

This was a gathering of friends; the conversation was crisp, full of fun and familiarity. There had been some ribbing about Shep being afraid of ghosts and some lighthearted jabs aimed at Jonathan, when he walked in sporting a bandage across his forehead. He explained he had cracked it running a cable under his desk in his office. This had prompted Hawk to launch into a well-worn story of one of his klutzier moments, and the room was filled with laughter. Even Reginald Cambridge was smiling and relaxed. He rarely relaxed, he explained, because Hawk was always getting into some kind of trouble that Reginald had to get him out of.

One of the strengths that Hawk had believed and taught as a leader was the importance of how a team spent time together. Strengthening relationships, allowing one another to catch a glimpse of doing life together, tightened the bonds that held a team together. Times when they could be relaxed like this were some of his favorite moments, and he had missed them because they had not occurred often over the past eighteen months. He had a sense that their lives were about to change again. The laughter subsided, as Hawk turned the conversation to the events of the day.

Once again they revisited the audio-animatronic pirates that had turned up in the Magic Kingdom. The pirate attack account was familiar to all but Jonathan, who sat amazed at what he was hearing. As Hawk relayed the story of what had happened in the Hall of Presidents, he could see Reginald straighten up and slide forward in his chair. Each expression darkened as Hawk recalled how the masked man had struck him and delivered the threatening warning, *One if by land, two if by sea, put out the lights and give us the key.* The mood lightened slightly when he explained how he was released and had improvised with a group of visiting students after they saw him sitting among the presidents. But as he finished his account, the tension in the room hung thick with the threat of what they might be facing.

Reginald bristled. "I knew I should not have let you wander through the park alone."

"It doesn't matter." Hawk leaned forward. "I'm not going to let you babysit me, and it turned out just fine. I'm not hurt."

"You aren't hurt this time." Juliette shook her head. "But remember what happened before. These people who want to take this key don't care what they have to do to get it."

No one said a word, but Hawk knew what they were thinking. Over a year ago, Hawk was trying to unravel the mystery of the key to the kingdom. Juliette had been kidnapped and threatened. If Hawk hadn't found her, they weren't sure how far her captors would have gone to use her to get Hawk to turn over the key. Those days and the quest to solve the mystery had deepened their friendships, but he knew they were all aware of just how dangerous people who desired power, control, and riches could really be. It was easy to ignore this looming threat when things were going well. But as with any moment in life, it only takes a quick reminder, and the events of the past crash back in around you.

Cambridge rose to his feet. "I'm going to call Al Gann. We need his assistance." Al was their liaison with the sheriff's department and a friend who had helped them on the first key quest.

"That's a good idea, but hold on a few minutes." Hawk motioned for Reginald to retake his seat. "We need to unpack our little ghost hunt tonight."

They compared their experiences in the Pirates of the Caribbean from earlier. The group explained to Hawk and Jonathan what they had seen on the security footage. Hawk then told them of his journey through the damp, darkened catacombs of the attraction and his encounter with George. He carefully recalled everything George had said to him. He summarized why he believed for certain that George was one of the original Imagineers who had helped Walt and Roy Disney design this plan for a key to be the driving mechanism for the progression of power and leadership of the company. He told them what George had told him to do: *unlock what never was, to protect what is yet to be.*

"What does that mean?" Shep interrupted.

"It means we have enormous problems." Again Cambridge got out of his seat and drew his cell phone from the holster on his hip like a gunfighter.

"Yes," Hawk agreed. "We may have problems, but we also have something else to do."

Cambridge paused once again. He lowered his phone. Each set of eyes looked at him, waiting for him to sit down once again so Hawk could finish. Relenting to the peer pressure, he took his seat, looking extremely uncomfortable.

"George told me to start in his tower." Hawk pulled the envelope out of his back pocket. "That is where I found this."

"What is it?" Jonathan nearly slid out of his chair trying to get close enough to see it.

"I don't know." Hawk spun the envelope in his hand so they could see it. "I wanted to wait until you all were with me so we could see it together."

"I already know what it is," Cambridge said guardedly. He allowed his stare to pause on the face of each person in the room. "It is going to be some type of clue. Which will lead to another clue. And then yet another. You don't realize how dangerous this game might be. But once you open the clue, it won't matter . . . you will willingly embrace the game and want to play it until the bitter end. You can't do it this time. There is too much at risk. Too much to lose."

Shep's eyes were dancing from person to person. "But we figured it out last time. It all worked out great. Hawk is now the chief creative architect, and—"

"That is exactly what I am saying," Cambridge slowly stated. "If you will remember, I was pursuing you on your last mystery-solving excursion." He leveled his gaze at Hawk. "And I almost caught you. If it hadn't been for your girlfriend, who turned out to be an enemy who was just playing you—" He slowed down, as though realizing his words may have hurt Hawk. "You turned my theme parks upside down with your disregard for rules, safety, and common sense. Only when it was over did I discover this grand and glorious adventure that you claimed to be on."

"But—" Hawk felt a surge of pain like he had just been punched in the gut.

"Wait." Cambridge held up his hand. "Let me finish. Since that time, I have come to understand why Farren Rales and the Imagineers helped the Disney brothers create this model for how to keep the company running. And I have also done my best to keep you safe, always knowing in the back of my mind that the same people who tried to stop you before, the same people who kidnapped Juliette before, and the same people who will stop at nothing to take your key to the kingdom, would one day try again."

The group was silent. Cambridge paced the room. He ran his hand over his forehead, paused, and looked down at the floor. After a few moments he inhaled deeply and continued. "Today they have managed to shut down four attractions in the Magic Kingdom. We don't know how they did what they did. They managed to kidnap you." He nodded toward Hawk. "And you walked right into it. They obviously knew that George the Imagineer was getting ready to contact you. More than likely that is why they used pirates today to send you a warning to give up the key. Just like before, they were watching and staying one move ahead of you. Grayson, they are better at playing this game than we are. They don't play by any rules. You have to take care of our guests, our resort, the rest of us, and yourself." He finally replaced the phone into its resting place on his belt. "We can't win on our own this time. We need help."

"He's right, Hawk." Juliette sank back in her chair. "This is serious stuff."

"I agree." Jonathan clasped his hands behind his head. "It's pretty risky. Juliette could have been hurt badly, and you could have been hurt. Shep and I were just trying to help you solve some clues, but you were in way over your head by the time we got involved."

"That is why I wanted you all here this time when I opened the clue." Hawk looked at the envelope he was still turning over and over in his fingers. "But you're right. It is pretty crazy stuff. We should let the professionals figure out who is trying to mess with us." He stood and placed the envelope back into his rear pocket. "Reginald, go ahead and call Al. I can give the envelope to him tomorrow. I have breakfast in the morning with Farren.

He might be able to shine a little more light on the mysterious George." He glanced at each person. "I don't ever want you to get hurt because of me. Let's call it a night. Thanks for coming. Thanks for being my friends."

The friends exchanged hugs, handshakes, and pats on the backs as they made their way to exit the Hawk's Nest. Cambridge left, Juliette followed, Shep lingered, and Hawk nodded at him, giving him permission to use the firefighter's pole that had been installed in the apartment. The trapdoor opened, and Shep slid down into the shop below, causing an audible reaction from the guests that drifted up into the apartment. Hawk was gazing out the window down to Main Street USA. He sensed someone still in the room with him and turned to see Jonathan standing in the doorway.

"You good, Hawk?" Jonathan asked.

"Yep, I'm good."

"And for tomorrow?"

"Yes, good for tomorrow. Looking forward to tomorrow." Hawk nodded and waved, reassuring it was alright for Jonathan to leave.

Tomorrow was Hawk's day to cover and participate in one of the worship services at Celebration Community Church. The sudden fame and notoriety of Grayson Hawkes had created some positive press for the church. As a result, the visibility of the church had been enhanced, and visitors flocked to see what was going on there. Now as one of the teaching pastors, Hawk would make an appearance at one of the worship events each week. Tomorrow was that day. He was scheduled to preach in an evening worship event. Worship and teaching was one of the things he looked forward to each week.

Jonathan spoke softly. "See you then." He closed the door and left.

Hawk turned back toward the window and gazed out at the guests exiting the Magic Kingdom at the end of another day. Walt Disney World was truly a magical place for him. He was living a dream. Deep inside, he prayed that his dream would not turn into a nightmare.

 *Day One*
Evening

HAWK'S THOUGHTS WERE INTERRUPTED by a knock on his apartment door. He crossed from the window to the door and absently called out, "Who is it?" as he clutched the door knob. Turning it and pulling, he opened the door to see Juliette, Shep, and Jonathan all standing there. Juliette and Shep were grinning. Jonathan had a more skeptical expression.

"You're going to open it now, aren't you?" Shep pushed past Hawk and reentered the Hawk's Nest.

"No," he replied sternly.

"But you are going to, right?" Juliette placed her hands on her hips.

"No, you said it was serious stuff." Hawk turned toward Jonathan as he closed the door behind him. "And you said it was risky."

"And you expect us to believe that you're just going to leave that envelope alone all night?" Jonathan pointed at the envelope still in Hawk's hand.

"And you won't open it?" Juliette raised her right eyebrow.

"Actually . . ." Hawk paused and looked down at the envelope. "I was waiting for you to come back up here." A grin exploded across his face as he raced over to the table and took a seat.

The three followed him to the table and huddled around him as he carefully worked his finger under the sealed edge of the flap. It gently released. Looking up at his staring friends awaiting the contents to emerge, he smiled. "Thanks for coming back up."

"Will you just look inside already?" Shep shook Hawk's shoulder to get him moving.

He reached inside and felt a thin, flat object. Tilting the envelope, he slid out the lone item within, a very old picture. As Hawk placed it on the table in front of them, they peered at it.

The black-and-white photograph showed wear and tear collected over the years. It was a picture that had been valuable enough to keep, but it had not been well preserved. There were three people depicted in it, seated on a front porch; the person in the middle was instantly recognizable. It was Walt Disney. The picture captured a moment in time when he was caught between a smile and a laugh, and his mouth looked as if he were getting ready to say something.

Holding a hat in his hand, Walt appeared as he would have looked during the 1950s. His two companions were huddled close and smiling brightly for the photographer. The woman on the left was seated beside Walt in a wooden swing suspended by chains, leaning in toward him for the picture. Shoved up right next to the swing was a wooden rocking chair. In it sat a smiling white-haired woman. All three seemed to be having a good time being together, without a care that this time of their lives was being captured in a photograph.

"A picture." Shep stated the obvious.

"A picture of Walt Disney." Jonathan added to the obvious.

"I would say an old picture of Walt Disney, but you guys are killing me with the obvious. Tell me something I don't know." Juliette leaned in even closer. "This isn't the standard kind of picture the studio would have had taken, archived, or released. This is from someone's personal collection. And that's not quite as obvious." She nodded, satisfied.

"That makes sense." Hawk studied it. "I wonder whose collection . . . Walt's or the people in the picture with him."

Juliette reached over Hawk's shoulder and picked up the picture. Bringing it closer to her face, she flipped it over in her hand to see the back. With a smile, she softly placed the picture back on the table face down in front of them. There was writing on the back of the photo.

"Aunt Jessie, Walt, and Irene," read Jonathan aloud.

But something else was written below that inscription. Clearly this notation was not a part of the original writing and not penned by the same person. This cleanly scripted note had to be a message that was intended for whoever opened this envelope and discovered this picture.

*Aunt Jessie has a special delivery.*
*Walt's grandparents are trying to Call you.*
*Go back to the roots to find your way.*

This was it. Hawk picked up the picture. He knew those three simple lines were about to propel him into something unknown. Juliette drifted away from the group and slumped back into a chair by the window. Jonathan moved a few feet and took a seat at the table with Hawk. Shep began pacing the apartment. All four were lost in thought and no one spoke.

"OK, I give." Juliette shook her head. "What does it mean?"

"It's a clue," Shep said. "It has to be."

"No kidding!" She rolled her eyes.

"It is a clue," Jonathan restated. "Which brings us right back to where we were before we opened it."

"What do you mean?" Hawk turned toward his friend.

"It's what we talked about." Jonathan's eyes locked on his. "This is another moment when you have to decide if you're going to go on some wild clue-finding, who-knows-where-you-will-end-up-or-what-might-happen scavenger hunt."

"Maybe it will be easier this time—or at least not as bad."

"Really, boss?" Jonathan got up and moved toward the living room area. "It was created by an Imagineer, like Farren Rales, who is trying to give you a secret created by Walt Disney. And let's not forget that there are some very connected, angry, and bad people out there who would like to stop you from finding it. . . . I think you just told us about your encounter with an upset president from earlier today."

Hawk placed the picture back on the table. His friends already knew what he was going to do. His drive for adventure and his commitment to protect what he had been entrusted with was one of his strengths . . . and might be where he was most vulnerable.

"You already have decided to solve this thing." Juliette forced a laugh. "I could have been killed last time."

"But you weren't," Hawk reminded her. "I found you."

"And you remind me of it . . . often."

"However . . ." Hawk raised his hands palms up and closed his eyes. "If you three, as my most trusted friends, tell me it is too dangerous and risky to get tangled up in this . . . then I will leave it alone."

"We told you a minute ago it was too dangerous and risky," Jonathan chided.

"Oh, yeah . . . you did." Hawk reopened his eyes. "I guess I just never listen."

"Let's solve this thing." Shep moved back to the table to take another look.

"What about Reginald?" Juliette's face turned serious. "You told him you would leave it alone and that he should call Al Gann."

"He needs to call Al . . . I told him I would give the picture to Al, and I will." Hawk smiled. "I'm just not going to tell him I am not ready to let it go . . . not quite yet."

"He'll be upset," Jonathan reminded them.

"He worries too much," Hawk countered.

"His job is to keep you safe and out of trouble." Juliette got out of her seat and moved back toward the table. "And you make that extremely difficult."

Jonathan also returned to the table, and once again the group settled into seats around it. Hawk slid the picture to the middle of the table, the three smiling faces looking up at them from the black-and-white image. The friends studied the picture and its inscription with great attention to detail.

"Let's all do a little digging into what the clue might mean," Hawk instructed. "We can compare notes tomorrow night at church."

"I've already been to church this week," Juliette said. "We went to the morning service this week."

"That's right, she did," Jonathan added.

"But I hear the preacher tomorrow night is very good," Hawk offered.

"Nah . . . I've heard him before." Juliette smiled. "Tim and I can bring the kids. They are always asking to go to Kid Church, so they won't mind going back again."

"I love Kid Church!" Shep *would* feel that way, since he was the one who'd created the special children's worship events at Celebration Community Church. "I can't wait to go there."

"It's settled, then." Hawk pushed back from the table. "We'll compare notes tomorrow night before church. I have breakfast with Farren in the morning. Maybe he can shed some insight on this little photo." Hawk glanced at the clock and knew it was going to be a sleepless night. He couldn't wait for breakfast to arrive.

## CHAPTER NINETEEN

## Day Two
## Morning

FARREN RALES REVERENTLY HELD the old black-and-white photo-graph in his hand. Squinting, he studied it closely. His eyes danced between the three people, but he lingered on the familiar face of the man in the middle of the photograph, Walt Disney, just as Hawk, Shep, Juliette, and Jonathan had done the night before.

While the Imagineer looked over the photograph, Hawk settled into a pivoting leather chair, finished off the pastry he'd picked up on Main Street USA, and gazed at the variety of security camera monitors and control panels lining both sides of this room. He turned slowly in the chair, taking in the state-of-the-art control room; it was also a bunker, safe and secure from all the activity taking place above them in the Magic Kingdom. This room, which Hawk had eventually found and unlocked, had been a part of the key to the kingdom. It was an auxiliary control center that could operate much of the Magic Kingdom if needed. Through a series of deliveries moved from nearby storage areas into this room, and then Farren's personally wiring the electronics and finishing it up, the room had been created in secrecy. There were only two people that knew this bunker existed, and they were both sitting in it right now, finishing breakfast.

While Hawk had been solving the mystery of the key, Farren had hidden away in this bunker and monitored Hawk's progress in unraveling the clues that eventually led him to his friend and the mind-numbing secrets this room protected. Upon entering it that first time, he found himself face-to-face with Walt Disney. As Mr. Disney addressed him by name and engaged him in conversation, he soon discovered that he was talking with the most advanced audio-animatronic creation ever made by the company, the AI-1000 Audio-Animatronic Walt Disney. But that wasn't the only surprise Hawk's key opened; it was a preview of coming attractions. That encounter with Walt Disney had welcomed him to this underground facility, but eventually he had made it to this control room, which contained the biggest surprise of all: Walt Disney himself.

The shiny silver cylinder in the center of the room glistened as the light emanating from each monitor bounced off its reflective surface. The cryogenic container held the body of the creative genius. Hawk had been amazed to find out that the often-repeated urban legend about Walt Disney's body being placed in cryogenic suspension was true. Not only was it true, but the legend had been perpetuated by those who knew the truth. Unlike the myth, however, the quest for Walt Disney was not to live forever or to be restored to life when medical science might find a way to do so—instead he was available if the need ever arose for him to come back to rescue, preserve, or reemerge within the company he had created. One of the main roles for Hawk as the keeper of the key to the kingdom was to make that decision, if it were ever a necessity.

His choice as the keeper of the key had also taken into deep consideration that as a pastor, with a heart for God, he would be wise and make the moral and ethical choice about whether such an action was the right thing to do. The secret was his to keep and protect. Farren Rales had chosen him for the task and was the only other person alive, insofar as Hawk knew, that had that knowledge. Now, as he watched Farren looking into the photograph of his dear friend, he wondered what Rales was thinking.

"Aunt Jessie, Walt, and Irene," Farren read the notation aloud. "Hmmm, then of course there is the note, 'Aunt Jessie has a special delivery. Walt's grandparents are trying to Call you. Go back to the roots to find your way.'"

"Yes." Hawk rolled his chair toward where Farren was seated along a counter below some monitors. "What does it mean?"

"I have no idea." Farren looked up at him and smiled. "I have absolutely no idea." He laughed out loud as he passed the picture back to a dumbfounded Hawk.

"What do you mean you don't know?" Hawk took the picture and reflexively looked down at it. "Who are these people in the picture?"

"The one in the middle is Walt Disney," Farren said slowly.

"I figured that one out."

"The other one . . . I am guessing the one on the right is Aunt Jessie, and then Irene is seated next to Walt on the left."

"Farren," Hawk sighed, not amused by his friend's laughter. "I guessed the same thing. I asked what it means."

"I told you, I do not know." Seeing Hawk's frustration, Farren tried to quell the smirk on his face. "Tell me where you found the picture."

Hawk launched into the detailed story of what had happened the evening before, after he had left Farren at the office in the Bay Lake Tower. He told him of the ghost story, the encounter with George, what George had said, and how he had climbed George's Tower in the Pirates of the Caribbean to find the envelope. He also recalled the reluctance of Reginald Cambridge to open the envelope, his promise to give it to Al Gann, and then the return of his staff members to see for themselves what was inside. Hawk recalled each moment with vivid detail. He paced the room as he talked, his eyes lighting up as he remembered details and acted out what had taken place.

"That is quite a story." Farren smiled as Hawk finished. "You told that story with such style, I could see every detail of it. It reminds me of the man in your picture there."

Suddenly speechless at the compliment he had been given, Hawk felt his face blush as he gazed back toward the picture in his hand. He had been waving it around absently as he told the story, using it as a prop to enhance the tale. He paused, took a deep breath, and returned to the chair he had been seated in. Looking from the smiling Walt Disney to Farren, he waited. His old friend had to know something about this picture, about the encounter the night before, and about whatever would happen next—or might be happening right now. He could not image Farren not having some perspective that would help him.

"So you met George last night?" Farren said mildly.

"Yes." Hawk leaned back in his chair. "And unlike the legend and the stories in the Pirates of the Caribbean attraction, George is not a ghost."

"In some ways he is." Farren leaned forward to Hawk. "In some ways, he is."

"A ghost?"

"I said in some ways. His name is George Colmes. I haven't seen him for years."

"And he is one of the Imagineers chosen by Walt and Roy Disney to protect the company and create the key to the kingdom?"

"Yes." Farren spoke softly. "He is one of the three Imagineers who helped to create this layer of protection for the company."

"Tell me about him." Hawk sat up straighter in his chair.

"George Colmes was one of the Imagineers that Walt and Roy selected to design this intricate plan of succession and survival for the Disney Company. How we accomplished our tasks was left to us. The only time we connected with one another about what we were doing was when we thought we were crossing over into an area that might impact what one of the others was creating."

"So your job was to find the keeper of the key."

"Yes, we believed if each person had a specific role and worked exclusively of the others, it would provide an additional layer of security, in case anything went wrong." Farren gestured toward Hawk. "You were my choice.

You now possess the key, the pieces of it I was tasked to give you, and you are now in a position of power in the company—and you now have Walt himself." Farren nodded his head toward the cylinder.

"So now I meet George, and he gives me directions to find a picture on top of a haunted tower, and you describe him as some kind of ghost." Hawk pursed his lips. "Did I summarize that correctly?"

"Pretty much." The old man smiled. "George Colmes, like all of us, had to do his best to protect what he had been entrusted with. He was very involved, as we all were, in developing the Florida Project. After Walt passed away, George was busy steering the developers who were trying to get the resort built and opened."

"I don't remember hearing of him before."

"You wouldn't have. George had a very different role than I did. Most didn't know him very well. He was a very close friend of Roy Disney. As Roy stepped up his leadership to get Walt Disney World built, George was a guide, a friend, and a strong influence behind the scenes in making things happen."

"So, with Walt gone, he and Roy probably worried about the future of the company and this plan that was being created?"

"Probably more than I ever realized. When Roy suddenly died just after the Magic Kingdom opened, George retired unexpectedly and was never seen or heard from again."

"Wait." Hawk leaned heavily on the arm of the chair. "Why did he disappear?"

"I always believed it was because he had lost Roy, which was just as emotional for him as losing Walt. He became like a ghost . . . I have not seen him or talked to him since 1971, the year the resort opened. He had no family that anyone knew of . . . he just disappeared."

"You say no one knows where he went or what he did after he retired? But he was a part of a select group of people like you . . . you had to have some idea."

"No, I really didn't." Farren shrugged. "Though I had suspicions, to be sure. Little things I noticed."

"Help me here. I'm not following where you're going."

"I know, my friend. I really am not trying to confuse you. Let me see if I can explain this to you." Farren rose and made a sweeping gesture around the room with his hand. "The things that I was busy doing were completed because of the people I trusted enough to help me. Although they never knew details of what they were doing, they completed the tasks I needed done. They never had enough information to understand the vastness of the projects I was a part of. Even if they suspected they might be involved in something bigger than I was letting on . . . they could only be suspicious. They had nothing else to run with, no more information to find, and no more places to find it. I chose them, like I chose you, because I trusted them. I suspect George Colmes probably operated in a similar way to do what he needed to get done."

"But you don't know what he was trying to do?"

"No. Eventually he would be responsible for making sure you would know or have or see or do whatever the Disney brothers had given him the task of passing on to you. But what that might be, I can only suspect."

"What do you suspect?"

"What did he tell you?" Farren rose to stand in front of Hawk.

"I told you," Hawk replied. "He told me to unlock what never was, to protect what is yet to be."

"Is that all he said?"

"Yes, that's it."

"No, Grayson . . ." Farren grabbed each arm of Hawk's chair and leaned in over him. "There had to be something else."

Hawk was taken back at the intensity of his friend. His mind rewound to the encounter in the caverns of the Pirates attraction. Thinking back, he remembered George had asked him a question. At the time he heard it, he thought it was misplaced or silly. Now he was trying to recapture the memory. Hawk lowered his head and tried to recall each line that was uttered. One of the reasons he had been so successful in solving the mystery that Farren had created was because of his ability to notice and remember details. In the world of Walt Disney, details always mattered and discoveries were always waiting hidden in plain sight.

"There was something else." Hawk locked onto the question he had momentarily lost. "George asked me something that I thought was odd. He asked me how I was going to unlock the kingdom."

Rales released the chair and straightened up. "And then he told you to unlock what never was, to protect what is yet to be?"

"Yes, and I thought it was an odd question, because when I found all the pieces you had hidden, and found this . . ." Hawk looked around the room. "Well, to be honest, I thought I already had unlocked the kingdom."

"No, my dear friend." Farren was smiling. "You have been given the kingdom. It is yours. But you have not unlocked it . . . yet."

 *Day Two*
*Morning*

"**WHAT DO YOU MEAN I HAVEN'T UNLOCKED** the kingdom yet?" Hawk rose to his feet and began to pace. "I found so many pieces of this incredible puzzle you put together for me. I did things to solve it because I was worried about you and thought something had happened to you. I put my friends at risk, my reputation on the line, and . . ."

"Someone you trusted betrayed you." Farren stated the part that Hawk was going to skip.

"I haven't forgotten." Hawk had wrestled with it more than anyone knew. Kiran Roberts had exploded into his life. He'd trusted her, and she'd helped him unravel some of the clues and get access to places he never would have found. Then he discovered that she had been using him to get the key for herself and her associates. "I just don't talk about her."

"Of course." Farren nodded.

"But now you're saying I'm not done yet? Last night Juliette, Jonathan, Shep, and I were thinking this was another mystery to unravel . . . but . . . seriously . . ." Hawk stopped pacing and looked at his reflection in the silver cylinder. "What else is there?"

"I don't know, I honestly don't know." Farren turned his palms up. "I only know what I was supposed to give you. George was given something by Walt and Roy that he was supposed to take care of until I chose the keeper of the key . . . that is you. Now George has decided it is time to give it to you."

"He gave me a picture." Hawk held up the photo.

"He gave you a clue." Farren moved to Hawk and took the picture from him. "I said earlier I didn't know what happened to George. Yet there were times I suspected he was still very active in the company. Just like I had people I could trust to help me, George had the same kind of influence. He has been very busy . . . or so I believe."

"Busy how? What kind of busy?"

Farren turned to one of the monitors and took a seat in front of it. Grabbing a nearby wireless keyboard, he began pounding on it using the two-finger method. After a series of keystrokes, he brought up an aerial view of the Walt Disney World Resort. He pointed at it, then circled it with his finger. "Do you know what this is?"

"The Walt Disney World Resort?" Hawk decided to play along. Farren was one of the greatest living storytellers, and when he unpacked ideas, they came in the form of stories. Farren believed—and so did Hawk—that stories can change the way you look at life and view the world. Each person lives out the story he was created for, and each day a new page of the story begins. You never know what lies on the next page, and you live life a word, a phrase, and a paragraph at a time. In life, there is no skipping ahead to the ending. Instead you have to take the journey to get there. If you do it right, you will enjoy the story.

The story of Hawk's life was radically different since he had met Farren. But he had enjoyed the story. There was a feeling in his gut that he might be at the first sentence of a new chapter that Farren was getting ready to read aloud to him.

"Very good." Farren paused, as he began to hunt and peck again on the keyboard. "It is not just the Walt Disney World Resort, it is your kingdom. The kingdom you possess the key to."

A new image appeared on the screen. This was Walt Disney World from a bygone time. The aerial view featured the familiar Magic Kingdom with only the Contemporary Resort and the Polynesian Resort. Massive amounts of undeveloped land surrounded it. Once again Farren traced it with his finger. "You recognize this?"

Hawk mentally unraveled the years, to a happy moment from his childhood. "Walt Disney World when it first opened."

"Exactly, this was what we looked like in 1971." Now as Farren hit a key, the image went from the original view on opening day to the current layout of the property. "Look at all the changes. We have made many changes and come a long way over the years. Walt Disney World is always changing, and changes happen fast. Sometimes people like the changes, sometimes they don't. But change is a constant here. We are always improving, expanding, and enhancing for the enjoyment of our guests."

"Right. That is what we are supposed to do . . . isn't it?"

"Sure, but have you ever wondered if there was a deeper meaning to some of the changes?"

Hawk looked at the images as Farren toggled between the resort of the past and the resort of the present. He pondered what he had just been asked. "I don't know. I always believed things were changed to improve them. I never knew I needed to look beyond that reason."

As soon as the words were spoken, Hawk realized it was what he had always believed . . . until he was given the key. Over the last year and a half, he had been noticing details about how the park changed that didn't always make sense to him. His mind unfurled a list of unasked questions he had been collecting. Perhaps it was time for him to start getting answers. Snapping his attention back from the mental list was the silence that had filled the room while his friend paused after his last statement. The quiet disappeared.

"Most don't. And why would they?" Farren left the image on the 1971 version of the resort. "You asked me what kind of business I suspect George has been up to. . . . I think he has been very active. I believe that he has continued to influence the changes and development of the resort."

"Why?"

"Simple, really. He was a part of the original design group that created what you see here, alongside Roy and his team." Farren pointed to the screen. The image then changed to the present-day resort. "It is easy to see how much things have changed, but . . ."

"But?"

"Stay with me here. . . . I have always wondered if some of the changes had a deeper meaning or purpose. I knew that, in order to create the elaborate scenario and structure you would need to become the keeper of the kingdom, I would have to get very creative. Clues hidden in plain sight, technology, things that had to be built. If George had something you were one day supposed to find, he would have to do the same thing."

"That makes sense . . . I guess." Hawk was locked in, trying to track alongside of Farren's trail of thought.

"So what if some of the changes were done for a specific purpose? What if George did the same things I did . . . hid clues in the details of the park? From time to time, they would need to be changed or updated as time or other things demanded."

Hawk looked closely at the differences in Fantasyland in the Magic Kingdom. The 20,000 Leagues Under the Sea attraction had disappeared years ago. Mr. Toad's Wild Ride had been revamped for Adventures of Winnie the Pooh. Inside the new attraction hung a portrait of Toad passing the deed to the property to Owl. Eventually, all of Fantasyland had gone through the biggest expansion in company history as new attractions, restaurants, shops, and details were added. He could see clearly in the snapshots of his mind the "Hidden Nautilus" that was carved into the rocks as a tribute to the old submarine ride. Could the changes mean more than just making things better for the guests? "What things demanded the changes?"

"Specifically, villains. People who were trying to find what was intended by Walt and Roy for you to find one day. George was very influential in development circles. As a matter of fact, he may have been the major reason that an entire area of the park was never developed."

Hawk straightened up and wrinkled his forehead. Glancing back at the screen, he swept off the dust in his mental library of Disney knowledge, trying to remember the projects that had died as unfinished dreams. "Which area are you talking about?"

"There was supposed to be a place called Thunder Mesa and the Western River Expedition. It was heavily advertised and promised to be in development."

"I've heard of it." Hawk could see the images of the attraction playing like a slide show in his mind. He was disappointed he hadn't remembered it before Rales mentioned it.

"Of course you have. Every Disney fanatic who really knows his history knows of it. People have always hoped one day to see it, but they never will."

"They might." Hawk bristled. He had the authority to put such projects into motion. His reaction surprised even him. He didn't like Farren stating something was impossible. It wasn't like him.

"No, they won't," Farren again stated firmly.

"Why?" Hawk had an icy edge to his voice that he hadn't intended.

"Officially, it would cost too much . . . but we have never had an idea so completely developed and ready to go that never happened. There were always rumors as to why it was never built, and there are other strange things that happened as well. But I tell you to help you understand that George was not just any Imagineer. He could envision things the rest of us could not."

Hawk was lost. He didn't know where Farren was trying to get him to go. He ran his fingers through his hair and shook his head. Exhaling loudly, he tried to slow his whirring mind to figure out what improvements to the resort had to do with an old Imagineer and him. There was some new mystery to solve, and Farren had him reeling over a project that had been kicked off the drawing board years ago. An old idea was not going to help him find what he needed to find now. Or was it? Urgency crept in from the edges of his mind. Walt Disney's kingdom might be at risk—the kingdom he was supposed to protect—and some very nasty people wanted the key to the kingdom immediately.

"How many things have been updated and remodeled since you became the keeper of the kingdom?" Farren asked suddenly.

"I don't know . . . a lot." Hawk shrugged at the unexpected question.

"And how many of those have you been a part of planning?"

"Some, but usually I'm just signing off on them."

"And where do those ideas come from that you are just signing off on?"

"From various departments within the company, driven by their desire to create a better guest experience—and of course there are always economic factors."

"That makes sense," Farren confirmed. "But you haven't really gotten too involved in that process. I would suggest to you that some of the changes and improvements might be happening to protect and preserve the company, and to stay one step ahead of those who have been trying since 1971 to control this place—and the same villains are trying to take the key you have been given as well. I would submit to you that what is happening is very serious. Make sure you know who you can trust, and don't assume that any place is out of these villains' reach. Even this place."

Hawk watched Farren gesture across the bunker for emphasis. He then flashed back to the face in the Hall of Presidents from the previous day. Those he was close to all agreed that once again someone was trying to make a play to take control from Hawk. Even George has sensed it and hinted at it, choosing this time to introduce himself to Hawk. George had told him to unlock what never was, to protect what is yet to be, as if there was some danger and urgency beyond just the control of the company.

"So for all of these years, George has been working behind the scenes, almost like a ghost . . . to influence the changes necessary to protect something that Walt and Roy had given him?" Hawk closed his eyes and rubbed his temples. "Attractions and areas may have been refurbished if something hidden there was discovered or someone was getting close to figuring it out?"

"Exactly." Rales smiled at Hawk's conclusion. "At least that is what I think. The G.C. that I knew would do that."

"Did you call him G.C.?"

"Yes, G.C. was the name his friends called him . . . why?"

"The initials G.C. were carved at the base of George's Tower in the Pirates of the Caribbean."

"As I told you, George is very much a ghost . . . mysterious, unseen, and yet . . . he seems to be doing things that are hard to explain . . . if I am right about how much influence he might have had through the years."

"I don't know, Farren, that all seems like a far stretch . . ."

"Really?" Farren cocked his head. "This, coming from a preacher who suddenly is the one person who knows Walt Disney's greatest secret." Farren pointed at the silver cryogenic chamber.

Hawk followed his motion and looked toward the chamber, then slowly turned back toward Rales. "Maybe I don't know Walt's greatest secret . . . and maybe you don't either, from what you are saying."

"Then it appears, my friend, that you have an even bigger mystery to solve."

 *Day Two*
Evening

**THE PARKING LOT OF THE CELEBRATION** Community Church was filled to capacity. Grayson Hawkes had to park on a side street to make it inside this church that had become increasingly popular in the Disney-created community. This small town, created as an experimental community, was now struggling with the same issues all towns face when dealing with the pressure of expansion in a popular, developing area. The church had become an anchor point for many families. Hawk, Jonathan, Juliette, and Shep had helped to lead the church to become that kind of ministry. Although the church was thriving, there still was a great transition going on as the responsibilities of the ministers and their day-to-day involvement had shifted over the past eighteen months.

Stepping into the lobby of the worship center, Hawk could hear the voices of those already inside waiting for the evening's worship to begin. He could feel the anticipatory buzz in the air. For Hawk that feeling was satisfying; he had tried to lead people into anticipating what can happen when you worship. He had communicated with passion that what you experience in a church environment is a choice. If you come with an expectation to encounter Jesus, then you will encounter Jesus.

People waved as they recognized the pastor entering the building. Instantly, it felt as if the anticipation increased as word began to spread that this evening was the designated service for Hawk to preach. The church policy was not to announce who the speaker would be at any particular service. Whether it was the best policy was not yet clear, because the church constantly took calls asking whether the chief creative architect of the Disney Company was the featured teacher on that night. Glenn Rogers, the church administrator who had been called to fill many of the leadership needs that arose in the aftermath of the staffing changes, walked across the lobby and caught Hawk's attention.

"I managed to get the camera crew squared away," Glenn stated with a smile.

"Camera crew?"

"*Total Access?*" Glenn's smile faltered as though he sensed he'd caught Hawk by surprise.

"Ah, yes . . . *Total Access*. Sorry, I had my mind on other things today. Are they tucked away where they won't be a distraction?"

"They are. I gave them the ground rules of what we expect and how our focus is on celebrating the Savior. I believe they will honor what we have asked."

"Thanks, Glenn." Hawk patted Glenn on the back as he moved away.

Glenn had done an amazing job in an almost impossible situation, helping the ministry move forward despite the changes that had suddenly unfolded. What had happened to Hawk had impacted the lives of so many. No matter how much he had tried to smooth the transition, there was no way to protect people from the consequences of the unexpected shift of the staff's lifestyle.

Hawk drifted into the hallway where his old office was located. Just past his old door was a conference room where he had asked everyone to meet him before the service started. Pushing the door open, he was greeted by Shep, Juliette, and Juliette's husband, Tim Keaton.

"There he is . . . the big cheese himself." Tim rose to embrace his friend.

"How you been, Tim?" Hawk looked at his buddy. "Long time since I've seen you."

"My boss has been working me too hard," Tim joked. Hawk knew he was kidding because Tim loved the direction, creativity, and freedom he had in his job. He had expressed it many times.

"If I see him, I'll let him know." Hawk smiled and took a seat.

"Did you bring the picture?" Shep cut right to the topic at hand.

"I did." Hawk slid the picture across the table.

"Did Farren have anything that might help us?" Juliette took another look at the picture as it was placed in front of Shep.

"No, he really didn't, but he had a lot to tell me about our ghost, George."

"You can tell us about that later." Juliette cut her eyes toward Shep. "It might scare you-know-who."

"Not funny!" Shep snatched up the picture and looked at it closely. "Well, Farren might not have had any info, but I found out a few things."

"Do tell." Hawk leaned forward.

"I found a copy of this picture online. It's a part of the State of Florida Division of Library and Services archive. It's called the Florida Memory Project. It doesn't tell us any more about the picture, but it's a part of the state historical archive."

"And that is important why?" Juliette asked.

"Because it lets us know the picture was taken somewhere here in Florida."

"Hey, that makes sense. Good work," Hawk complimented.

"Hang on, boss, there's more." Shep tapped his fingers on the table, creating a drum roll. "The picture is of Walt Disney's aunt Jessie and his cousin Irene from his mom's side of the family. Flora Disney, Walt's mom, moved from Kansas to Florida when her family relocated here. Apparently there was a young man who was interested in Flora. He moved to Florida with his family at the very same time and became a citrus farmer."

"Was that young man named Elias?" Hawk took the picture back from Shep.

"You guessed it. Kepple Disney moved his family here as well. Kepple's son, Elias, married Flora here in Florida on January 1, 1888."

"That's a nice way to start a new year." Tim Keaton leaned in to get a better look at the picture.

"They were married in Kismet, which is right next to Acron, which means nothing to me since this is nothing but a lost piece of history. A real ghost town."

"Another ghost?" Juliette smirked.

"I said ghost town." Shep curled his lip. "But Walt's parents were married here in Florida. Eventually they would move away, but Flora's parents and a lot of their family remained close."

Hawk's mind started to churn the information. He gestured for Shep to hurry up with the rest of the information.

Shep nodded and cleared his throat. "It appears that the Disney children would come down and spend some time each summer with their Aunt Jessie and her husband, Albert. Walt and Roy grew up spending their summers right here in Florida."

"How far from here did they live?"

"Best I can guess?" Shep placed a finger alongside his temple and tapped lightly. "Forty or fifty miles north of here."

"But the town they were married in is gone." Tim restated.

"Yes, but a very small community is still there, off the beaten path, a real undeveloped area of the state. Today it's known as Paisley, Florida," Shep added.

"So, realistically," Hawk thought aloud, "all of those stories about Walt searching for an East Coast location were probably made a little less complicated because he had some fairly solid Florida roots, actually Central Florida roots."

"That kind of changes some of the official story about how Project Florida came to be, doesn't it?" Juliette looked at Hawk as she asked.

"A bit. It's an added chapter of the history that most people don't remember." Hawk was intrigued. "Shep, are any of the family still living up near . . . what was the name of the ghost town?"

"Kismet . . . and no. At least, I couldn't find any using the search tools I had access to online."

"So I can't go talk with any of them, then." Hawk shrugged. "But according to the note on the back of the picture, 'Aunt Jessie has a special delivery. Walt's grandparents are trying to Call you . . . go back to his roots to find your way.' What do I do with that?"

"I don't know what you do with it, but let me tell you the rest." Shep slid forward to the edge of his chair. "Walt's Aunt Jessie was Flora's sister. She inherited a job from her husband, Albert Perkins, after he passed away."

"A job?"

"Aunt Jessie was the postmaster of Paisley, Florida."

"Who better to get a special delivery from than the postmaster?" Juliette stood, her eyes gleaming with excitement.

"That's what I thought." A satisfied grin crossed Shep's face. "And although I couldn't find any information about the family still being around, I did find information about where some of the family is located."

"Come on, Shep . . . what does that mean?" Hawk leaned forward, placing both elbows on the table with his hands tightly clasped together.

"The cemetery." Shep slammed his fist down dramatically on the table. "What I did find is that some of the family is buried in an old cemetery called Ponceannah, near the town of Paisley, Florida."

"I can't go talk to someone in a cemetery or pick up a special delivery there . . ." Hawk was trying to piece together information. "Can I?"

"Well, I guess I should tell you one more thing that might help a bit," Shep said, in a quiet voice. "Do you know what Walt's grandparents were named?"

"No, but you're going to tell me, aren't you?" Hawk looked directly at Shep.

The door burst open, and Jonathan entered the room. All eyes turned toward him. He looked at each of them, his expression growing serious, and closed the door behind him. "Did I interrupt something? What did I miss?"

"I'll catch you up on all the details later," Juliette answered. She turned back to Shep. "Continue."

"As I was saying, Walt Disney's grandparents on his mother's side were Charles and Henrietta Call."

The names hung in the room. Smiles began to break out on each face as this next piece of information clicked into place. Hawk noticed Jonathan looking from person to person, so he summarized the other pieces for him.

"So Walt Disney's Aunt Jessie, who was the postmaster in Paisley, Florida has a special delivery for me. Walt's grandparents on his mother's side of the family are trying to Call me. In the note, the *C* in *Call* was capitalized, and their last name was Call. Charles and Henrietta are trying to *Call* me. And I have to get back to his roots to find my way." Hawk reached out and shook Shep's hand. "You, my friend, are awesome. Give you a computer, and you are a genius. All I need to do is figure out what getting back to the roots means and we have this figured out."

"Hold on." Jonathan held up his palm. "Based on past experience, I would venture to say we haven't figured out anything yet. This may just be a start to a far more complicated scenario. Remember, you promised to give the picture to Al."

"I'll give it to him tonight, if he's here," Hawk promised.

"He is. I just saw him come in," Jonathan replied. "But you didn't warn me about the television crew."

"I didn't remember, to tell you the truth." Hawk shrugged.

"Well, I wish you would have. I hate being on television with this Band-Aid still on my head." Jonathan smiled as he touched the bandage they had given him a hard time about the day before.

"Did I tell you I was preaching out of Numbers 11, about how we shouldn't complain and gripe so much? That sure did sound like a complaint to me." Hawk tapped the Bible that he had placed on the table when he came in.

"You didn't let me finish. I was trying to say I hate being on television with this Band-Aid on my head, because I don't want to distract anyone from being able to worship by worrying about my injury. . . . See, it wasn't a complaint, just voicing concern for the congregation."

"Nice recovery," Tim whispered to Hawk.

"So what are you getting ready to do?" Juliette looked toward him. "You've started to figure this out, right?"

"Hold on just a minute." Tim raised his hands in front of him. "This time, see if you can keep my wife safe from the bad guys out there, will you?"

Hawk knew Tim was kidding him. After Hawk had rescued Juliette from her captors months earlier, Tim had promised Hawk to be his protector and bodyguard for the rest of his life. Although they had often joked about it, the situation could have turned out badly. That they all could be in the same room today, laughing and talking, was a blessing.

"This time, I'll be a bit more cautious." Hawk nodded.

"You don't know how to be cautious." Juliette shook her head. "I have to watch out for all of you in this room on most days. When you get together, you guys think you are indestructible."

For the second time, the door burst open. It clanked into the doorstop, revealing a breathtakingly stunning brunette. The interruption caught them all off guard, and no one spoke for a moment. The woman at the door surveyed the room with confident green eyes that stopped when she saw Hawk. She extended her hand toward him as he continued to stare.

"Dr. Grayson Hawkes, I am Kate Young from *Total Access*." She granted him a brilliant smile.

"Uh, hi . . ." Hawk stood as he shook her hand. "I'm Grayson Hawkes, you can call me Hawk." He realized that she had already said his name, but there was no way for him to take it back after he had repeated it.

"Nice to meet you," Kate said boldly. "Looking forward to getting to know you. We will be spending a lot of time together over the next few days." Taking a quick glance around the room, she nodded slightly. "Just wanted to say hello. I'll let you all get back to your business."

Just as quickly as she entered, she turned on her heel and exited. The room remained silent as they all stared toward the empty door.

Juliette, however, was not looking at the door. *Men*, she thought. She studied their reaction with an amused grin. Tapping on the table to get their attention, she cleared her throat.

"Is there something wrong, gentlemen? Are you just starstruck or did you decide to be rude and gawk at Ms. Young? Seriously, you act like you've never seen a glamorous woman before."

Shep opened his mouth to say something, but Juliette cut him off with a wave of her hand. Raising an eyebrow, she smiled at Tim, who smiled back at her. He quietly moved his index finger toward his eye and then pointed it toward her. It was his way of saying *I only have eyes for you*. Her smile grew wider. She turned her attention to Hawk. With a playful snap of her fingers to get his attention, she continued.

"Hawk, did you forget that you have company with you this week? *Total Access* means that she has total access all week long. This is the behind-the-scenes interview that all America has been waiting for. You remember this, right?"

"Yes, of course I do." She noticed he quickly cut his eyes away from hers.

"Can I have a word with you alone, please?"

Jonathan moved to the door and waited for the room to empty. Pausing, he looked at the preacher for the evening. "I'm going to go ahead and get started, if that's alright. Don't be long. The music set is about twenty-five minutes, give or take."

After Hawk nodded, Jonathan silently closed the door.

Juliette came around the table to where Hawk was standing. He raised his hands in an attempt to wave off what she was getting ready to say. She stopped, slid out a chair, and sat down slowly. With a smile, she lifted her hand and invited Hawk to join her at the table. Squinting a puzzled eye toward her, he took a seat.

"That was a . . . um . . . very smooth introduction to Kate Young a few moments ago." Juliette continued to smile to soften her comment.

"Yes, don't know what happened. We were talking about solving this clue, and she caught me by surprise."

"Well, Hawk, about that . . . I have tried to warn you about this *Total Access* thing. This is an important week for you, for the company, for the Disney shareholders. You have burst onto the national scene and so far have been very selective about who has had access to you. Now that you're venturing beyond the company's television networks and news outlets, we won't be able to handpick and control your dealings with the media as much. We have been taking some criticism for that . . . as you know."

"I know," Hawk stated matter-of-factly. "You have been doing a fantastic job at keeping—"

"Stop." Juliette offered a backhanded wave. She knew he was going to say something nice and try to turn the conversation into some type of encouragement for her. It was one of the things he always did for those around him. "I'm not fishing for a compliment. I know you appreciate what I do, and you know I'll keep you out of trouble to the best of my ability. But as I told you before, Kate Young did not get where she is today by being a lightweight news journalist. She's the best there is. She has power, she has influence, she has clout. If she senses a weakness, she is going to go after it like a shark to blood. I don't think she has a preset agenda. To the best of my knowledge, *Total Access* is not trying to do a damaging piece, and it doesn't have an ax to grind. But listen to me, Grayson . . ." She used his given name so he'd know she wanted his full attention. "She will bury you in the interviews and slice you up in this behind-the-scenes special if you don't bring your A game. Got it?"

"I've got it, coach." Hawk smiled reassuringly. "Got it."

"As far as our little mystery here, let's figure out the clues we have, and as soon as they pack up their cameras and Kate gets back on the plane for New York City, then we will unravel this puzzle . . . alright?"

"Sounds good." His eyes widened, and he grinned from ear to ear.

Juliette laughed. "You're lying. You are not about to wait to solve this mystery. You are too tenacious, and you can't let it go . . . can you? Then at least let me know what you're doing so I can run interference for us. Promise me you'll do that."

"I promise." Hawk looked like he meant it. "Really, I promise."

"Fine." She sighed deeply and slumped back in her chair. "Remember you have your first formal sit-down interview with Kate Young tomorrow morning at ten o clock."

"Yes, I will be there."

"She's pretty, isn't she?" Juliette slowly rose from her chair to leave.

"Who?"

"She who!" Juliette narrowed her eyes and nodded toward the door, where Kate Young had entered.

"I didn't notice." Hawk waved her off.

"That is twice in a matter of moments. It's bad form for a pastor to lie to a friend. You need to work on that, preacher man."

"Don't know what you are talking about."

"That's the third lie." Juliette was unusually cautious as she continued. She knew how deeply Hawk had been hurt by Kiran's betrayal months before. Deliberately, she had avoided asking him many questions about his female friends or acquaintances. "She is pretty, isn't she?"

"Yes, I suppose she is . . . in a glamorous, beautiful, television-personality kind of way . . . if you find that kind of look attractive."

"If you find that kind of look attractive." Juliette shook her head, relieved he had responded playfully.

"Exactly."

 *Day Two*
Evening

**THE WORSHIP SERVICE ENDED,** and as always, people lingered, laughed, talked, and greeted one another. The lobby of the worship center was spacious and featured a coffee bar that became a gathering place for families and friends after the worship event ended. Hawk mingled and stayed busy greeting people but kept his eye open for his friend Al Gann. Al worked for the Orange County Sheriff's Department and was the point man for any and all activity related to law enforcement on Disney property. Although Disney had its own security force, it interfaced closely with the sheriff's department. This structure had been in place for years and had been very effective. The Walt Disney World property was one of the safest places you could ever visit.

The two men found a high-top table in the corner, away from the crowd. Standing up and leaning onto it so he could be heard over his flock's chatter, Hawk slid the picture, now tucked back inside the envelope, across to Al.

Taking the envelope from Hawk, Al opened it, glanced at the picture silently, then looked back up. "Reginald told me about this." He turned his head side to side before he spoke again. "Is this another one of those great treasure hunts?"

"It could be," Hawk admitted. "Farren Rales seems to think so. I can't imagine it would turn into the same type of, well . . . problem that it did before."

"Hmm . . ." Al raised an eyebrow skeptically. "You have a way of getting involved in some fairly complex situations."

"What?" Hawk allowed his jaw to slump open. "Why do people always say that about me?"

Both men laughed. Al was a church member who, eighteen months earlier, had become involved when the quest to find the key had gotten out of hand. He had bought Hawk the time he needed to solve the mystery before law enforcement had to become actively involved. Al was also a friend of Reginald Cambridge, which allowed for easier communication between the two offices. Sometimes the informal communication was more essential to keep things running safely and smoothly than were the official lines of communication and procedures.

"So what are you going to do with this?" Al held up the envelope.

"I suppose I'll see if I can look into what it might mean, just a little bit."

"Can I help?"

"Yes. Did Reginald tell you about my little run-in at the theme park yesterday?"

"He did." Al leaned heavily against the table. Speaking so softly that Hawk had to strain to hear, he said, "That is serious and dangerous. I don't like what we are dealing with here."

"I don't either." Hawk leaned in as well. "But we know what they want. Right now, there is no danger. They want me to give them the key. They're going to try to intimidate me to get it. But they also seem to be doing this now because another part of some big picture is getting ready to fall into place."

"And this has to do with that ghost guy . . . George, who you met last night, who gave you the picture." He patted his head with the envelope. "I don't know why these Imagineer guys just don't come out and tell you what they want you to know. Their mysterious puzzles are a little too risky, if you want my opinion."

"It's because this is a chapter in a bigger story. A story they have been a part of for a long time. They are the ones telling the story, and now we are a part of it. Solving the mystery is the next segment of the story."

"That sounds crazy. You've been hanging around them too much."

"It may be crazy, but it has been a pretty crazy and unbelievable eighteen months since I found the key, hasn't it?" Hawk asked lightly.

A sudden change in the noise level of the room caught their attention. As they turned to see what was happening, the people in the lobby seemed to gravitate toward the set of doors on the far side of the worship center. Camera phones were raised in the air, and the two men stood up straighter to see what had caused the commotion.

Kate Young had just entered the lobby and was instantly swamped. Allie Crossman was at her side, trying to gingerly navigate the crowd and keep the fans from being overly aggressive. Kate smiled, shook hands, waved, and signed a couple of napkins from the coffee bar that had been shoved in front of her. Slowly she began to make her way to the front doors of the building.

Al turned toward Hawk. "You know Kate Young?"

"Nope, sure don't."

"Pretty girl."

"Hadn't noticed." Hawk wrinkled his nose in mock dislike.

Now the crowd followed Kate and Allie to the doors. As Kate spoke with people, she looked up across the lobby. Her eyes met Hawk's. Rising up on her tiptoes, she flashed a blazing smile that brightened the entire lobby. She waved at him and then stepped out the door.

"I thought you said you didn't know her." Al stuck his elbow in the preacher's ribcage.

"I don't . . . no kidding."

"Well, it looks like she knows you."

"That's what I am afraid of." Hawk frowned.

Juliette and Shep slid up behind him and immediately were caught up in watching the famous reporter leaving the building. Shep soon glanced at Al and then nodded in approval, letting Hawk know he'd noticed that Hawk had actually given Al the photograph as planned. While Shep began to give Al some of the information he had shared with the group earlier, Juliette turned toward her boss.

"You look nervous. Any reason?" She tilted her head inquisitively.

"Maybe this *Total Access* thing wasn't such a great idea."

"It'll be fine. She's just a beautiful woman. Don't let her intimidate you," Juliette reassured him.

"You're the one that said she was tough. I think you used the phrase *shark to blood* or something like that, didn't you?"

"Just trying to get your attention."

"You got it." Hawk turned back to the door, as the lobby was now quickly emptying out. "Juliette, you asked me to let you know what I was up to . . ."

"Yes?" Concern crept into her voice.

"I am going to see what special delivery Walt's Aunt Jessie has for me."

"When?"

"Now." Hawk strode across the lobby without another word, and before anyone could say anything to dissuade him, he was out the door.

 *Day Two*
Night

THE WINDSHIELD WIPERS DRUMMED a steady beat as they tossed water back and forth across the windshield of the Ford Mustang. Hawk had aimed the car away from Celebration and was following his GPS toward the rural town of Paisley. Twenty minutes into his drive, he'd been hit by wave after wave of heavy rain that now fell in sheets around him. Drops pelted the roof of his car, and the noise drummed around him. Squinting his eyes to catch a glimpse of the road after the wipers opened up a brief view, he slowed his speed.

County Road 42 was a two-lane winding road that snaked along the border of the Ocala National Forest, which gobbled up a huge portion of north Central Florida like a black hole. Dense and dark, it was easy to lose your way in, if you moved off the beaten pathways that cut through it. Many a person had gotten lost in the depths of the forest, and Hawk silently prayed he would find the cemetery before he had to venture in too deep.

The GPS could not seem to locate the road he was traveling on. No streetlights and no other cars on the highway made the trip more intimidating. Hawk wondered why he hadn't waited until tomorrow to make this journey. Passing the marker that beckoned him to turn into the Clearwater Lake area, he slowed into a series of turns.

A deer darted across the road in front of him. The headlights illuminated the animal for an instant, and then the water on the windshield caused it to disappear from view. Hawk swerved to keep the car under control on the slick black asphalt.

He felt the car slide off the shoulder, and he slumped to his right, grasping the wheel hard as the tires sank in the ground just off the paved road. As the wiper swiped back across the glass, the deer was gone. His tires churned, then grabbed, and he felt the car come back under his control as he steered back onto the county road. The road twisted to his left, and he caught a glimpse of motion just past the tree line. The Mustang bounced across a dirt road intersecting the highway. A black wrought-iron fence jutted out into his path. Instinctively, he pulled the car to the left, trying not to jerk the steering wheel with too much force and cause the car to careen out of control or flip.

The Mustang's fender grazed the black iron fence. Sparks showered into the air, illuminating the rain drops into an impromptu light show. Depressing the brake, he tried to bring the car back under control. Finally, it came to rest along the side of the fence.

Lightning flashed, as if on cue, lighting up a white oval gate just in front of him. To his right, Grayson Hawkes saw a blackened expanse of property, accented by monuments of granite and rock—tombstones. This was the entrance to a graveyard.

Surely this had to be it. He had not just found it, he had run into it. Sitting in his car in the glow of the dashboard panel lights, he contemplated what to do next. He was sweating from the sudden rush of adrenaline surging through his system. Exhaling loudly, he turned again and looked out into the darkened cemetery. He questioned why he had been so eager to find it now, but he was here, and he was going to go in.

"This may not be the best idea you've ever had," Hawk said aloud.

Opening the car door, he was hit by the onslaught of the downpour. Instantly, he was soaked. He pushed the front seat forward to survey the backseat for a jacket. There was none, but he did spot the flashlight he kept back there. He slapped it against his palm, and the beam cut through the darkness, only to disappear in the shower of raindrops. His shoes sank into the mud as he made his way to the gate, and he could see deep gashes in the soil where his car had come off the road and crashed into the iron fence. Further back, he saw a deer staring at him.

"Thanks a lot." Hawk raised his voice over the rain. "You about got us both killed."

She flicked her tail and bounded into the forest.

Shaking his head, Hawk turned back toward the cemetery. Red letters sprawled across the white archway, confirming he had found the right place: *PONCEANNAH*. He traced them with his light a couple times, reading and rereading the name. Then he stepped forward below the arch and allowed his light to move into the inkiness of the cemetery. Another deep breath, and he took his first step along the mudded out pathway leading into the graveyard. His light jittered back and forth at the ground in front of him, then he cut the light beam to look at the grave markers. Just inside the gate, the beam came to rest on the statue of an angel.

A lighting flash with an explosion of thunder illuminated the angel brilliantly for a moment. The hair on his arms stood on end, and the air crackled

JEFF DIXON

with energy. He read the inscription. *Shed A Tear But Do Not Cry. Safe With Lord, Above The Sky, To All Who Rest At Ponceannah.* This marker served as a welcome to the cemetery. Standing in the rain, he wondered how you shed a tear but not cry. He thought that once a tear fell, you were officially crying. A quick shake of his head turned him back to the task at hand. *Get busy, find what you came looking for . . . and then get out of here.* On cue, the lightning danced across the blackened sky as thunder again rolled over his head.

At first glance, the cemetery appeared to be a typical rural Florida grave-yard. Many small communities throughout the state of Florida were still off the beaten path despite heavy development elsewhere. They attempted to hold on to their identities, with some community members living there all their lives. Family heritage could be traced back for generations among the stronger family units. Many of these families would end up here.

Hawk began moving into the cemetery. Through the rain he could see a mixture of old tombstones and grave markers right next to newer, more ornate ones. His light flicked across a gazebo to his right, just off the path, perhaps erected in memory of someone. As he got closer, he could see it covered a picnic table and was lined with benches on each side—a place for people to rest and find relief from the Florida heat on a cemetery visit.

Stepping under the covering, Hawk found an instant break from the deluge. He was able to orient himself in the pitch-black graveyard. It appeared the cemetery was surrounded by woods on all sides, and there were shadowy clumps of thick trees scattered over the property. The rain did not appear to be letting up, so he knew if he was going to find anything he would either need to start looking now or come back at a later time. It had taken him well over an hour to get here, and he was determined not to waste the trip.

He decided to circle the perimeter of the graveyard, looking at the tomb-stones.With each trip around, he would tighten his spiral until he ended up back in the gazebo. Lunging back out into the rain, he wasn't really sure he had a great plan for covering the entire cemetery because he wasn't sure just how big it was. But at least it was a plan.

He moved from the gazebo, along a dirt path lined with tombstones, with the intent of staying on it until he hit the outer edge of the cemetery. He played the flashlight beam over each marker, looking for the name Call. He hoped the Call family from years ago had been prominent enough that a number of family members might be buried here. If that were the case, it might make Walt's grandparents easier to find, especially if they were located in a family plot.

In a few minutes, he reached what must be one edge of the cemetery. Another dirt path broke off the one he was on, which had come to an end.

He could turn right or left. The right turn looked like it would take him back toward the front of the cemetery, where his car had tagged the iron fence. The left would take him deeper into the graveyard toward the back of the property. He chose left. Here, the plots were overgrown and weedy. The graves to his right backed up to a fence marking the edge of the cemetery. Unlike the iron fence that lined the highway, this was made of wire, draped between wooden poles. A dirt road just beyond the fence cut though the dense forest. The wire had been torn off the poles there, giving access to the cemetery from the dirt road. As Hawk moved along the path without a fence, he felt somehow vulnerable and exposed.

*You are being silly*, he thought as he continued to walk. He sensed that the rain was getting harder and the storm surrounding him was settling in for an even more intense soaking of Paisley, Florida. Reaching the back of the graveyard, he saw a huge pile of flowers, wreaths, and various other items used to decorate gravesites. Apparently, the old decorations and memorials were discarded unceremoniously in this pile of trash. Following the path to his left again, he made a sharp turn that placed him on the back side of the land.

There were fewer grave markers along this path, and the woods encroached on the property line. Hawk shivered as he continued to search the names. As a pastor, he had been in many cemeteries, conducted too many funeral services to remember, and had never found the places people were buried frightening. He knew what remained was just a shell of the person that once lived. He did not believe in or fear ghosts and found those that did amusing. Their fears were unfounded.

But in this moment, walking in the old cemetery in the rain, his senses were on heightened alert. Perhaps it was from being detained and threatened in the Hall of Presidents; it might have been the trouble with the pirates being found in the Magic Kingdom; it could have been his encounter with George, or the strange way Farren had described George Colmes. No matter the reason, he was amped. *Keep it together and just keep looking.*

Stopping and sweeping his light around him, he noticed something that seemed out of place. A white pillar rose from the ground like a naked tree trunk among the scattered tombstones. The pale white was the same color as the majority of the grave markers that decorated the cemetery, but it was unusual enough that he decided to explore it more closely.

Lightning flashed across the sky, lighting the entire cemetery for just a moment. Hawk froze in his tracks as he saw a shape dart behind a clump of trees across the graveyard. In the dark, he never would have seen the movement. The timing of the lightning had been so precise that he was looking right at the trees when he had seen whatever it was move.

Standing and wishing the lightning would strike again, he could see nothing among the dark shapes of the trees barely visible in the rainy night. Thunder bounced through the sky, causing him to cringe. *It must have been an animal. Probably more afraid of you than you are of it.* But he'd been sent here for a reason. He had to know.

Hawk swallowed hard and began jogging toward the clump of trees.

 *Day Two*
Night

**THE HEADLIGHTS CAUGHT THE MUSTANG** parked against the wrought-iron fence. The driver instantly cut them off. Easing the car to the side of the road and pulling to a stop at the corner of the fence, he clicked off the ignition switch, plunging the interior of the car into darkness. The heavy pummeling of the rain echoed inside the vehicle, as the passengers strained their eyes toward the car parked outside the cemetery.

"This is his car, right?" Kate Young leaned forward with both hands against the dash, trying to see from the passenger seat.

"Vintage Mustang with a vanity plate that says HAWK? It's his car." Kate's assistant, Allie, answered matter-of-factly from the backseat.

"The question is, what is it doing here?" The driver, Punky Zane, wondered aloud. "Is he in it, did he wreck?"

"I can't see anyone inside." Kate pressed her face as closely to the window as possible, trying to see out of the window.

The three had followed Hawk from the moment he had pulled out of the Celebration Community Church parking lot. Kate Young was playing a hunch. She had listened outside the door before she made her unexpected appearance in the conference room at the church earlier in the evening. Her investigative nature made her curious, some would say nosy, but she had overheard a discussion about some kind of message that Walt Disney's aunt was trying to get to Hawk and some concern about Hawk not being safe and the need to be careful. She had nearly been caught eavesdropping when the worship leader of the church had come down the hallway. She managed to slip into the restroom as he passed by, and eventually made her entrance to introduce herself to Grayson Hawkes.

*Total Access* was not here to do a scandal piece of gotcha journalism about Grayson Hawkes and his mysterious rise to power in the Walt Disney Company. From all indications, the new leader of the company was a genuinely good man. The things he had said earlier in the evening about striving to follow Jesus had been a positive affirmation of that. Kate was already planning on using some of the footage from the sermon in the special when it aired. But, as often happened to her when she got a piece of information, her curiosity kicked in and she instructed Punky to follow the preacher when he left. The farther they had gotten away from the Disney Resort, the more she knew her instincts had been correct. Something was going on.

When Hawk began his journey down this country road, they had dropped way back and fallen off the pace, out of sight, and pulled off the road so he wouldn't spot them. Trusting they would find him by coming along behind him later, they took a chance that there were places to stop along the deserted roadway. They had assumed they had lost him and were getting ready to turn around and go back to Walt Disney World when they happened to spot his car. Kate Young had learned a long time ago that to be successful in business took a mixture of sheer determination, a curiosity that never stopped asking questions, and a good dose of dumb blind luck to get a story everyone else would miss. Once again, her instincts and luck appeared to be leading her to that kind of story.

"Are we sitting next to a graveyard?" Allie asked from the backseat.

Kate and Punky both turned and looked into the cemetery, not having noticed where they had parked until this moment. The rain streaked the windows, making it nearly impossible to see anything. Kate leaned back in her seat and turned again to the front window, looking out toward Hawk's car.

"So what do we do, Kate?" Punky watched her as she peered through the rain.

"We're not getting out of the car . . . here . . . are we?" Allie shifted nervously in the backseat.

"Kate?" Punky asked again.

"Let's get out and take a look." Kate reached for the car door. "Punky, do you have your mini-cam in case there's something to see?"

"Always." Punky reached into his pocket for the small surveillance camera he usually carried. The quality wasn't great, but the footage it captured had the hidden-camera style look that sometimes was needed to break a great story. It was encased and safe from the elements, had a night vision setting, and was designed to work perfectly in inclement weather.

Kate opened her door, then immediately closed it. "What kind of shoes are you wearing?" She glanced toward the backseat. Allie always dressed more casually than she did and would rather stay in the car anyway. "Let's trade."

"Heels, just like you. We just all went to church, remember?"

"Do you want me to take a look while you wait here?" Punky offered. "Neither one of you are dressed for a walk in the rain and mud."

"Through a cemetery," Allie added for emphasis.

"Nope, I'm going." Kate opened the door, slid her shoes off, and got out. The soles of her feet sank into the soft, muddy ground. "But I'm not going to ruin my Jimmy Choos." Walking barefoot, she headed toward Grayson Hawkes's car parked some twenty yards in front of them.

Punky handed the key ring to Allie. "Crawl over the seat and be ready to crank it up if we need to get out of here."

"Do you think there's going to be a problem?" Allie's hand shook as she took the keys.

"We're with Kate, following one of her hunches, in the middle of Nowhere, Florida." Punky smiled. "Not only is it pouring down rain, but we're getting ready to check out what looks like an abandoned car next to a cemetery. Only Kate could turn a trip to Disney World into a night of fright." He opened the door and hustled to catch up with the investigative journalist, who was now standing next to Hawk's car, peeping in the windows.

 *Day Two*
Night

**HAWK JOGGED TOWARD THE TREES,** trying to create enough noise to scare away any animal that might have sought a break from the storm under the branches. Lightning ripped across the heavens, causing him to slow his pace for a moment. Trees were a horrible place to be in a lightning storm, and he tried to decide whether or not to keep heading toward them. Good idea or bad, he was sure he had seen something moving in them, so he accelerated.

He also ran toward the tree because he lived with a philosophy of life that had always served him well. Never run from danger and difficulty; instead, run toward it. This credo had allowed him as a leader to tackle things head on, acquire a reputation of being tenacious, and it didn't allow problems to fester and become worse than they needed to be. Usually it didn't apply to graveyards, in a storm, at night. Nevertheless, he found himself arriving at the trees and yelling over the storm.

"Who's there?" He cut behind the trees where he had seen the shape disappear.

There was nothing there. Just the sound of rain hitting the tree branches all around him. Playing his light over the ground, he saw no footprints in the mud, no trampled blades of grass, no broken twigs. He searched, ducking under tree branches, until he was satisfied his eyes had been playing tricks on him earlier in the blasting light of the storm. Then he stepped out from underneath the foliage and began retracing his steps to the white pillar.

As he approached it, he was still struck by how out of place this pole was in the midst of the gravestones around it. It was an oddity, and in all of the years in ministry, he had never seen anything like it in a cemetery. It was surrounded by a series of concrete markers that formed a large rectangle indicative of a boundary for a family plot. He walked past a double headstone as he approached this white tree-shaped object. Shining his light toward the ground, he saw a name on the tombstone by his feet. The marquee across the top of the stone read *Perkins*. The name on the left read *Albert* and the name on the right read *Jessie*.

Hawk's mind locked back onto the information Shep had given them earlier in the evening. Aunt Jessie was Flora's sister. Flora was Walt and Roy Disney's mom. Their Aunt Jessie had become the postmaster in Paisley, Florida after the death of her husband, Albert Perkins. This was where Walt's Aunt Jessie was buried. Stepping around to face the tombstone, he shone the light across both their names. *Aunt Jessie has a special delivery. Walt's grandparents are trying to Call you. Go back to the roots to find your way.*

Hawk thought, *OK, Aunt Jessie, I am here, what do you have to give me?* The gravestone had some artificial flowers on it, which indicated it had been visited in the not-too-distant past. Hawk knelt at the grave marker and inspected the flowers to see if there might be a card attached to them. There was nothing.

Rising to one knee, he looked around on the wet ground. He still saw nothing. Over his shoulder, he glanced again at the unusual pole rising up from the ground. He turned his flashlight toward it and traced it in the beam. His eyes blinked against the rivulets of rain running down his face, and he noticed a vine and leaves engraved upon the pole. It not only looked like a tree, it was supposed to be a tree. A concrete tree.

The statue had been created to look like the branches had been cut off. *What a strange . . . gravestone?* Hawk stepped around and explored the front with his light. Halfway up the trunk, he found words carved on the marker.

*Charles Call*
*Born March 22, 1823—Died January 6, 1890*
*Henrietta Call*
*Born July 23, 1837—Died February 21, 1910*

This gravestone, the weirdest one he had ever seen, marked the final resting place of Walt Disney's grandparents. With the last name of Call, they were trying to *Call* him. But what did that mean? Hawk looked back toward the tombstone of Aunt Jessie, just a few feet away, then at the tree-shaped tombstone of Walt's grandparents. He thought back to eighteen months before when he'd solved the intricate clues that Farren Rales had left for him. Every word mattered and was necessary to figure out the meaning. George Colmes was an Imagineer just like Farren, and their promise to the Disney Brothers had been the commitment of a lifetime. The words in the clue meant something. Now, standing in front of the gravestone, he had to know what.

*Go back to the roots to find your way.*

JEFF DIXON

Hawk inhaled deeply. Lightning flashed and thunder rolled across the cemetery. He slowly walked to the back side of the tree-shaped tombstone. *Go back.* He now stood at the back of the grave marker, closer to where Aunt Jessie was buried, dissecting the next phrase of the clue, *to the roots to find your way.* Roots would be at the bottom of the tree. He dropped to his knees and examined the back of the tombstone. Around the base, he saw nothing that looked unusual or out of place. But neither did he see anything that looked like roots at the bottom of the tree-shaped marker. Again he turned back to the tombstone of Aunt Jessie and thought for a moment. He played out each segment in his mind. A special delivery from Aunt Jessie; he was here, and Aunt Jessie had something for him to find. Walt's grandparents had Called him. He was at the grave marker of the Calls.

He was now at the back and had to go to the roots to find his way. He stared down at the ground. The thought crossing his mind sounded crazy, even as he thought it. It was reckless, it was dumb, it was foolish, and yet he was contemplating it. All for the sake of solving another puzzle that had something to do with Walt Disney and unlocking his kingdom.

He needed to start digging at the back of the tombstone. He reached down and grabbed a clump of grass and pulled. It tore away from the muddy ground easily. He reached down again and scooped up a handful of dirt from the base of the concrete and pulled it away.

 *Day Two*
Night

"**WHAT IN THE WORLD IS HE DOING?**" Punky zoomed in on Hawk digging at the base of a cemetery monument, through the lens of the camera.

"How weird is this?" Kate leaned in over his shoulder and watched through the rain.

Kate and Punky had trudged their way into the cemetery. After pausing in the gazebo, they noticed a flashlight beam moving near the rear of the cemetery. Carefully and quietly moving from under cover, they had passed an old well, crouched behind a few grave markers, used a tree for a sight block, and gotten as close as they possibly could without being detected. As they first started tracking the beam of light, it was moving from a row of trees toward a clump of tombstones. They had both noticed the unusual tree-shaped object rising out of the ground—the very object they now watched Grayson Hawkes digging at.

Soaked completely through, they hid behind an oversized tombstone and watched with curious disbelief.

"What is he digging with?" Kate spoke quietly.

"His hands," Punky whispered.

"So he didn't come here planning to dig."

Kate Young had always been smart and had an ability to cut through the clutter to get at the heart of a situation. That was a trait that had made her a powerful interviewer. At times it overwhelmed the people she was interviewing, but in other moments it had created some memorable and moving moments that were captured forever on film. Time would be the judge as to what kind of moment they were capturing right now.

"Apparently not," Punky agreed. "And he's looking for something that must be very valuable. Or why not wait until it isn't raining or come back when it's daylight to find it?"

"Whatever he is looking for, it must be important." Kate repositioned herself, as her foot sunk in the mud. "Because the chief creative architect of the Walt Disney Company is on his knees, digging in a graveyard, in the middle of the night."

"It will be a surprising documentary, won't it?" Punky smiled, as he continued to capture the images.

"Look!" Kate pointed excitedly. "He found something."

The camera lens zoomed in, as Hawk pushed back some additional dirt and pulled out a buried package. It was about a foot long, wrapped in some type of cloth, and secured with a rope wrapped multiple times around it. Hawk slumped forward for a moment, then carefully and respectfully began replacing the dirt. A few minutes later, he was patting down the ground, on his hands and knees, to make it look like nothing had been displaced.

"Now he's refilling the hole," Punky commented as he watched the close-up he now had in frame.

"Did you hear that?" Kate whispered.

Punky jumped a little. "Hear what?"

"I just heard what sounded like a branch break." Kate was urgently looking around, trying to stay hidden while searching for the source of the noise.

"How can you hear anything over the rain?"

"I'm telling you, I heard something besides the rain."

 *Day Three*
Midnight

**HAWK HAD REVERENTLY AND METICULOUSLY** tried to put all the dirt and grass back in place. He had felt uncomfortable digging in the graveyard. He understood how people were buried in Florida and knew that digging at the base of the gravestone was no worse than digging in your own backyard. Yet it was a graveyard, and something about digging there just didn't sit right. He had been almost ready to give up when he touched the cloth wrapping. Quickly he had traced the shape and dug it out. He had no idea what he had found. It was a foot-long cylindrical package, wrapped in burlap and bound excessively with a rustic, thin rope tied off at one end. Finishing his impromptu landscaping project, he'd immediately turned his thoughts to getting out of the cemetery. He would open the package in the car.

Straightening his back and rising to his feet, he securely gripped the discovery in his left hand. Absently shaking his other hand, he attempted to shake some of the dirt and mud off from his excavation. Aunt Jessie's special delivery had been found. It was time to get out and go home.

Hawk felt the air rush out of his body, as he was struck from his right side. Something had come flying out of the darkness and hit him. As he crashed to the ground, his brain tried to process the alarms sounding inside his body. There was somebody on top of him. He had been blindsided from his right. Someone had hit him in the ribs and driven him to the ground.

Hawk felt his grip tighten on the secret package. He rolled to his stomach beneath his attacker. Struggling for leverage, Hawk got one knee supported on the ground beneath him, which allowed him to drive an elbow backward. The chief creative architect felt his elbow connect with something solid, and the person behind him moved off.

Hawk spun to his right to await the next onslaught. As soon as he started to move to his feet, he was hit again, this time from the front, and driven backward. Hawk instinctively wrapped his arms around the attacker and pulled back, using the momentum of the attack to buy him a few precious moments. His back hit the ground, and the air rushed out of him for the second time in a matter of seconds. He felt his left hand open and the package slip from his grasp on the ground.

Tightening his right hand into a fist, Hawk continued to keep his arms wrapped around his attacker. He aimed the fist at the side of his assailant's head. The punch landed with more effect than Hawk had thought it would, and the attacker rolled off him.

Hawk was now trying to force air back into his lungs as he turned to his side. His mind was barking out dueling instructions to his body. First, reclaim the special delivery from Aunt Jessie before his assailant could grab it. Second, incapacitate his attacker and find out who it was and why they were here.

The attacker's ski mask had been knocked askew. He was busy straightening it, giving Hawk a chance to scour the ground for the cylinder.

Much to Hawk's disappointment, the attacker was lying on top of it. In that instant, the enemy finished straightening his mask, and a grin slowly formed in the mouth hole of the mask. Reaching underneath him, he grabbed the package and, with a quick glance at Hawk, sprang to his feet and sprinted across the graveyard. He was heading for the side of the cemetery where the fence was torn down.

Scrambling to get his legs under him, Hawk was on his feet and running after the man. Lightning flashed, illuminating the entire cemetery once again. Mud flew as Hawk gave pursuit, thunder bounced through the black clouds. In the next flash of lightning, he could see he was gaining on the assailant. Through the darkness, Hawk saw the attacker was heading toward the opening in the fence near all the discarded trash. Hoping he was correct, he veered to his left and tried to take a shorter route.

Lightning danced across the sky and picked up intensity, as the thunder shook every tree in the graveyard. The lightning again gave Hawk a strobe-lit glance across the gravestones, and he saw another figure running alongside his attacker. The second man leaped toward the masked man, knocking him to his knees.

Hawk changed direction again to cut off his assailant. As he ran, he watched the masked man rise to his feet and swing wildly at the second man. The second man absorbed the blow and staggered backward. Hawk blinked, trying to see through the rain, waiting for the next flash of lightning. In the next blast of brilliance from the stormy sky, Hawk no longer saw the second man; he had vaporized into air as quickly as he had materialized. Only the masked man could be seen, still heading for the side of the cemetery. However, Hawk had the angle and was going to catch him.

The last few strides gobbled up the distance between them, and Hawk went airborne to tackle the fleeing man. Hitting him in the small of the back, he felt the man buckle and begin to fall. Hawk drove him to the ground and, in one motion, snatched the package from his hand. The assailant kicked wildly, and he deflected each kick, looking for a way to get closer to launch a second attack.

"Help!" A female voice called through the rain.

Hawk turned in the direction of the cry for help. That momentary distraction allowed the attacker to scamper to his feet and continue toward the edge of the cemetery. Hawk had the package, so his instinct to give chase was placed on hold to answer the cry for help. Getting to his feet and moving toward the cry, Hawk heard the engine of a car fire to life in the distance. Turning back, he saw the interior lights of a car glow as the attacker jumped into a waiting vehicle sitting in the dark, on the dirt road beside the cemetery. A tidal wave of dirt flew out from behind the back tires, as the car sped away toward the main road, leaving a cloud of dust that was being picked apart by the projectile drops of rain falling from the sky.

Pushing on, he saw a woman standing in the graveyard. As Hawk drew closer, he recognized her: Kate Young. Drenched by the rain, standing in the cemetery, barefoot and still wearing what she had on when he had met her at church, she looked more than out of place in the stormy weather. She turned and was looking down at something. At what, Hawk could not yet tell.

"Kate?" Hawk called out as he approached.

"Hawk, we need your help." She waved him over.

Closing in on her position, he noticed she was standing next to a gaping hole in the ground. He realized it was a freshly dug grave that you couldn't see until you got right up on it. Arriving at the graveside, he followed her finger as she pointed down into the hole. There, stretched out in the bottom of the hole, was Punky Zane. Hawk stopped at the side of the grave and looked down.

Kate grabbed his arm. "We need to get him out." She pulled back her wet hair from her face.

"Mr. Zane?" Hawk placed his hands on his knees and looked into the hole. "Are you hurt?"

"Not bad, I don't think." Punky shifted to his feet and looked up into the rain, toward the two above him. "I messed my arm up, but other than that, I'm fine . . . I think."

"What are you doing here?" Hawk looked at Kate, knowing they had followed him but hoping for a less complicated answer than the one he suspected.

"We followed you, of course." Kate wrinkled her forehead. "We saw you get attacked, and we were trying to stop whoever it was." Then she stepped back and gestured down at her outfit. "Punky was doing most of the trying to stop him. I couldn't really keep up. It looked like Punky hit him, but then just disappeared. When I caught up, I found him here."

Hawk had heard of people who asked reporters to bury a story. Facing Kate in the driving rain, he wondered if he could convince her to leave what she had just seen here in the graveyard. Instantly, he knew it would not be that easy.

"I didn't see the hole in the dark." Punky waved to get their attention. "If you could give me a hand please, I need some help getting out of here."

 *Day Three*
Early Morning

THE RAIN SUBSIDED, AS THE MUSTANG CUT through the rolling fog that had come in behind the storm. The headlights threw a blast of brilliance against the cloud that enveloped them. After pulling Punky Zane from the empty grave, the three had emerged from the cemetery, much to the relief of Allie Crossman. Although she had not seen anything that had transpired, she had been startled by a car appearing from a side road that nearly struck her vehicle as she waited. Upon seeing Hawk, Kate, and Punky exit the graveyard, she was shocked at how dirty they looked. Covered in mud, soaked from the storm, and with Punky supporting his arm with his other wrist, the three looked as though they were walking out of a battlefield.

As they arrived at the car, they concluded that Punky was not hurt too badly. Hawk suggested he have the arm x-rayed, but the director balked at that idea. After a few moments of silent awkwardness, the four prepared to leave Paisley. Kate suggested she should ride back to the resort with Hawk. Hawk tried to suggest she should go back with her *Total Access* crew. He reminded her they were officially scheduled to begin shooting video tomorrow. She countered by reminding him that according to her watch, it was now after midnight, which technically meant the tomorrow he had been referring to was already upon them.

Her satisfied smile convinced him she was not going to settle for any other arrangement. He relented—Allie would drive Punky back to the Contemporary Resort, where Hawk was taking Kate as well.

Now Hawk intensely studied the road in front of them. Visibility was limited but not impossible, and he felt himself growing more uneasy now that they were in the car together. He became aware that Kate was paying no attention to the road but looking directly at him from the passenger seat. "It's rude to stare," Hawk said matter-of-factly.

"Oh, thanks for pointing that out." She continued to look at him.

Hawk shifted in his seat and looked at her longer than he had intended. He noticed again how disheveled she was after her excursion through the graveyard. He also noticed that she was a beautiful mess, but a mess nevertheless.

"Eyes on the road, mister." She pointed her manicured index finger toward the windshield. "We already look like we've been in a wreck. Let's not get in one now so we don't merely look the part."

Hawk knew once they had broken the silence, the questions would start coming. He wasn't prepared to answer them. Especially since she had been there at the cemetery. He had hoped to control the interview, and although Juliette had warned him of what to expect, he had hoped he could limit the access Kate and her production crew would have to him. Now they were in a car with a fair distance to travel, and he couldn't escape her interrogation. He would have questions if it were him. He braced for what was getting ready to rocket across the seat toward him.

To his surprise, Kate remained silent. She sat in the passenger seat, slightly turned toward him, continuing to stare. The gaze made him feel incredibly uncomfortable, and occasionally he would cut his eyes in her direction. Since her reprimand earlier to keep his eyes on the road, he had done just that. The silence was deafening, and he found himself weighing whether it was better to ride in awkward silence or have her peppering him with questions he did not want to answer. If she was as good as Juliette had said at being an investigative journalist, then what she was doing right now might actually be a part of a well-thought-out strategy to get him to talk. He never should have agreed to the documentary.

She raised her chin slightly. "I bet right about now, you're wishing you had turned down our request to do a special about you . . . aren't you?" she asked, as though she already knew the answer.

"Trying to read my mind?" he parried, a bit stunned that she had nailed the very thought he had been wrestling with.

"I would be having second thoughts if I were you."

"OK, so I'm having second thoughts."

"So what are you going to do?"

"What do you mean?" Hawk let the words linger before he continued. "What am I going to do?"

"Yes, what are you going to do?" She smiled and pointed back to the windshield to get him to look at the road. "Are you going to have us thrown out and cancel? You can do that, you know."

"I might." Hawk pondered what she said. The thought had crossed his mind. That solution might be the best.

"Of course . . ." She leaned in a little closer and spoke softly. "Then I would have this footage of Grayson Hawkes digging up a grave in an old cemetery . . . that I would have to create my own commentary for and draw my own conclusions about. . . . I just don't see how that plays out very well for you."

"Hmmm . . ." Hawk felt his pulse coursing in his throat. She was right. The possibility of sending them away disappeared into the fog shrouding the car.

"What's in the package you found?"

"Don't know, haven't opened it yet."

"Let's open it now."

"Nope."

"So . . . what were you doing in that cemetery?"

"Paying my respects, of course." He shrugged. "What else do people do when they visit cemeteries?"

"Your respects?" She laughed. "Most people don't pay their respects in a blinding rainstorm, in the middle of the night, by digging up a grave."

"I didn't dig up a grave." He measured what he was about to say next. "I was digging around a tombstone."

"OK, fair enough . . . you were digging around a tombstone." She shook her head. "Whose tombstone and why?"

They were back on Interstate 4, the main thoroughfare through Orlando, Florida. Eventually, as they exited the city, they would find the multiple exits that would lead them back to Walt Disney World. He didn't answer her question. He simply drove. The fog began to melt away and the night became clearer, as he pushed through the downtown area. Kate Young continued to stare at him. He knew she was waiting for an answer, but he wasn't sure what answer to give her. Minutes passed, and still they were silent. Finally, she broke that silence once again.

"Did you not hear my question?"

"Yes, I heard you." He paused, rolling his shoulders backward to chase away the tension. "Is this off the record?"

"Off the record?" She burst into sincere, rich laughter. "You're kidding, right?" She studied his face as though calculating whether he was making a joke, then gave him a minute nod. "I find the chief creative architect of the Walt Disney Company braving a storm, driving an hour to visit a cemetery in the middle of the night. He digs around a tombstone, finds a package, gets attacked, I capture it all on film . . . and you want to know if the conversation is off the record? Seriously?"

"I am serious." Hawk jerked his head toward her with his jaw set. "Off the record."

"Hawk, all I have to do is show the footage we grabbed of you tonight, and you will spend the next three months trying to clean up and spin it."

JEFF DIXON

She exhaled loudly. "I'll just explain how we got the footage, what happened when you were attacked, and you will have to deal with the firestorm that follows. You can't explain what we saw by just saying 'no comment.' You really don't understand how to deal with the press, do you?"

The exit to Walt Disney World was in front of them. Hitting the blinker arm with more force than he had intended drew her attention away from his face to the steering wheel. Her eyes grew huge as he cut it sharply and twisted the car onto the exit ramp without decelerating. He maintained his speed and handled the curve masterfully, as he had learned at the Richard Petty Driving Experience on the Walt Disney World Speedway. It was one his favorite things to do.

The speed of the car threw Kate off balance, and she rocked toward him and then back toward the passenger side door. She held her hands out to steady herself as they approached the archway to the Walt Disney World resort. Now Hawk stepped forcefully on the brakes, pulling the car off the side of the road and shifting her forward against her seat belt. As the car screeched to a halt, he removed both hands from the wheel and spun in his seat toward her.

"You're right, I don't know how to deal with press." He leaned toward her and narrowed his eyes. "So since I am obviously so bad at it, here is how I am going to deal with you. You saw something tonight you were not supposed to see. There was no great evil plot unfolding in the cemetery. You just saw something that is none of your business." His lip curled. "I can't do anything about that. You saw it, you filmed it, what's done is done."

He lowered his voice to an intense whisper that scraped in his throat. "So you can take that footage and brag about how you got total access and show it to the world. Your ratings will skyrocket, and my life will get much more complicated than it already is. But that is all you get, and you are done. If you want a shot at finding out what really was happening, if you want any hope of getting more than some hard-to-explain footage, and if you might just believe you have stumbled across a more interesting or important story . . . then, Ms. Young, we are going to have some off-the-record conversations. Some will need to be *way* off the record."

He shoved the car back into gear and hit the accelerator, driving a surprised and silenced Kate Young back into the high-backed leather seat. Her silence was exactly what Hawk had been hoping for. Baiting the investigator like that was a risk, and he was banking on her curiosity to carry the moment. He hoped he had thrown her off track. He could sense her gathering her thoughts as the car raced past the gate of the Magic Kingdom, headed for the Contemporary Resort. The road sloped downward as they swooped into a tunnel below a canal.

"I take back what I said." The smile reappeared across her face, more brilliant than ever. "You do know how to handle the press."

Hawk wanted to grin, but he didn't. He knew she was playing a game with him. He had managed to stun her for a moment and buy himself a few minutes, but that was all he had done. She had some very damaging footage of him and wasn't above using it, and she had admitted as much. What made him nervous was that she had seen something that would make for a great story, and the journalist in her might not be able to resist going public with it.

They pulled up to the security station of the Contemporary, and Hawk produced an identification card that released the gate to let them in. The security guard in the building one traffic lane over recognized the car, and Hawk waved at him. Kate nodded and waved. The guard tried unsuccessfully to look unfazed. The gate lifted, and Hawk drove into the resort at a slightly more sedate speed.

"Congratulations," he told Kate, glancing down at his watch. "I bet he's wondering who was in the car with me at three o'clock in the morning."

"Don't flatter yourself. He saw me and wondered why I was stuck in a car with a guy covered in mud who scared me to death with his driving and then pulled over to yell at me on the side of the road." Her eyes danced across his face, searching for a reaction. "It's easy to see that I could do better."

He wheeled the car through the general parking area and into a section marked Service Vehicles Only. Screeching to a halt, he turned off the ignition and opened his door. Kate remained seated and watched as Hawk walked around the front of the car and made his way back to her door. Grasping the handle, Hawk looked across the parking area for any unusual activity. Other than his car, all seemed quiet.

He opened the door like a gentleman, despite her provocation, and held it while she swung her legs out and stood. Hawk and Kate were a sight to behold. Both looking like storm survivors, mud caked in clumps on their bodies and clothes, accented by faces smudged with rain-streaked dirt. If someone managed to grab a picture of them in this moment, it would be the lead story on some scandal news website by morning.

Taking her by the arm, he led her toward an unmarked doorway. He used his security card once again, the door clicked open, and they stepped inside to a very industrial utility area at the base of the resort. Gently guiding her with a hand on her arm, he led her forward. Their footsteps echoed in the deserted concrete passageway.

Hawk kept his voice flat and emotionless. "You would have been bored."

"What?" Kate's voice raised in pitch ever so slightly as they walked.

"You said a few minutes ago that it was easy to see that you could do better. That is very true, but I was pointing out that you would be bored."

"Oh, you think?"

"I *know* . . . because right now you don't know what to do, Kate Young. Do you run with the footage you have and offer some half-baked, lame story that will get you great ratings? Or do you roll the dice and see if you can come up with something even better?" Hawk now allowed a smirk to flash across his lips. "What to do? What to do?"

"Why, Grayson Hawkes . . ." Kate stopped, forcing Hawk to stop as well. "I said it before and I'll say it again. You do know how to handle the press, don't you? You're teasing me . . . daring me to figure out what was going on and not running the footage I have . . . yet." She tilted her head.

He couldn't tell whether she was impressed, intrigued—or acting.

Hawk shook his head and resumed walking, motioning for her to follow. She caught up with him in just a few steps. In silence they traveled the length of the hallway and ended up at an elevator. When he pushed the button, the door opened instantly due to the lack of traffic at this time of the morning. They stepped inside, and he hesitated at the control panel. He didn't know which floor her room was on. She smiled, brushed past him lightly, and pushed the button for floor number five. They both stood watching the lights change as they climbed from floor to floor.

"You brought me in the service entrance and up the freight elevator so we wouldn't be seen," she said.

"I figured we could stay out of the main lobby, be seen by fewer people, and then have fewer people talking about us . . . looking like we do."

"I appreciate your thoughtfulness," she said drily. "Thank you."

"You're welcome."

The elevator made a ringing sound as they arrived at the fifth floor. The door opened and Kate stepped out. Hawk stepped in front of the door, to keep the sensor engaged so it wouldn't close the door, and pointed at the set of doors to his right.

"Go right though there, and you'll end up in the guest area. You can find your room from there." Then he looked down at her feet. "And try not to track mud all through the corridor of my resort."

Looking down at the mud and then back at him, she said, "I'll walk lightly."

"Good night, Kate." Hawk stepped back and the doors began to close.

Her fingers caught the door before it shut completely, and she came back into view as the door reopened. "I believe we have an interview scheduled in the morning at ten. I will get my story, Hawk. I'll figure out what was going on tonight."

"Good night, Kate." Hawk smiled, the door closed again, and he began the ride back down to the ground.

 *Day Three*
Morning

THE POUNDING ON THE DOOR ROUSED HAWK from a deep sleep. He rolled over in his bed, swung to the side of it, and his feet found the floor. The early morning stagger carried him out of his bedroom and into the living room as the pounding thundered louder. Blinking to focus his eyes, he trained them on his Mickey Mouse watch. It was 7:05 a.m. The pounding continued, and he unlocked the door of his Main Street apartment to see Reginald Cambridge with his fist raised, ready to pound again.

"Good morning, Grayson. We need to go."

"Hi, come in." Hawk stepped away, leaving the door open. He moved off toward the kitchen to make a cup of coffee. After dropping Kate off at the Contemporary, he had parked his car at the Bay Lake Towers, walked back to the Magic Kingdom, hopped across the fence, and made it back to his apartment by four in the morning. He had decided not to open the package he had found in the cemetery, even though the curiosity was killing him, until he could get Shep, Jonathan, and Juliette together. He had excluded them last time he tried to solve a mystery, and this time wanted to include them as much as possible. It was probably safer and wiser to do it that way.

His encounter with Kate had distracted him enough that he hadn't had time to dwell on his discovery. He was worried about what she was going to do with the footage and more concerned as to how to handle the situation. She was not going to disappear, and he had no idea how he could persuade her to ignore what she had seen. The coffee dispensed into the cup at the push of a button as he leaned over the kitchen counter, waiting.

"Want a cup of coffee or something to eat?" Hawk yelled into the living room.

"No, but thank you for asking." Reginald seated himself on the couch. "I am not eating breakfast today."

"Why?" Hawk emerged from the kitchen carrying his mug of java.

"I appear to be having some type of dental issue this morning." Reginald pointed toward his jaw. "I am dealing with some discomfort and have decided it is probably best not to create additional discomfort."

"You'd better get to a dentist." Hawk raised the hot cup to his mouth.

"I was going this morning until I had to detour to pick you up. Again, I repeat, we need to go."

"Where?" Hawk stood to slip into something more appropriate than the pajama pants he was wearing.

"Epcot." Reginald looked grim. "We have another situation we need to check out."

Hawk hurriedly brushed his teeth, threw on a pair of jeans and a button-up shirt, and rushed back into the living room carrying his shoes. Sipping his coffee and gesturing toward the door with his shoes, he left his apartment with his friend. They headed to Cambridge's SUV waiting just behind the doors that carried the pair out of the eye of the public guest area. Sliding gently into the front seat, Hawk balanced his coffee mug and put on his shoes as Reginald began to give him details.

"This morning, as our cast members were getting ready to send one of our attractions through a pre-opening test sequence, they noticed something on a security monitor," Reginald explained.

"Oh, no . . . not another ghost."

"Not exactly, but some might classify it as that."

"Stop." Hawk sat up in the seat as the vehicle hit a stretch of roadway to take them toward Epcot. "What attraction are we talking about?"

"Soarin'. There were already guests seated on the attraction."

"But the attraction wasn't opened yet."

"Exactly, sir."

Soarin' is one of the most popular attractions in Epcot. On a busy day, the wait can grow to ninety minutes easily for guests unable to secure a Fast-pass. Yet line up they do. The technology is genius. Figured out on a holiday weekend by an Imagineer who constructed a model with an erector set he had played with as a child, the ride seats guests in multiple rows under a winged canopy. A cantilever hoists the vehicles forward and into the air so the guests' feet dangle beneath them. The ride vehicles are lifted forward into a concave movie screen that, in essence, surrounds them and puts them into the movie. The effect—feeling like you are in flight—is popular with all ages.

The SUV moved into a backstage service area of Epcot, behind the pavilion known as the Land, where Soarin' is located. Cambridge and Hawk left the vehicle and jogged toward the door, which put them inside the Land. Moving across the huge dining area that consumed the bulk of the floor space of the pavilion, they moved through the still-empty queue lines. Following Cambridge's lead, Hawk stayed close behind, and they were greeted by a young woman who had been waiting for them. Her name badge read Melinda.

"We were just doing our normal morning maintenance," she informed them with a strong southern accent, "when we found our surprise passengers."

"Thank you very much." Reginald stopped her at the entrance to the ride area. "We will take it from here."

"But I just wanted to show you." She tried to follow them inside.

"I think we can handle it."

Hawk slipped past them both and went into the ride area. Normally people would file in, fill up each row, and then wait to be hoisted up in front of the screen. The ride moved with the film; the Imagineers had designed it so smells could be pumped in, and the multi-sensory experience was one most guests never forgot. In the dimly lighted area, Hawk slowly stepped to the front of the room, near the screen, and surveyed the passenger area. What he saw took him aback.

Cambridge entered without Melinda, Hawk noted. He closed the door, and now only he and Hawk stood in the room. Scattered throughout the seats of the flying vehicles were audio-animatronic figures. This time, however, they were not pirates. Instead, strapped into the seats of the flying kites, as though waiting for the ride to take off, were a number of United States presidents.

"Welcome aboard flight 5505," Hawk muttered.

"What was that, sir?"

"Flight 5505." Hawk looked toward Cambridge. "That is the imaginary flight number for this ride. It opened on May 5, 2005, so the flight number pays homage to the opening date."

"I see."

"How many presidents do we have here?"

"According to my count, we have ten guests." Reginald moved to one and began to unbuckle the presidential figure. "As you can imagine, this was quite startling to see on a security monitor. And with the figures being presidents dressed in their period costuming, it is as if ghosts from the past have attempted to take over the ride. Which is why I stated they could be classified as ghosts."

"Yes, I got the connection there, Reginald."

Hawk watched as Reginald released President Teddy Roosevelt from the bench, carried him to the back of the room, and placed him by the door. Hawk walked back and forth across the front of the room, looking at the presidents still seated.

"Are all the presidents still on display in the Hall of Presidents?"

"Yes." Reginald, answering instantly, must have anticipated the question.

"I had a detail check out the Hall of Presidents, and all is as it is supposed to be. It appears that these figures came from one of our storage areas. Like before, according to all of our records, there are none missing. But I believe we will make the same discovery we made with the pirates from yesterday. There will be some we can't account for. I have Clint Wayman checking once again."

"What about the other attractions with the presidents?"

"I'm not following where you are going."

"The models for the figures used in the Hall of Presidents can be found in various attractions throughout Disney World. If you look closely, sometimes they look familiar. On Spaceship Earth alone you can find Teddy Roosevelt as an Egyptian Priest and also a Roman politician. James Buchanan—" Hawk pointed toward the president seated in front of him. "—is Gutenberg in the other attraction. You can also see Dwight Eisenhower as a lute player and Ulysses S. Grant as a sculptor." Hawk gestured toward the president. "Make sure these really did get plucked out of a storage warehouse."

"I will check," Reginald said, setting down another president and stepping toward the front of the attraction where Hawk stood.

"How did they do this?" Hawk's curiosity was causing his mind to race.

"They took their time, and that is what troubles me, Grayson. This did not happen quickly." Reginald turned slowly and looked at the presidents still seated on the ride. "Someone was able to move these into the building, seat them on the ride, and then get back out. They have too much access, and they are not afraid of getting caught. And they are disrupting our operations."

"Why is today a day for presidents?"

"I think clearly it is to remind you of the warning they sent you yesterday."

"I haven't forgotten, but I am growing tired of their little displays."

"I imagine that would be what they are hoping for, sir." Reginald scowled. "Whoever is doing this is trying to show you they can do things that you can't stop. They have threatened you, and they are trying to show you they have the means to create real havoc in the theme parks . . . if you don't give them what they want."

"That's not going to happen."

"I understand that, but we can only anticipate they will heighten their malicious activity. I want to assign protection for you."

"No, you can protect me if I need it."

"No, I can't," Reginald grumbled. "As I have told you before, you are prone to doing the unpredictable, and that makes it impossible for me to cover you *and* find whoever is doing this."

"I appreciate your concern." Hawk patted his friend on the shoulder. "Have your team get the place checked out so we can open on time today.

Heighten our security in every area. I'll authorize you to bring in extra manpower for the next few days. We have to keep our guests safe."

"It will be taken care of." Reginald nodded. "I will get additional security for you as well."

"Thanks for the concern, but I will be fine." Hawk turned and headed for the exit. "I have an interview to get to. All things considered, I'd better not be late. And you get to the dentist and take care of yourself, got it?"

"Indeed I will." Reginald almost smiled and nodded toward his boss as he exited the ride area.

Hawk took the final strides toward the door and heard a hollow noise at his foot. Looking down, he chased the source of the sound with his eyes as it rolled away from him. He spotted it and crouched to get a closer look. Reginald, who had paused at the door, walked over to see whatever it was his boss had discovered. Hawk stepped to the wall where the object had come to rest and picked it up. After tossing it in the air and catching it again, he inspected the white golf ball that he had inadvertently kicked. He smiled, noticing it was a Mickey Mouse golf ball and tossed it to Cambridge. Reginald snatched it from the air and inspected it just as Hawk had.

"Someone must have dropped this," Cambridge stated.

"Or it was dropped on purpose," Hawk quickly responded.

"I'm not sure what you are driving at."

"Good choice of words, Reginald. Not sure what I'm driving at . . . golf ball . . . driving . . . that's good."

"Hmm." Reginald did not smile. "You think this means something?"

"It could. Have you ever ridden this attraction?"

"Yes, when it first opened I rode. It was well done."

"I agree. You remember the scene where a golf ball flies at you while you're soaring over the golf course?"

"Yes, it comes straight at you."

"If you're real quick, you see there's a Mickey Mouse on that golf ball . . . but the real message to me may be who hits the golf ball."

"You know who hits the golf ball in the film?"

"I do. It's the ex-CEO of the Disney Company. Michael Eisner."

"So the message is?" Cambridge frowned at the ball.

"This is my final shot or I will become an ex-leader of the company . . . just like Eisner."

"Do you really think that is what it means?"

"Hard to know for sure, but details do matter. . . . They do matter." Hawk nodded curtly and shoved open the doors of the attraction.

 *Day Three*
Morning

HAWK EXITED EPCOT AND CAUGHT the first monorail of the morning. As it snaked its quiet way along the highway in the sky toward the Transportation and Ticket Center at the Magic Kingdom, Hawk stared out the window. A few guests sat in the car with him. They whispered, as guests regularly did when trying to figure out if Hawk was indeed who they believed him to be. Arriving at the Ticket and Transportation Center meant he would have to change monorails and jump on another one that would make stops along the resort hotel loop.

He disembarked at the Contemporary, then crossed over to the Bay Lake Towers, where the first of the formal interviews with *Total Access* was scheduled to take place. He walked into the lower floor of his office at exactly ten o'clock, and Nancy Alport smiled and said good morning. Hawk wasn't sure whether she was glad to see him because she liked him or because he was actually on time for this appointment, as opposed to the disastrous day he'd had yesterday. Bounding up the steps toward the offices, he crested the stairs and could see the conference room had been gutted and set up for the interview. Chairs set against the backdrop of the picturesque view of the Magic Kingdom, lights strategically placed to illumine the interviewer and the interviewee without causing reflection off the glass.

Three different cameras would capture the interview from every angle. A control center, where both director and producer would watch the events unfold and make notes to make editing easier in postproduction, was positioned along the wall. As he moved past the door, he could see Kate Young in front of a mirror with Allie, applying makeup and going over notes. Pete Brady stood in the doorway, going over production notes with Juliette and Punky.

"Good morning, Dr. Hawkes." Pete smiled and nodded, as Hawk moved toward his office.

"Good morning," he said pleasantly. "Punky, how is the arm?"

"I think I'll live, thanks." Punky was sporting a wrapping on his wrist. He had either gone to have it checked as Hawk suggested or had self-treated the injury.

Juliette excused herself from the meeting with the director and producer and followed Hawk into his office. He'd known she would, and was waiting for her to come in and close the door. She did so with a look of concern crossing her face.

"What don't I know?" Her eyes narrowed toward him. "What happened last night?"

"It was bad, I messed up." He felt a fleeting quiver in the pit of his stomach as he admitted it.

"I told you to be careful." Juliette raised her hands in exasperation. "How bad?"

"Well, it could be catastrophically bad." Hawk lowered his head.

"Tell me."

"They have footage of me digging in a graveyard in the middle of the night and then getting attacked by an unknown assailant."

"Oh, that silly kind of stuff." Feigning nonchalance, she lowered her face for a moment. When she raised it again, her eyes blazed at him. "Have you gone insane? They have footage of you in a graveyard? What did you tell them was going on?"

"Nothing yet. When I brought Kate back to the Contemporary last night, she was hammering me and trying to intimidate me pretty tough." He looked up and tried to reassure her. "I pushed back, and we were at a standoff when the night ended."

"So what is your plan?"

"We may have to give her the story of a lifetime."

"You're going to tell her everything?"

"No, I didn't say that. But we may have to give her a story if she'll wait to run it under the conditions we set. I'll need your help on this if it works."

"Alright, what do you want me to do?" She sighed, looking slightly more relieved than Hawk felt about his beginnings of a plan.

"Get Jonathan and Shep to meet us later. Right now I have to survive this interview. We're going to ask her about last night and find out whether she's going to do a 'gotcha' interview."

"And if she does?"

"Then we shut it down and start trying to figure out how to spin it."

"Is there a good way to spin it?" Her voice lifted hopefully.

"Not that I see."

"Great."

A knock on the door ended their conversation as Juliette went over to open it. Allie stood there asking if they were ready to begin. He noticed the circles below her eyes. She had been up all night, and he hoped it was not from reviewing the footage they took in the cemetery. Juliette turned toward Hawk, who nodded and got up out of the chair to make his way over to the conference room. Stepping with him into the hallway between the two rooms, Allie inquired if Hawk needed to apply some makeup before the interview. He waved her off; early on in his new role, he had promised himself that whether it was a filmed interview or a photo shoot, he would not wear makeup. Juliette considerately stepped between them, as Hawk breezed into the conference-turned-interview room. Kate Young stood there, looking perfectly rested, watching him enter with her usual dazzling smile on display.

"Morning, Hawk."

"Kate." He acknowledged her with a nod. "How'd you sleep?"

"Good, just not enough of it." He heard the slightest crack of fatigue in her voice. "And you?"

"Excellent." He took a slow breath and tried to exhale away his own weariness without her noticing. "Just enough to be ready for the day."

"Glad to hear it." She waved Hawk toward a chair, then indicated a second one. "This will be your seat. I will sit here. The cameras will roll constantly, but we'll take a few breaks and give you a chance to relax and for me to go over any notes. Understand?" She pointed out where everyone would be stationed in the room. Juliette would be joining Pete and Punky behind the makeshift control booth. Allie would be the guardian of the door in case someone needed access while they were filming. As Kate explained, she described what was—in her words—standard stuff.

Hawk felt like her instructions would never end. He wanted her to speed it up and get the entire event over. His mouth felt dry as he tried to pay attention. She then took her seat and crossed her legs opposite Hawk. Leaning toward him, she whispered, "I had a good time last night."

"No, you didn't. You were frustrated and didn't get what you wanted." He smiled as Punky fitted him with a microphone and then hid the wireless battery pack.

"I'm hurt you would think that."

He tried to read the emotion in her pale green eyes but could not. Pete was reminding everyone to turn off their cell phones, and that reminded Hawk he needed to get a new one. He jerked his head to Juliette, who must have been thinking the same thing. She nodded and gave him a thumbs-up. The lights clicked on, and the room turned to shadows beyond them.

The countdown for the interview started.

Kate leaned in to Hawk and motioned to him to lean toward her. He did, and she whispered in his ear. "Just remember, Hawk, this isn't personal."

## CHAPTER THIRTY-ONE

*Day Three*
Late Morning

THE INTERVIEW HAD BEEN A LIVELY GIVE and take between Hawk and Kate. He had not been surprised by her questions as she probed into his background. They had talked about the church, his faith in Jesus, his call to ministry, and how he viewed life. The first break allowed them a chance to grab a drink of water and then shift gears for the second portion of the interview. During the second portion, they had talked about Disney. The company, the state of the company when Hawk took the helm as chief creative architect, and the success they had experienced in the eighteen months that followed. He'd answered questions similar to this in many of the interviews he had endured.

"You're doing great." She nodded encouragingly.

"Thanks."

Kate removed her mike, then wandered over to consult with the producer.

Formal interviews drained the life out of Hawk. Probably because of the nerves and the effort it took to make the interview look natural. They had been at it now for hours, and he was getting tired. He yawned in an attempt to exhale the fatigue. Standing for a moment, he stretched, wishing for an extended break.

"One more segment for this formal interview today if you're ready," Pete called out.

"She is really not covering any new territory." Juliette confirmed what Hawk had been thinking. "Maybe you have her curious enough to wait and see if there's a bigger story out there for her to find."

"I hope so." Hawk watched as Juliette moved back to the control booth and Kate reseated herself across from him. The investigative journalist reached out and patted him on the knee as the countdown started.

"Just remember what I said earlier." She flashed her smile at him once more and moved into the interview as the count reached one. He felt his heart crawl toward his throat when her question began. "Now Hawk, there has been much speculation about your life prior to becoming the chief creative architect for the Walt Disney Company. We have talked about your background, but tell us a little bit about your family."

Hawk shifted in his seat and battled back the urge to get up and leave. He looked through the darkness toward the outline of Juliette as she nearly dropped the bottle of water she was holding. He knew immediately where this was going. Kate was getting ready to try to peel back one of his most private chapters. Only his closest friends knew, and it was never discussed among them. This was a portion of his life that was closed because it was extremely painful. The emotion was still real, and it was something he constantly battled. His personal demons began clawing at the surface of his world.

"Not much to tell." Hawk smiled cautiously. "I grew up here in Central Florida, loved it, just a well-rounded Florida kid whose mom and dad taught him right from wrong, taught him to love Jesus, and to believe you can change the world. Not much that your viewers would care about."

"I disagree. I think our viewers have a great curiosity about your life. How about a wife or children?"

Hawk felt his throat tighten. The silence in the room echoed in his ears. He could sense the unseen control booth, where he knew both Punky and Pete would be leaning forward, anxious to see where this question might take them. Juliette would be getting ready to move in and stop the interview immediately. Before she could do so, he decided to answer.

"No." Hawk smiled a crooked smile and leaned back in his chair.

Kate leaned forward as if on a hunt. "No? No wife or children? Or no, you don't want to talk about it?"

"No." Hawk tried to slow his rapidly beating pulse.

"That really isn't an answer, is it?" She scrunched her face in a choreographed expression of confusion. "Somehow this is a topic that has never come up in any of your background interviews. I think our viewers would love to know more about who you are and what makes you tick. So you've never been married or never had children?'

"Well, I don't talk about it." Hawk again turned toward the people off camera behind the lights. Although he knew he had a friend back there, right now he was alone. Kate was fishing and had a hook in him. She was now just reeling in the line. He could stop it and end the interview. Or he could hold on and try to keep it together and survive. Hawk understood she had gradually worn him down through the earlier segments. He should have known this question was coming.

"Why don't you talk about it, Hawk?"

"It's private. It is a part of my life that is in the past. I've worked hard to move forward beyond it." He was telling the truth. This was his standard answer if someone got too close. Usually it was the answer he gave when he was digging in and not going to give any more details. It was enough for most. His past was deeply hidden; many speculated, but few knew for certain. Hawk now was fighting to stay alive in the interview, not knowing how much Kate really knew.

"But you are now a very public figure, Hawk. People care about the backgrounds and the pasts of those who make their living in the public eye. So tell us, why you don't talk about your wife and kids?"

"I don't have a wife and kids." He stared at her, willing her to let it go.

"But you did." She smiled and nodded as if to prod him along. He now knew that she knew. *Just remember, Hawk, this isn't personal.*

"I did." But with a tilt of his head, he stopped short of offering any more information. "But that was a long time ago."

"Indeed it was. But according to our research, you were married at one time and had three beautiful children. Isn't that correct?" Her eyes bore into his.

He was determined not to give her the satisfaction of knowing how painful this was.

"If that's what your research says, then I guess *Total Access* can't be wrong." It was a weak response, and he knew it as soon as he said it.

Kate paused, glanced down at her notes, and then refocused on him like a lioness ready to spring. "Why don't you tell us about the accident?" Her tone softened slightly.

"I don't remember much about it." He looked directly into her eyes and said the next words very slowly, measuring each one. "Why don't you tell me and your viewers what you think you know."

"You were a young seminary student, traveling with your wife and three children back to Orlando for a family vacation in Walt Disney World. You'd just finished your final exams for the semester, and you had been doing what most students do . . . cramming and using every minute to study." Her pale green eyes were riveted on his as she unpacked the narrative, each word driving into his heart like a nail. "Right after the last exam, you loaded up the car and started the twenty-three hour trip to Orlando. Does this sound about right? Please tell us what happened."

Hawk never broke his connection to her eyes. He was desperately trying to see beyond them to her motivation. Was this really all about getting a story? Was she hoping he would stop her and tell her she was wrong? Was she just guessing at his background and trying to trick him into divulging more information than she really knew? He was going to wait for her to tell the story. But he was not going to help her. He repositioned himself in the chair and listened.

"Your wife had suggested that you rest a bit or delay the trip until the following day, hadn't she?"

Hawk thought back to those moments years ago. His wife had asked him to wait, but the kids were excited, he was excited, and he was so ready to have a break from the studies and have time to play with his family. No matter how deeply he tried to bury the memories, they were always just a heartbeat away. He heard Kate's voice again, dragging him back to the interview.

"But you didn't wait, did you? You were excited and anxious to get to Disney World. So you drove. You didn't have much money as a seminary student, and you needed all the funds you had for your vacation, so you decided to make the trip without stopping, you decided to drive it straight through."

This time there was no pause to ask a question. Kate had figured out he would not answer. He continued to explore her eyes with his and felt his begin to sting a bit around the edges. He saw her green eyes moisten as she continued her story.

"It was in the panhandle of Florida, along Interstate 10. It was a long stretch of dark, lonely, isolated highway. Everyone else in the car was asleep. You felt your eyes get droopy. You found yourself fighting to stay awake. And then you dropped your head and went to sleep. Out of sheer exhaustion, you had pushed yourself to the limit and you couldn't stay awake any longer."

Hawk clenched his jaw. His face tightened, and that sensation ran down both sides of his neck and across his chest. Blinking away the stinging in his eyes, he kept his gaze connected to Kate's, locked in a battle of wills. He was going to force her to look away before he gave her the satisfaction of seeing him crack under her questioning.

"The car careened off the road into a ravine along the interstate. The police investigation later would report that you went to sleep and for an extended time stayed on a straight stretch of the highway. But by the time the car left the road, you were traveling in excess of ninety-five miles an hour. The vehicle rocketed into the woods along the highway. It cut through a tree and came to rest deep in the forest. Your car was so deep in the woods, and so badly damaged, that you and your family remained trapped inside for three days before someone found you.

"You were the only survivor, and you spent the next four weeks in the hospital in critical condition. The rumor at the time of the accident was that you may have been driving under the influence. Due to the catastrophic nature of the wreck, those charges were never filed. It was a horrible and tragic accident." She paused. A small tear rolled down her cheek.

She glanced down at her notes. Once she looked away and broke eye contact with Hawk, he turned toward the window and looked out toward the Magic Kingdom. She had told the story in perfect, heartbreaking detail. He had spent years wrestling with guilt, remorse, and the knowledge that his own stupidity and reckless lack of judgment had taken those he had loved the most from him. It was his fault; he knew it, he owned it, and he couldn't forget it. It haunted him. He knew that God had forgiven him. He knew it was an accident. But forgiving himself and moving forward, that had been and would always be the struggle.

He turned his attention back to Kate, who was allowing him time to gather his thoughts. They were not done yet. He thought about getting up and walking away, but it was too late. He never should have agreed to the *Total Access* project.

"Did I get the story right, Hawk?" He heard a softness to her voice he had not heard from her before.

"Does it matter?" His voice trailed off as he glanced toward the ground before looking back at her. A numbness settled over him. He had always worried about the moment when everyone would find out about his past mistakes, and he realized that very soon this interview would be seen by the entire world.

As a pastor, he had walked through crisis with people many times as they had to come to grips with mistakes of their past. He had explained that falling never hurt anyone; it was the stopping when you land that really hurts. Now it was his turn, and he was in an emotional free fall, without a parachute. The looming impact was terrifying. Kate would tell the world about the moment that changed him forever, and he was about to find out if he could move forward once people knew. As he tumbled through his thoughts, he heard her voice.

"I'm sorry." Kate spoke softly. "I didn't hear you. I asked did I get the story right."

"I said—" He cleared his throat, searching for more volume. "—does it matter?"

He saw a slight hitch as she took in her next breath. His response was not what she had expected. He was not going to admit or deny the account. She knew it was what had happened. Her research was as good as it could have been. He knew she had checked the facts and verified them as accurately as she could. After all the years, he knew that eventually someone would unearth the report. It had been buried for years.

When Hawk had stepped into the public eye, a retired policeman from a small community in the panhandle had contacted him and asked if he was the same Grayson Hawkes that had almost died on the highway. Juliette had stepped in and followed up with the man and told Hawk not to worry about it. He assumed this was Kate's source, and once she had the overview she was able to confirm much of the rest. That was why Juliette had been so careful to keep him in front of handpicked interviewers. He knew she had been terrified of his meeting Kate Young, and now he understood why. Juliette, having set up this interview out of necessity, had warned him, trying to protect him from himself—and he hadn't been smart enough to let her.

Kate studied the man sitting across from her in the hot seat. Over the last couple of minutes, she had painted a horrific story of a tragic event that would have shattered the life of anyone it had happened to. When he'd asked whether it mattered, it caught her off guard. He had spoken so softly, she wasn't even sure if the microphone would have picked up what he said. He had repeated it, and she had heard him correctly. It took her a moment to register what he meant.

"Of course it matters." Another tear leaked from the corner of her eye and streaked down her cheek.

She tried to find something besides him to focus on. She hadn't expected to say that. Glancing down at her notes again, she shifted in her chair and decided to shift the subject matter too. Normally she would work to change the topic in such a way as to completely throw off the interviewee, causing him to reveal information he had never planned on giving up. Grayson Hawkes had not given her anything. She knew she was right. She could see it in his eyes, could read the expression; she saw what the camera did not. She had hurt him. Not because she wanted to, but because it was her job. This was a secret that Hawk and the people he had surrounded himself with had hidden from the world. But Grayson Hawkes had chosen to live large in the public spotlight, and the cost of celebrity is privacy.

"I have a video clip for you to see," she announced. She produced a small handheld camera. She wanted to see his reaction to the clip that would be edited into the segment.

"Can't wait." Hawk leaned up to look at the camera.

She was surprised that he bounced back and responded. Her fear was that she had not only hurt him, but that something in him had broken and he could not continue the interview. He was much stronger than she had thought. The clip began to play, and she knew it was not what he had been expecting to see. Instead of the shot of Hawk on his knees digging in a cemetery in the rain, this clip was from a few days ago.

She watched as he saw himself leaping from boat to boat in the Pirates of the Caribbean and then jumping into the water as the city burned around him. The clip ended, and she lowered the camera. Someone had used a cell phone to capture Hawk's heroic efforts to reach the body in the water and had gotten the clip to *Total Access*.

"According to reports, a body was found floating in the famous Pirates of the Caribbean attraction this week." She smiled her famous smile, but this time with less enthusiasm. Tiredly she asked, "Was there a body found in the attraction?"

"No, I promise you." Hawk's voice burned with intensity. "There was not a body in the Pirates of the Caribbean this week."

"This footage was captured by a park guest in another boat. The rumor was there was a body. However, a number of people reported seeing you move into the attraction and, well, literally jump in to solve the problem. What are we seeing here?"

"One of our very expensive audio-animatronic figures ended up in the water. It looked like a body for sure." He smiled. "But I assure you, it was not a person. Just something of our own creation."

"So all is going well in the world of Disney for the chief creative architect?"

"All is well." His nod was in stark contrast to the alarms still screaming in his head. The revelation of his tragic past, his being seen digging in a cemetery, and now realizing that someone had footage of the unfolding battle raging around him had his senses on fire and ready for a fight.

Kate immediately stood to her feet and turned to the table hidden in the darkness behind the light. "Are we good?" she asked into the blinding light.

"We're good, Kate," Punky said from the darkness.

"Cut the lights," she ordered, as she removed her microphone from her jacket.

The sudden change in lighting left Hawk blinking. Kate stepped in front of him, snatched off his microphone, and covered it with her hand. Leaning in and placing her mouth right next to his ear, she whispered, "The questions about the accident are my job. I don't always enjoy it, but I do the job better than anybody else. You shouldn't have tried to hide it. But Hawk, the video I showed you is my gift to you. I could have shown you what we filmed last night, but I didn't. You were on the ropes, and I could have destroyed you." She paused, and he could hear her swallow. "But I didn't, remember that."

Kate tossed both microphones into the chair she had been sitting in and rushed toward the door. Allie moved across the room to meet her, but Kate waved her off and exited alone.

Hawk sluggishly got to his feet and placed a hand on the back of the chair as he looked toward the control table. Juliette came around the table, reached out and grabbed Punky Zane by the injured arm. He winced, and she released her grip.

"Was it necessary? You could have frontloaded where she was going." Juliette hurried toward Hawk. "You alright, boss?"

"Sure, how'd I do?" He forced a smile, knowing that there was no way they could derail the *Total Access* train that had left the station.

"I'm sorry, we never should have said yes to their request." She wrinkled her nose slightly and smiled apologetically.

"Nope, it's not your fault. You tried to warn me. It happened, and hearing Kate's questions reminded me that when you're reckless, people you love get hurt. I'm the one who's sorry. I did this."

The two friends stood and looked out the window toward the Magic Kingdom. After a few moments of silence, Hawk noticed Juliette had turned and was waiting for him to look back at her. He shifted his stance to face her, and she tilted her head and raised her eyebrows.

"Well." She held her palms up. "We always knew this day would come."

"We did." His stomach felt heavy, as he squeezed her hands and then let them go. "So what happens now?"

She paused thoughtfully, placing her hands on her hips. "I suppose I need to start preparing a strategy to deal with this new information that the popular and charismatic CCA of the world-renowned leader in family entertainment has a past . . . and in that past, had a tragic accident and lost his entire family."

"That is just the start of it." Hawk felt sick. "I didn't just lose my family. The way the story is about to be told, I'm responsible for their deaths. And we tried to hide the story."

"It was an accident." Juliette looked at him seriously. "People will understand why this is a part of your life that you never have made public."

"You really believe that?"

"Believe what?"

"That people will understand?" Hawk allowed a smile to crack his solemn face.

"No." She laughed sadly. "The press will eat this story up, and there will be reporters and critics coming out of the woodwork to paint you as some kind of monster." She raised her index finger between them. "But I will figure out a way to protect you."

"I know." Hawk nodded. "While Kate was finishing up her dissection of my life, something else dawned on me."

"What?"

"I realized it when she showed me the clip of me in Pirates of the Caribbean. If the people who are trying to steal the key and organization from me knew about the accident, they would have used it to blackmail me into giving up the key." He watched as Juliette's mouth opened slightly as she understood where he was going with this line of thinking. "The truth is, my enemies don't know about the wreck. So who is the most dangerous person or persons in my world right now? These enemies who want the key or Kate Young? Because she knows something that they don't know."

Juliette furrowed her brow. "And I wonder where Kate got the footage of you jumping around on those boats in Pirates."

 *Day Three*
Evening

**GUESTS ENTERING THE MAGIC KINGDOM** emerge from the tunnel under the Walt Disney World Railroad and step into turn-of-the-century America on Main Street USA. They first enter the Town Square, complete with a City Hall and Fire Station. The lettering on the station reads Engine Co. 71, the number commemorating the year the Magic Kingdom opened. The Fire Station is located right across the alley from the Harmony Barber Shop. This is a real working barbershop with old-style barber chairs where haircuts and beard trims are offered. Standing on the corner in front of the barbershop, a person can look back across the street at the station and notice a long set of steps that run up the side of the building to a door on the second floor. Each day, people stand in front of the barbershop, not just to wait for haircuts, but also to catch a glimpse of Grayson Hawkes as he enters or leaves his apartment.

Shortly after he had converted this space into living quarters, the rumors began to circulate that, just like Walt had done in Disneyland, a new resident lived above the Fire Station in the Magic Kingdom. Once Hawk had descended the fire pole into what used to be a gift shop, guests began to wait for a chance to greet or get an autograph from the chief creative architect of the company. This day, there was a small group of people calling out to Hawk as he came around the building to head upstairs. He stopped and chatted with the guests that were there waiting. After a few minutes, he turned and raced up the steps to his home.

He had invited Juliette, Shep, Jonathan, and Farren to meet him so he could show them what he had found the night before in the cemetery. Now, after spending some time with the guests along the street, he was late. They would probably all be there waiting for him.

He stepped into his apartment, and his friends turned to greet him. Their faces showed concern, and he knew that Juliette had told them about the emotional interview with *Total Access*. He had decided to make the best of the bad situation and move forward. He was about to speak, when his focus shifted from them to his place of residence.

Stunned, he slowly stepped toward the center of the room and turned his head to take it all in. It appeared as if a bomb had exploded in the apartment. Papers and books littered the floor. Every piece of furniture had been turned over. The bottom of his couch, each cushion, the chairs, and each pillow had been slit open, and much of the stuffing strewn across the floor. Lamps lay on their sides, and shards of glass littered the small living space.

Moving toward his bedroom, he saw more of the same damage. Pillows, mattress, and bed linens were slashed. Clothes were tossed about; drawers from the dresser had been removed, emptied, and thrown across the bed. It looked as if nothing was left untouched. His stomach was churning as he silently walked back into the living room, where his friends were waiting.

"It looks like I'm probably going to have to stay in a hotel tonight." He masked his rising frustration with a grin. "Anyplace around here I can find one?"

"Boss, I am so sorry," Shep said, as Hawk continued to take in the damage. "I got here just before everyone else, and the door was ajar, so I just pushed it and found . . . well, this."

"I'm sorry, Hawk." Juliette's eyes rimmed with tears. "This has been a horrible day for you."

"Yeah, Juliette told us about Kate Young." Jonathan came over and grabbed his friend by the arm and gave it a squeeze. "You hanging in there?"

"I'm fine, it's not that bad." Hawk did a double-take at Jonathan's face and pointed his finger at it.

Jonathan cocked his head. "What?"

"Your eye, it's all puffy." Again Hawk pointed toward it. "This is nothing to cry over. Interviews and messy apartments are a part of life . . . now."

"I'm sad, but I'm not crying." Jonathan reached up and touched his eye. "Allergies, I guess. Woke up this morning and barely could see."

Juliette straightened up a chair. "Well, if you're allergic to things, then with all the junk that's been stirred up in here, you'll be having fits."

"What were they looking for, Hawk?" Farren asked, as he moved over and took a seat in the chair Juliette had picked up.

"I'm going to assume they want the special-delivery package Aunt Jessie left for me."

"They didn't get it, did they?" Shep ran his fingers through his hair.

"No, of course not." Farren pointed toward Hawk. "You're much wiser than that, aren't you?"

They all turned toward Hawk in anticipation. He shrugged and then widened his eyes and cut them back and forth as if checking to see if anyone was watching. Reaching behind him, he lifted up his shirt and removed the discovery from the night before, which he was toting in his back jeans pocket. Pulling it around and holding it in front of himself, he smiled.

"Yes, I am wiser than that."

He gestured for them all to grab chairs, and they slid back what remained of Hawk's belongings with their feet, making space. Seating themselves in a circle, they passed around the package Hawk had been hiding like they were playing a children's game. As the cylinder went from person to person, each studying it, the anticipation in the room crackled.

"So someone trashed your apartment looking for this." Jonathan passed the cylinder to Farren.

"It looks like it," Hawk said. "Good thing this isn't my first mystery."

"A very good thing." Farren weighed the discovery in his hands. "Are you ready to open it?"

"Why don't you?" Hawk offered.

"No, that is not my role. I helped design one small piece of this secret. It is your quest, your challenge, and your responsibility now . . . to figure it out, to do what needs to be done. What was it George said to you? 'Unlock what never was, to protect what is yet to be.' That was it, wasn't it?" Farren offered the discovery back to Hawk.

Footsteps in the open doorway jolted their attention away from the conversation. Stepping inside was Kate Young, followed by Punky Zane holding a mini-cam and shooting footage. As soon as they entered the room, their faces slackened in shock. Punky immediately panned the camera across the entire wreckage of the apartment. Kate swung her head, and Hawk saw her begin to take inventory of what she was seeing and create her conclusions. He had been robbed, and she stopped looking at the mess and turned to face Hawk, as Jonathan and Shep jumped up and started moving toward them.

"Turn the camera off and get it out of here," Jonathan said, as he headed toward Punky. "Now!"

"You have a lot of nerve coming here uninvited." Shep zeroed in on Kate. "You need to leave."

Punky did not stop filming fast enough for Jonathan, who snatched the camera from Punky and shoved him backward. Holding the camera in one hand, Jonathan gestured toward the door. Punky looked back at Kate, who was standing her ground as Shep approached. As Shep stepped up and stood nose-to-nose with her, all motion suddenly stopped. Shep probably wasn't going to push her, and Hawk guessed she would back toward the door.

Kate Young was always unpredictable and seemed unfazed by Shep's bluff of force. Taller than Shep, her height accentuated by her heels, she looked down on him but did not back away. Punky waited for a cue from Kate, but she gave him nothing. He glanced nervously at Jonathan and took a step back.

Hawk rose to his feet and walked toward the tense activity taking place just inside his doorway. He took the camera out of Jonathan's hand. With a pat on the back, he stepped past him and handed the device back to Punky.

"Leave it off for now," Hawk said, before releasing it into Punky's clutched hand.

"Sure," Punky said, and took another step back toward the door.

Now Hawk placed a hand on Shep's shoulder and gently tugged back. Shep got the signal and backed up a full step from where he had been standing facing Kate.

"Hello, Kate." Hawk angled himself in between the pair. "What can we do for you?"

"We were trying to get some moments with you at home." She looked over Hawk toward Juliette. "This was on the schedule for today."

"As you can see, we have been distracted by some unforeseen circumstances." Juliette motioned across the room. "I hadn't had a chance to talk with Hawk about the schedule yet."

"I still have to get the footage for the show." Kate tilted her head and shrugged.

"Kate, this is not a good time," Hawk said to her.

"Hawk, that is not how this works," She replied gently.

Hawk spun back toward the door. Motioning to Jonathan for help, he pointed toward Punky, who had taken yet another step closer to the exit.

"Punky, you take your camera and get out now. Wait outside." Hawk turned toward Kate. "And you, follow me."

Kate nodded toward Punky. "I'll be fine here. Go back to the resort. I'll call later." He slid out the door with his camera and was gone.

He walked through the damaged apartment and realized there was no place to go that was not demolished. Taking the clearest path he could find, he edged into the kitchen, where every cabinet had been gutted and left open. He stepped over the clutter and leaned against the counter, facing her. He tried to read her, and her chin jutted out slightly as if getting ready for battle. Well, he imagined she had been through this type of encounter before.

"Kate, can you just back off a little bit?" He kept his voice calm and his tone soft. "You have taken some pretty good shots at me today. And tonight I walk into this . . . in my home."

Her lips parted, and her gaze softened. "You're not going to rant and rave, end the agreement, and involve *Total Access*'s legal team?"

When she looked like that, he paused, almost wanting to reassure her. He realized then just how good she was at getting her story. "Not just yet. But cut me some slack here, OK?"

"Hawk, look . . . I am sorry that today got a little rough for you. Like I said, it's my job. It was not personal, it was never personal. I backed off, and I hope you're going to continue our agreement and give me total access. That means whatever is happening here, right now, is a part of that."

Hawk looked over his shoulder at Juliette, who got up and made her way in their direction. Farren smiled kindly at Hawk, and Jonathan stood with his back against the door like someone was going to break in at any moment.

Hawk took a deep breath. "You aren't catching me at my best. This is a mess, and my life is . . ."

"Your life is exactly what I'm here to see. So far, I've seen you preach and teach with a clarity that I've never, ever heard in church before. I think you actually believe that you can change the world. I've seen you drive into the middle of nowhere into a storm to go digging in a cemetery to find something. Which, by the way, looks a lot like that round package that the older gentleman is holding right over there." She pointed toward Farren. "Before we can get out of the cemetery, someone attacks you and tries to take what you found. Listen to me: The chief creative architect of the Walt Disney Company is attacked in the middle of the night and someone tries to steal something from him, and I get it on tape. But then it gets even better . . ."

Kate started pacing the kitchen, trying to avoid the obstacles all over the floor. "You fight back. You go after this guy that attacked you. And you fight pretty well, by the way. My crew tries to help you, and you end up with your discovery. But you don't ever mention calling the law, you get irritated at me and hint there might be something really big going on, and if I will just play nice, you will let me know 'off the record' all about it."

Now standing across the small kitchen from him, she placed her hands on her hips. "Then today I let you know I've uncovered some deep dark secret from your past, and you don't want to answer my questions, but I give you the chance." Her voice was getting louder. "It broke my heart to watch you squirm in the interview . . . and for just a few moments, I hated doing my job. But I let you off the hook. I still don't know why . . . but I didn't show the cemetery footage. I knew you would be spinning and trying to recover from the media coverage of that for months." She waved a hand at Juliette. "I know you don't want that, and I don't want you to have to do that . . ."

Kate turned back to Hawk. "Then tonight I come here, as I had asked to do, and find your private apartment on Main Street USA in Walt Disney World, in the theme park mind you, has been broken into. And you are mad and irritated at me. Short stuff over there—" She gestured toward Shep. "—acts like he's going to punch me, and you start shoving around my cameraman . . . who, in case you forgot, helped you last night when you got attacked." Stepping back, she waved both arms in a grand gesture. "If you haven't taken inventory of your life lately, Grayson Hawkes . . . it is a mess! I can see it, and I have only known you for two days."

Silence spilled over the apartment. Kate was breathing hard. Her gaze was fixed on Hawk, and all eyes in the room were cutting between Kate on one side of the kitchen and Hawk on the other.

"Well, when you put it that way, I guess it is a mess." Hawk slowly rolled his eyes and stepped past her, moving back into the living room and taking his seat across from Farren. He watched her from the corners of his eyes.

Kate placed her hand over her forehead, stretched her fingers across her temples, and started to laugh as though she hadn't expected him to agree with her. Juliette snickered. Shep rocked up on tiptoe in an attempt to look taller and drifted back toward where they were seated. Jonathan turned the lock on the apartment door and pushed off it to make his way back. Juliette left Kate in the kitchen and joined the circle of friends. Hawk settled in his seat and looked up into the pleasant face of Farren Rales, who was still clutching the package. He had not moved throughout the entire exchange. He once again held out the cylinder for Hawk to take from him.

"Unlock what never was, to protect what is yet to be," the old Imagineer said, as Hawk took the wrapped package.

"What am I going to do about her?" Hawk gestured with a thumb over his shoulder toward Kate, who he could still see watching them from the kitchen.

 *Day Three*
Night

"COME IN HERE AND JOIN US, Ms. Young." Farren motioned Kate into the living room. "Perhaps we should give her what she really wants . . . the story of a lifetime." Farren then whispered to Hawk, "Within reason, of course. Some secrets are best left secret."

"Agreed," Hawk said.

Jonathan pulled another chair from where it had been tossed onto the floor, and Kate sat down next to Hawk. Farren cleared his throat.

"Let me introduce myself. I am Farren Rales. I am officially an ambassador for the Walt Disney Company. I am an Imagineer. Some consider me a legend. Others, my dear . . . well, they just consider me old." He smiled. "I am a storyteller and have been around a long, long time. But you are here looking for a story and trying to get the untold story of how a preacher could become the chief creative architect of the Walt Disney Company. So, considering all that has happened and some of the things you have seen . . . you need some type of explanation to understand it all. Correct?"

"That would be helpful." Kate nodded.

"Because if we don't help you understand, then you will draw your own conclusions and tell some type of story that might damage the reputation of Hawk or even this company."

"I'm not here to do a hatchet job."

"But you will." Farren reached out and patted her arm. "What else could you do with what you have seen? However, it would be mutually beneficial for all of us if we could have a better story told. Better for us, because it would help you understand that our leader is not just the average everyday grave robber; better for you, because the story we have to share is a classic Disney story that is nothing short of fantastic."

"I can hardly wait." Kate smiled at the old Imagineer.

"There is one request you must grant before we go any further."

"There always is . . ." She sat back in her seat expectantly.

"No cameras. You get to be a part of the story, and then when you have it all . . . then you decide how best to tell it to others."

"*Total Access* is a production. We are visual, and we have made our reputation on the footage we capture and on the way we use it to tell a story."

"I understand how to tell a story. This is a story that you will discover is worth doing differently." Farren glanced to Hawk, who was listening, puzzled. "Trust me, what you will find will amaze you."

"But no cameras?" She looked skeptically at the people seated around her. "What happens if I don't agree to this new arrangement?"

"Then I am sure that *Total Access* and Juliette can argue about what happens next, but I can promise you this, you will miss out on the story of a lifetime." Farren's eyes sparkled. "But if you are willing to take a chance, you might just find a story that is . . . beyond belief."

Silence drifted across the room as Kate pondered her options. Hawk knew she was intrigued by the invitation Farren had just placed before her. His mind whirled, rooting through the information circling his brain as he processed the old Imagineer's strategy . Hawk understood they were in a mess. *Total Access* could not realistically back away from the story it had stumbled into by following him to the cemetery. Added to that was the information about his past—tragic and embarrassing, the story would become a feeding frenzy for scandal nuts and haters. Then the footage of him jumping from boat to boat in Pirates of the Caribbean with the hint that something was wrong in the theme parks, and now a break-in at his private residence right on Main Street USA. Sadly, in a matter of hours, Hawk had generated enough bad news to leave the media talking heads with their tongues wagging and shareholders of the company more than a little jittery.

If Kate Young could be an ally and not an adversary, it would make this new mystery easier to solve, because he wouldn't be distracted by trying to keep *Total Access* from gaining access. Hawk realized that Farren was taking a chance that might just backfire, but the risk at this point had to be worth it. In just a couple of days, his magical eighteen-month run at the helm of this company that he loved had begun cracking around the edges.

As the soundtrack for the evening parade began to play, a tremor shook the room. The parade began in the alley right outside the Fire Station. The route looped through Town Square, past the Train Station, and past the Town Square Theater, before it went straight down Main Street USA toward Cinderella Castle. The window of Hawk's apartment provided a unique view of the parade that few ever had the chance to see. The lights of the parade floats shone through the window and sparkled off objects in the room. On this night it improved the disastrous condition of the Hawk's Nest. With the parade providing the background music, the group waited for Kate to make a decision.

"I'm in." Kate glanced at Hawk and then looked back toward Farren. "Tell me a story."

"Our friend Grayson Hawkes was chosen by Walt Disney himself to lead this company," Farren said with a huge grin.

Kate sat back in her chair and crossed her legs. She tilted her head. "So Hawk got the job because Walt Disney wanted him to have it?"

"Ultimately, yes." Farren leaned forward and lowered his voice. "But the selection process was left to me."

"You've got me." She clasped her hands in her lap. "I suppose you can convince me of this, right?"

"Of course I can. I will be happy to fill in the details for you. But for now, you are going to have to learn as you go, I'm afraid." He nodded toward Hawk to open the package. "For right now, we have work to do."

Hawk, taking the signal from Farren, began to unwrap the discovery he had made in the cemetery the night before. Slowly unwinding the rope that encased the burlap, he freed the last wrapping. Then, gingerly peeling back the layers of burlap, he released the prize inside.

It was a figurine. Approximately eleven inches in height. An intricately detailed figure of a cowboy; shirt, jeans, and scarf, with his left arm extended to hoist his cowboy hat in the air in celebration. It was a work of art, displaying a high level of craftsmanship. Hawk raised his eyebrows and turned it over in his hands, studying it. The rest of the group leaned in closer, and Hawk held the figure up in front of them so they could get a better view.

"That was the special delivery from Aunt Jessie?" Shep asked.

"Aunt Jessie is Walt Disney's aunt," Hawk said, for Kate's information, as he slowly maneuvered the figure, looking at it with a 360-degree perspective. "Aunt Jessie was the postmaster of Paisley, Florida. She's buried in the cemetery. Actually, in the family plot where I found this."

Hawk continued to study the figure, as he quickly rattled off details about Walt's grandparents, the picture, the words written on it, and how he had figured out where to look for the special delivery. He noticed Kate would get a curious look on her face and want to ask something but refrained. He continued to explain how he'd ended up in the cemetery, hoping it would keep her intrigued in the mystery.

Kate reached out to take the figure from Hawk, but he pulled it away from her and handed it to Farren.

"Hold on," Kate blurted. "So you have this puzzle you are trying to solve and you find that? What is that? A cowboy doll?"

"A clue. Come on, Kate, you're going to have to keep up," Hawk chided, as he waited for Farren to finish examining it. "A clue that I hope will help me find whatever it is that Walt Disney is trying to tell me."

Kate's mouth dropped open slightly. Juliette touched her sleeve to get her attention.

"Now, didn't we tell you this would be a story almost beyond belief?" Juliette smiled brightly at her.

"I haven't seen this in . . . well . . . since 1975." Farren smiled, and his eyes grew misty. "Isn't it a work of art? This was a model designed by Imagineering legend Marc Davis. It is a model piece from the Western River Expedition attraction."

"The Western River Expedition that was the main attraction in Thunder Mesa? The same one that George Colmes worked on or stopped from being built?" Hawk leaned forward.

"One and the same."

"Who is George Colmes?" Kate asked.

"A ghost," Shep answered.

"Is not." Juliette folded her arms. "He is another seasoned Imagineer, but I don't know what he has to do with anything yet. Just hang on. Listen to the story."

"You can learn a lot by paying attention and getting the real story," Hawk said to Kate without looking at her.

"If this is what I think it is . . . it hasn't been seen since 1975." Farren passed the figure to Kate. "Thunder Mesa was a heavily advertised area being developed at Walt Disney World. The main attraction was the Western River Expedition. It was to be a better version of Pirates of the Caribbean. Created especially for Florida. It was going to have other rides as well, but it would have been an expensive development, and it was put on hold so other attractions would be ready for opening day in 1971. Still, in the books that explained the Magic Kingdom to people when it opened, Thunder Mesa and the Western River Expedition were heavily promoted as a coming attraction."

"Why hasn't this been seen since 1975?" Jonathan asked.

"Eventually, officially, the plans were delayed indefinitely because it was too expensive to build. People in Florida wanted the Pirates attraction, so it was built, then Space Mountain came along and became the first roller coaster in the park. However, one of the ideas for Thunder Mesa was a mine train, and then eventually Big Thunder Mountain Railroad was built. The plan kept getting pushed back, and finally it seemed like nothing more than a dream. George Colmes was an Imagineer who, like me, was close to the Disney brothers. George was extremely close to Roy, who, of course, pushed the Disney World project to completion. After Roy passed away, George disappeared, and the hope of Thunder Mesa and the Western River Expedition became the stuff of legend and Disney folklore."

Farren paused, shrugged his shoulders. "Most people didn't realize that the entire area had been created in a model. After the project was finally axed, the model was stolen from WED Enterprises."

"WED stood for Walter Elias Disney Enterprises?" Kate asked.

"Very good." Farren clapped. "I believe this is one of the original pieces from that model. It is . . . it is priceless."

"Hold on." Hawk raised a hand. "I think I have seen something similar to this figure before, haven't I?"

"Yes, you have." Farren was caught up in the story. "You and I viewed it once together in the Imagineering Research Library at WDI in California. There was a second model, a partial model, right here in Walt Disney World that was on display in the post-show area of the Walt Disney Story attraction right here in Town Square. When the 1981 rehab was being done, the workmen decided it was too much trouble to take down the elaborate display. There was a talking owl named Hoot Gibson that was an animatronic host. He introduced people to the coming attraction, and the preview featured a model of what a portion of the show would look like. The workmen decided to put a wall up over the display. They just covered it up and left the lights on in the windows and lanterns of the model. Thirteen years later, when we were getting ready to reuse the area for the twenty-fifth anniversary celebration, the wall was opened up and the model found. Since the original model had disappeared in '75, these pieces were treated like gold. The owl must have flown away, because to this day there is no Hoot Gibson . . . but this cowboy that you found . . . it is one of the originals. George Colmes must have had it."

Jonathan looked toward Hawk. "And he left it for you."

"Why? What does it mean?" Kate asked Farren.

"That is what Hawk must figure out," Farren replied. He stood and stretched. "Well, it is getting late. I hope you are just a little bit intrigued by our story. If you would like, there are some more details I can share tomorrow over breakfast. Since you are staying in the Contemporary, I will be at Chef Mickey's at 8:00 a.m. One of the perks of being an old timer with the company is that I have a reserved a table there. Just ask a cast member, and someone will get you to me."

Hawk walked Farren to the door. He helped to kick a path through the clutter that until earlier had neatly decorated his home. Hawk unlocked the door and shook his friend's hand.

"Thanks, Farren. See you tomorrow?"

"If you need me." A look of concern crossed his face. "You, my dear friend, be careful and don't worry about Ms. Young. I will tell her enough, but not too much. I think it is about time for us to tell the world *some* of your story."

With a wink, the old Imagineer closed the door.

 *Day Three*
Night

KATE WAS FIRING QUESTIONS AT JULIETTE, Jonathan, and Shep, only to have them shrug, offer an excuse for not giving her answers, or tell her to ask Hawk or Farren. She was getting exasperated, while the others seemed amused by her discomfort. After closing and securing the door, Hawk made his way back toward her across the apartment.

"Haven't you guys gotten this place cleaned up yet?" he joked.

"We didn't know where you wanted to put everything." Juliette looked a little overwhelmed at the catastrophe encircling them.

Kate stood, holding the figurine. "You know, I have a ton of questions."

"And you will get answers to most of them . . . eventually," Hawk assured her. Some assurance *that* was. She had a show, and a show needed content.

"Well, how about this one? What is the significance of this figurine? Other than its being priceless?" Kate shook her head. "Which should be answer enough I guess, but somehow I think it is more than just priceless. If it's a clue, what does it mean?"

"I really don't know yet." Hawk pointed at the statue. "But it means something. We'll figure it out."

"Hawk, I don't mean to be a party pooper, but I need to get home." Juliette stood. "I can get a team in here tomorrow to help clean this up if you want."

"Sure that would be . . . great." But he looked around the room, then back toward Juliette, and shook his head.

"It's OK, Hawk," Juliette reassured him. "You're going to need help with this. It will take you forever to do it alone."

Hawk paused again, sighed deeply, and then nodded affirmatively.

"First, I have a feeling we should call Reginald and let his boys get in here and look around." Jonathan opened his cell phone. "He's going to be ticked if we don't."

Shep also got to his feet. "And I'll go home and find out more about this

Western River Expedition. I have heard of it, but I don't really know the whole story. I might be able to find something in the history and archives to help us." He headed to the door.

"What are you going to do?" Juliette asked Hawk.

"I'll get Kate back to the Contemporary and then find a place to stay for the night. I'll probably camp in the office."

He walked his friends to the door, and they said their farewells. Kate observed him as he watched them go down the steps to the empty Main Street USA. She had heard him say he would spend the night in his office. He was in charge of the most popular vacation destination resort in the whole world and could stay anywhere he liked. Instead, he would stay in his office. Her career had allowed her to meet some of the most powerful people in the world. Hawk was the king of a magical kingdom but acted like he was somehow just lucky to be in that position. He was a man who certainly had his ego in check and was not fascinated with himself. She found that disarming.

If it was an act, then he was very good at it. If it was real, then it intrigued her more than she wanted to admit. When he returned to the trash heap his apartment had become, Kate made sure she was intently studying the cowboy figurine. She let her attention turn to Hawk as she noticed him absently wandering around his apartment. All of the possessions in the apartment had been broken, rifled through, or tossed about like they junk. He looked like he didn't know what to pick up first or what to look for in the mess.

"Hey." She smiled sweetly after she had his attention. "I'm sorry about your apartment. It's a one-of-a-kind location for sure."

"Location, location, location," he quipped. "It's just stuff."

"Maybe, but it is your stuff."

"No, it isn't."

"Explain whose stuff it is, please."

"I said, it isn't my stuff. It's God's stuff." He placed his hands on his hips and looked around sadly.

"God's stuff?" *Was he for real?*

"You heard me, Kate. It is God's stuff." Hawk picked his way through the room, pointing at things as he went. "That cup over there, the plaque on the floor, that torn-up couch cushion, all of it . . . is God's stuff. Everything we have is something that God entrusts to us to manage and use for Him. We don't really own it, we just have it on loan from God."

"So you don't own anything?" She thought of her sleek apartment in New York, her elegant Lexus.

"Not really, in the big picture. I prove my non-ownership when I die because I can't take any of it with me. Everything I have is a blessing from

God. I have to use it wisely, enjoy it, and share with others so the blessing doesn't turn into some kind of curse. I think sometimes people take the blessings of God, and instead of worshipping Him and thanking Him for them, they worship the blessings He gives and . . ." He noticed her staring at him. "Sorry." He held up his hands. "Was I starting to sound like a preacher?"

"A little, but you sure aren't like any preacher I've ever met before." She gestured over the room. How could he not be going ballistic over the invasion? She didn't understand him at all. But she wanted to. "So this really doesn't upset you?"

"A bit. It makes me sad that so much stuff got ruined, but it's just stuff. What really bothers me is that someone came in here and destroyed the place looking for something. I guess they wanted what is in your hand right now."

She looked at the cowboy with the upraised hat once again. It looked like just a figurine. Looking back toward Hawk, she saw him moving toward the door of the apartment. He unlocked it, opened it, then paused.

"Kate, I'll take you back to the resort in just a few minutes. I need to do something real quick first. Take care of our cowboy figurine and don't let anyone in, please. I'll be right back. Um . . . make yourself at home."

The door closed behind him with a click. She heard the bolt turn and slide into place. Getting up and finding a path across the room, she pulled back the curtain to the window overlooking Town Square. It dawned on her on how amazing it was that she was actually looking out on Town Square from this perspective. Below her, Hawk emerged from the side of the building and starting walking toward the Emporium on the corner of Main Street USA.

She had so many questions about him. He seemed so genuine and real, but she had not yet managed to wrap her mind around the mysterious side of him. He was somehow dangerous, and she was wary of him; but at the same time his adventurous spirit fascinated her. He slowed and glanced back up toward her as if he knew she would be watching him leave. She wiggled her fingers in a wave. He returned the wave and then bounded around the corner down the street.

*Who are you really, Grayson Hawkes?* Kate realized she was smiling at him though he was no longer there. The smile on her face slowly melted away, and she released the curtain, allowing it to fall back into place. Reflexively, she pulled it back once more and touched the glass pane of the window as if reaching out for him. A lump formed in her throat as she wondered what was going to happen next.

There was a story here. Every instinct she had was telling her she was onto something big. She hoped she could tell the story without hurting him.

After all, she was in a place where they believed in **happy** endings. But no matter what the ending was destined to be, she was going to find and tell her story. That's what she did. That's who she was.

 *Day Three*
Night

**HAWK TREKKED DOWN MAIN STREET USA.** Two blocks long, the street stretches from the WDW Railroad Station all the way to the Central Park Hub and was inspired by one of Walt's boyhood homes in Marceline, Missouri, where the Disneys lived on a forty-five-acre farm. Although Walt had been young, the days in Marceline imprinted themselves into his memory, and forever it became his image of what a hometown in America should look like.

The theme park had closed shortly after the parade made its way down the streets of the Magic Kingdom. The guests were gone, and the evening shift was moving into the park to begin the nighttime maintenance. They would work all night, and, as the sun rose in the morning, would be wrapping up their efforts to have the park ready for another day of guests. At this time of night, there was no place like Main Street. All the lights were shining, and it was a chance to see some of the details on the street that you would never get to see when it was jammed with people.

Passing the Main Street Athletic Club, Hawk looked up at the famous windows on Main Street. These second- and third-story windows honored those who had made great contributions to the development of the theme parks and Disney history. The one he locked his eyes on now always made him smile. It read, "Magic Kingdom Casting Company—It Takes People to Make the Dream a Reality." It was a tribute to the WDW cast, and Hawk knew the saying on the window was true. The public never saw the way the evening crew moved in and spent the entire night sprucing up the park, but the crew kept the look and magic of the park alive for the guests each day. On some nights, in the early hours of the morning, Hawk would venture out into the streets and open up the Ice Cream Parlor and treat every person working to free ice cream and conversation.

A cast member working on the door of a gift shop waved at Hawk as he passed. The CCA slowed and walked over, patting the maintenance crew member on the back.

"Can I borrow a Phillips screwdriver from you?" Hawk asked.

"Sure, got one right here." The maintenance man handed over the tool. "I'd be happy to help you out if need me to, boss."

Hawk checked the man's name badge so he could answer. "No thanks, Sean. I've got this." At the corner, he walked past the Ice Cream Parlor and veered to his right. Finding the cast member door leading off stage, he pushed it open and stepped inside. A rack of various cast member uniforms hung on the wall. Spying a light jacket, he slipped it on so he'd be dressed like other cast members. He wasted no time, and stepped back through the doors into the theme park.

Causally flipping the screwdriver in his hand, Hawk continued toward the Central Park Hub. Another reason Hawk liked moving through the park after hours was that people assumed you were supposed to be there. Only staff members went about their business at the end of operating hours, so most people were good about sticking to their own tasks and not getting overly concerned with what others were doing.

Hawk needed a few moments of not being noticed right now. His senses were in hyperdrive, taking in all of the activity around him. He was searching for anyone or anything that looked out of place. As he arrived at his destination, he slowed down and busied himself doing some meaningless tasks to see if there were any unwanted eyes following him. After tying his shoe, checking a trash receptacle, and then picking up a few scraps of paper, he decided to move forward.

Stepping into the hub, he looked up at the famous *Partners* statue. The smiling Mickey Mouse was looking up at Walt Disney, who was pointing with outstretched arm down Main Street USA. Most speculated that Walt was pointing boldly to the future, but Hawk knew better. Not only was Walt pointing toward the future, but he was also pointing at something very specific. Figuring that out had been helpful for Hawk in unraveling a mystery months before. Jumping up into the flower bed surrounding the statue, he was careful not to trample any of the meticulously manicured residents growing there. Crouching, he faced the plaque at the base of the statue. "*Partners*—We believe in our idea: a family park where parents and children could have fun ~ Walt Disney."

Quickly inserting the screwdriver into the screw in the upper right-hand corner, he gave it a sharp turn to the left. It gave, and he took out the screw and repeated the routine with the three remaining screws. The plate was now free, and carefully lifting it away from the base, he revealed an opening behind it. Reaching into the chamber, he pulled out a shiny metal box with a Mickey Mouse emblazoned across the top.

The lid clicked open, and inside he found four metal bars and an ancient skeleton key tucked away. He had come after the key itself. This was the key to the kingdom, given to him by Farren Rales. This old key, he had discovered, opened locks that he'd never dreamed it could open. He was sure that the thieves that had busted up his apartment were looking for not just what he had found in the cemetery; this was the real prize they were after, the key they were looking for. Shoving it into his pocket, he replaced the silver box and reattached the plate on the statue. Standing up and jumping out of the flower bed, he glanced around and saw, as he had hoped, there was no one in the area and no one had paid any attention to him.

He had carved out this hiding place for the box a few months after he had found it. The contents of the box and the key itself were all necessary to open some of the things he had found, along with additional codes that he had memorized and written nowhere. He had a growing sense that he might be needing the key in the near future, especially since there were clues to be found. This key was the original key Walt had held in his hand when he recorded a secret film explaining that he had set up a leadership plan to be carried out in the future. Hawk had a copy of that film hidden in the secret bunker control room below the Magic Kingdom.

He retraced his steps and returned the jacket to the peg on the wall where he had found it. Emerging from the supply area, he returned to the street and looked to see if anyone had noticed. As before, he saw nothing unusual. Jogging back down Main Street, he spotted the man he had borrowed the tool from and returned it. With a few pleasantries, he headed back to the Hawk's Nest to pick up Kate and take her back to her hotel.

 *Day Three*
Night

HAWK OPENED THE DOOR TO HIS APARTMENT. To his surprise, he found Kate picking up some of the clutter thrown about in the break-in. He thought she blushed a bit, as she explained she was just trying to make the place look a little better and put some of God's stuff away. He thanked her and moved to help her slide his couch back into a more orderly place in the living area. Once it was in place, she sat down and patted the seat next to her.

"Hawk?" Her expression was difficult to read. "What do you know about QR codes?"

"Uh, well . . . uh . . ." The question had come from so far out of the blue that his brain was clicking, trying to process it.

"You know what a QR code is, don't you?"

"Yes, of course." Hawk was catching up. "A QR code is the little squares that you find imprinted on everything these days. QR is short for Quick Response. They're used to take a piece of information and put it into your cell phone.

"Very good." She smiled. "You aren't an expert on just Disney-related things."

"I try." He continued, realizing he was telling her something she likely already knew but unable to stop trying to impress her. "You see QR codes in magazine advertisements, on billboards, toys, products of any kind at all, even on T-shirts. You can scan them with your cell phone app, and that takes you to more information about that item, usually using a link to a website. They are pretty incredible. We use them here all the time." He paused and sat back on the sofa. "Why do you ask?"

"Because I have something to show you." She got up from the couch and walked over to the chair where she had placed the cowboy figurine. Picking it up, she came back to the sofa. "While I was waiting for you, I took a closer look at this cowboy." She turned it so the soles of the miniature boots were pointing at Hawk. "What do you see?"

Looking at the bottom of the boot, Hawk saw something they all missed when they had been examining the cowboy earlier. Stuck to the sole was a QR code. Now that he was looking, it was easy to spot. He couldn't imagine why they had all missed it before. Reaching out, he took it from her and turned the cowboy figure to a better angle for lighting. He smiled at her for a moment and then looked back toward the boot. He reached into his pocket for his cell phone but remembered that he did not have one. He still had not replaced his phone from a few days before. Seeing him reach for a phone only to come up empty, Kate shook her head in disbelief and held up her smart phone, waving it back and forth.

"Want to borrow mine?" she asked, with a glint of excitement in her eye.

"That would be helpful." He reached out to take it from her, and she pulled it away, teasing him. "Hey . . ." He leaned across her and took it from her hand as they both laughed.

"So this is going to be some kind of clue?" Kate asked. She had decided to allow the story to unfold and was determined to catch up with it. If that meant she had to become part of the story, then she was willing to jump in, at least deep enough to find out whether it was worth chasing.

"I hope so." Hawk fumbled with the phone, looking for the barcode scanner application. He found it and turned the camera toward the bottom of the boot. "There's only one way to find out."

The scanner moved across the QR code information square, and the screen captured a still image of the black-and-white data box. Then little points of light began to dance across the code and across the viewer. The display screen flashed twice, and then they both put their heads next to one another as a video began to flicker, in the style of an old film, on the modern screen.

"Greetings, Hawk. As the man who holds the key to the kingdom, you now must unlock what never was, to protect what is yet to be . . . . Listen carefully. You will only hear this once . . ." The image of George Colmes smiled as he spoke. He was in motion, as though filming himself in a moving car or ride. The familiar background flashed by quickly, but Hawk was focused more on the face and what he was about to hear just once.

"Who is that?" Kate whispered.

"Shhh, just listen." He waved gently to keep her attention on the small screen on the phone.

"Walt reminded us . . ." George spoke slowly and carefully. "It was all started by a mouse . . . . Go back in time to where and when it all began on a steamboat . . . and a foot became a year." George smiled, lowered his head slightly, and the screen went blank.

"Let's see it again." Kate whirled her finger in a replay motion.

"OK." Hawk touched the screen, but there was no replay icon available for the film. He aimed the camera again at the QR code on the boot. The scanner moved across the square, and the screen captured a still image of the box. The little points of light began once again to dance across the viewer, and then it went to black and displayed the message "The Information You Are Searching For Is No Longer Available."

"I've never seen one that did that." Kate peered at the message on the screen.

"He said he was only going to say it once. I guess he meant it." Hawk handed the phone back to her. "He probably created it that way so no one could steal or intercept the clue."

"Who was that?"

"That was George Colmes." Hawk watched as she connected the dots to the information she had heard earlier in the evening.

"And he just gave you a clue . . ." She smiled. "I bet you know what it means."

"No, I don't." Hawk got up and started pacing the room over and around the stuff. "Not yet, but I think I know where to start."

"Let's go!" She jumped to her feet, eyes sparkling.

Hawk stared at her a few seconds longer than he intended to and glanced away nervously before answering. Inside he felt like rushing out the door to solve the clue—and he wanted her to go with him. But common sense was calling him back to be cautious. He had been burned before when he had let a stranger in on his adventure. He was determined not to be singed a second time. "You want go? Don't you need to go back and explain to your crew the change in plans for the documentary?"

"They can wait." Kate stepped over to him. "And you have to convince me that this is worth doing this way. *Total Access* has an agreement that protects you from giving away proprietary secrets, and ensures the security of guests isn't compromised by our being here. The burden of proof is on you and the company to make that clear to us. You would be surprised at how often someone tries to tell us we can't use our cameras or finish the work we have under contract to do, because it gets too hot for them to handle." She pointed her finger at him. "I promised no cameras and to alter our original agreement with the promise of something bigger happening. So far, I am intrigued. But you have to show me something . . . so, like I said, let's go."

His mind whirred through the potential pitfalls of taking her with him. If Farren was right, then they would have to give her a story. How much of a story and what she would do with it made him hesitate. Sighing, he resigned himself to what he was about to do.

"Do you remember what ole ghost George told us?"

"I think I can remember most of it." She cocked her head. "And you?"

"I've got it." Hawk gave her a huge smile and turned toward the door. "It's what I do. I remember details."

 *Day Four*
Early Morning

**BUENA VISTA DRIVE IS THE MAIN ROADWAY** that runs through the heart of the Walt Disney World Resort. Hawk guided his Mustang along the nearly empty road heading for Cypress Drive, which would carry him into the behind-the-scenes locations of Disney's Hollywood Studios. Kate rode in the passenger seat. He glanced toward her and noticed she was taking in the sights and trying to get her bearings as the car pulled up to a security booth. The roadway was blocked with cylindrical barriers that protruded from the pavement. The security guard inside the booth recognized Hawk but inspected his identification anyway. He glanced down toward the passenger seat and stepped back into the booth. In seconds, the barriers descended into the pavement. Once they were completely below the driving surface, the horizontal gate arm rose, and the security guard motioned the vehicle through.

Hawk steered the car to a backstage parking area and swung open his door. Popping the release on the trunk, he motioned for Kate to put the cowboy figurine in the compartment. She carefully placed it inside, covering it with an old sport coat he kept stashed in the trunk, then Hawk closed it. The beep-beep of the key ring secured the car and set the alarm. Kate followed in silence. Being accustomed to backstage areas in public places due to her celebrity status, she would know that any moment they would immerge right in the middle of an unexpected place.

Hawk was fascinated by the things that happened onstage and the things that happened behind the stage that helped make the magic the public would see possible. He never tired of understanding and trying to appreciate the work of the cast that made the guest moments possible. Hawk wound his way through a couple of turns that took them between buildings and down what looked like a long alley. When he got to the door he was looking for, he pushed it open, and they stepped into Disney's Hollywood Studios, right beside the Hollywood Tower Hotel. The hotel, inspired by three different famous California hotels, the Mission Inn, the Biltmore, and the Chateau Marmont, was known best for its attraction name: the Twilight Zone Tower of Terror. This ride would take you to the top and then, in an elevator malfunction, send you plummeting toward the ground multiple times. Each fall was carefully controlled, and the thrill ride was a favorite among Studio guests. Hawk looked up at the massive attraction as they passed, and leaned over to Kate to speak.

"If you ever go into this hotel, make sure you take the stairs. The elevators sometimes have glitches." He laughed and pointed toward the top of the hotel.

"Are you going to let me know what we're doing?" Kate asked.

"I'm trying to unravel the clue George gave us," Hawk said as they continued to walk along Sunset Boulevard. A hammering noise coming from the Anaheim Produce market to their right captured their attention, as a team of cast members repaired a sign that was askew.

The late-night activity in this theme park was similar to the activity that took place in all the theme parks. Workers would clean, paint, and repair things to get the park ready for guests the next day. Eventually, each street would be pressure washed and cleaned. It was shortly after midnight, and the night crew was hard at work. The attitude here was the same as in the other parks. If you were here at this time of the night, there was a reason and you had a purpose. For the most part, the staff members stuck to the tasks they were trying to accomplish.

Hawk and Kate moved toward the corner where Sunset intersected Hollywood Boulevard. Slowing his walk, he began to explain to Kate what they were doing. Or at least what he thought they were doing.

"The phrase George used about unlocking what never was to protect what is yet to be has something to do with whatever it is I'm supposed to figure out. But I believe his specific clue started right after that. Remember what he said?" Hawk turned and looked at her as they moved along the street.

"Walt reminded us that it was all started by a mouse."

"Right, then what?"

"Go back in time to where and when it all began on a steamboat . . ." She raised her hands slightly. "I think."

"You've got it." Hawk swept his arm across their pathway. "I have found from experience that these clues are very precise and yet vague at the same time. To go back to where it all began means that we have to go back to Hollywood. This is as close as we can get."

"But we also have to go back in time," Kate reminded him.

"True, and that's where it gets a little bit more confusing." Hawk continued to point out sights as they moved. This time he directed her attention to the Carthay Circle Theater. "For example, this is modeled after the theater where *Snow White and The Seven Dwarfs* premiered. The Studios were created to capture an era of Hollywood history that has long passed. A golden age of remembering the Hollywood that never really was but people always hoped for and believed in."

"And that means?"

"By being here, we have kind of stepped back in time."

"So we are where and when it all began?" Kate absorbed her surroundings like a sponge and added, "You know, I kind of like being here at this time of the morning. You can see a lot more. It really is beautiful."

Hawk had noticed when they left his apartment that she took a lingering glance down Main Street USA in the Magic Kingdom. If they could find the time, he would try to give her a guided after-hours walk through the park of her choice.

"Do you know what the steamboat part of the clue meant?" Hawk quizzed her.

"I am guessing that if it all started with Mickey Mouse, then the steamboat was the movie *Steamboat Mickey*, right?"

"Almost. The movie was *Steamboat Willie*, and it starred Mickey Mouse as Willie."

"Silly of me, I should have known that." She waved her hands dismissively.

"Ah, but that is where you have to be careful. Because around here, the details matter. They're here on purpose, and if you can figure out why, then you have an entirely different guest experience." Hawk stopped as they reached the corner of Sunset and Hollywood Boulevards. "Like right here."

"Here?" Kate looked around.

"Right here." Hawk tapped his foot on the concrete. "I think we have to start looking here to solve the clue." He knelt and motioned for Kate to kneel down as well.

She struggled to squat in her high heels but didn't hesitate to join him on the sidewalk. After getting down next to him, she giggled. "What are we getting ready to do . . . pray?"

"Nope, though maybe we should. We need to figure out the clue, and divine intervention wouldn't be a bad way to figure it out." Hawk smiled and pointed down. "Look here."

He ran his hand across the ground, showing her a semicircular imprint in the concrete next to the curb. Kate placed her hand next to Hawk's and softly traced the outline and a few of the letters in the concrete.

"Mortimer and Company." She moved her finger from the words stamped in the arc of the half circle and pointed to the bottom of the imprint. "Contractors, 1928," she read. "Mortimer and Company Contractors, 1928."

"This imprint pays tribute to Mortimer Mouse."

"Mortimer? Silly name for a mouse," she stated. Hawk glanced at her, and she added, "If you ask me."

"Funny, that's exactly what Walt's wife said."

"Smart woman."

"Indeed. When Walt first drew his new lovable character, he named him Mortimer. Mrs. Disney said that he looked more like a Mickey than a Mortimer. So Mickey Mouse was born." Hawk pointed to the year. "The 1928 refers to the year *Steamboat Willie* premiered. It was the year Mickey became a star."

Resting her hands on her legs, she looked down again at the imprint on the concrete. When she glanced back up at Hawk, he could see the wheels were turning as she rolled over the information.

"It was all started by a mouse, Mickey, also known for a brief time as Mortimer. We are where it began . . . in Hollywood, and back in time when it began . . . 1928." Kate looked at Hawk expectantly. "So what did we find?"

"I don't know . . . nothing yet. But this is the place to start." He stood and extended his hand to Kate.

She placed her hand in his, and Hawk pulled her easily to her feet and held on while she steadied herself on her heels. When he released her, they both brushed the sidewalk grime off their hands. Hawk noted that this had not been pressure washed yet. It was too early for the cleaners to have been by. He put his hands on his hips as he studied the imprint, thinking. Then he took a step so he was right on top of it, facing the oversized sorcerer's hat directly in front of them. Tilting his head as he looked toward the hat, he slowly stepped back and looked down toward the imprint again.

"What are you thinking, Hawk?"

"The last part of the clue is throwing me. It all began on a steamboat . . . and a foot became a year. That doesn't connect. Steamboat Willie came out in 1928, so we have the time and the place. But there's nothing here except the imprint. The last part has to mean something."

"So how does a foot become a year?"

"I'm not sure. Let's check more 1928s." Hawk smiled at her, rested his hands on her shoulders, and turned her around. "See?"

Kate's eyes traced the tall building before them to the top, where its name read *Pacific Electric . . . World's Wonderland Lines*. Her eyes widened, and she pointed to a spot right below the circular sign with the building name on it. There on the building was the street number for the Pacific Electric Building: *1928*.

"Glad you figured it out." Hawk grinned.

"Then we must be onto something, right?"

"I don't know. Tell me how a foot becomes a year." Hawk began pacing the sidewalk. He would pause and look down at the imprint then step back and look up at the 1928 on the Pacific Electric Building. Turning toward Kate, shaking his head, he shrugged. "I'm not seeing it here."

"So what do we do?"

"Like I said, we check out more 1928s." He moved back down in the direction they had come from originally. A few seconds later, he heard the hurried clicking of her heels.

"You mean there are more references to the year *Steamboat Willie* came out?" Kate asked as she fell in step with him.

"Sure, if it all started with a mouse, then that year was a very significant year. I believe I remember hearing or reading that the Imagineers have placed numbers to commemorate that in a variety of places. The real question is going to be, if we can find them, will they show us how a foot can become a year."

They made their way back down toward the end of the street where they had entered. Sunset Boulevard dead-ended into two major attractions, the Twilight Zone Tower of Terror and the Rock 'n' Roller Coaster starring Aerosmith. The area was themed to look like a historic area of Hollywood and called Sunset Hills. As they got to the end of the street, Hawk paused and pointed toward the metal sign affixed to the stone entranceway at the edge of Sunset Boulevard and Gower Street. Streetlights illuminated the street names posted on the traffic light supports.

Kate stepped off the sidewalk and walked to the entrance, where she gazed up at the raised lettering on the metal sign. *Sunset Hills Estates. Established 1928.* Turning back toward Hawk, she motioned for him to come over. He did, and she stepped away from the sign.

"Another 1928 . . . but how does this have anything to do with a foot becoming a year?"

"Don't know, Kate. I just don't know . . . yet."

"Maybe we're missing something, Hawk. I mean, we have three 1928s, but they don't seem to connect to the last part of the clue."

"We haven't found the right 1928 yet." Hawk took Kate by the arm and gently nudged her back down Sunset Boulevard.

She picked up the pace. "So, let me make sure I'm getting this right. Walt Disney chose you to be the new head of the company?"

"Yes. Farren will give you the details tomorrow at breakfast." He offered nothing else.

"And solving clues or a mystery is how you got the . . . "

"How I got the what?" Hawk knew she was fishing, but he had made the mistake once before of giving someone too much information too fast. That mistake had been named Kiran Roberts, and she had been trying to take the kingdom key from him.

"I don't know . . . I was just looking for more info."

"I know you were." He was impressed at her admission and felt a bit sorry for her. He could read the confusion on her face. She was a woman who had built her career on finding answers. Right now she had very few.

Cutting across Hollywood Boulevard, they moved down a half block to Vine Street. With Kate still in tow, Hawk stepped up onto the curb and looked across at the Hollywood and Vine Diner. Kate followed his gaze toward the diner.

"Another 1928—the address is 1928 right there on the building." She smiled in satisfaction.

Hawk nodded confirmation of her discovery. This building had been a stop in his original quest to find the key to the kingdom, but this time he saw nothing that seemed to help. The outline of Roger Rabbit on the window made him smile. The reference to Eddie Valiant right next to it connected the two main characters from the innovative film *Who Framed Roger Rabbit?* But this time there seemed to be no secrets here to discover. This couldn't be the right 1928 reference.

He stepped back out into the street and looked around. Wordlessly, he began to backtrack toward the corner where they had first started. Arriving in moments back at the contractor's stamp in the cement, he stood on the corner and gazed around the Studios.

"Are we out of 1928s?" Kate asked quietly.

"Kate, I'm sure there are more. I'm just trying to remember." He scratched his head. "Mickey Mouse was born that year, and so there are references to that date scattered through the park. But none of the ones we've found so far seem to fit the clue."

As he finished speaking, he turned his head at an angle and scanned the street to his right. He pointed toward the dining area he saw, and they stepped off the sidewalk.

"The Brown Derby?" she asked, referring to the restaurant they were now walking toward.

"Yes, do you know when it was opened?"

"I have no idea. Was it 1928?"

"Maybe. Let's see if we can find out."

Together they walked down the sidewalk along the restaurant and then took a right toward the front doors. There was a crew of people inside, cleaning the floors of the eating establishment. Beside the door, a golden plate with raised letters read, "This building is inspired by the Vine Street Brown Derby, originally built in Hollywood, California in 1928."

Hawk waited while Kate read and reread the words.

She turned to face him with a strange look. "How do you know this stuff?"

"What do you mean?"

"We're wandering around looking for the year 1928, and you find numbers on the sidewalk, numbers on buildings, you remember the year the Brown Derby was opened . . . how do you know these details?"

"I'm not sure. I guess I just love details." Hawk smiled. "And if you're a detail person, then there's no better place to be looking than Walt Disney World, because they are everywhere. There are trivia, tributes, hidden Mickeys, and secrets hidden in plain sight and not-so-plain sight . . . all waiting to be discovered if you just look. Sometimes they aren't that important, but every once in a while, paying attention to details can unlock a brand-new discovery or piece of information."

"So you're unlocking what never was, to protect what is yet to be?"

"Pretty much." He stepped back from the doorway to the Brown Derby. "People don't notice details anymore. We're in too much of a hurry to get to the next thing, the next moment, the next stop . . . and sometimes we forget that the details matter. It's the little things about places and people that matter. If you don't take the time to slow down and look . . . well, you just don't care that much about them."

Kate stepped back away from him half a step and then looked him over from head to toe. "I have never met anyone who says things like that. I know as a reporter I look for details to collect information, but you notice the details because you want to know something or someone better . . . because you really care."

"I guess." He shrugged, never having thought about it like that.

"So, what details have you noticed about me?"

"Well . . ." Hawk stopped himself. "Uh . . . I've . . ." His face got hot.

"No, you goofball." Kate grabbed him by the chin and held his head straight. Spreading her index and middle fingers, she placed them under her eyes and then pointed them toward his and then back again. "Not about how I might look . . . but the details you have come up with about who I am."

A face suddenly appeared, glaring at them through the glass of the doors of the Brown Derby. Hawk flinched. Kate jumped back and darted behind him. The face peering back at them was covered by a presidential mask. It was the face of Jimmy Carter.

 *Day Four*
Early Morning

THE MAN IN THE RUBBER MASK PUSHED the door of the Brown Derby outward and lunged toward Hawk and Kate. Hawk reared back and kicked the door just above the handle as hard as he could. The door slammed back, trapping the masked figure between it and the door frame, and the man grunted as the door caught him in the chest. Glass shattered at the impact. As hard as Hawk had kicked it, he knew he had knocked the wind out of the man or had perhaps even cracked a rib. As the man slumped toward the ground, Hawk did not hesitate. He whirled and grabbed a stunned Kate Young by the hand and pulled her with him away from the incapacitated attacker and the door.

They ran from the restaurant and circled behind the iconic Sorcerer's Hat. Hawk was headed toward the Great Movie Ride inside the Chinese Theatre. They hustled toward the attraction, and as they raced through the gateway, Hawk glanced back to see if they were being pursued. It did not surprise him to see another man wearing a ski-style mask was now giving pursuit, along with the man wearing the Carter mask, who needed some assistance and was slowing down his partner. Hawk looked side to side for help, and it dawned on him that he saw no other people in the area. No workmen on the night crew, no other activity at all, except for the floor cleaners they had seen inside the restaurant. Those floor cleaners, he surmised, were the people chasing them now.

As they ran, he gripped Kate's hand tightly, pulling her along. Her shoes were making it difficult for her to run as fast as he would have hoped. With his other hand, he readied the key to the kingdom he had picked up a short time before. He knew he would need it now, as the doors to the attraction should be locked. They were. Hawk quickly unlocked the door, and they raced inside. As he closed and locked the door behind them, Hawk could see that their pursuers were picking up the pace.

Hustling through the lobby where the attraction queue line often began, Hawk unclipped the barriers, letting them fall to the ground behind them. They burst through the doors of the large theater, where guests would weave back and forth in line, waiting to climb aboard the massive vehicles that would carry them through the ride. Bypassing that waiting area, Hawk and Kate now ran into the loading area, and Hawk raced to the control panel. He powered up the panel, and the light started flashing green on the massive button.

"Get in the vehicle." Hawk pointed toward the car.

Kate climbed over the side and into the front seat. He leaped over the side into the driver's position, activated the drive, and the vehicle began to move slowly forward. They moved into the beginning portion of the ride, which, in the early hours of the morning, was dark and silent because the attraction was closed. Hawk kept looking behind them as the vehicle snaked away.

"We were running faster than this, Hawk," Kate said, as she looked behind them for their pursuers as well.

"I know." Hawk smiled at her. "Look, there's Gene Kelly." He pointed at the motionless audio-animatronic figure hanging on a lamppost from Singing in the Rain.

"You picked now to give me a private tour?" She looked up at him, confused.

"Why don't you just stay low in the seat. There are Julie Andrews and Dick Van Dyke." He moved his head toward the two figures they were passing under. "Now we move into the underworld, where the gangsters rule." Hawk focused on moving toward the doors ahead of them.

Kate leaned to see what he was doing to the driving mechanism of the vehicle. He blocked her view as he crouched in front of it, and the doors opened in front of them as they glided into the old western set.

"OK, Kate, let's hop out." Hawk brushed past her and bounded out of the still-moving vehicle. She stood to follow, and he lifted her over the side as the vehicle kept going. They stood facing the audio-animatronic John Wayne, then Hawk grabbed her by the arm and hustled her toward the doorway, where Clint Eastwood stood lighting a cigarette when the figure was operating. Hawk led her past Clint, through the swinging doors, and they ducked behind the wall of the set, under the window, next to the Eastwood figure.

"What are we doing?" Kate whispered in Hawk's ear.

"Waiting."

Hawk had hoped that by activating the attraction and moving the car, he would entice their pursuers to follow them into the ride itself. He figured they wouldn't get into a ride car because they are slow, but he was hoping to make it appear that he and Kate had. That would force the two chasing them to follow. They had to, because they couldn't risk that Hawk and Kate were riding a car through the attraction. They also could wait for the car to come out, but that would take too long, and Hawk and Kate might have done exactly what they did, get off on the ride. The pursuers would have to be sure; they would have to follow. Hawk peered over the window and saw the men bust through the doors into the western set.

Putting a finger to his lips signaling Kate they were here, he waited, listening.

"They are already past here," one of the men said. "Let's catch the ride vehicle, then if they aren't in it, we backtrack."

Perfect. They were doing all they could to find them, as Hawk had hoped. When the men giving chase had moved into the scene from Alien, Hawk peered again out the window. Making sure they were gone, he grabbed Kate and headed across the vehicles' pathway to the western set on the other side of the street. Kate followed closely as they went up the wooden steps and onto the front porch of the western building. He led them through a door into the backstage area.

"This is where our live actors move in and out, switching drivers for the ride vehicles. You ever been on it?" Hawk asked.

Kate shook her head no.

"You need to do that during your stay."

"What are we doing?" Kate spoke over his shoulder.

"Getting away. There is no way they can navigate backstage as quickly as we can, and where they committed to go in the ride does not give them any shortcuts out. When they find we aren't in the car, they have to backtrack and look at every place we might be hiding. By the time they get out, we'll be long gone."

Kate smiled as she followed. "You are resourceful."

"I pay attention to details." He smirked softly. "There's too much track for them to cover to be able to figure out where we're hiding or whether we got—" He stopped abruptly.

"What is it?" Kate turned to look behind them. "Did you hear something?"

"No, I didn't hear a thing." Hawk now changed direction and led her down a narrow corridor. "But I did figure out the clue."

They pushed their way out the side door to the attraction then snaked their way back toward the front of the theater. Rushing to the massive archway, Hawk hurriedly looked from side to side. Seeing what he was searching for, he raced toward a massive pillar and pointed Kate toward a bronze-colored plaque near the bottom.

"What does it say?" he asked as he continued to search.

"This facade is a re-creation of the Chinese Theatre originally built in

Hollywood, California in 1928." Kate saw the year and smiled. "Another 1928. . . . Is this our 1928?"

Hawk came around the edge of the pillar. "I think so. It's how a foot becomes a year."

"I don't follow you . . . so help me out here." Kate stepped next to him and looked back to see if they were being chased again yet.

"The famous Chinese Theatre we see all the time in Hollywood films didn't open in 1928, it opened in 1927. You've seen enough around here to know that our Imagineers do not make that kind of mistake. So you have to ask yourself why they put the wrong date on the marker."

"Because it's a clue?"

"Sort of . . . it means something. When we were inside, I remembered that when the attraction was built, they discovered that the track was 1928 feet long. So when it came time to put the marker up, with all the references to 1928 everywhere else, they decided to tweak the facts just a bit . . . on purpose. It's an inside joke."

"Yes." Kate furrowed her forehead.

"So the extra foot of track became the year they put on the marker. In essence, a foot of track became a year they added to the actual date." He motioned toward the marker.

"A foot became a year! So this is it."

"It is." Hawk crooked his finger toward her to follow. "Come here."

Stepping past the poster advertising the Great Movie Ride attraction, they came to a massive display case. Inside, there was a vase that looked like a Chinese artifact. At the base of the display cabinet, in the back corner, was a figurine of a sleeping cowboy. It looked similar to the figurine Hawk had found in the cemetery. Kate pressed her hands against the glass and peered inside. She reached up to open the cabinet, but it was locked.

Hawk stepped to the lock and used his kingdom key to release the locking mechanism. The door opened quietly, and Kate reached in and grabbed the figurine. The detail on this one, like the first, was amazing. The cowboy was asleep or passed out and snoring. She held it up for Hawk to see closer. He checked around the corner first.

"There is the ride exit. This is the main entrance." He pointed at both access points. "The guys following us are going to come out of one of those two doors. My guess is they'll split up, so they'll probably hit both doors." Hawk carefully closed the glass door of the cabinet. "We need to get out of sight, and I know a pretty good place to hide for a few minutes. It's close."

Hawk noticed Kate was listening but distracted. She turned the figure of the cowboy back toward him and was fiddling with something attached to it.

Surprisingly, it let loose from the adhesive holding it in place. She gently held it up between her fingers.

It was a pin. A collectible pin in the shape of Mickey Mouse. Smiling, with a hand on one hip, the other extended, he was inviting someone to join him . . . somewhere. The pin was about two inches tall, made of metal, designed like the pins that were collected and traded by people all over the world. As Kate flipped this pin over, they both saw it at the same time. A QR code on the back of the pin. They looked at each other, and Hawk instantly knew they had found what they were looking for and more.

"Let's go." Hawk motioned her to follow him as they moved off toward the right-hand side of the attraction, through an ornate arch decorated to match the exterior of the classic theater, and down a set of stairs.

As they descended the steps, Hawk heard voices emerge from the theater. He knew it had to be the people chasing them; they seemed to be arguing. About what, he couldn't tell, and he couldn't risk stopping to attempt to listen. He sensed Kate slowing down behind him as she heard the voices too. Turning back toward her, he again motioned for her to follow as they reached the bottom of the steps and turned down their destination. Although he was moving silently, his mind was filled with a cacophony of messages blaring through his head.

The people trying to take the kingdom from him were better than he had judged them to be. They had tracked him here, and he hadn't told anyone where he was going. That meant they were watching him more closely than he'd thought.

He felt Kate's hand rest on his shoulder as if pushing him forward. He worried about whether it was a good idea to have her with him. Her presence gave him one more thing to be concerned about as he tried to protect the kingdom . . . by unlocking what never was . . . whatever that might mean.

 *Day Four*
Early Morning

**ONE MAN'S DREAM WAS THE ATTRACTION** Hawk had a special soft place for. This was the place where Walt Disney's life and career were put on display for guests to enjoy. In the months since he had been in charge of the company, he had returned here many times. He always told the cast working here it was because he was looking for inspiration, which was partially true. But he returned often because this was the place where his life had been forever changed.

When Farren Rales had given him the key to the kingdom, he had no idea what it was for. Eventually, he figured out that it was leading him here, to this attraction that kept many details about Walt Disney's past. It also contained the original desk Walt used in his office when *Snow White* was produced and released. It was where Walt thought and worked, and in it had been the first clue Hawk needed to begin his incredible journey to become the chief creative architect of the company.

He also visited the attraction after hours, usually after the maintenance cast members had finished their jobs for the evening. He liked to walk, look, and think uninterrupted. In those moments, he wondered what Walt would do in a certain situation or how Walt would handle a decision that Hawk was trying to make.

They'd entered through the front doors of the attraction using the kingdom key, and he now used it again to open a security door that would take them behind the public viewing area of the attraction. Squeezing through the narrow hallway, they moved along the back side of the exhibits until they came to a corner where the space opened up into a wider area and the passageways intersected. Turning to face Kate, Hawk held out his palm to look closer at the pin. She placed it in his hand, and he flipped it over and studied it. As a collectible piece, it was magnificent. Pin collecting was a huge hobby worldwide, and there were pin collectors who spent their days at Disney showing their pins, trading their pins, and purchasing new ones to add to their collections. It was affordable; cast members participated, which gave them an additional way to interact with guests; and Hawk had implemented a plan that allowed all cast members to build initial pin collections so they would have pins to trade.

This gift, a cast member lanyard that contained ten pins, changed each month depending when the member was hired. The parks were now full of cast members sporting lanyards with pins, just waiting to trade. This pin was not one that you could just pick up anywhere. The detail and craftsmanship was different, the style was different, and it was slightly larger than other pins.

The QR code on the back was stuck to it in a similar fashion as the QR code had been attached to the boot of the cowboy he'd found in the cemetery.

"So it looks like we have a matching set," Kate said, examining the sleeping cowboy. "Who were those guys chasing us?"

"Probably the same people who busted up my apartment and tried to steal the package in the cemetery."

"I've got that figured out. I asked who they were."

"If they wanted us to know, they wouldn't be wearing masks." Hawk winked.

"No, don't try to be charming right now." Kate pressed, "Why are they trying to stop you?"

"Simple." Hawk sighed. This is where he had made the mistake in telling someone too much once before. It had been in this attraction under another stressful set of circumstances. "If they can figure out whatever it is *we* are trying to figure out, they might be able to grab power and maybe control of the company."

"Because they solve a puzzle? How valuable is whatever we're looking for?"

"Priceless."

"How valuable was what you found before?"

"Just as priceless. I went from being a preacher of a local congregation to the chief Imagineer in the most magical company in the world. Overnight, it seems. That's why you're here, remember?"

"Oh, trust me, I haven't forgotten."

"I'm sure you'll get more details from Farren," Hawk assured her.

"I'd rather hear them from you." She smiled at him.

He looked at her and thought seriously about saying more. He had learned a long time ago as a leader that mistakes and bad judgment happen to everyone. Great leaders learn from the mistakes and do their best not to make them a second time. Hawk was not going to make the mistake of telling someone too much too soon ever again.

Kate touched his arm. "Are you afraid to tell me because someone has betrayed and hurt you before?" She took in a deep breath before exhaling. "Or are you afraid to tell me because I hurt you earlier in the interview?"

Hawk looked into her face. She stared back at him, her crystal-green eyes inviting him to search for an answer. She blinked. The silence hung between them.

"Can I use your phone?" Hawk asked.

Kate's expression became carefully neutral. She nodded her head and handed him her phone, and he pressed the button, bringing the touch screen to life. Finding the icon for the numeric touchpad, he pushed it and then dialed the phone number. He listened as the phone rang, and just before the call should have gone to a voice messaging system, he heard the line connect at the other end.

"Cambridge here."

"Reginald." Hawk said, relieved.

"Grayson, where are you?"

"Hollywood Studios, where are you?"

"I was in bed."

"Sorry to wake you." Hawk looked at his watch, which now read after three o'clock in the morning. He had wondered what took Reginald so long to pick up.

"Not sleeping. I was concerned about you. I had a team in your apartment admiring your new interior decorating. I am extremely agitated that people dared to break into your private quarters in the theme park."

"Yes, I am too."

"And you—" Reginald lowered his voice. "You seem to be getting into some kind of trouble again. I had asked you not to do that. I suggested we involve law enforcement."

"I did, Reginald," Hawk insisted. "I promised you I would give the picture to Al Gann, and I did at church. Just like I said."

"And then?"

"Then I found something. And well, that is where the trouble seems to have started."

"It is difficult to protect you and to protect our guests when you continue to—"

"I believe we used the phrase *go off road*?"

"Yes, off road. You are in Hollywood Studios now?"

"I am, and my friend in the president mask, plus a buddy, are trying to rough me up a bit. I lost them in the Great Movie Ride. Can you see if you can catch them before they get out of there?"

"I will make a call and get some people there right away. I will be there momentarily as well." Reginald took a slow, long breath. "Where are you going to be?"

"I don't know yet."

"Whose phone are you using? I didn't recognize the number."

"Kate Young's." Hawk had to remember to get his phone replaced. "I'll talk to you later. Thanks, Reginald."

"Be very careful, Grayson. Good-bye."

He assumed Kate had been able to hear most of the call because of Reginald's powerful voice resonating from the phone's speaker. Turning the phone in his hand, he activated the bar-scanning application and waited while she held up the Mickey Mouse pin. The app scanned the QR code, and then, just like before, after a series of flashes, the same style of film came to life on the view screen of the phone. Tilting the screen so they could both hear it, they stood shoulder to shoulder and watched as the face of George Colmes once again filled the screen. His head bobbed and weaved again, indicating he was in motion. He was riding in some kind of tunnel, yet light streamed in from both sides. The place was familiar, but it was only a background to the face that spoke to him.

"Hello, Hawk. Congratulations on solving the clue. Since you're watching me now, you have been successful. You must really be as good as Farren Rales believes you to be. Very well, just like before, you will only hear this once . . . so listen closely. Where toys stand guard over one hundred acres of woods . . . make the time your time . . . . It will almost rock you to sleep."

The screen went dark, and the message came to an end. Hawk was already thinking about what they had just heard as he handed the phone back to Kate, then paced in circles, thinking about what he just heard. He replayed the clue over and over in his mind a few times so he would remember it, then he started to unwind it.

"Well?" Kate broke his train of thought.

Coming to a stop, he looked at her. "I don't know, Kate. Give me a few minutes to think about what he said."

"That isn't what I'm asking about."

"It isn't?" Hawk blinked a few times. Then what *was* she talking about?

"I asked you a moment ago why you were afraid to tell me how you ended up here . . . now . . . doing what we are doing . . . and you got real quiet and then asked to use my phone." Kate shook her head and frowned. "We have had two moments when I almost got to see the real you. Remember outside the Brown Derby when I asked you what details you've figured out about me?"

"Yes."

"And after I got you to start focusing on answering me, we were interrupted. And then just now, when I give you a chance to tell me what makes you tick . . . you interrupt that moment by wanting to use the phone. But you know exactly what I'm talking about because you're smart and you pay attention to details. You're not going to tell me."

"Kate, I don't know you." He reached out and grabbed her by the shoulders, holding her at arm's length. "Right now I am involved in a fight to protect Walt Disney and every dream he ever dreamed. And you are here involved in that. I don't know if that is good or bad, but it doesn't matter, because I can't do anything about it. But you know a lot more about me than I know about you. And you're trying to find out even more about me right now."

"And what happens if I do?" Her eyes wouldn't let his gaze escape.

"I'm not sure. I do know that usually when you find out information, you use it in a documentary. Just because there are no cameras doesn't mean you aren't working." He tried not to look as confrontational as he knew he sounded. "You were the one who told me there are no off-the-record conversations with you."

"So . . ." She looked to her right and then her left, at his arms holding her shoulders. "It is better for you to keep me like this? At arm's length?"

Hawk lowered his arms. Something within him wanted to tell her what she wanted to know. Still, the experiences of the past and the intensity of this current set of circumstances had his senses on high alert.

She dropped her head and studied the ground for a few moments. When she raised it, he saw a smile cross her face.

"Take me back to the Contemporary please, Hawk. I have breakfast in a few hours with Farren." Her expression brightened. "Maybe he'll give me a few more answers."

"I'll take you back in a minute. First, follow me." He gently took her arm and pulled her closer to him. He led her down the hallway to a door that opened into a display.

She opened the door and looked inside. It was the office of Walt Disney. He motioned for her to step inside; she did, and he followed her in. He watched as she looked around at the inside of this exhibit with a chance to see it like few ever have. Guests would stare through the plate glass window to see what Walt's office looked like on the day he passed away. Most of the objects in the display were re-creations, with the originals in California. However, some of the items were very real, and all were placed where they were for a reason. To many who pass by, it appears to be a simple display, but this was the work of Imagineers, archivists, and historians.

Hawk allowed Kate to take her time; Cambridge had said he was sending a team, and Hawk trusted they'd quickly find the men pursuing Kate and him. He went over and pulled out Walt's chair and invited her to have a seat. She did, and he pushed the chair under the desk, then went to stand on the opposite side.

"Can you imagine what it was like to be Walt Disney and sit in this office?" Hawk glanced around the office.

"No, I can't." She admitted reverently. "Walt Disney was so creative—a genius—he actually changed the world and created things no person had ever created before. His legacy is huge, and his influence shaped our culture . . . it's, well . . ."

"Incredible?" Hawk grinned.

"Yes, incredible is a word for it."

"Kate, you're digging at me, trying to figure out what makes me tick." He held out his hands in a gesture of surrender. "Here is part of it. Through an unbelievable set of events, I now get to lead the world that Walt Disney created. In some ways, I sit in the chair you are sitting in right now. Not the actual chair, mind you . . . but you already know that I was chosen by Walt to keep his dreams alive and on track. You know what I do when I sit where you are right now?"

"No." She blinked slowly. "Please, tell me."

"I sit there and think about all the responsibility and expectations and pray . . . God, please don't let me mess this up." He motioned for her to get up so they could leave. "I take what I do seriously. We are the best storytellers in the world, and the influence we have stretches around the planet. I just don't want to mess it up . . . so, if I'm not as forthcoming with information as you'd like, that is why. If I don't want you digging into my past, that's why. People are counting on me to get it right and always be right. Even Walt and Roy Disney are counting on me."

 *Day Four*
Morning

HAWK AND KATE MANAGED TO GET OUT of Hollywood Studios without further incident. On the way out of the theme park, the previously empty streets had become a beehive of activity. It was not just the maintenance cast at work; Hawk also saw security moving through the park and stationed at various places along the street, monitoring the activity during the early morning hours. He was confident that was at the instruction of Reginald Cambridge.

The ride back to the Contemporary was quiet. Kate sat speechless, and Hawk wondered whether she was tired, upset, or just thinking through the events of the night and trying to decide how to move forward with the *Total Access* project. He enjoyed being with her, and in many ways wished he could tell her some of the things she wanted to know. But her aggressive curiosity reminded of him too much of his adventure eighteen months before when he had been hurt so badly by Kiran.

He walked Kate into the lobby and escorted her to the elevator so she could go to her room. This time they didn't use a service elevator, and she waved her fingers in a good-bye as the doors slid closed. He took the escalator to the main floor of activity in the Contemporary, although there were not many people moving about in the early hours of the morning. Hawk moved across the walkway to the Bay Lake Towers and headed to his office, which featured a private living area where he occasionally spent the night when he'd worked too late and was trying to avoid the crowds and noise of the Magic Kingdom.

His shower and stretching out in bed did not relax him or usher in sleep. He rolled the latest clue over and over in his mind. Thoughts of Kate kept creeping in. He was worried about what she was going to do with her story, what Farren would tell her, and what she would do with that information; part of him was distracted by the fact that she was gorgeous and not afraid of adventure. She had proved that in the Studios. After allowing himself to be distracted, he would return to the clue . . . *where toys stand guard over a hundred acres of woods . . . make the time your time . . . it will almost rock you to sleep.* He told himself to break the clue down, take it in segments; he knew enough about the trivia and the details of the resort to figure this out.

Sometime before daylight, he dozed off, to be awakened by sounds coming from the office suite. Glancing at his watch, he realized that Nancy would be at work by now; she was always early, and he could hear her talking.

Stepping into the main office downstairs, he was greeted by not only Nancy, but Reginald as well.

"Good morning, sir." Nancy smiled and stood. "Can I get you some coffee?"

"No, thanks. I'll have some coffee, but I'll get it." Hawk waved her back to her desk. "Reginald, can I get you some?"

"Nancy has graciously already taken care of that." He raised his steaming cup in display.

Hawk moved to the counter and found himself staring back at Reginald. He didn't look right. He couldn't immediately deduce what was wrong or different, but he knew he didn't look like he normally did. Reginald reacted by shifting his gaze down at his shirt as though checking to see whether he had spilled coffee on himself. When Hawk returned to take a seat across from him, Reginald looked up.

"We did not find anyone in the Great Movie Ride last night." Reginald set his cup on the coffee table in front of his chair. "We did find the ride mechanism was left on, and there was an unaccounted for ride vehicle that had been rigged to keep running without a driver. Sound familiar to you?"

"Oh, that. I forgot to tell you about that." Hawk hadn't even thought about it since they had escaped. "I was trying to distract the bad guys. Did I break anything?"

"No, everything is fine, I am told. But that is not the main concern. The main problem is that there are bad guys you are trying to avoid. There are people who want to take control of Disney away from you, and you are treating it like a game."

"It is not a game." Hawk grew deathly serious. "I know what's at stake, Reginald. They can only play their hand so fast. They can do criminal things, but they can't cross the line. They need to make me look bad, help me to make a mistake or have an accident." Hawk lowered his tone even more. "They know exactly what they are doing, and so do I. If I don't figure out this new puzzle, and they don't have me to put the pieces of the entire thing together, they have got nothing."

"So you don't believe they are trying to hurt you?" Reginald shifted in his seat with some difficulty.

"They want to hurt me and they want me to give up and quit. They're trying to get me to believe they're going to hurt guests, hurt our operations, and me."

"It is my job to keep them from hurting you." Again, Reginald moved uncomfortably. "And you are making it incredibly difficult and frustrating."

"Are you OK?" Hawk asked, looking closely at him. "You don't look so good, Reginald."

"I'm fine. I just don't feel very well. I'm coughing and having trouble breathing today."

"Maybe you should see a doctor. First it was a headache, then a toothache, now you're battling some kind of congestion. Reginald, something might be seriously wrong with you." Hawk turned to Nancy. "Nancy, call our medical team and get someone up here."

"Strike that! Please . . ." Reginald found a way to position himself that seemed to bring relief. "To be honest, you are the source of my stress, Hawk. I don't know how to help you. The headache is better, the dentist fixed the tooth, and this discomfort has a name—it is Grayson Hawkes."

"Should I make the call, sir?" Nancy asked.

Reginald shook his head no. Hawk took another sip of coffee and leaned back and stared at his friend. He was worried about Reginald. Hawk had put him through an exhausting year, and being a member of Hawk's inner circle carried a tremendous responsibility. The strain was showing, and Hawk didn't want anything to happen to him. Hawk, too, waved Nancy off on making the call.

"This is against my better judgment."

"Better judgment!" Reginald broke into a hearty laugh that was cut short as he began to cough. "You don't have any better judgment within you." He again laughed with more restraint.

"Be that as it may, you are going home." Hawk got up to signal the conversation was over. "Get Clint or Chuck to make sure I can find them if I need them, and you go home . . . now . . . and get feeling better."

Hawk walked to the door of the office and patted Reginald on the back as he left. He had never seen Reginald feeling bad, so he was concerned. In his mind, he had seen Reginald as indestructible. He furrowed his brow as his friend left. Moving back into the office reception area, he asked Nancy to get Shep, Juliette, and Jonathan on a conference call, then headed up the stairs toward his office. By the time he got to his desk, turned on his computer, and picked up the phone, Nancy was already waiting for him on the line.

"Sir, I wasn't able to get them all," Nancy reported.

"What do you mean?" Hawk moved the receiver to his other ear.

"Juliette is unable to be on the call right now because Tim is home sick today, along with one of the children. She said she would call you back as quickly as she could. She said she was sorry. Jonathan is sick today as well. His wife said he was up nearly all night, congestion, coughing, trouble breathing . . . he is asleep right now, and she didn't want to wake him."

"Of course. What is the outbreak we have going on around here?" Hawk said to her. "What about Shep?"

"I'm on the line," Shep informed him over the phone line.

"Thank you, Nancy," Hawk said, and he heard Nancy leave the conversation with a click.

"You doing alright, boss?" Shep asked.

"Good, had a busy night."

"What did you figure out?" Shep's voice grew excited.

Hawk debriefed Shep on the night's activities from the time they'd left his apartment. Shep was silent as Hawk filled him in on the details. The use of the QR codes gave Shep reason to ask many more questions. After they had all been answered, Shep reported back to Hawk the discoveries he had made about the Western River Expedition. Apparently, in Disney circles, this was a topic that was both loved and hated. Considered to be the greatest attraction that was never built, this was going to be, at least in its original design, spectacular. From the boat ride, to the shopping areas, to the runaway mine train, this was a place one could imagine being the greatest thing Disney ever would have built.

Shep went on to explain that the disappearance of the original model had been a huge scandal. Most believed it had been removed as a revolt by Imagineers who were upset that the project had been kicked to the curb as it had been. The complete model, of which Hawk now had two pieces, had in its original creation comprised over one hundred figurines. It was massive, and the last time anything had been seen of the model was a few years ago when some of the figures showed up in an auction. They sold for a fortune, and some hoped more pieces would emerge. They had not, until Hawk found the cowboys.

Thirty minutes later, they concluded the two-person conference call with Hawk going over his thoughts about the last clue with Shep. He promised Hawk he would call if he had any more thoughts on it but agreed with what Hawk was thinking. It then dawned on Hawk that he still didn't have a cell phone, so Shep couldn't call him. That realization came after they had ended the call.

Hawk left his office and headed downstairs, where Nancy sat at her desk with a phone next to her ear. Seeing her boss, she excused herself from the conversation and ended the call.

JEFF DIXON

"Nancy, did Juliette drop by a cell phone for me anywhere?"

"No, she may have not had the chance, dealing with her sick family," Nancy reminded him.

"She said she was tracking one down for me, but if she's busy, how about you finding me one?"

"Happy to do it, sir." Nancy grabbed a notepad and scribbled a note.

"Leave it for me in my office, please. I'll grab it later."

"Yes, sir. Are you leaving?"

"Off to Epcot . . . be back later."

"Very well, sir."

In a heartbeat, Hawk was out the door and moving across the walkway to the main building of the Contemporary. He decided to take the monorail to Epcot. It would take time and slow down his travel, but it also would keep him in and around people. That might offer him two things: The chance to disappear in a crowd if he needed to, and the protection a crowd could offer if things got a little dicey.

He took the escalator to the monorail station and jumped on board a monorail. The front was one of his favorite places to ride and allowed him to avoid being caught up in the rush of people getting on and off. Guests were not allowed to do this, but his request was granted immediately by the cast member who recognized him at the gate. As the doors closed and the monorail started to move, Hawk looked down into the lobby.

From his vantage point, he could see into the dining area below. Seated at a table in the corner of Chef Mickey's was Farren Rales, talking with Kate Young. Kate was laughing aloud as Farren regaled her with what Hawk presumed was the legend of how Grayson Hawkes had come to be the CCA of the Disney Company. He trusted Farren, but he wished he knew what and how much he was telling her.

The monorail streaked out of the Contemporary Resort into the bright Florida morning.

## CHAPTER FORTY-ONE

*Day Four*
Morning

IT HAD TAKEN HAWK LONGER THAN HE THOUGHT to get into Epcot and make his way back toward the World Showcase. Walt Disney had believed and managed to instill into those who worked with him that the more we understand about one another, whether it be similarities or differences, the better equipped we are to find mutual ground with each other and to move into the future with less difficulty. That idea—or, as some viewed it, a dream—was the focus when the World Showcase of Epcot was created. The World Showcase drew its inspiration from the early world's fairs, which had featured participation from many nations in a bygone era when that somehow was easier to accomplish. Epcot, in many ways, is two distinct theme parks in one. The World Showcase offers guests a trip around the world, and Future World is loaded with attractions and innovations of a bright and shining future of the world as it could be.

Although far from the vision that Walt had when he talked about his Florida Project, Epcot was still visionary in its approach and design and inspired people of all ages with the experiences that could be found on any given day in the park. On this day, the crowds were heavy early, and people recognized Hawk, stopping him to ask for pictures, autographs, and to talk about Disney. Hawk did his best to accommodate each request. His accessibility was one of the things that set him apart from his predecessors. He had also made headlines when it was announced how little he made in salary.

For Hawk, the perks of his job were well worth it. Instead of the inflated salaries that were so often criticized when made public, Hawk had chosen to steer away from that controversy. He believed the high-powered executives were probably worth what they were paid. But he remembered where he had come from, trusted God for what he needed, and was blessed to be living a very comfortable life with more than he needed. Most were stunned to find out that he was not the highest paid executive within the company. This, too, had given him a connection with many of the guests, who saw him as someone very much like them—an average person, albeit in a very big job.

Moving to his right as he reached the start of the World Showcase, he headed through Canada toward the United Kingdom. The journey through the United Kingdom pavilion was designed as a trip through time. The building facades lining the streets gave people who walked through a chance to see England as it might have looked in various eras.

Hawk had pulled so many possibilities through his mind, he'd lain sleepless during the early morning hours. Finally, an idea settled and he couldn't let it go. That was what he had to pursue now. Shep had confirmed that he might be on to something; now, he had to know for sure.

*Where toys stand guard*, the clue had said. Hawk remembered there was a toy store in the United Kingdom. He had walked through it a number of times but never paid as much attention as he should have. Right now, he was running on a wing and a prayer. The toy store was called the Toy Soldier. Surely that would fit the first part of the clue. The rest of the clue, he would figure out in real time inside the store. Reaching the pavilion, he stepped back into the streets and immediately was swept away to another place. The United Kingdom design always managed to take him into another world, and this showcase, in particular, was loaded with details.

The Toy Soldier was near the back of the street section. As he made his way to the door, the crowds became lighter. The park tended to fill up from the front to the back, so it took longer for people to get where he was now. The World Showcase also opened later than Future World, so there was always a lull in the way people moved into each area. The shop itself wasn't scheduled to open until eleven, an hour away.

Hawk knocked on the window, and a cast member getting ready for the day saw him. Opening the door and seeming very nervous that the boss was there just to look around, the cast member busied himself at a manic speed. The shop was much as Hawk remembered it. Loaded with classic English toys that included wooden trains, castles, toy soldiers, and assorted books and games, it was a great little toy shop.

The books featured in the shop were the works of P. L. Travers, author of the Mary Poppins books. Walt Disney had spent years trying to convince Helen Lyndon Goff, who wrote under the pen name Travers, to let him produce the film. It had become a huge success, and now in this shop many of the Poppins stories were available. The other author featured was A. A. Milne, the creator of the Winnie the Pooh stories. The shelves of the shop were lined with the various adventures of the bear always in search of honey.

It was the Milne collection that had brought him to the store. The Hundred Acre Wood is the fictional land inhabited by Winnie the Pooh and his friends. The clue had mentioned *over a hundred acres of woods,* and he hoped he might be on the right track. Seeing nothing that stood out to him, he navigated through various gifts from the British music invasion that influenced the culture of the 1960s. He drifted toward the back of the shop and found a library that had been set up on the shelves. The library opened up into the last room of the shop, which was used primarily as an area for guests to meet characters and take pictures.

Moving through the doorway, Hawk glanced around and then whispered to himself a triumphant yes.

To the right, he looked through a massive wall of windows into a cartoon forest. The Hundred Acre Wood. Flipping through the pages of his memory notebook for what he knew about the world of Winnie the Pooh, he began remembering facts and trivia. Some of it he tossed to the side, while others items he began piecing together to form a picture. The Hundred Acre Wood was the area where Christopher Robin, the boy in the story, would go out to meet his friends, and together they would have amazing adventures. These adventures were the stories of the books and movies. But Hawk was trying to find something beyond the commonly known facts of the story. He remembered that Milne's son was named Christopher Robin Milne, and the books and poems were created by the author to be the adventures of his son. Now, as Hawk turned quickly, he knew what the Imagineers had built. They had built Christopher Robin Milne's bedroom as the last room of this toy shop.

He scanned the room. There was a boy's desk, a dressing wardrobe, and toys displayed throughout. Next to the window was a bed, and as he looked up on the shelf above the bed, he saw two toy soldiers standing guard over there the boy would have slept. *Where toys stand guard . . .* and immediately to the right was the window looking out over the woods . . . *over a hundred acres of woods.*

Refocusing, he saw that at the foot of the bed was a giant toy chest with a chess board on top of it. His eyes darted to the toy horse, a riding horse, next to the chest. At first glance, it looked like a rocking horse, but then he noticed it was mounted to a frame with no rockers. It was indeed a riding toy but not a rocking toy. The clue had said, *it will almost rock you to sleep.* A horse that almost rocks, but doesn't, at the foot of the bed. Now it made sense.

Directly behind the horse stood a miniature wooden grandfather clock, a detailed prop that fit perfectly into this bedroom setting. *Make the time your time . . .* Hawk raced across the room and popped open the front panel of the clock. Inside, there was a shelf with two wrapped packages perched neatly on it. Bound together with a thin rope, the packages looked like they had been shipped together as one unit. The only markings on the paper covering the packages were two words: *hurry* and *rush*. Both references to the urgency of time. *Make the time your time . . .* these had to be what he was looking for.

Hawk grabbed each of the packages and moved to the cash register, where the cast member struggled to look busy and not look nosy at the same time. With his heartbeat quickening, Hawk asked if he had a pair of scissors. Once he had them in his hand, he cut the rope and unwrapped the first package. The larger of the two contained another figurine from the Western River Expedition collection. This time it was a dancing girl, a cancan dancer with leg extended into the air. When he turned her around, he found a collector pin fastened to her back with adhesive.

"Do you have a bag back there?" Hawk asked the cast member, who was obviously very curious.

The bag was produced, and Hawk placed the figure inside. Now opening the second package, he found a black box. The box was simple yet sturdy, and when he opened it, Hawk knew immediately what it was for. It was box to hold collectible pins. About an inch thick and four inches square, it was nearly the same size as the silver-plated box that contained the discoveries from his first quest into the world of Disney. Counting quickly, he spotted places to put five pins. He had just found his second pin, and he was willing to wager it had another QR code on its back. Stuffing the box into the bag, he said good-bye to the cast member, who continued to stand there looking shocked that the CCA had just come and opened up what was thought to have been a decoration. Hawk pushed the door open and returned to the streets of England.

Now the crowds had begun to arrive in the World Showcase. Squinting into the morning sun, Hawk sought out a place to inspect the pin he had just discovered. Stepping across the main pathway, he looked over at the Rose and Crown Pub and Dining Room. It was too early for them to be serving guests yet; but inside, the cast members would be getting ready to open. He glanced up at the motto of the establishment posted above the doorway: *Otium Cum Dignitate*. People always wondered what the phrase meant, and when they found out it translated to *leisure with dignity*, they were impressed. He smiled to himself because he knew that at the time the phrase was actually coined, most people could not afford the luxury of leisure activity. In that era, they defined the word *dignity* as *being worthy*; as a result, members of the upper class thought they should live a life of dignity because they were worthy.

Sometimes what something says and what it actually means are entirely different. That is what Hawk always tried to remember in dealing with people, and immediately he thought of Kate. He tried to once again figure out the details and intricacies that were hidden in plain sight all around him. As he often told people, details matter. Right now, they mattered a great deal.

The door to the restaurant was locked, and he tapped on it, catching the attention of a young lady moving through one of the dining areas. She looked toward the door and waved him away, mouthing that they were not yet open. Another woman inside noticed what was happening and stepped past the younger woman to make her way to the door. *This must be one of the managers*, Hawk thought, *and she recognizes me.* The door unlocked, and she opened it. Hawk noticed her nametag read Amy and her hometown was London, England.

"Good morning, Amy." Hawk greeted her before she had a chance to speak. "I am—"

"I know who you are, sir," Amy said in a Cockney accent that would make Eliza Doolittle proud. "I am Amy, one of the managers at the Rose and Crown. How can I help you today?"

"If you wouldn't mind, I need a place to hide out for a few minutes. I was thinking somewhere I could be out of your way, maybe by the water?" Hawk enjoyed eating a meal here, sitting in the outdoor doing area overlooking World Showcase Lagoon.

"Why of course, sir, follow me."

Amy led Hawk through the Rose and Crown, and the cast members getting ready for the day all paused as their special guest entered. He smiled and waved. Each one returned the wave and quickly went back to work trying to look busy. His unexpected visits to attractions and places throughout the resort were common knowledge, but the resort was so big that most never really expected him to drop in on them. Amy guided him outside and offered him the table right along the wall by the water's edge.

"Can I get you anything this morning?"

"Ah, yes." Hawk suddenly remembered something he needed. "Do you have a cell phone I could use for a few minutes, preferably a smart phone?"

"Well, sir . . ." Amy hesitated. She would know that the use of such items was not allowed in guest areas when you were on the clock. Her reluctance was an indicator to Hawk that she took her job seriously. On any other day he would be pleased, but today was not that day.

"Amy, I know it's against the rules for you to use one. I promise you this is not some kind of test." He tried to reassure her. "But I imagine someone has a phone back there I can borrow. I would consider it a personal favor if I could."

"I suppose." Amy turned her head and twisted her mouth slightly. "You can use mine. I'll go get it."

"Thank you. Trust me, it's going to be just fine." Hawk patted her arm as she turned to go.

Seated along the water, he closed his eyes and took a deep breath. His mind was cluttered. He had to clear his head to think about what he was doing. There was this crazy treasure hunt he was on again, there was an unknown group of people trying to stop him, there was a new Imagineer who had emerged as a ghost from the fog, and the people he was closest to all of a sudden were unavailable to help, with the exception of Shep. He was very concerned about Reginald and how bad he looked—Hawk feared something might be seriously wrong with him. And then there were *Total Access* and Kate. He wondered how her breakfast with Farren had gone and how much he had actually told her.

Opening his eyes, he looked back toward the people moving past the entrance to the Rose and Crown. His gaze stopped on a man wearing an oversized hat and dark glasses. The look was not unusual, as tourists would wear an amazing variety of garb into the theme parks. Fashion was not foremost on most of their guests' minds. What caught his attention was that this man seemed to be staring right at him. He couldn't be sure because they were not close enough in proximity. As Hawk looked at the man, he did not turn his head away or move a muscle. He was just standing, looking in Hawk's direction. *He might be looking at something else or lost in some deep thought*, Hawk reasoned. But still he did not move, and now the prolonged statuesque pose began to make Hawk uncomfortable. The man was too far away for the CCA to distinguish any features; he was nothing but an oversized hat and shades.

"Here you go, sir." Amy returned, tentatively offering her cell phone to him.

"Amy, you are awesome. Thank you." Hawk took the phone.

Having his attention diverted for a moment, Hawk looked back to the man who'd been watching him, only to find he was gone. Letting his eyes roam the crowd of people, Hawk did not catch a glimpse of him as he searched the tops of heads for the hat the man had been wearing. He stood and looked again. With all that was going on, he might be a little paranoid. Satisfied the man was gone and that he was overreaching to think the man was watching him, he sat down and opened the package from the Toy Soldier.

The cancan dancer was of the same design and craftsmanship as the other priceless Western River Expedition figurines. This would be the third in his collection that was being stored in the trunk of his car. He had no idea if that was any more secure than anywhere else right now. When he got the chance, he would stash them in the control bunker for safety. But he hesitated to do so yet, remembering Farren's warning. In the short term, his trunk was the spot. The Mickey Mouse pin he had found was in his pocket; in a moment, he would put it in the box designed to hold it.

Laying the box on the table, Hawk opened it and put Mickey in the upper left-hand corner. Now, carefully removing the pin placed on the back of the figurine, Hawk took a better look at it. It was Minnie. She, like Mickey, was a high-quality collectible pin. She was crafted facing to the viewer's left. Which meant that if she was side by side with Mickey, she would be facing him. This was a common design in creating a piece of art that included them both. Flipping the pin over, he saw the QR code stuck to its back.

He turned on Amy's phone and did a quick check of her apps to see if she had a scanner. She did, and he used it to read the QR code. The lights flicked in small points across the screen, and then with a flash, the screen changed. The face of George Colmes appeared again. Instantly Hawk was struck with the same thoughts he'd had each time before. The video had the look of an old film, but the background was in motion. George was giving these clues as he was riding in something. The background suddenly went dark. George's face was now in shadows lit by the light on the camera he was using to film.

"Good to see you are still with me." George smiled. "Your adventure continues with the host of the showcase . . . when you are followed by the airplane as far as you can go, then you find a lesson for the future . . . Listen to the teacher . . . her story is your story and where you will find a word . . ."

The screen went dark. Hawk scanned the QR code again just to see if the video would no longer be available to watch again. He wanted to pay attention to where George was. Each time, he'd had too little time to focus on the background—but each time, he'd noticed it enough to be curious. The scanner tried to read the code, only to find it was no longer available. He carefully placed the Minnie Mouse pin in the top right slot of the box and shut it. Hawk got to his feet and reloaded the shopping bag with his discoveries. Rolling the bag up tightly, he shoved it under his arm and picked up the phone to return it to Amy. He found her busy getting ready to open, though he was sure she'd been keeping a curious eye turned toward him as he used her phone. He was also sure she would check to see if he had placed a call. Of course, he had not.

"Amy, thank you so much. You saved me a trip back to my office, I don't have a phone with me." He handed her the phone. Stuck between the phone and his thumb was his business card. She took it and looked at it and then looked back toward him. He tilted his head. "If you ever find that you need anything, that card contains my direct office phone number. You have been very helpful, and I'd like to return the favor if you ever need one. Don't be afraid to use the number."

Hawk hurried out the door.

 *Day Four*
*Morning*

**HAWK MOVED TO HIS LEFT TO MAKE HIS WAY** around the World Showcase. The first part of the next clue seemed simple: *Your adventure continues with the host of the showcase.* Hawk was heading toward the American Adventure. Located in the middle of the World Showcase, the USA served as the host nation. When Epcot was built, much thought was given as to how to present America as the host of this festival where the world comes together. The American Adventure, built in the center to welcome the world with outstretched arms around the World Showcase Lagoon, was the answer.

The colonial-style manor house captures a period in American history that defined the direction of the nation. Red, white, and blue show up time and time again in the decor, whether in banners or flowers. Hawk remembered a great Walt Disney quote, "I get red, white, and blue sometimes." He smiled and realized he felt the same. The American Adventure as an attraction was a place that allowed him to revisit history and remember the foundations the country had been built upon.

The crowds touring the nations were growing but were not overwhelming at this time of the morning. With room to move, Hawk walked quickly with his head down and without making eye contact with anyone. This was not his norm, but he was trying to get somewhere fast and didn't want to be sidetracked by cast members or guests who might steal his attention. Before he realized it, his pace was nearly a jog and probably was drawing more attention than usual on a morning when he was trying to avoid it. He slowed himself down and purposed his pace to be more even. He moved through Japan and emerged into the USA Pavilion.

Nearing the entrance of the American Adventure, he was greeted by two cast members dressed in colonial-style costumes who informed him the first showing was not for another forty-five minutes. He assured them he was just there to look around for a project he was doing some work on. They held the door open for him. Hawk paused as he entered, and asked the two cast members if they could please keep everyone else outside for about ten minutes, even cast members. With puzzled faces, they confirmed they could; with a reassuring smile and a thanks for both of them, he moved inside.

The USA Pavilion's rotunda was beautiful and contained many treasures that most guests would never slow down to notice. The rotunda was adorned with a marble-and-gold floor and encircled by high columns. It was a masterpiece of design and detail . . . and the details once again were the reason he was there. Hawk had easily clicked on the first part of the clue, but his memory was a little cloudy as to what the next part might mean. Now inside, he was forced to put his memory to the test. *When you are followed by the airplane as far as you can go, then you will find a lesson for the future.*

Hawk stepped toward the center of the room to get his bearings. He thought he remembered a picture of an airplane hanging in the room. He revolved slowly, focusing, then he saw it. Rushing toward it, he inspected it closely. One of the original paintings created for the attraction depicted a moment in history from World War II when the B-17 bomber was being constructed. The picture was of a factory where the planes were in various stages of assembly. Not all the mechanics shown working were men, because at that time the men were gone to war, and the women picked up the factory work. The primary focus of the painting was the larger of the planes to the left-hand side of the picture.

Moving parallel to the painting and staring at the nose of the B-17, he walked the length of the picture, then back again. Slowly his eyes began to focus, and he saw the unique effect almost leap out of the picture. This Imagineering masterpiece was created by R. Tom Gilleon, who had painted the image of the plane in such a way that the aircraft seemed to turn and follow you wherever you walked. The bomber always faced you. *When you are followed by the airplane go as far as you can go, then you will find a lesson for the future.*

The picture of the plane was on the left side of the rotunda. The plane following him fit the clue; he was moving, and the plane was, in essence, following him. So now he had to find the lesson for the future. He moved along, looking carefully at each piece of art he passed. Arriving at the back of the rotunda along the left-hand wall, he spotted a painting featuring a teacher sitting under a tree, teaching her class of students. In the background was a one-room schoolhouse. She had a book open in her lap and was reading to the students and telling them a story.

Hawk flashed back to formative moments in his life when he remembered teachers reading to him. It was where he first developed his fascination with books and the art of telling a story. That ember of interest had been fanned into flame as the years passed. He realized that he liked this painting yet had never noticed it before. Perhaps because it was at the back of the rotunda. To find it, he had gone *as far as you can go . . . then you will find a lesson for the future . . .* and in the picture, the teacher was teaching a lesson to the future generation of young learners. This must be what George was referring to. But in a quick glance, there was no figurine tucked away in the corner, no package, no pin to be seen . . . just a painting. He looked closer.

A huge grin broke across his face, and he lightly smacked his forehead with the palm of his hand. He had missed the obvious. The plaque at the bottom of the portrait offered the title of the picture: *Lesson for the Future.* Now he went back to replaying the clue in his brain. *Listen to the teacher . . . her story is your story . . . and where you will find a word . . .* Leaning in, he inspected the picture more closely. His vision came to rest on the book in the teacher's lap. Getting as close to the picture as possible, he tried to focus. Then he pulled back and moved toward it again, looking for the perfect distance to see with the most clarity. He could barely make it out; he read it and then rubbed his eyes. Now he looked again to make sure he got it right. *Her story is your story . . .* the story she was reading was *The Swiss Family Robinson.* And if that was where he was going to *find a word* then he had to go back to the one place that connected to this particular story. The Swiss Family Robinson Treehouse in the Magic Kingdom.

Straightening up, he glanced around to make sure he had not missed anything. He shook his head in disgust, as he had almost missed the most obvious part of the clue, the title of the painting. He moved back toward the front door and glanced back at the B-17 bomber. Sure enough, the closer he got, the more aware he was that the image followed him as he walked. It really was a masterpiece.

As he reached the doors, rechecking to make sure he still had his shopping bag securely tucked under his arm, he looked through the windows. Something outside caught his eye. The oversized hat and sunglasses peered at him from in front of the American Gardens Theatre, directly across from the attraction. Hawk made a decision to find out if the person was really watching him, and he pushed through the doors to rush toward him. As he emerged, the cast members who had been there when he entered stepped in his way.

"Did you see what you were looking for?" the female cast member asked.

"We told our cast to wait until you were done to enter the attraction," the male cast member added.

"Yes, thanks," Hawk said, looking past them. "You did great." He saw the man in the hat start to run. "I've got to get moving."

Instantly, Grayson Hawkes was in a dead sprint. Legs churning, he shifted the package to the crook of his arm like a football. His eyes traced the tops of the heads in the crowd in front of him. The hat bobbed up and down as the man wearing it moved away from him. Hawk chased him and momentarily lost him. Moving quickly through Italy and into Germany, Hawk skidded to a stop and leaped onto a bench to get a better view of the crowd. People were staring, and some pointed at him in recognition. He scoured the crowd, then picked up the moving hat once again.

Its owner was at the boat launch, boarding a boat that would take a guest across the World Showcase Lagoon. There was no way Hawk could get to the boat before it left, but he wondered if he could beat it to the other side of the lagoon. He jumped down from the bench and began to sprint through the edge of the Germany Pavilion into a fairly open and largely undeveloped area of the World Showcase. The boat had pulled away from the dock and was making its way across the lagoon. The boats were a great way to get around the showcase if you knew where you wanted to go. They were not extremely fast but much quicker than taking a leisurely stroll. Hawk was banking on getting to the other side quicker.

Hawk knew that from Canada, at one end of the World Showcase, to Mexico, at the other side, was one and a quarter miles. He was a half mile away and intent on getting there first. He raced along back into another pavilion. The sounds of China echoed up toward him as he weaved, skipped, and ducked through the crowd. A pocket of tourists slowed his progress, and he tried to find a better path to take. A display was just releasing the attendees from the area, and the slow-going bumper-to-bumper traffic of strollers began to clog the pathway.

No longer able to run due to the log jam, Hawk tried to keep some kind of pace and moved to his far left to find the boat. He spotted it, but was still stymied by the influx of people along the path in front of him. The crowd seemed to be bottlenecking, and there was nothing he could do make them move any quicker. Again he looked back toward the boat and realized if he didn't get moving, he would not get there first. The thought occurred to him that even if the boat beat him, it always took a few minutes to secure the boat and disembark. He could still get there in time. He felt a sharp pain in his shin, as he stumbled into a stroller.

"Come on, mister, get to the right-hand side." The frustrated woman pushing the stroller used it as a miniature battering ram to navigate the crowds. "You're going against the flow, come on and move it."

She shoved the stroller into his shin a second time.

 *Day Four*
Late Morning

**THE MAN IN THE OVERSIZED HAT** looked out from his seat along the rail of the boat, as it skipped across the waters of the World Showcase Lagoon. He had hoped his ridiculous disguise would allow him to blend into the crowd, but he had become too careless and too curious. He knew that Hawkes began his excursion by shopping at the Toy Soldier; he had seen the bag when he left the store. Somehow he couldn't imagine the CCA of the Disney Company just dropping into a store to pick up a few things.

Watching Grayson Hawkes enter the Rose and Crown Pub and Dining Room had caused him to make his first error. Trying to get a glimpse of what he was carrying in the shopping bag, he managed to find a good place to see where Hawkes was seated. The problem was that Hawkes had caught him staring. He tried to fool the chief creative architect into thinking he might be looking at something else, and when the waitress came to the table, he managed to disappear.

He did not see what Hawkes had in the package. Instead, he waited across the street, looking aimlessly in the shopping areas of the pavilion until Hawkes came out of the restaurant. He was able to stay out of sight by looking through the window of a shop as Hawkes went past. From there, it had been fairly easy. Hawkes seemed to be in a hurry, moving quickly through the crowd with his head down.

He could have walked directly behind him if had chosen to, but he hadn't. He was content to keep a view from a distance. Following him to the American Adventure was easy, but after Hawkes had moved inside, once again, he could not see what he was doing. Deciding to wait across the walkway at the theater allowed him a clear view of the door. That was when he made his second error. He didn't plan on Hawkes's still being alert and looking for him.

That's when he decided to run. He did not have great confidence that he could outrun Hawkes, so he hurriedly tried to come up with another plan. Then he noticed the water taxi boarding just outside of the Germany

Pavilion. He lowered his head and tried to zigzag through the crowds until the last possible moment before boarding the boat. His timing was perfect. He was going to get away.

Then Hawkes did the unexpected—he gave pursuit; he actually thought he could outrun the boat to the other side of the lagoon. For a moment, the man in the hat and glasses believed Hawkes would be able to—until the unfortunate run-in with the stroller in China.

The memory of that caused the man in the hat to smile, as the boat bounced up against the dock. From behind his sunglasses, he watched the people get off in front of him, and he glanced along the shoreline to confirm that Hawkes had not done the impossible and managed to beat the boat. He was not there, and the man smiled again, imagining him still pushing his way through the people trying to get to the boat. He left the boat and moved back across a bridge toward a building called Odyssey Center. By the time Hawkes reached the boat, he would be long gone, and very soon, he would be out of the theme park completely.

Crossing in front of the building, he followed a small group of people as they made their way along the sidewalk. A roar burst from the building in front of them. Looking up, he saw Test Track, as a car raced on a track above his head on the outside the building. Moving past it and picking up his pace, he entered an area where people were waiting to board a ride called Mission: SPACE. He finally relaxed, as he moved down the pathway and under the covered path that carried him past the Electric Umbrella, a restaurant that was filling up for lunch time.

His hat jerked to the side and then pulled him backward, as if he were caught on something. Twisting his head, he pulled back against whatever had him caught. The wide brim of his hat slid down over his eyes, effectively blinding him. Then it was lifted away, and hands gripped him firmly, spinning him a hundred and eighty degrees. As he fumbled to readjust his sunglasses, he saw he was standing nose to nose with Grayson Hawkes.

Hawkes didn't look happy.

 *Day Four*
Noon

"YOU ARE FAST." The man in the sunglasses glared up at Hawk. His breath whistled in his throat as he spoke.

Hawk reached out and took the glasses from the man's face, folded them up and placed them inside the hat, then shoved them at the now recognizable Pete Brady, the executive producer of *Total Access*. Without a word, Hawk steered him to an open table and pushed him into a seat. Taking the seat opposite him, Hawk leaned forward.

"You forget, you are running around in my theme parks. You don't have to be fast." Hawk shrugged. "You just have to know where to go. Now, let's cut to it. Why are you following me?"

"It's what I do."

"You follow people?" Hawk laughed. "You need to get better at it. Your disguise is terrible."

"It's what we do at *Total Access*." Brady set the hat with the glasses inside it on the table. "I saw you get on the monorail this morning at the hotel. I followed you while you went shopping, and then you spotted me. So I dropped back, then you spotted me again.

"Are there cameras out there somewhere?" Hawk looked side to side. "You got Punky hiding in a tree over there?"

"No." Brady waved off the notion. "There are no cameras out here today."

"Did Kate put you up to following me?"

"No." Brady wrinkled his forehead. "Just the opposite. She met us this morning and told us to shut down production for the day and clear the calendar for the rest of the shoot. There had been a change in plans."

"Really?"

"Really. Kate informed us we could take a few days off and wait for her to tell us what to do with the stuff we already had captured."

"Really?" Hawk repeated.

"Yep, that is exactly what I said." Brady interlaced his fingers and set his hands on the table. "It's like this, Dr. Hawkes. I know you had a rough day in the interview yesterday, but that's what we do. Kate is the best. *Total Access* is the best. Then this morning, our star and boss tells us we're going to back off and take a different approach. That means something is wrong."

"Wrong?" Hawk leaned forward and cut his eyes toward the streams of people passing by their table. He wished he had found a more private place for this conversation. "How is that wrong?"

"That is not the way we work. We have enough footage of you to get the weird factor with that cemetery stunt you pulled. We have the scandal covered with that little story from your past—which, by the way, you did not confirm or deny—and then there's that whole criminal slant we picked up when you were attacked in the cemetery." Brady laughed. "My own cameraman and the star of the show got involved in that. In other words, we have our special whether you want to help or not. But then Kate tells us to back off. Like I said, something is horribly wrong here. That is why I am following you."

"And what did you find out by following me?"

"Basically that you went shopping. What's in the bag?"

"Nothing that would interest you." Hawk tightened his grip on the bag.

"Oh, I have a feeling I would be very interested." Brady stood. "And I am very interested in what in the world is going on around here."

Hawk rose to his feet along with Brady. Extending his hand in a conciliatory gesture, he waited to see if Brady would shake. He did, and Hawk spoke.

"Enjoy a few days in the resort. You need to relax and enjoy your time here."

"I'll enjoy it more when I know what is going on." Brady released the handshake.

"Have a magical day." Hawk winked and walked away. Pausing, he turned and added, "You really need to get a better hat. That one makes you stand out in a crowd."

Hawk imagined Pete Brady momentarily staring at his hat as he walked away from him. Stepping through an unmarked access door, Hawk disappeared backstage. Streams of emotion churned within him. He was pleased Kate had given the word for the production crew to shut down. That meant she was being true to her word. However, he had not considered that the rest of the *Total Access* team might not follow her instructions.

If they decided to go rogue, then he would have to keep looking over his shoulder for a camera around every corner. And then there was this mystery he was racing to solve, along with the people trying to stop him. Those streams converged in a raging river of danger. He felt his adrenaline surging to keep pace with it.

 *Day Four*
*Afternoon*

THE DOOR OF HIS OFFICE GAVE A SILENT CLICK as it opened. Grayson Hawkes walked in and waved to Nancy, who was, as usual, on the phone. Quickly bringing the call to an end, she handed him a stack of messages.

"Are they important?" He flipped through them quickly.

"They always are important, sir." She smiled, probably because she knew he would hand most of them back to her to find out more details before he called them back himself.

"Have you heard any more from Reginald? How is he feeling?"

"I haven't heard. Do you want me to call and check?"

"Please do." Hawk nodded as he handed her back the entire stack of messages. "What about Tim and Jonathan? Any word on them?"

"Nothing. Should I check on them as well?"

"If you get the chance." Hawk turned to head up the stairs to his office.

"Sir, I left your new phone on your desk."

"Thank you. You're the best, Nancy," Hawk said, from two steps up the staircase.

At the top of the stairs, he pivoted and headed into his office. Once inside, he hit the light switch, which not only turned on the overhead lights but also illuminated all the display cases with various Disney collectibles that were part of his ever-growing collection. Reaching the desk, he picked up the new phone and powered the device up, relieved that once again he would be connected to the people he needed. After the phone had time to boot up, he discovered that Nancy had managed to set it up with all his contact numbers and most of the same applications that had been on his previous phone, prior to its dunking in the Pirates attraction.

He scrolled through the numbers and stopped at the one belonging to Farren Rales. Tapping it, he listened as the phone dialed and connected to his number. An automated voice system answered, and Hawk waited for the tone to leave a message. "Farren, this is Hawk. Just wanted to touch base with you and see how your breakfast went. I also wanted to give you an update on a couple of things I have discovered. Call me if you get the chance. Thanks."

He walked behind his desk, set the package he had been carrying down on it, and reminded himself to put the new figurine in the trunk of his car when he left here today. That would keep the set together. He opened the black box containing the two pins. He needed three more, and then he would have . . . Well, that was the problem: he would have a set of pins, and beyond that, he had no idea what he would have. Looking up from his desk and through the open door, he could see that the door to the conference room was open. Usually it was closed. He imagined that after all the activity and moving of furniture to convert it to an interview set, perhaps some of the *Total Access* gear had been moved out already this morning. He got up and moved through his office, carrying the collectible pin box, and stepped inside.

He caught the soft scent of a perfume he had smelled yesterday when he walked into this room, and he breathed deeply. He looked at the two interview chairs placed in front of the window and saw Kate Young seated, with her back to him, staring out the window at the view of the Magic Kingdom. Gone were the massive lights and the covers used to diffuse them. They were stacked in the corner; the equipment had been broken down and was in various stages of being packed. The room was empty—except for Kate, who sat motionless.

Stepping around her chair and easing into the seat across from her, he flashed back for a brief moment to the day before, when this had been a hot seat and the mood between them was tense. In the early hours of the morning, when he had last seen her in the Contemporary, her mood had been somber; she had said little after they left Walt Disney's office in One Man's Dream. Now here she sat, lost in thought, gazing toward the Magic Kingdom. He took an extra moment to really look at her. She was as stunning today as she had been every other time he had seen her. It was safe to conclude that stunning was normal for her. Erasing that rabbit trail of thought, he sat back in the chair.

"Kate? Is something wrong?"

Silently, she remained staring out the window. After an extended pause, she breathed deeply and then slowly exhaled before breaking into a pleasant smile. Still not looking at him, she spoke. "Seeing the Magic Kingdom from here is magnificent." She crossed her legs and turned toward him with her hands clasped across her knee. "I hope you don't mind my being here. I told Nancy not to tell you I was here. I wanted to surprise you. If that's not OK, it's my fault."

"That's fine." He raised an eyebrow. "You wanted to surprise me?"

"Yes, but not in a bad way. I don't have a camera hidden somewhere. I just wanted a few minutes to talk with you . . . just the way you want to talk . . . off the record."

"But there is no 'off the record' with you, *is there*?"

"Today, right now, there is." She grinned but warned him, "Just don't get used to it. It won't last."

"Fair enough." He watched her look back toward the window. "How was breakfast?"

"Very . . . enlightening." She turned her gaze toward Hawk once again. "Farren Rales is one of a kind. He told me of his life and career and how he was friends with Walt Disney."

"Farren is the best," Hawk agreed.

"And, in case you didn't know. . . " She laid a hand over her heart. "He really loves you."

Other things he'd anticipated, but not that. He decided to wait and see where this conversation might be going.

"You know that, right?" She nodded at him as she moved her hand back to her knee. "He loves you like his own son, he is incredibly proud of you, and he thinks you're the greatest person ever . . . since Walt Disney."

"A lot of people think he's getting old and maybe senile when he starts saying things like that." Hawk laughed.

Kate did not. "I'm serious. To think that he chose you to become the visionary leader for the company that Walt built. He spent time getting to know you. He spent time looking at your life, your friends, listening to you teach, and watching how you lived. Then he sent you on an incredible adventure that sounds like it went horribly wrong for a while." She paused, studying his face. "But you did, in his words, what had to be done, and figured it out."

"Just how much did he tell you?" Hawk grew very guarded.

"He told me there always has been a group of people on the fringe, vaguely aware of Walt and Roy's plan, that would stop at nothing to sit at the top of the company where you are now. He told me about Juliette getting kidnapped and how you were the one who found her and brought her back safely."

"I think he's making it sound more heroic than it really was."

"Sounded heroic to me." She cocked her head slightly and lowered her voice. "He told me about Kiran Roberts."

Hawk inhaled sharply. "He did?"

"Yes, and he told me she used you and tried to steal the kingdom right out from underneath you. He told me how much it hurt you and how that had been the first woman you have had feelings for since . . . well . . ."

"I think Farren talks way too much." Hawk felt beads of sweat start to form along his neck as he looked toward the window.

"He needed to tell his story, which is now your story." Kate stopped, looking at her hands. "I'm sorry she hurt you. She was stupid and evil."

Hawk turned back toward Kate and said, hoarsely, "She was evil, but she wasn't stupid. She knew what she was doing."

"And you now have in your possession something that Walt himself designed for you. Now don't panic, he didn't tell me what it was . . . but I'm guessing part of what he gave you is that key you were using last night to open every door we needed to open."

He shrugged. "That was just a master key."

"You are a horrible liar." She leaned closer to him. "And that key you have is what everyone is after. At least, that's how I see it. They won't know what to do with it if they get it, because without all the rest of the things that only you are aware of, it doesn't mean anything . . . does it?" She waited. Hawk looked back at her but said nothing. "And you aren't about to give it up, because you are Grayson Hawkes and you are tenacious, strong, smart, and you follow Jesus with so much passion, you think you can change the world, and you think being in charge of the most influential storytelling company in history will help you make the world a better place."

Hawk whistled. "That's a good story, Kate."

"I heard it from a great storyteller." She sat back in her chair.

"Sounds like he gave you an earful."

"Indeed."

The two sat there across from each other, trying to figure out exactly what to say next. Kate watched, as Hawk began to squirm in his chair. Finally, he broke the silence.

"And what are you supposed to do with the story he told you?

"What do you mean?" she asked coyly.

"What now?"

"Well, Farren told me he had an amazing story to tell me . . . and that he would tell me as much as he could. He promised I would be amazed." She grinned. "And I must admit, I am amazed. It's next to impossible to believe. But he told me I couldn't tell the story to anyone . . . until you figured out how I could and should tell it."

His skin began to tingle, and he jerked his head back slightly. "What?"

"How I tell this story all depends on you. He told me you would fill in the gaps I needed filled in, and you would know how I could tell the story in the best possible way. Because, according to him, you are the man when it comes to how to take care of a story."

Hawk was having a difficult time slicing through his fuzzy thoughts. "I don't know what he was talking about, Kate."

"You know, he said you would say that." She was still smiling. "Amazing. Oh, and he also said that you are extremely attracted to me, but because of your past you're overly cautious."

"He did, did he?" He wondered if Farren really was going senile. Not only had he dumped a lot of information in Kate's lap, but he was going to leave it to Hawk to figure out how she would tell the story. If that wasn't enough, his old friend was trying to play matchmaker.

"He did. He also said that you were not as confident as you appeared around me, because I make you nervous because I am a big, mean, nasty reporter. And . . . that I should get to know you because I would like what I find."

"Sounds like he was rambling . . ." Hawk felt his stomach sink.

"Oh, there's more. He also said that I hurt you very badly in the interview yesterday. Whether I meant to or not, whether it was my job or not, it was uncalled for, and that I owe you an apology, but you were way too kind ever to tell me that."

"Again, I say—"

"So . . ." Kate reached out and grabbed both his hands and held them tightly. "I am sorry I hurt you. It was wrong and I was wrong. I should have found a better way to tell the story about you."

"Kate, it's . . ."

"Hey!" She looked intently at him. "I'm not done yet. And if you feel the need to keep me at arm's length, I understand . . . because, after all, I am a . . . big . . . mean . . . nasty reporter. Okay, now I'm done. You can talk."

"I don't . . ." Hawk laughed. "I don't know exactly what to say."

"That would probably be because I make you nervous. Right?"

"Uh-huh." He rolled his eyes. "I'm sorry I asked how your breakfast went."

"Breakfast was good." She let go of his hands and sat back in the chair. "And what happens now really does depend on you. No kidding. I told the *Total Access* crew to cool their heels, and we'll reconfigure what we're doing with you. I told Farren that in exchange for what he told me, I would not do anything until you and I together agreed on how to best tell this story. So I'm either going to sit here and look out the window while you stare at me—which I don't mind, by the way—or you're going to tell me what we're looking for next and what the game plan is . . . and for now, it's all off the record."

He held up his hand. "Whoa, go back a second. When you said, 'Which I don't mind, by the way,' were you talking about me staring at you or you just sitting here looking out the window?"

"I'll bet you'd like to know, wouldn't you?" She laughed, and Hawk thought he noticed a twinge of nervousness. "Now, why don't you tell me what's in that black box you placed by your chair when you first came in here?"

 *Day Four*
Late Afternoon

**HAWK AND KATE MOVED THROUGH** the Magic Kingdom, weaving their way toward Adventureland and the Swiss Family Robinson Treehouse. After giving Kate a chance to examine the pin box and the Minnie Mouse pin, he had told her most of the details of his morning. As soon as he had stashed the latest Western River Expedition figure in his car, they walked across the red-brick walkway from the Contemporary to the Magic Kingdom. He had not told her about his run-in with Pete Brady. If Pete had decided to do some investigating on his own, then Hawk did not want the responsibility of being the one to give that information to Kate.

He decided he would leave that to the executive producer to volunteer. As they walked, he told her about the latest clue he had been given and explained what he had done to unravel it. The painting with the B-17 fascinated her, and she expressed a desire to go see it for herself. Then he went on to make the connection from the painting featuring the teacher, the book she was reading to the students, and why they were now heading into the Magic Kingdom.

*Her story is your story . . . where you will find a word* was the last portion of the clue they were now pursuing. Thunder rattled across the Florida afternoon sky. Hawk looked up and saw ominous clouds rolling above them. It rained often in Central Florida, but the beauty of an Orlando rainstorm was that it never lasted very long. The bad news for them was going to be at the tree house. When lightning dancing across the sky, it was ill-advised to allow guests to move into the heavens in an artificial tree, daring the lightning to strike. Usually, the attraction was closed until the sky was clear and guests could safely navigate the steps and tour the exhibit.

The Swiss Family Treehouse is based on the 1960 live-action Disney feature film "Swiss Family Robinson." Making the connection to the book in the painting had been an easy one for Hawk. Although the attraction was not a thrilling one, it was one Hawk loved just because of the creativity, and as always

. . . the details. Trying to recreate a model of the home the Robinson family built in the movie was no easy feat for Imagineers. They ended up building a tree house, and it doesn't include an elevator. That means navigating the one hundred sixteen steps every time you visit. Hawk and Kate walked past the entrance and over to a shop across the plaza. Once inside, they absently flipped through clothing racks while they looked over the streets of Adventureland.

"Are we going to climb a tree?" Kate asked as they faux shopped.

"Did you know that tree is a Disneyodendron eximus?" Hawk asked her, as his eyes moved through the crowds, searching.

"A what?"

"It means an out-of-the-ordinary Disney tree, or something like that. It's man-made, with concrete roots. The fourteen hundred limbs are constructed of cement-coated steel. Three hundred thousand plastic leaves were attached by hand. The tree is ninety feet high and sixty feet wide."

"How do you keep all those facts in your head?" She looked at him with a mixture of puzzlement and amazement.

"Scary, huh?"

"I'll say." Kate looked back toward the tree. "Are we going up it?"

"Well . . ." Hawk looked at her outfit. "Is that really how you dress to visit a theme park?"

"You don't like my outfit?" Kate looked down at her usual stylish blouse, skirt, and heels. "This is how I dress every day."

"I didn't say I didn't like it." He smiled. *I like it a lot.* "But it makes it tough to blend into the crowd with you dressed up."

"Who likes to blend into a crowd?"

Hawk listened as the thunder rolled again. This time it was closer. He walked to the cash register and bought two of the opaque plastic ponchos that miraculously showed up in every merchandise store when inclement weather appeared over the resort. Umbrellas were discouraged in the parks—they were too dangerous, and someone might get poked—so ponchos and raingear became the dress of the day. He made his purchase and came back to where Kate was standing at the clothes rack.

"They've closed the attraction." Hawk nodded toward the entrance of the Swiss Family Robinson Treehouse. "It's too dangerous to climb it with the lightning and rain."

"So what do we do, just wait out the storm?"

"No, I'm not the most patient person. I don't like to wait. I get bored."

Hawk moved Kate out of the shop, into the covered pass-through that allowed guests to move from Adventureland into Frontierland and Liberty Square. There were restrooms and the entrance to a gift shop located in the walkway. Once the rain started, people began to gather en masse inside. As the rain fell even harder, the people pressed in, and the passageway became a sea of humanity trying to stay dry. The more people that packed into the passage, the louder the noise became. The sound of the hard, steady rain and the elevated voices of everyone trying to be heard made it almost deafening to wait there.

Hawk leaned in, positioning his mouth at Kate's ear, and began whispering to her. As she listened, she would occasionally pull her head away from him, look at him, then nod, and then lean back into him to keep listening. She reached over and grabbed his arm tightly and mouthed, "Be careful." Then he slipped out of the crowd, onto the street, merging with the poncho-covered people determined not to let the rain spoil their vacation. On a sprint through the rain, he arrived at the entrance, and ignoring the sign indicating the attraction was closed, he jumped the gate and ran across the bridge to the steps.

Thunder shook the tree as he hit the bottom of the steps. The design was simple and genius. The steps would carry you up into the tree where Imagineers had re-created rooms and props that were a part, or could have been a part, of the live action film. *Where you will find a word.* That was what he was now looking for . . . a word . . . whatever that might mean. Arriving at the first room, he saw the re-created living room, which featured an organ, tables, chairs, and bookcase. Pressing his face against the window to get the widest view of the room's interior, he let his eyes explore the space for another figurine or something a figurine might be hidden in. The word portion of the clue had not yet connected; he was hoping it would all fall into place as he searched, because he had no other lead to pursue. Seeing nothing in the living room that alerted him, he skipped up the next section of steps that wove their way through the branches.

Lightning flashed bright and close, a spectacular yet frightening blaze of hot white across the darkened late-afternoon sky. As he squinted against the light, the thunder clapped, shaking the walkway beneath his feet. *I'm glad we shut this down in bad weather,* he thought, as he arrived at the bedroom of Mother and Father Robinson. Again placing his face against the window so he could see inside, he started at the nightstand by the bed and moved his gaze across the room. He stepped back for a moment and then leaned forward again. Straining to see with better clarity, he noticed that one of the books in the room had the word Holy Bible on the cover. That was two words. As a pastor, he often referred to the Bible as the Word of God. People in Christian circles would utter the phrase that they needed a word from the Lord.

The Bible, he believed beyond any doubt, was God's Word. The book was the word. The door to the bedroom was located behind a rail that kept guests out of the display and secured by a rope system that he quickly released. It swung open. Hawk stepped into the bedroom. He lightly walked over to the nightstand and bent down to look at the Bible closer. From this new vantage point, he could see what was under the nightstand. It was a cylinder-shaped object, wrapped in a burlap cloth, similar to what he had found in the cemetery during another rainstorm. He snatched up the package and began to unwrap it right there, out of the rain.

Just as before, he unwound the cloth until he saw another figure, a bit smaller than the others because this person was designed to be seated. The cowboy's hands were extended with the fingers pointing down as if playing a piano. Flipping it over in his hand, he saw a collectible pin attached with the same adhesive. He gently pried the pin free, and tossing it over in his hand, saw it was one of his all-time favorite characters: Goofy. After placing the Goofy pin in his pocket, he carefully rewrapped the cowboy figure, then stepped back out onto the stairs.

Despite the weather, he couldn't resist the temptation to steal a rare, spectacular glimpse of the park. He climbed up the next flight, which led to the bedroom set of the boys from the film. This was the highest point of the attraction, then the steps would unwind themselves down the tree and take you past other things to look at on your descent. Hawk paused and looked out over the park.

The height of the tree gave an amazing perspective of the Magic Kingdom, and particularly of Adventureland. In the rain, the streets had become a steady stream of hooded, opaque Mickey Mouse ponchos bobbing as the guests moved to the next stop on their journey. Then he saw the movement at the bottom of the tree.

There was someone wearing a black hooded rain jacket scuttling into the exit area of the tree house. Hawk descended a few steps and peered closely, trying to see the face. When the person turned to look up toward him, the only detail Hawk could see was a black ski mask, shadowed by the black hood. Not a good sign, but also not a surprise.

In the pass-through earlier, Hawk had whispered to Kate that he was sure he would be watched by those trying to stop him. They had threatened them, they had chased them, they had tried to stop them; and so far, they'd had no success. They were getting desperate, because the more time Hawk had to look, the closer he would be to finding whatever was out there to find.

Hawk reversed himself and went back up the way he had come, cresting the stairs by the boys' bedroom, then heading back down toward the entrance. Swinging around the corner, he came up short. A man wearing a black hooded jacket was coming at him across the bridge. Staring directly at him, Hawk could see under the hood the presidential mask he had grown tired of seeing. The hooded man stopped when he saw Hawk pause on the steps and waved a finger in the air from side to side at the CCA, as if telling Hawk he was in trouble now.

Hawk backed up the steps. There was a hooded man coming up the steps toward him from either direction. He had no place to go. The lightning streaked the sky again, and thunder rattled the tree to its concrete root system. Hawk twisted on the landing at the top of the tree, peering downward. The men were closing in on him. He wiped his rain-streaked face with his hand and tried to think. They would reach him in moments.

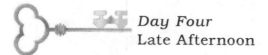 *Day Four*
*Late Afternoon*

**THIS IS INSANE WAS THE THOUGHT** that ran through Hawk's head as he leaped over the railing and landed on top of the tree branch stretched out in front of him. The jump was not far or that difficult, but the height of the tree and the branch now made slick by the rain created an additional challenge. After making sure he was secure, he scooted out on the branch and looked back at the two men coming after him up the steps. They were still standing motionless, watching him move out on the branch. Their reaction was exactly what he had hoped for. They waited to see whether he would hang on or slip and fall into the water below.

Hawk looked down and thought about the possibility of falling. It did not appeal to him. If he fell, he would bounce through the concrete-and-steel branches before finally clearing them and plopping into the water below. He wasn't sure, but he knew the water, like much of the flowing water in the park, was not nearly as deep as it appeared. If he didn't die bouncing through the branches, he would probably be severely injured as he hit the too-shallow water. This plan had better work.

Once again, multiple streaks of lightning flashed around him and thunder shook the tree. Now that he was trapped on the limb, the men chasing him resumed their ascent with renewed speed.

Hawk began to drag himself across the branch, focusing on the limb slightly lower than his perch. To reach it, he would have to jump perfectly and grab the one section that looked like the best place to connect. The men had reached the place Hawk had leaped from. They both stood and watched him carefully. Hawk felt behind him and made sure the wrapped package was still tucked securely in the waist of his pants, where he had placed it moments before his jump. He had no doubt they could see it there as well.

"Why don't you come on out here and join me?" he yelled over his shoulder, loud enough to be heard over the sheet of rain.

Then, pulling himself up into a crouching position on his branch, he jumped out toward the next one. His feet slid just as he left the safety of the tree limb, and he knew immediately he was going to be short of his distance. As he plummeted through the air, time seemed to slow down, and his brain ran through a series of possibilities and calculations in that fraction of a second so his body would know what to do.

He lobbed his forearm over the extended branch, immediately tightening his grip, trying to pull himself closer to the length of concrete while bracing for his full body weight to sail below it. Once that happened, he felt himself start to slip around the branch while he anxiously lunged toward it with his other hand. Getting a handhold, he now hung below the branch, tightly grasping it with both hands.

Looking down, he saw that the attention of the poncho-clad passersby was being drawn toward him. A few, then a few more, and then a crowd began to notice the man hanging from the branches of the Swiss Family Robinson Treehouse. Exhaling, he pulled himself up to the branch in a chin-up. Now he was able to stretch out a hand and grip a smaller branch to pull himself upright. Another glance over his shoulder allowed him a glimpse of the two men who'd been chasing him. They now seemed as enthralled as the rest of the crowd.

Perched on the second branch, Hawk reached behind him and grabbed the wrapped package. Holding it in his hand, he looked carefully across toward the crowd below him. What he was about to do was risky, but no riskier than what he'd just done. He pulled back his arm and with a side-armed heave, launched the package into the air, whirling it like a boomerang. The old joke played across his brain as he watched the package spin. What do you call a boomerang that doesn't come back? The answer was always . . . just a stick. But the stick he had just tossed was a priceless piece of art. He watched as it sailed through the raindrops and landed just where he had been aiming. It hit the branches of a tree lining the walkway near Bwana Bob's. The package hung up momentarily in a branch and then dropped and bounced until it hit the ground.

A carefully manicured hand snatched it up and hid it under a poncho. Just as they had planned, in case someone decided to try and stop him, Kate had been waiting below. Now he could no longer spot her in the flowing sea of ponchos moving along in the Magic Kingdom. The package was safe, and she was, for all practical purposes, invisible in the crowd. Twisting his head back, he turned in time to see the two hooded pursuers already heading down the tree. They would be too late; she was already gone, and once again they had been foiled.

While he watched them move away, he reached into his pocket and carefully removed the Goofy collectible pin. Holding it tightly between his wet fingers, he inspected it to see if it had a QR code attached; it did. He retrieved his new cell phone and punched the button to power it up. Sliding his finger over the touch screen, he scrolled over the apps until he found the barcode scanner. He brought the scanner to life and aligned it over the black-and-white-patterned square. Flecks of light danced over the code, then the screen blinked and the old-style film began to play. Hawk remembered to focus quickly and try to catch a glimpse of the background as George spoke. This time, George appeared to still be moving inside a tunnel. Light shone across one side of his face. The screen shot was a tight close-up, and again Hawk knew that where it was filmed had a familiarity to it that, as of yet, he just couldn't figure out.

George spoke. "You are still on the adventure . . . good for you. Don't give up . . . not yet . . . you are getting closer. I will say it once, listen closely. Follow the ghosts of the past when the floodwaters flow . . . under the pressure of clouds . . . on your quest you will go."

It appeared that George had taken a sudden and sharp turn. The background behind him went dark. Then the screen went blank, and the message was done. Shoving the phone and the pin back in his pocket, he replayed the clues once in his mind so he would not forget.

Sighing and placing himself flat against the tree branch, he laid down his head and closed his eyes. Feeling the rain soak him, he knew that this time he had pushed a little too close to the edge. A sharp crack of lightning caused his eyes to immediately spring open, and he remembered he was lying on a concrete-covered steel tree in a storm. He slowly began to pull himself along the branch, back toward the trunk of the tree.

JEFF DIXON

 *Day Four*
*Evening*

**ROGER E. BROGGIE CRAWLED INTO THE FRONTIERLAND** Train Station. The *Roger E. Broggie* was one of four locomotives that chugged around the Magic Kingdom on the Walt Disney World railroad line each day. Named after the man who'd led the effort in acquiring the locomotives, he was a trusted friend of Walt's and one of the Imagineers who had helped make Epcot a reality. The train named in his honor let off a burst of steam as it stopped in Frontierland. There was a flurry of activity as passengers disembarked at this station, which placed them at the entrance to Splash Mountain on the edge of Frontierland. After those getting off had cleared the loading platform, the gate was opened for guests who were boarding. The rain had made people reluctant to leave the train, and it was now the resting place for passengers who had decided to ride out the storm under the cover of the passenger cars.

Grayson Hawkes made his way through Frontierland Station to board the train. His climb down from the Swiss Family Robinson Treehouse had been far less harrowing than the trip out onto the branches. Yet the climb down had not been without difficulty. The jump from the limb back to the safety of the guest area had been farther than he thought. Luckily, by the time he got to the lowest part of his climb in the branches, three cast members and four members of the security team had positioned themselves to meet him. When they realized it was the chief creative architect coming down the tree, their focus had narrowed from getting him down safely and escorting him out of the park to getting him down safely. The security detail had questions, and Hawk had deferred them all to contact Reginald Cambridge. They informed him that Cambridge was not in the parks today, and Hawk told them to direct their questions to Clint Wayman instead.

After making sure he was OK and that no one had actually been hurt during his little adventure, Hawk left the befuddled bunch at the base of the tree and quickly donned his poncho. Sliding the plastic hood over his head, he cut through into Frontierland to get on the train. The cast member let him pass through the gate to climb aboard, and he headed to the last car. He had given Kate specific instructions to meet him on the last row of the last car on the train. That way he was assured of only one person being behind them: the cast member responsible for getting passengers on and off. From the vantage point in the rear compartment, they could see who got on and off, they could see any unusual activity in front of them, and the train was noisy enough that they could talk without being overheard. It was the concept of hiding in plain sight that had developed this plan.

For the first time since boarding, he looked up and saw Kate Young seated in the last row of the back car, her head still covered in poncho plastic, looking at him. He slid into the seat next to her, where he was greeted by a surprisingly powerful punch to the arm.

"Have you completely lost your mind?" She reared back to hit him again.

"What are you talking about?" He tried to twist away from the second punch but was not fast enough.

"You scared me to death." She hugged him as he gripped his aching upper arm.

"So, you decided to hit me *and* hug me?" he asked as he strained to breathe in her viselike embrace.

"When you said to wait for you to get me the figurine, I didn't know you were going to climb the tree." She finally released him. "I thought you were going to fall. Are you alright?"

"It's a little late to ask that now, after you've been whaling on me." He rubbed his arm where she had punched it.

"You big baby," she scolded. "If you're tough enough to swing from a tree, then you can handle a girl punching you. Quit whining. Now tell me, are you alright?"

"I'm fine." He smiled. "Worked just like I had planned."

"Really? So that was you being in complete control?"

"Yep, pretty much . . . impressive, huh?"

"I was afraid for you. It was risky and crazy." She slid closer to him.

"I underestimated how difficult it was going to be. But it worked."

"Yes, it did." She removed the wrapped package from under her poncho. "Did you get the pin off of it before you threw it?"

"I did." Hawk looked back over his shoulder to see where the cast member in the conductor's stand had his attention directed. Sure he was not paying attention to them, Hawk continued. "Yes, and while I was in the tree, I played the clue. George said, 'Follow the ghosts of the past where the floodwaters flow . . . under the pressure of clouds on your quest you will go.'"

Taking the Goofy collectible pin out of his pocket, he passed it over to her. She studied it and turned it over to the QR code on the back. This was pin number three, and the storage box he had been given had room for five pins. Hawk breathed deeply and noticed that Kate was no longer looking at the pin but looking at him.

"You sure you're OK?" she said with concern.

"Couldn't be better. Just trying to think through the next clue." He scratched his chin. "And I guessed right about us being followed. I just wonder where they picked us up."

"They aren't wandering around the park wearing their masks." She tightened her lips. "So they could be anyone and anywhere. When they decide to move, they must slip on their masks and emerge from the crowd."

His plan was for them to meet and hide on the train for as long as they needed to. The train ride looped the Magic Kingdom continuously, making stops at each station and for water as needed. As an operating steam engine, the water stops were frequent and scheduled like clockwork. Each time, the passengers had the option of staying on board and continuing their ride or getting off at the station. By not having to move and leave, they had the chance to talk, to rest, to plot their next move, and to work on figuring out the next clue.

As they rode, they kept their heads bowed so they would not be recognized and spoke in hushed tones. One loop became two, two became four, and after their seventh trip around, they decided to give up their seats. The rain stopped, and as they got off, they took off their ponchos. Hawk promptly threw them in the trash so they wouldn't have to carry them around in the crowds of guests moving through the streets. Dusk had fallen, and the park's lights made the Magic Kingdom glow.

Frontierland was darker than other areas. The light came from re-creations of streetlamps and lanterns from the western frontier. As Hawk and Kate made their way down the stairs of the train station, he kept scanning the crowd, looking for anything that seemed suspicious or out of place. His senses were on high alert, and Kate was right on his shoulder, doing the very same thing.

"Why are you so quiet?" Hawk asked Kate, as they cautiously traveled through the frontier town. He knew that because she was an investigative journalist, her brain was in overdrive trying to process what had just happened at the tree house.

"Just wondering . . ." Hawk tried to read her expression. As she stared back at him, he couldn't tell whether she was worried, frightened, puzzled, or a mixture of all three, creating a trifecta of turmoil.

"Wondering what?"

"What I don't know." She shook her head slowly. "There is much more to the story than Farren told me. Only you can fill in those gaps. But whatever those gaps are, they're so big you're willing to risk your life to protect them. You won't ask law enforcement to help. And what we're doing is dangerous."

"Kate, I—"

She held up her hands in front of her. "Hawk, I'm not asking you to tell me right now . . . but I do want you to tell me."

Hawk's cell phone went off in his pocket. When he saw it was Reginald, he answered, hoping to head off Reginald's inevitable chiding for his exploits in the theme park. "Hey, how are you feeling?"

"I was feeling a bit better until I heard about the head of the company jumping from limb to limb at the Swiss Family Robinson Treehouse," Reginald fired back.

"An event that was exaggerated by whoever told you, I am sure."

"Are you unharmed?"

"I'm just fine. Everything is under control here." Hawk watched Kate contort her face and roll her eyes. "I need you to get feeling better and get back here soon."

"I can be there right away."

"I'm not saying you need to rush over here now, though I can use your help to keep me out of trouble." Hawk reassured him, "Until you get back, I'll be fine."

"You were the one who told me to go home," Reginald reminded him.

"That's because you were about to keel over."

"Or could it have been to get me out of the way so you could turn the theme park upside down with your outrageous behavior?"

"Would I do that?" Hawk laughed. He heard Reginald laugh on the other end of the line and then go into a coughing jag. "Reginald, seriously . . . I am fine. You get feeling better. I can use your help, but not until you're feeling good."

"Are you doing what you are doing alone?" Reginald's voice grew quieter and deeper.

"No." Hawk cut his eyes toward Kate. He didn't want her to notice a change in the conversation's tone. "Kate Young is here with me."

"I know there is no need for me to remind you of our experiences eighteen months ago." Reginald spoke slowly. "Be careful and take care of yourself." His concern for Hawk's well-being physically and emotionally carried over the phone connection.

"It's good. Don't worry." Hawk paused, "Thanks, Reginald. Feel better. Bye."

Ending the call, he looked back toward Kate. He angled his head in the direction they had been going before.

"Reginald is still sick?" Kate's voice was soft with concern.

"Yes, he sounds awful. I don't know what's wrong with him, but I was very worried about him earlier today. He looked horrible. He can't breathe, he has pain, he's coughing . . ."

"But he's worried about you?" Kate asked.

"Yes, he was going to come here now."

"Hawk, you have a lot of good people who will help you. If we need them, let's get them here." Kate lowered her head. "I don't want you falling out of a tree and killing yourself."

"I'm done with climbing that high for the day." He exhaled loudly. "That was tough."

"So where are we off to now?" She lightly bit her lip to suppress a smile.

"Right here . . . I think."

Hawk walked up the incline with Kate, then they turned left and headed toward the Big Thunder Mountain Railroad. After walking past the entrance and moving up the hill toward the exit, they stopped in an isolated viewing area and photo spot overlooking the attraction that raced along the track and through the curves in a re-creation of Monument Valley.

"The Big Thunder Mountain Railroad?"

"Yes, do you know the story behind it?" Hawk gestured to the roller coaster in front of them.

"You mean the backstory? No, I haven't heard it . . . but I am finding out that with you and at Disney, it's *always* about the story."

"In the late 1800s, gold was discovered on Big Thunder Mountain. Overnight, it started a gold rush, and the little town of Tumbleweed became a booming mining town. Mining was good, the gold veins were rich, and an extensive network of mining trains was set up to move the gold. Sadly, what the settlers and miners of Tumbleweed didn't know was that Big Thunder Mountain was sacred to the local Native Americans. And according to legend, the mountain was cursed."

"Of course, you gotta hate those curses." Kate smiled.

"Because the townspeople didn't care, and the miners didn't stop their desecration of the mountain, things turned tragic. The curse caused earthquakes, mines collapsed, people were hurt, and a flash flood destroyed the town of Tumbleweed. The people fled, the mines were closed, and the town became a ghost town. There were a few people who remained because they got stuck, they held out hope things would get better, or they had no place else to go."

"You know, this is kind of a depressing story," Kate observed.

"You have no idea," Hawk continued. "As the legend goes . . . later, it was discovered that the old mining trains were running by themselves. Racing along the old tracks without drivers. Some said ghosts were driving. Others said the trains were possessed. Eventually, the mining company set it up so tourists could ride the trains and view what was left of their mines and the old town of Tumbleweed."

"That is quite a story." Kate looked as the mine train zoomed past. "Sad and spooky, but quite a story."

"Well, how else do you explain mine trains that run with no drivers through an old ghost town and deserted mine?"

"Hey, Hawk?" Kate touched his arm. "You said a minute ago when I called it depressing that I had no idea. Did that mean something more than you've told me?"

"Wow, you must be a reporter." He smiled. "You don't miss a beat. The Big Thunder Mountain Railroad is similar to what was planned for the Thunder Mesa and Western River Expedition areas. When Big Thunder Mountain was created, it became pretty clear to most that the Thunder Mesa plan would never really happen. So not only is the story about a haunted mine train, but it's also a story about the ghosts of good ideas that never made it."

"And this is where the next clue brings us?" She watched as another mine train streaked past.

Hawk nodded. "We have to visit the ghost town of Tumbleweed."

 *Day Four*
Night

HAWK STEPPED THROUGH THE GATE of the attraction along with Kate and a nervous security team member. After a brief meeting with the ride manager, the decision was made to shut down the ride for fifteen minutes, giving Hawk and Kate the time they needed to take a walk in Tumbleweed. The manager of the attraction and then the manager of Frontierland had decided that a security team needed to be brought in to make them feel better about shutting down the attraction without emptying the queue lines. Hawk had insisted he would be quick; the managers were edgy about guests seeing Hawk and Kate wandering about the attraction.

The security officer named Neil fiddled with his collar and straightened his shirt repeatedly. He had asked why he needed to guard the chief creative architect of the company as he took an unplanned walk into the Big Thunder Mountain Railroad. His question had gone unanswered. To make matters worse for Neil, he recognized Kate Young and didn't know why there was a reporter tagging along. She was prettier in person than she was on television, he had blurted, before suggesting someone with more seniority should be assigned this task. Hawk had reassured him there was no time to get anyone else and they needed to hurry.

They walked into the attraction through a side entrance, in view of the guests in line. Some of the guests recognized Kate and then Hawk. They called their names and waved. Eventually Kate smiled to the crowd, stopped, and waved back at them. The ripple through the crowd was visible. They wanted to know why the head of the company and the star of *Total Access* were walking through the attraction. Seeing the crowd push against the side of the queue lines for a glimpse made them move quicker. The flash of cameras meant there would be evidence of this field trip and questions to answer.

Hawk pointed toward the crowd and waved. "You're here to make sure that they all stay up there and feel safe," Hawk said to Neil as they rounded the corner out of the view of the crowd. "If you'll stay here, we'll be right back."

Hawk and Kate moved deeper into the attraction and stepped carefully over the realistic and rocky terrain. Hawk helped support Kate by giving her his hand as they moved forward.

"You know that someone up there who just got a picture is posting it on Facebook right now. On Twitter, someone is going to be asking what we were doing out here."

"Probably," Hawk agreed. He realized they were walking hand in hand, and he noticed what a nice fit her hand was inside of his.

She tightened her grip against his palm. "And I have to wait for you to help me figure out what story to tell them?"

"That is the deal." Hawk smiled. "Or you can just tell them we went for a walk."

"What was the clue again?"

"*Follow the ghosts of the past* . . . I think that is as much a reference to the legend of the ride as it is to the history of the theme park. The ghosts may be the ghosts of Thunder Mesa." Hawk kept moving them forward, stepping cautiously. "*When the floodwaters flow* is a reference to the legend of how Tumbleweed was destroyed. That was the easy part."

"Have you figured out the hard part yet, or are we just out here making it up as we go?"

Hawk opened his mouth to answer, paused, then decided to say nothing. In a sense, he *was* making it up as he was going. Once he had enough of a clue or a trail to follow, he was ready to track it. He was willing to risk being wrong if he did make a mistake, but in most situations, he found another piece of the puzzle to keep him moving forward. He was guessing he knew just enough to stay on the right path.

Stepping over the red rock, they moved into Tumbleweed. The set was positioned where tracks passed nearby on both sides. The town featured a variety of details guests would easily miss as they blew past on the mine train. The silhouettes and shapes of people moving and dancing in the saloon now shined through the windows, a detail that could be seen only at night. A little hill and a quick turn meant that the guests would pass through Tumbleweed in a hurry.

Hawk pointed to a cart where a man stood bent over and bailing water with a bucket.

"That's Cumulus Isobar. See his name on his wagon?" he said over his shoulder, steadying Kate to make sure she didn't fall. "*Under the pressure of clouds on your quest you will go*. His name is the answer. *Cumulus* is, of course, a type of cloud."

"Of course." She stumbled, and Hawk tightened his grip on her hand.

"*Isobar* is a measure of barometric pressure. So under the pressure of this cloud on our quest we go. I'm guessing that the next thing we're looking for is in that wagon. If it is, this has probably been our easiest clue yet.

"Yep, that is just what I was thinking." Kate caught up to him. "How much easier could this clue be?"

Hawk looked at her and laughed and then crawled into the cart past Cumulus Isobar, the rainmaker. Inside, he found the package, wrapped like the others, lying on the floor of the wagon. He retrieved it, crawled back out of the wagon, and waved it toward Kate.

"You want me to throw this one at you too?"

"No, just hand this one over," she said.

Kate took the package and waited for him to jump down from the wagon. They moved back to the old abandoned storefronts and had a seat. He nodded at Kate, who began to unwrap the package. As she was untwisting the cloth, Hawk's phone rang. This time the caller ID read Nancy.

"Hi, Nancy."

"Hawk, I am going to go home for the day, if that's OK, sir."

"Sure." He glanced at his watch. "Why did you stay so late?"

"It's been pretty crazy with things happening in the parks, *Total Access*, the extra activity going on around here. I just wanted to stay in case you needed something."

"I appreciate that, Nancy." Hawk knew that most of any information she had, she picked up in passing. After her years of working with Rales, her transition to working with Hawk had been easy in most ways, with the exception of this layer of secrecy that had been unfolding.

"I also talked with Juliette. She said Tim and the kids are getting better. She'll try to see you sometime tomorrow. Jonathan's wife said he still was no better. She was going to have drag him back to the doctor, although he didn't want to go. I didn't get in touch with Reginald."

"I talked with him," Hawk interrupted.

"Very well," she continued. "And Shep wanted me to remind you that he had a meeting tonight and would be out of pocket all evening."

"OK. Thanks, Nancy. Go home and have a good night."

He hung up the phone, noticing peripherally that Kate had unwrapped the next western figurine. This one was a saloon girl, attired in a frilly dress with her hands on her hips.

"Something wrong?" Kate asked.

"I don't know. Nancy said that Shep had a meeting and would be unavailable. I just don't remember him telling me he wasn't going to be around."

"You've been a little preoccupied, don't you think?"

"I guess, but it's just a little odd that while I'm out on this dangerous treasure hunt, all the people who are close to me are unavailable to help."

"I'm helping you." She tilted her head. "Aren't I?"

"Yes. That's not what I'm talking about." Clouds of concern formed in his mind. "At the break-in, none of them hinted that they wouldn't be around. They know what the stakes are and what we're doing."

"Are you worried about them?"

"Last time, Juliette was kidnapped. And this time, there's no one at all around. It's weird, that's all."

"But is everyone accounted for?" Her concern showed in her eyes and her voice.

"Yes, everyone is accounted for, no one is missing . . . They're all just busy or not feeling well."

"So what do you want to do?"

"Nothing . . . yet." He looked toward the saloon girl figurine. "We've added another to the collection."

Kate turned it over, and like before, there was a collectible pin attached. The priceless work of art released the pin with a gentle tug, and Kate held it in her hand. The Donald Duck pin was intricate and detailed just like the others. Spinning it around, she displayed the QR code attached to the back. Hawk already had his phone out and was touching the screen. He scanned the code. After the usual few seconds of processing, the old film appeared on screen. Hawk tilted it so they could both see, and the image of George Colmes began talking directly to the camera. He was still in motion, the background a blur behind him, but this time Hawk noticed a familiar landmark, a post that passed behind George in a wave of motion, and then the camera jumped unsteadily.

George spoke. "Don't let this clue throw you off track. This light on the water will show you the way . . . but beware the dog and the gators . . . don't let them swamp you as you search . . . " The screen went black. After a few seconds, Hawk rose to his feet, then helped Kate to hers. Wordlessly, he motioned for her to join him. They retraced the treacherous pathway back toward where they had entered, and upon rounding the corner, he heard the crowd waiting in line once again clamor for their attention.

Kate again acknowledged the crowd with a wave. Raising an arm toward Neil, Hawk swirled his hand in a circle, giving the signal to crank up the ride. His watch told him they had shut the attraction down for only thirteen minutes. They pushed through the gate, back into the streets of Frontierland.

 *Day Four*
Night

"**IS THIS DANGEROUS?**" Kate asked, as she and Hawk crept along the train tracks.

The ground was sloped, and occasionally she would bump into him or he into her as they walked along the edge of the railroad tracks circling the Magic Kingdom. They had emerged from Big Thunder Mountain Railroad and now headed back to the Frontierland Train Station. It was extremely dark in some sections of the walk, and then an occasional light would shine through. As they walked past the opening that gave train riders a chance to glimpse the mine cars of Big Thunder Mountain Railroad, they were able to look back across at the expertly crafted scene of the town of Tumbleweed, where they had just been.

"Only if a train comes by." Hawk turned to see if she was really concerned or just wanting to talk.

"I figure you already have this next clue figured out?"

"I'm working on it, but I have an idea."

"Do you know as much about other things as you do about Disney?"

"Probably not. I am such a huge Disney fan. Have been for as long as I can remember. I listen to podcasts, I read the books, I notice and explore the details. I did all of that long before Farren Rales ever turned my life upside down." He smiled at the memories. "The Disney parks are the greatest places to spend time."

"I will say, to be honest with you . . . I have never had a trip to Walt Disney World like this one." Kate shook her head. "Or had a trip this fascinating and confusing."

"Well then, we won't be asking you for a celebrity endorsement, will we? Come to Walt Disney World for the most fascinating and confusing time of your life!"

They both laughed but were interrupted by the sound of Kate's cell phone ringing. She answered it, and Hawk could hear only her half of the exchange.

"This is Kate . . . Oh, hi, Allie . . . Really? Tell me more."

Hawk saw Kate's expression grow dark. Her eyes narrowed.

"That is interesting. . . . No, I don't know anything about it."

Kate now cut her eyes toward Hawk. He saw them flash with anger as they met his.

"The answer is no . . . There is no way under the stars we are going to that, and I don't care what they threaten . . . We can let the one segment go viral online."

Hawk felt his insides crumble and sink to the pit of his stomach. He didn't know what she was hearing, but it wasn't good. The way she was looking at him made him feel guilty, but he wasn't sure what he might have done.

Kate stopped, her voice snapping, emphasizing each point with her hands, although the person on the other end of the call would never see.

"You make sure it's locked away . . . No one sees it, no one touches it. Got it? Thanks, Allie." Kate ended the call and remained in place with her eyes closed. When she opened them, her gaze was burning.

He thought he'd start with the obvious. "Something is wrong."

"*Total Access* just got an interesting call."

"A call?"

"Yes." Kate placed her hands on her hips. "The call was from the Walt Disney Company, requesting we turn over all of the footage we've taken of you during our stay here. Since we are no longer going to complete the project we came here under contract negotiations to do, we are not allowed to use any of the footage we have taken. That would include the cemetery footage, the footage of you in Pirates of the Caribbean, and the interview footage."

"That's . . . interesting."

"Is that all you have for me? That's *interesting*?" Kate's words sliced at him with a sharp edge.

"You think I know something about this?"

"You're the head of the company."

"But you've been with me—I've been running around with you. I didn't place the call."

"Of course you didn't do it yourself." She stepped toward him, invading his personal space. "I did what you asked me to do." Her voice was shaking slightly. "I lived up to what I promised. Together we were supposed to decide how to tell the story. But that does not mean I am turning over the footage I have so that your company can lock me out of my story or try to renegotiate our deal later."

"Calm down. Who did the call come from?" he asked.

"I don't know. Allie didn't say. It came from your staff." Standing this close to her, he could see a vein on the side of her neck twitch with her rage.

"Kate, I'm sure this is some mistake or some formality." Hawk held up his hands. "It probably came from Reginald's office. He's not up to speed on what we're doing and what we have agreed on. Your deal with Farren is an agreement we will honor. To be honest, I haven't figured out how yet. But like you, I'm willing to work it out. It's a mistake. Keep the footage, hang on to it. We don't want it."

They stood there facing each other in the darkness. Hawk could see her chin held high, hear her breathing, and tension radiated from her. He understood but had no idea who might have placed the call or why it had been placed. Normally, Juliette would be the point person for matters like this, but she wouldn't have placed the call without covering it with him first. In the clash of Kate's anger and his confusion, he wanted to reassure her.

"I've already told you to keep the footage. I will get it straightened out later. Alright?" Hawk waited, but Kate remained silent.

He saw her body grow slightly less rigid, and she relaxed. She nodded her agreement and then waved her hand for him to continue along the tracks. Walking side by side, they covered ground at a fairly brisk pace. The uneven terrain slowed them more than he had hoped, but eventually they wound past the edge of Monument Valley, then entered the curve that took the train along the outside of the Rivers of America. After a few minutes of walking in silence and trying to concentrate on their footing in the dark, they moved away from the tracks a few feet to nudge closer to the tree line.

"So what did the key that Walt Disney sent you unlock?"

He knew he needed to answer carefully. "Kate, it was similar to what we're doing right now. It sent me on a search for a number of things. When it was all done, I had to take all the pieces I had found and learned, and then I had the resources I needed to figure everything out."

"What was the *everything* that you figured out?" Kate tossed the question that Farren had deferred to let Hawk answer.

"I discovered," Hawk answered slowly and methodically, "the deepest, the most important, and the most private secrets of Walt Disney, of Roy Disney, and of their vision for the company."

"Like what?"

"That is where it gets tricky." Hawk felt obligated under Kate's relentless gaze to offer her as much of the truth as he could risk giving. "I am leading while unpacking what I have learned and discovered a little bit at a time. So eventually what I have learned, everyone will find out. Does that make sense?"

"I suppose." She continued to watch him, riveted. "That's just not very . . . satisfying."

"For a reporter, I guess it isn't. But don't take it personally." Hawk chuckled. "The thing is, the people so intent on taking control, whoever they are, don't even know what they are trying to take or how to use it if they get it. And now we are trying to unlock what never was, to protect what is yet to be."

"And what exactly does that phrase mean?"

"That is what we are trying to figure out, Ms. Young. . . . And when we do, then and only then will we understand."

Coming to an opening in the trees, they looked down to their right and saw the Rivers of America, the waterway that surrounded Tom Sawyer's Island, which, in the daytime, was full of tourists. Closing at dusk, the river was quiet, and the activity around it was calm. Hawk turned to his right and began making his way down to the water, and they drew closer to the back of a wooden cabin. Visible from the train and from the *Liberty Belle* steamboat that circled the river each day, this cabin had been viewed by guests for years. Sensing Kate dropping back behind him, Hawk turned and looked back up the hill toward her.

"Everything alright, Kate?" he whispered, although he didn't know why.

"I saw someone sitting there." She pointed toward the cabin. "On the other side, on the porch, by the water."

"It's OK, he's expecting us."

"What?"

Hawk held out his hand for Kate to keep making her way down the hill. Carefully finding her footing, she made it to where he was waiting and clasped his outstretched hand. Together they moved over the grass that was growing damp and slick in the evening air. The breeze off the river blew cool and sent a shiver over them both. Reaching the back of the cabin, they walked around to where the man sat motionless in a chair. Once they moved to the side, they both had a good view of the white-haired man in the chair, and Hawk smiled as Kate saw he was not real.

"Kate, I'd like you to meet Joe." Hawk made the formal introduction. "And Joe, I'd like you to meet Kate." Then Hawk leaned into the life-sized figure sitting on the porch and added, "But I wouldn't talk to her too much— she's a reporter. My advice would be to say nothing." He smiled, pleased with himself.

"You are not as cute as you might think," she scolded. "And we are here because this is part of the clue, right?"

"It is. This old guy here has been sitting on this cabin porch forever. As a matter of fact, his face can be seen here at Walt Disney World in Pirates of the Caribbean and the Haunted Mansion. But George said, '*Don't let this clue throw you off track.*' That is what caught my attention—the *off track* is a reference to the train track. The clue didn't throw us *off track*, he drew us *off track*. It means the train track, which is right there." He pointed up the hill to where the track ran past them.

"Then George said, '*The light on the water will show you the way*,'" Kate added. "Hawk, there are no lights out here. As a matter of fact, it's so dark, we've been stumbling around."

"But you're wrong. There is a *light on the water*." He was impressed she remembered the second part of the clue so exactly. "The figure has a name. His name is Beacon Joe. A beacon of *light on the water will show you the way*."

"OK." She stepped up closer to Hawk as they looked at Beacon Joe.

"*But beware the dogs and the gators . . . don't let them swamp you as you search . . .* The rest of the clue is right in front of us." He pointed to their left, where a display portrayed a dog standing in a boat, catching fish as they jumped past. "His name is Rufus."

"I didn't even notice the dog."

"The rest is right here." He pointed to the sign on the shack itself. It read *Alligator Swamp*. "The swamp and the gator would be right there, wouldn't they?"

"So the clue must be . . ."

"Inside the swamp shack," Hawk said, as he opened the door and stepped into the dark interior of the shack.

 *Day Four*
Night

**HAWK STEPPED OUT OF THE SHACK,** holding another burlap-wrapped package in his hand like a conquering hero would raise a sword. Kate clapped her hands together without actually allowing them to touch, and he laughed at her overdramatic silent celebration. Hawk immediately held out what he already knew must be another priceless figurine, to allow Kate to unwrap it.

The voice from the side of the shack sounded like a rifle firing in the blackness of the forest. "Give me that package and the one you have tucked in your belt, if you wouldn't mind."

Out of the darkness emerged a man dressed in the now-familiar presidential mask that Hawk had first seen outside the Hall of Presidents. Stepping onto the porch, he stood at the edge of the shack with his hand outstretched, waiting for Hawk to pass him the discovery. Hawk smiled and, with a shake of his head, took a step back. Hearing a sound of struggle behind him, he turned and saw another man in black, face covered in dark mask, grab Kate from behind and lift her off the ground. With her arms pinned behind her, she was securely held in place. Fear flashed in her eyes.

"As I said, give me the package, or . . . well, let's not talk about what will happen. Both of you could so easily have a tragic accident, but this doesn't have to become a tragic kingdom for either of you." The masked figure gestured for Hawk to comply. "It would have been so much easier if you would have just given me the key when I warned you. Trust me, you will not only give me what you have found, but you will give me the key as well. Let's start with the package . . . Now."

The train whistle blew in the distance as the train pulled out of Frontierland Station.

"Perfect timing," the masked figure said in a muffled voice. "When the train passes and the whistle blows, no one will hear Kate Young scream." He stepped closer to Hawk. "It doesn't have to be that way though. Just give me the package."

Grayson Hawkes once again was facing what he dreaded the most. Someone he cared about was now in harm's way because of him. Whoever this enemy was, he was good, *but not good enough.* There was no way Hawk was going to lose the kingdom or the girl—not here, not tonight, and not this way.

Hawk held out the newly found package toward the man, who reached out to take it. In the same way children play practical jokes with one another, he drew the package back just before the masked man could close his hand around it. Hawk snickered, and the man in the mask raised his head from the package to look back at him.

"Kate, run!" Hawk yelled as he spun toward Kate and her captor. He sent a right hook whistling through the air, narrowly missing Kate's face. His fist flew over her shoulder and buried itself to the knuckles in the mouth of the man who had pinned her arms. The captor's head snapped back, and he released her arms instantly.

Raising her foot, she sent a spiked heel crashing downward, on the top of the man's foot as he stumbled away, causing him to cry out in pain.

Kate was now loose, and Hawk lunged toward the man in the Jimmy Carter caricature mask. In one fluid motion, Hawk spun and jumped into the air, throwing an elbow that caught the man in the jaw.

The man snarled and kept coming.

Hawk aimed low, sending a shattering blow into the man's midsection. The recoil was instant, and the man groaned, staggered backward, then fell off the porch into the water.

Not waiting to see what happened next, Hawk took two quick steps around Beacon Joe and then past the other assailant, who was crumpled on the ground and holding his foot. The man reached out in a halfhearted attempt to trip Hawk, but the CCA hurtled over the man's arm as it swiped past him.

He headed up the hill toward the tracks behind Kate. She was struggling, and one of her shoes had fallen off.

"Faster," Hawk urged her.

"Take my shoes." She kicked off the other one to run barefoot over the wet grass up the hillside.

Hawk grabbed both shoes as he passed them and scrambled to catch up with her. She was able to run faster now, and the train was thundering around the corner as they drew closer to the tracks. The engine passed them, and the passengers in the nearly empty cars were startled to see two people heading toward them from the river.

"The train, Kate, get on the train."

As she arrived at the crest of the hill, she began to run parallel with the train. Hawk was behind her, giving pursuit. He could see Kate was having trouble reaching out to grab the bar of the passenger car to pull herself in. He increased his speed and sprinted past her toward the moving train. Reaching out, he grabbed the bar, leaped aboard the train, tossed the wrapped package and her shoes onto the empty seat, and swung around. He held the bar with one hand while extending his opposite hand toward her. She grabbed it and ran a few steps alongside him.

"Jump!"

She closed her eyes and jumped toward him. He heaved against the speed of the train and pulled her up and into him. As their bodies collided, she embraced him, and together they fell back onto the seat in a heap. A voice crackled through the speakers above them in the car.

"For your own safety, please remain seated at all times when the train is in motion. Please keep your hands, arms, and legs safely inside the passenger compartment."

Through heavy breaths, she whispered, "You sure are some tour guide, Grayson Hawkes."

The train whistle screamed, as the locomotive chugged around the corner toward Tomorrowland.

 *Day Four*
Night

**THE TRAIN MADE ITS LOOP** and steamed back to the Train Station in Town Square. This had been the final trip of the night, and the pair waited for everyone else to leave and head down the exit ramp. As guests disembarked, they strained to catch a glimpse of the two who had run alongside the train and jumped aboard, along the shore of the Rivers of America, like a scene out of an old western movie. The gawking lasted only a moment or two, as Hawk and Kate kept their seat and waited for everyone to leave.

The conductor stepped up and told them it was time to go, then recognized the leader of the company.

"Hawk, or Mr. Hawk, sir . . . that was quite a way to get on board the train." The conductor nervously thrust his hand toward him. "Are you OK? Are either one of you hurt?"

Hawk shook the man's hand. "I think we're fine, thanks for asking."

"I've never seen nothing like that before, been here a lot of years, but that was a first." The conductor tilted back his hat. "You two sure you're OK?"

"We're good." Hawk stood to exit. "We're going into the station for a few minutes to take a look around. You have a great night, and thanks for doing such a good job here."

It was the time of night when guests started leaving the park, and a steady stream of people was flowing through the traffic tunnels below the train station. Now that the train was shut down for the night, the station would be empty and locked. Using the key to the kingdom, Hawk unlocked the door and opened it for Kate. She strode past him, and with a quick look from side to side, he checked to see if there was anyone watching them. All appeared quiet on the train exit platform where they had entered through the back door of the train station.

Kate moved across the station, found a wooden bench, and crumbled onto it. Hawk could see she was tired and still shaken from the encounter on the dock at Beacon Joe's shack. He handed her the still-wrapped discovery, and she silently began to unwind the wrapping from the figurine. This work of art was of a cowboy with his six-shooter raised up into the air in celebration. Hawk barely gave the priceless long-lost figure a second glance, as he waited for Kate to find and pull off what he knew was the last collectible pin.

The black box had space for five pins. He had found four, and this would now be the fifth. As Kate pulled it away from the figure and held it between her fingers, Hawk saw it was Pluto. The five pins they had found were of the Fab Five; Mickey, Minnie, Goofy, Donald, and Pluto. The classic anchor characters of the company. All characters that Walt had input into creating, even giving voice to Mickey Mouse in the early years. He now had completed the pin collection as the box was full. The question was, what was he supposed to do with them?

Using his phone to scan the QR code just as before, they connected to an old-film-style video that featured George riding something with a familiar, yet hard-to-discern, background blazing past him. Hawk studied it and saw support poles going past. Again he thought they were something he had seen before. Then the video went black with an eerie light casting shadows on George Colmes' face. His voice echoed as he went through some type of tunnel.

"Walt had a dream . . . a dream about tomorrow . . . a vision you can see . . . a vision as it was meant to be . . . a living blueprint of the future where people can actually live a life they can't find anyplace else in the world. . . . I can see the vision from here. . . . Go to it. . . . Find that vision. . . . Stick with it."

The video flashed, and the screen went to black. George was gone, and Hawk sat thinking about what they had just heard.

"He was talking about Epcot, wasn't he?" Kate turned on the bench toward Hawk. "All he was saying sounded like Epcot."

"Yes, it did, didn't it?"

"But where at Epcot? Last time I checked, it's a pretty big place." She slid to the edge of the bench like she was ready to go there immediately.

Hawk got out the black box and carefully placed the final pin of the collection into place. After he closed the box, he held it up and thought carefully before he spoke.

"We now have this set of pins and a clue that is about Epcot . . . and that is all we have to go forward with." Hawk stared past her longer than was comfortable for either of them. "You're right. Epcot is a big place, and we didn't get a whole lot of information in that last clue."

"You mean to tell me you haven't figured this one out yet?"

"No, not yet. And you?" He tried to hide his angst because this clue had not yet clicked into place at all in his head. With a bit of direction, he could move forward, but she was indeed correct. Epcot was an awfully big place.

"Nope, but I am not the knower of all things Disney. That is you." Kate reached out and patted his arm. "By the way, thank you for not letting me drown in the Rivers of America back there."

"You're welcome. That was a little intense, wasn't it?"

"A little intense?" She laughed. "That's one way of putting it. Today I've seen you being chased up a tree, doing an insane limb-to-limb jump, hiding under a poncho, getting attacked on a dock, and jumping onto a moving train. I can't wait to see how you figure out this next clue and figure out how to help me tell this story."

"You're right, it has been a very busy day. And I can't wait to figure those things out either."

"So is your life always like this?" Kate eased back and crossed her arms. "Is there always someone trying to catch you, hurt you, take what you have?"

"Not always, but I guess in my life, just like in a great Disney story, there are heroes and villains. I'm just trying to be one of the good guys, doing what I was asked to do."

"By Walt?"

"And Farren."

"Hawk, I think they both would be very proud." She leaned toward him. "And today you have been very heroic. Thanks."

"You're welcome." Hawk got to his feet and held out his hand. "Now I need to get you back to your resort safely. I have to call Reginald and make sure they quit hounding you guys about turning over the film footage, and I have something to do yet tonight."

"And what would that be?"

"I'll tell you tomorrow, but for right now, it's safer if you don't know."

"So what's the plan?"

"I'd like to get my team together in the morning. I have to figure out how to understand this last clue. So, you'll be at my office in the morning?"

"Oh, am I a part of your team?"

"You are now." Hawk grinned.

Kate took his hand and got to her feet. "Are you asking me to be on the team, or are you telling me I'm on the team?"

"Are you always asking questions because you're curious or to be difficult?"

He headed toward the doors of the train station, with her next to him.

## CHAPTER FIFTY-THREE

## Day Five
## Morning

**MORNING BROKE SPECTACULARLY** over Central Florida. The coolness of the sky was lit by brilliant streaks of Florida sun. Grayson Hawkes had had a very short night. After making sure Kate Young had returned to the Contemporary safely, he had stashed the newly found figurines in the trunk of his car and hidden the collectible pin box where he believed no one would find it. In the early morning hours, he shuffled his way back into the Magic Kingdom to go home. The security team had finished looking over his apartment, and he had managed to kick enough things out the way to find his bed. After a quick shower and change of clothes, he headed to meet Farren and Reginald for breakfast at Downtown Disney.

As he drove toward the shopping resort, he formulated his strategy for the day. He would have Nancy get in touch with Juliette, Jonathan, and Shep; hopefully, he could get them all together this morning, including Kate. His intention was to go over the clues and findings with them, to see if they could help him determine where to search next and if they had any idea what George Colmes was trying to get him to find and why. Idling the car at the traffic light, Hawk quickly reviewed, for his own clarity of thought, the events of the past few days, just as he had eighteen months before.

He had doggedly tried to solve and find each piece of an Imagineers puzzle so he could have the prize, the prize that Walt Disney had wanted him to have. He was continually troubled by the ever-present group trying to stop him. He had always believed that they would create trouble, they would threaten, and they could cause great difficulty for him; but he'd thought there was a line they would never cross. Last night, when the two men met them at the shack and threatened Kate, much in the same way they had threatened Juliette months before, he knew he had once again underestimated his enemies. They were operating with a set of rules he did not yet understand.

Steering the car into the parking lot, he moved into the far right parking area and pulled to a stop next to an elevated security tower. Here, guards could watch over the parking lots during peak periods. He had asked Reginald to make sure this particular tower was manned even at this early hour. Getting out of his car, he glanced up and saw the cast member sitting inside, behind a tinted window. He wanted the guard to make sure the contents of his trunk stayed safe and that there was added security near him this morning. *Later, I'll need to call Al Gann as well.*

The Earl of Sandwich was a popular restaurant that served breakfast, lunch, and dinner in Downtown Disney. He cut past the front doors of the toy store where Buzz Lightyear greeted guests and saw that Reginald and Farren were waiting on him, seated at an outdoor table on the far right-hand side of the patio area. They had some privacy at that end of the dining area at this time of the morning. Reginald had balked at his selection of where to meet, and Farren loved the idea. Hawk personally just liked the food.

Farren greeted him with a wave and a smile. "Hawk, welcome. I ordered your sandwich and got you some coffee."

"Thank you. Good morning." Hawk slid out his chair. "Mornin', Reginald, how are you feeling? Any better yet?"

"I don't have time to be sick. But if I weren't feeling poorly already, I would be sick with worry over your antics in the park." Reginald took a deep sip of his black coffee. The steam off the liquid curled up around his nose as he drank.

Hawk took the next few minutes to make sure both Reginald and Farren knew what he had been doing and what he had found. He needed their help, their thoughts, and their input, so he wanted them to have all the information they needed to be successful. That was a leadership concept that always showed up as Hawk led and moved people forward. He wanted them to have what they needed to be successful. He had learned a long time ago the information may not be as much as they want, but it would be as much as they need. That is what he offered to Farren and Reginald.

When he finished giving them an overview of the day, he took a bite of his breakfast sandwich, giving them time to think about what they had heard. He swallowed, then spoke.

"Did you know that in 1762, John Montagu, the fourth Earl of Sandwich, was one busy guy? He was the First Sea Lord of the mighty British Navy. And he was a noted explorer, a patron of the arts, and a gambler who liked to take risks."

"I am sure there is a reason you are telling us this?" Reginald asked.

"There is." Hawk took another bite, chewed, and then swallowed. "The dude was too busy to eat. So he came up with the ingenious idea of putting meat between two slices of bread. From then on, it didn't matter if you were inspecting the fleet or laying down a royal flush—you could eat great food without too much fuss. Cool, huh?"

"The reason?" Reginald asked, as he took another sip.

"I have been running so crazy the last few days that I haven't had time to eat or think, and I've gotten very little sleep. I wanted you guys here to slow me down and help me make sure I'm not missing something." Hawk nodded at his friends, then added, "And to tell you that the sandwich was named after its inventor, the fourth Earl of Sandwich, in 1762. Just in case you didn't know."

Reginald frowned.

Farren laughed at Reginald's irritation and at Hawk's penchant for sharing trivia, both of which Hawk loved to do in a playful and respectful way. "Well, for not having had too much sleep, you are in rare form."

"Yes, that is what I want to talk about . . . your rare form." Reginald set his cup on the table and tapped his fingers on the surface. "You could have gotten killed yesterday in the very large tree you were jumping around in. Not to mention the two men who attempted to grab you—not once, but twice yesterday."

"What was I supposed to do, wait for you to get to feeling better before I went looking?"

"No, you were supposed to let the sheriff's department do the looking for you." Reginald did not change his expression.

"They would have needed me to figure it out—more obscure clues and Disney trivia references."

"But you found everything?" Farren clarified.

"Up to this point. I don't really know what else I'm looking for."

"Have you secured everything you've found?" Farren inquired.

"Safe and sound at the top of the world."

"Go over the last clue again with us."

"*Walt had a dream . . . a dream about tomorrow . . . a vision you can see . . . a vision as it was meant to be . . . a living blueprint of the future where people can actually live a life they can't find anyplace else in the world. . . . I can see the vision from here. . . . Go to it. . . . Find that vision. . . . Stick with it.*" Hawk repeated the clue exactly as George had said it on the film.

"That sounds like Epcot. The answer is in Epcot," Reginald stated.

"That's what it sounds like," Hawk affirmed.

"But where in Epcot?" Farren stared at his napkin and twirled it on the table as he thought.

"I have no idea." Hawk smiled. "I was hoping you might."

"Grayson," Reginald interrupted. "I think we have to take care of these intruders who are trying to take the company for themselves. They have gotten awfully close to you, and you have been fortunate to this point."

"What do you mean, take care of them?"

"I think—" Reginald coughed, which turned into another, and both men could see he was visibly in pain. Reginald clutched his chest and waited for the spasm to pass. "I say it is time to give them what they have asked for."

"You are not serious, are you?" Farren's mouth opened slightly.

"I am serious. I think it is the only way." Reginald looked across the dining area to see if anyone was paying extra attention to them. "However, giving them what they asked for and then giving them what they want may not be the same thing."

"I'm listening." Hawk leaned in closer.

"What was the signal they told you to give in the window of the Hall of Presidents?" Reginald looked toward Hawk.

"*One if by land, two if by sea, put out the lights and give us the key.* Then I'm supposed to wait in the Hall of Presidents."

"I propose that we honor their request. It is time to turn out the lights and tell them to come get the key." Reginald smiled slightly. "However, when you turn out the lights of Paul Revere, what they won't know is that we are going to have our own little revolution."

Hawk's eyes widened. "Keep talking."

"You will be there waiting for them to show themselves, but we will be there as well. We will apprehend them and be rid of them. Perhaps then you can finish solving your little Imagineer puzzle, and we can get back to normal around here."

 *Day Five*
Morning

**THE THREE MEN CONTINUED** their conversation around the break-fast table, as Reginald laid out his rough idea to spring a trap on the people who so desperately wanted the key. Hawk was to have the lanterns snuffed out, and then, as the park closed, make sure he was waiting in the darkened attraction. Reginald would station himself inside. Out of sight, he would strategically place additional security. Hawk would be the bait, luring the predators into their trap. It was simple in design and made sense to everyone around the table. It should work.

It was then that Reginald voiced a concern.

"What is troubling me is the ease with which these people have been able to find you."

"Ease?" Hawk leaned back.

"Yes, they seem to be able to find you as though they know where you are going and what you are doing. They have easy access in the parks, which means either they are insiders, like we have dealt with in the past, or they are not afraid of being caught, which is also troublesome. I fear . . ." Reginald slowed and lowered his voice. "Someone who has gotten close to you might be involved."

"What?' Hawk threw his head back and laughed. "You get in my face about solving this mystery, and you have your own conspiracy theory. Seriously?"

"Hold on a moment, my friend." Farren held out his hand toward Hawk to quiet him. "His thought has merit. What are you thinking, Reginald?"

"It appears to me that someone knows what you are going to do before you do it. Someone understands how you think, how you operate, how you do things . . . your inner circle."

"You have lost your mind." Hawk pushed back from the table, his voice rising more than he intended. "You really think someone close to me is try-ing to steal the key."

"Let's go through the inner circle, your Warriors of the Kingdom . . ." Reginald leaned in and spoke in hushed tones. "There are the three of us, Juliette, Tim, Jonathan, and Shep."

Hawk's jaw was set in stone as he listened. Farren reached over and gave him a reassuring pat on the back and nodded for him to keep listening.

"And is there anyone else that you have allowed access to your world recently?"

"Oh, come on." Hawk rolled his eyes. "You don't mean Kate, do you? I am not being duped by another mysterious lady that has entered my life. It couldn't happen again."

"Perhaps not." Reginald shut his mouth.

Silence settled over the remains of their breakfast. Farren looked at Hawk, then lowered his eyes to the table. Reginald allowed his gaze to move between both of them.

"I may have misjudged her and told her too much." Farren spoke softly. "I thought it was a safe thing to do, and eventually, we have to figure out ways to tell our story and answer the questions people have. I thought she could help us . . . help you."

"No." Hawk looked from Farren to Reginald. "You are wrong, Reginald. Kate is not playing me. It isn't happening again."

"I hope not," Reginald said. "But let me ask you, who set up this in-depth interview with the most well-known documentary team in the world?"

"Juliette." Hawk knew what he was implying. "Reginald, you are out of line. Not just a little out of line, you crossed the line a few minutes ago."

"Then let me finish, since the line seems to have been ignored." Reginald's eyes grew fierce. "These men who have chased you have not been faring so well in their encounters with you. They are finding you to be more resilient than they had thought. Where has Jonathan been the last few days?"

"This is nuts." Hawk shook his head. "Jonathan has been ill."

"Yes, I know, and while anyone can be ill, think about the evidence."

"What is your evidence? You've been ill too." Hawk attempted to derail his train of thought.

"You are correct, but if you remember, I was with you yesterday. It was you who insisted that I go home . . . much to my displeasure."

"Hawk, let him finish." Farren was riveted to Reginald's words.

"According to your accounts of what has happened, you head-butted your captor in the Hall of Presidents, and the next day we see Jonathan with a bandage on his head."

"He hit his head moving equipment," Hawk defended.

"Of course, but then you had your fight in the cemetery and cracked your attacker in the face with an elbow, I believe you said. Jonathan shows up with a visibly puffy and bloodshot eye . . . due to allergies." Reginald leaned forward and gripped the table. "Yesterday, his wife called in sick for him because he was congested and sick with something that gave him trouble breathing. But that could also be from getting slammed in a door at the Brown Derby."

"Now I suppose Shep is a suspect as well." Hawk felt his face growing warmer. "Tell me why *he* makes the most-wanted list."

"I am suggesting that there is something amiss. Shep is the one who figured out the picture, and you use him as your information source to help figure out clues. He would know where you are going and have an idea of when you will be there."

"And Tim? Is he out to get me as well?"

"It would be safe to assume that if Juliette were involved, he would be as well."

"Unbelievable. So tell me, Reginald, why? Why would all of my closest friends in the world turn against me?" Hawk again had to check the elevated tone in his voice.

"I did not say all of your friends have turned on you. I am suggesting that there is someone who may not be what he or she appears to be." Reginald took a deep breath. "You need to be alerted to the possibilities."

"Are you buying into this, Farren?" Hawk turned toward the Imagineer.

"The case is compelling. Someone has inside information as to how you are operating."

"Stop it!" Hawk pushed back from the table. "I have heard all I am going to listen to. Reginald, we'll set the trap tonight after the Magic Kingdom closes. I'll turn out the lanterns and see you there."

"Grayson," Reginald called after Hawk, as he stormed away from the table.

Hawk stopped, jaw clenched.

"I know you are angry with me. My role is to keep you safe." Reginald Cambridge looked away briefly, then brought his eyes back. "I hope I am wrong."

"You *are* wrong, and I will prove it tonight."

 *Day Five*
Morning

HAWK WAS FURIOUS, as he entered his office in the Bay Lake Towers. He had driven back and taken a long loop around the entire Disney property. He rumbled through his conversation with Reginald and Farren over and over again. He was convinced that the people closest to him were his friends. They had shared too much of life together. Reginald had become a conspiracy theorist, his dark assumptions putting a cloud over the people he loved and trusted. A preacher had once told Hawk a lesson he had often used and tried to live by— never doubt in darkness what you have seen in the light. He knew his friends were loyal and would never hurt him. But the one telling him these things was a friend as well. He trusted Reginald with his life. And another who was telling him to consider these things was his friend also. Farren was the one who had first started him on this adventure, and now he was telling him to listen to Reginald. All these thoughts pressed in, as he closed the door behind him.

Nancy wasn't at her desk, and the phone was ringing. Ignoring it, he went to the stairwell and bounded up the steps as he did each morning. His office door was open, and as he walked in, he saw there were people already inside waiting for him. Juliette stood just inside the door and she hugged him hard as he entered.

"We were so worried about you," she said, relief saturating her voice as she released him.

Shep made his way across the room and hugged him as well. "I was starting to get nervous when I couldn't get in touch with you."

"It sounds like you had quite an adventure last night." Juliette nodded toward Kate, who was seated on the sofa.

"I didn't tell them everything, but I think I hit the highlights." Kate looked at him closely. "Are you doing OK this morning?"

Hawk let his gaze move from person to person as he walked across the room and settled in behind his desk. After rubbing his temples and then his eyes, he looked back up.

"Where is Jonathan this morning?" Hawk asked no one in particular.

"He's still sick. Something has gotten ahold of him, from what it sounds like." Juliette looked concerned. "Nancy told me she talked to him this morning."

"I was going to have Nancy get you all together this morning," he said.

"That's what I told them," Kate said. "I came over after breakfast to see if you were in yet, and they were both here looking for you."

"What do you mean, looking for me?"

"We haven't been able to get in touch with you." Shep went back to his chair. "We called you off and on all day yesterday, to see where you were and what you were doing. Never could reach you."

"What are you talking about? You were out of touch yesterday. No one could find you."

"Huh? I was with Juliette and Tim part of the day, trying to figure out what you were doing since we couldn't reach you."

"Juliette, I thought you were taking care of your sick family." Hawk looked toward her.

"They had a twenty-four-hour bug, but they were all better yesterday." She rubbed the base of her neck and shrugged. "I must have called you twenty times."

"I heard you were still with your family and you were out." Hawk pointed toward Juliette and then to Shep. "And you were just unavailable. Kate can tell you I had my new phone with me all day yesterday. If you were calling, I would have answered."

"That's what we thought." Juliette came over as Hawk pulled his phone out of his pocket. "But we called and called, and you didn't answer. To be honest, we thought something had happened to you, and we were about to call Al if you weren't here. Then Kate came in and told us about some of your day."

"That doesn't make sense. Nancy got this new phone for me and told me that you were all out and unavailable."

Shep got out his phone, pressed a few buttons, and held it to his ear. Listening, he waited, then held it out like everyone should be able to hear it. "I just called you, Hawk, and the message said that you were not available, please leave a message."

Juliette took Hawk's phone. "But your phone didn't ring, Hawk." She touched the screen and scrolled through to find Shep's number on speed dial. Touching the screen, she called. Shep's phone began to ring.

Shep looked at his phone and held it up again so everyone could see the screen. "This is a different number. You have a new phone and a new number, Hawk."

"Well, that explains why you couldn't get in touch with him." Kate smiled with relief.

"So you never would have been able to reach me because you had the wrong number. Nancy didn't just get me a new phone, she got me a new number." Hawk scratched his head and got up from his seat.

He paced the room. His mind was whirring, trying to understand the information that he had just been given and to align it with what Reginald had been saying earlier. He stopped his pacing in the center of the room and turned to face them.

"But why did Nancy tell me that you were unavailable and that you were out sick?" Hawk looked to Shep and Juliette, who'd taken a seat.

"I don't know." Juliette crinkled her lips. "I don't remember talking to her yesterday."

"Come to think of it, I didn't either," Shep added.

"So Nancy intentionally told you they were not available and failed to give them your new number." Kate slid to the edge of the couch and was using her finger to connect dots in the air, her investigative instincts coming to life. "So there was no way they could find you, and she knew you wouldn't bother them. Nancy was trying to keep you out of touch with your friends yesterday."

Hawk pondered this, then looked to Juliette. "You said Nancy told you about Jonathan. She was here when you got here?"

Juliette nodded yes.

"Where did she go?"

"Don't know. She left when I came up here."

"She was gone when I arrived." Shep looked toward Juliette. "After I got here, Kate showed up."

Reginald hadn't listed Nancy in his conspiracy, but perhaps he should have. Forgetting to give out his new phone number would have been an uncharacteristic mistake, but understandable. Lying about his friends' not being available or out of communication seemed intentional—no matter how many ways he tried to explain it away in his head. Hawk locked eyes with Kate. She smiled at him and nodded as if she already knew what he was thinking.

"Have either of you actually talked to Jonathan? Do we know he really is sick?"

"I haven't," Shep popped back.

"Not me." Juliette slowed her speech. "Nancy is the one who told me he was sick."

Hawk felt his mouth go dry, as he opened his phone and called Jonathan's number. There was no answer, and his excitement ebbed. He left a message and said to call him back.

"So we don't really know that Jonathan is sick," Hawk said, "and he didn't answer his cell."

"Let me call Sally." Juliette was dialing Jonathan's wife. They watched as Juliette shook her head, indicating there was no answer.

"So none of you have heard from Jonathan?" Hawk asked. They shook their heads no. "Isn't that a little odd? He knows what has been going on. He knew what I was up to, saw my apartment, and he hasn't checked in with anyone for the last two days?"

"Do you think something has happened to him?" Shep asked.

"I don't know." Hawk's thoughts grew dark. His mind went back to the conspiracy that Reginald had suggested earlier. He had seen Jonathan with the bandaged head and the puffy eye. He'd thought when he saw his eye that it looked more like Jonathan had been slugged in a fight than having an allergic reaction. Jonathan would have checked in with someone if everything were normal. And if he were sick, someone would have answered the phone, because he would have been home.

Kate joined Hawk in the center of the room. "What are you thinking?"

Hawk looked at her, then at Juliette and Shep. He had to look away from them because he didn't want them to guess what he was thinking. He didn't want to think that Jonathan was involved in this. Cambridge had to be wrong. But there was something . . . something . . . that was just not right.

 *Day Five*
Night

HAWK HAD SPENT THE REST OF THE DAY pondering, trying to unwind the last clue George had left for him. He was unhappy with the pieces that were falling into place. Nancy had never returned to the office after she left in the morning. From all indications, she had misled him about his closest friends, leaving him to believe they were all unavailable and were not to be disturbed for various reasons. The new phone had made it impossible for his most trusted friends to reach him. No matter how many ways he tried to reason it away, he couldn't escape the fact that her deception seemed intentional.

Jonathan Carlson had been his friend for years. They had lived a lot of life together and had worked in ministry together for a long time. Hawk had been told he was sick, very sick, and struggling to get over whatever bug was plaguing him. But neither he nor his wife, Sally, were able to found. If he was so sick, then he should have been at home. Juliette had followed up by calling some of the local hospitals to make sure it had not been something far more serious, but they had all known that if Jonathan had really been that sick, one of them would have heard about it by now.

The conclusion Hawk was leaning toward was the one Cambridge had suggested. That conclusion was in conflict with what Hawk knew about his friend. He felt awful for thinking that Jonathan might be a part of a movement to steal away Walt's kingdom. Still, the evidence, although completely circumstantial, was bothering him. He tried to shove those thoughts of a friend deceiving him out of his mind.

Juliette and Shep had kept in close contact all day. They made that pact in the morning and were checking in on one another at regular intervals. Each one was on heightened alert, and their stress levels were through the roof. Months before, the search for the kingdom key had turned dangerous; now it appeared that, once again, the danger increased the more they knew and the closer they got to solving this puzzle. Hawk made the strategic decision not to tell them the clue he and Kate had received from George. Not because he didn't want them to know, and not really because Reginald had put them all under a dome of suspicion; the less they knew, the safer they were at this point.

Kate had been with him as he listened to the clue, and at lunch at the Columbia Harbour House in the Magic Kingdom, they talked about what it might mean. She came to the same conclusion that he, Reginald, and Farren had come to: the clue contained an Epcot reference. After they were done, he made sure that when evening arrived, the lanterns burning in the window over Liberty Square would not come on. This would be the signal that he was ready to put an end to the upheaval at the resort and give this group of invaders the key. Of course, he had no intention of really doing that. He and his friends would be setting a trap.

The afternoon was spent putting the pieces of the trap together. Once the Magic Kingdom was closed for the day, Hawk would move into the Hall of Presidents and wait. He was the bait, and although that didn't make him happy, he knew it was the best—and perhaps the only way—to flush out some of the villains. As soon as the attraction was closed for the day, other things began to happen as well. Clint Wayman, one of Reginald's top security men, dressed in a suit they had secured from costuming and took a seat on the stage with the audio-animatronic presidents. His role was to sit there and not move, to blend into the background, and when needed, spring to life to do whatever had to be done. Chuck Conrad was hidden along the edge of the stage, tucked away behind the massive curtain that covered the front of the performance area. Out of sight and out of the way, he could still hear everything that happened as Hawk waited in the front row of the theater for someone to show up. Reginald stationed himself across the street in Ye Olde Christmas Shoppe and kept a close eye on the building itself. His part was to move inside as soon as he saw anyone enter. To make it easier, they left all of the access doors across the front of the building unlocked.

Hawk took the plan a step beyond that, and Reginald agreed, seeing the value in it. Shep, Juliette, and Kate were all there as well. Hidden in alcoves in the lobby of the attraction, they would wait until something happened. Hawk was running under the principle that by keeping everyone close, they could all be there when the trap was sprung, and then would no longer be under suspicion of being involved. Hawk did this for Reginald as much as for himself. The longer the day had gone on, the surer he was sure his paranoid thoughts were more suggestions from a concerned Cambridge and Rales than founded in fact. The only one who would not be there was Jonathan. The last call to Jon had been made just before they moved into position. Both he and his wife once again had not picked up their phones.

Hawk waited in Ye Olde Christmas Shoppe with Reginald until the streets cleared. The lights were extinguished in the window, and they watched each of their team move into place. With a pat on the back, Cambridge told Hawk it was time.

He stepped out the door and paused under the Liberty Tree. Hawk then moved across the street and opened the front door to the Hall of Presidents. As he walked through the lobby, he traced the room with his eyes and spotted Shep, wearing black as they all were, standing to the right side of the lobby. Close to him was Juliette, also disappearing into the background of the room. Getting closer to the door, he saw Kate standing along the wall, shielded by a pillar, and watching him as he moved. She nodded to him slightly as he passed and entered the auditorium.

The huge theater was cavernous and, in the dark, looked even bigger than when it was operating in the daytime. He could not see where Chuck was hidden but knew he was inside, having watched him come into the building. Clint was onstage, motionless and blending in, seated among the presidents, who now all seemed to be standing watch over the scene that would play out in the moments ahead.

Making his way to the front, Hawk eased along the plush carpet flooring and took his seat front row center. The soft chair welcomed him, and he slouched into it, allowing himself the chance to relax. He didn't know how long he would have to wait and had no idea what was about to happen. But he was confident that this plan was going to work.

The silence of the theater swallowed him, and he again looked to the stage and saw Clint still seated there. He glanced toward the curtain, where he knew he would see nothing but also knew Chuck was back there, listening. He ran the clues George had given him over in his head, then focused his mind on the final clue to see if he could determine where to go to find the answers in Epcot.

He did not have the key with him. The key he had in his pocket was a key ring he'd picked up in a Disney gift shop. It looked like an old key with an iconic Mickey Mouse-shaped end, from which the bar of the key extended as a normal key would. If push came to shove, he would offer this key to whomever needed it. The real key was tucked away with the collectible pins in the black box. He had no concept as to what purpose the pins played in finally solving the puzzle but knew they had a place to be sure. The figurines had been moved in the afternoon and were now tucked away in his secret bunker below the theme park. In spite of Farren's warning, this now seemed like the safest place. These priceless works of art from an unfulfilled vision now were perched on a shelf, safe and secure.

The minutes slowly ticked away, and Hawk became restless. He got up from his seat and paced along the carpeted floor. He stretched, to kill a few seconds. His mind kept drifting back to his friend Jonathan and how he might be something he had not appeared to be. Hawk pushed this aside again, then immediately the suspicion Reginald had presented to him came back again. After he had head-butted his captor in the Hall of Presidents days ago, Jonathan had shown up with a bandaged forehead. After Hawk had escaped the attack in the cemetery by blasting his attacker with an elbow to the side of the head, Jonathan had shown up with a puffed-up eye like he'd been in a fight. The report they had that Jonathan was having congestion issues and trouble breathing after Hawk had slammed his assailant in the door of the Brown Derby fit as well, although the source of the last report was now suspicious herself: Nancy Alport. He wished he could have reached Jonathan and found out what was really going on.

He walked back to his seat and sat down again. This would be the place where it would all unfold. He was ready, he was tense, and he was aching to find out who was behind this. He knew everyone else would be getting as anxious as he was, and he was positive that Reginald was ready to charge the moment anything happened.

A stream of thought trickled across the jumbled rocks of his confusion. Hawk suddenly blinked in the darkness like something had flown into his eye.

Reginald Cambridge's behavior was just as suspicious as everyone else's, although earlier in the day, Hawk had dismissed the thought because he had been the one who insisted Reginald go home. Reginald had shown up after the head-butting incident in this attraction, and he'd been complaining of a headache. Hawk had thought there was something familiar about the voice, but it had been muffled by the ridiculous rubber costume mask.

The day after the cemetery clash, Reginald had been complaining about a toothache—but why couldn't the sore jaw have been caused by the elbow Hawk used to punish his attacker? When he had trapped his pursuer in the slamming door at the Brown Derby, Hawk had known he had done some damage. With his heightened adrenaline and anxiousness, that door had slammed hard enough to break a few ribs. When Hawk had met Reginald the next day, he had wanted to call the medical team to come and have a look, since the complaints had been of chest pain and breathing trouble. Reginald had been insistent on that not happening and then had done the unthinkable . . . he had actually done what Hawk suggested and gone home.

If the medical team had been allowed to check him out, Hawk thought, they would have determined right away that this illness was not a cold, congestion, or worse. It would have been broken ribs. Last night, when Hawk had again hit his attacker with a blow to the chest that sent him into the water, he felt the man crumble easily. He was already injured. Today, Reginald had been far worse and was coughing even more. Broken ribs and an unexpected splashdown in the water could have caused that.

Hawk leaned forward in his chair and took his phone out of his pocket. He quickly went through his call log. He stared at the call from Reginald last night. How had Cambridge known the correct number when everyone else had not? Thinking back over their conversation, he recalled Reginald mentioning to Hawk that it had been Hawk who insisted Reginald go home. He had said the same thing at breakfast this morning when Hawk turned the spotlight of suspicion toward him. Why was Reginald so intent on making sure Hawk owned the responsibility for his absence?

He leaped up and paced lines into the carpet in front of the seats. His mind was whirring with thoughts that were cutting into his conscience and making him disgusted at each thought that sliced through him. Disgusted that he was even thinking it, but more disgusted that it made sense.

Suddenly, one more thought collapsed across his brain, and Hawk stopped. At breakfast, Farren had asked if Hawk had secured everything he had found, and Hawk had replied, "Safe and sound at the top of the world." Reginald had heard him. Reginald knew where the box of pins and the key were hidden. Spinning around toward the stage, Hawk threw a glance toward Clint that caused him to break character and move.

"Everything alright?" Clint called.

"No, nothing is alright." Hawk snorted, as he pulled out his cell phone and dialed Reginald's number. The call went directly to voice mail.

"What's up?" Chuck pulled back the curtain at the sound of the activity on the main floor of the auditorium.

"Nothing. There is nothing happening because there is no one coming." Hawk ran toward the entrance of the theater.

He busted through the doors with such force that the doors themselves sounded like a cannon shot when they hit the doorstops. Juliette, Shep, and Kate met Hawk as he burst into the lobby.

"What happened?" Kate anxiously looked around, then glanced back into the theater.

"Nothing. There's no one coming."

"How do you know?" Juliette fell in step with Hawk as he hurried through the lobby.

"Because we have been set up!" Hawk turned to face them. "All of us."

"What do you mean all of us?" Shep shook his head. "By who?"

"Reginald." The name boomed from his mouth, shattering their expressions the way a bomb's explosion destroys a landscape. "He tried to convince me that each of you was trying to steal the key, but in reality, the one in charge of this conspiracy to steal the kingdom is him."

"Where are you going?" Juliette asked, as they reached the exit doors.

"To get Cambridge. He knows where I hid the pins and the key. Shep, go across to Ye Olde Christmas Shoppe, just to be sure he isn't there anymore. I'm guessing he left as soon as we went inside."

Shep raced across the street, while Hawk continued to unleash the things that had clicked in his mind. "Juliette, find Jonathan. Do whatever it takes. Reginald created a very convincing argument that Jonathan was trying to steal the key. Find him."

"He's gone," Shep yelled from across the street.

"I knew it."

"How does he know where the black box is?" Kate's voice was calm but intense, like she was on the verge of uncovering a mind-numbing news story.

"I told him." Hawk sneered. "Not on purpose, but I know he figured it out."

"I'm going with you." Kate stepped closer, as tense as a boxer just before the bell rings.

Juliette pulled out her phone as they crossed the bridge back into the Central Plaza Hub. "I'm going to call Al Gann and tell him what you just said. Do you know where Reginald is?"

"Spaceship Earth at Epcot." Hawk broke into a run, with Kate close behind.

 *Day Five*
Night

HAWK CLAMPED HIS JAW, his gaze drilling into the darkness as he nailed the accelerator of his car. The Mustang streaked between the attendant booths and through the parking gates of Epcot so fast Kate recoiled in the passenger seat. Kate looked toward him but said nothing. Swinging the car through the turns into the parking areas, Hawk was heading right toward the main gate. Looming in front of them were the monorail station, the ticket booths, and Spaceship Earth.

"You probably need to slow down," Kate suggested, gripping the dashboard.

Still silent, he continued to race toward the end of the road. In moments, they would be crashing over the sidewalk into the guest areas where each day, thousands entered the amazing theme park. Stomping on the brake, he cut the wheel to the side. Drawing on the skills he'd learned from the Richard Petty Driving Experience, he kept a steady calm in vehicular chaos.

Smoke trailed from the tires, and the squeal of rubber on asphalt split the night air as Hawk guided the car's controlled skid, then slid to a stop and threw open the doors. The interior dome light burst the darkness, and Hawk jumped out onto the sidewalk. Kate followed suit, chasing him as he sailed over a turnstile. When he'd landed on the other side, he turned back toward her, helped her over, then snapped his attention back toward Spaceship Earth.

They ran toward the massive geodesic dome. The iconic structure is just as recognizable as Cinderella Castle and instantly known by people all over the planet; 11,324 individual triangular panels made of an aluminum alloy, each one custom fit, form the outer sphere. The attraction inside takes guests through the passageway of time, eventually ending up at the top of the domed roof, where the ride vehicles spin and passengers make their descent back to the ground by traveling backward. The ride is not thrilling, but its use of technology, audio-animatronics, music, and great narrative storytelling make it a classic in the truest sense of the word.

"We get in through the side door." Hawk pointed to a door, as they ran to the left side of the massive ball.

"How do you know Cambridge is here?" Kate asked, as Hawk opened the door.

"I inadvertently told him. He heard me tell Farren I had hidden what we had found at the top of the world."

"Nice move."

They stepped inside, then through another door, and began traveling up a flight of steps. Those steps ended at a landing that gave them the choice of moving off in one of two directions. Hawk paused at the top and thought about which path to use.

"This backstage network of hidden corridors is tricky. The shape of the building makes it impossible to figure out, if you aren't used to it. Sometimes cast members will draw along the walls with pencil, leaving a trail so they don't get lost." He pointed to a random pattern of hand-drawn lines along the wall.

"Isn't the top of the world what they call the top floor of the Bay Lake Towers?" Kate waited as he spoke.

"It is, and it used to be what we called the 'restaurant at the top of the Contemporary,' but we always refer to Spaceship Earth as the world when we talk. On the other side of the world, to the right-hand side of the world, and stuff like that. When the attraction breaks down, we say the world has stopped moving, or if you want to get out of the rain, you go stand under the world . . . . "

Hawk chose to go right. "So Cambridge knows it's hidden at the top of the world."

"When you say the top of the world, do you really mean at *the* top of the world?"

Hawk glanced back at her and nodded, then continued his winding, confusing, and steady ascent around the perplexing backstage corridors of Spaceship Earth.

Kate raised her fingers to trace the lines on the wall. "Like trails of bread crumbs," she said, drawing closer to him as she followed.

They reached another fork in the passageways, and this time, without hesitation, Hawk plunged to the left.

"When we get to the top, near the tunnel where the ride cars travel, you'll see a scissor lift platform. It's real old and has been here ever since Epcot was built. It's just beyond the edge of the central core of the sphere. It was used years ago in a commercial to get Mickey Mouse up on the top of the sphere. It's very unstable, but it wasn't practical to move it, and no one is ever up near it."

He pointed, and they changed their angle and kept going up. They were nearing the top of the dome. "I made sure it was working. Spaceship earth is really two spheres. There's an inner sphere that's covered in a thick rubber blanket for protection. Then there's a small gap of a couple of feet between that and the outer aluminum sphere."

"OK, all of that is good to know . . . and why do I need to know it?"

"Because there's a hatch at the very top of this structure, big enough for a person to crawl through—like the hatch on a submarine. You open it, then a few feet later, there's another hatch you open and you are literally on top of Spaceship Earth."

"Like outside on top?"

"Yes." Hawk stopped. "I hid the box of pins and the key on the very top of the sphere. I knew it was the safest place. No one would ever look there, and most people couldn't figure out how to get there if they knew."

"And you think Cambridge knows how to get up here?" Kate asked, breathing more heavily as the angle of the walkway steepened.

"I know so." Hawk paused and pointed, as they rounded the curve past a tunnel where the guests would ride in the vehicles.

The scissor lift was extended up, its platform sitting empty below an open hatch. The sight was terrifying, even for Hawk. The old lift was not mechanized, and from the platform he would have to use the hand crank to raise and lower it. The extensions off each leg had been deployed to steady it, but even at that, it looked very fragile stretched up into the top of the dome.

Hawk grabbed the metal bar at the base of the lift and pulled himself into the zigzagged cross pieces of the lift mechanism.

"What are you doing? Are you going to climb it?" Kate sounded stunned.

"Yep, you wait down here. I'll toss the pins down to you."

"No, no, no. Wait for Cambridge to find the pins. He has to come back down the lift. We'll get them from him when he gets back down."

"No, he won't come down with them." Hawk pulled up to the next cross piece. "If I know Reginald—" Hawk grew solemn. "—and I thought I did. But I'm guessing he has some kind of backup plan in place. Stay alert, and if you see anyone, and I mean anyone, hide—and stay hid until you see me."

She didn't look happy about being left behind, but she found a vantage point near the back of a set piece and gave him a thumbs-up.

Hawk placed one foot against the crosspiece and pushed himself up, carefully wrapping his arms around the next one. He could feel the lift shimmy as he got higher and his body weight climbed into the upper reaches of the mechanism. Finally he made it to the top, where he was going to have to reach out and swing on the platform and pull himself upward. Then he could slide on the platform to get to the hatch. Glancing down, he fought off a wave of dizziness at the height.

Beads of sweat rolled down the side of his face. Refocusing his attention on his target, he battled to ignore the gravity of his situation along with the gravity threatening to gobble him up if he missed. He leaped toward the edge of the lift platform and grabbed it. His legs swung below him like a pendulum, causing the extended piece of machinery to shudder violently.

The racket of the scissor lift shaking gave him reason to think he might have knocked it over when he had jumped. He looked down toward the noise below him, while holding on tenaciously to his precious handhold. Kate stepped away from it, then moved underneath Hawk as if she might be able to break his fall if he lost his grip.

With a groan, Hawk pulled himself up to the edge, then threw a leg over the side. This foothold allowed him to hoist himself over the platform. He rolled over, lay there on his back, and realized what he was seeing. He was looking up through the hatch of Spaceship Earth at the nighttime Florida sky. He had made this trip up in the daytime when the attraction was closed, but he had never seen this view at night. Getting to his knees, he stood up.

His head rose above the inner sphere and beyond it, until he was looking over the edge of the aluminum sphere. On the lip of the edge of the hatch opening, two industrial climbing hooks were attached. Reginald had been smart. He had brought anchors to make sure he would not fall. Hawk pulled himself through the opening.

Hawk heard a cough and turned toward the sound. There, crouched on the top of Spaceship Earth, with the black box in a gloved hand, was Reginald Cambridge.

"You shouldn't have followed me up here my friend," Reginald spoke with what was almost a smile. "But somehow, knowing your propensity to get into trouble, I knew you would."

Hawk now saw that Reginald was wearing a climbing harness and had secured himself to the climbing hooks with a sturdy rope. There was little room to move on the top of this dome. It stretched 180 feet above the ground. Due to its massive size, you could navigate a short distance on top, but you could not traverse far or the angle would be too steep and you would fall.

Hawk had hidden the box in a container he attached to the top of the sphere. When he hid it earlier in the day, he had opened the hatch, laid on his stomach, stretched out at far as he could reach, and affixed the container to the dome with a clip that hooked the edge of one of the panels. Inside the container, he had placed the black box containing the pins and the key. Reginald was positioned over the place where the now-empty container was attached.

"Care to tell me what the pins are for?" Reginald asked. "Or have you not figured that out yet?"

"What do you think?"

"I think if you know, you aren't going to tell me. No matter, I have them and the key."

"What are you going to do with them?" Hawk pulled himself free of the hatch and crouched on top of the sphere as well.

"Simple. I will take them, and along with my very powerful group of friends, have you removed as an executive of the company, then replace you with the people that can use this key to determine the direction we go into the future."

"Just what do you think the key does?" Hawk said, as the breeze picked up across the top of the silver ball.

"It opens all those secret places you have hidden your plans, all those places that Farren Rales and George Colmes have hidden Walt and Roy's roadmap for the future. And most importantly, the key represents power and control." Cambridge spit those last two words. "But the best part will be seeing you removed from your post in disgrace. Who wants a man who has no experience, has killed his own family, digs up graves, and can't keep company secrets running the biggest entertainment empire the world?"

Hawk felt his jaw clench and tried to steady himself with slow steady breaths. He saw Cambridge shake his head and then cringe as though even that slight movement caused him pain. He was tougher than Hawk realized to have climbed all the way up here with broken ribs. "Over the last six months, you have been making changes . . . that just aren't going to work. It has made you a hero, except to those who understand the bottom line . . . and now with these new issues . . . the shareholders will demand you go . . . and you will go . . . and a new team of leadership will step into place."

"Sounds like you have a plan." Hawk rose to his feet on unsteady legs and stood on the metal triangles next to the open hatch.

"Just what do you think you are getting ready to do?" Cambridge chuckled. "Are you planning on taking this box from me?"

"That's what I am thinking. And by the way, your plan is dumb." Hawk took a wobbly step toward Reginald.

"It will work. There are already pieces in place, and we will end this freak show of the last eighteen months with you in charge. Like I told you before, you should have been content being a preacher . . . that is what you are good at. You have no idea how to run this company, and the way you are trying to change it is embarrassing." Cambridge cocked his head slightly as he watched Hawk take the next step toward him. Although the distance between them was short, because of the wicked slope of the dome, there was very little room to move and navigate. Holding his hand out, indicating Hawk should stop, the security chief rose to his feet and stood as the wind continued to whip around them.

"This is going to end badly for you, Grayson." Cambridge held the black box in his hand. "In some ways, I am sorry about that. When I first met you, I chased you around the entire resort, not to stop you, but to keep you moving. I knew that the crazy old Imagineer had finally decided to implement the outrageous plan he had been working on for years. To think that Walt Disney would have created a plan to insure the future of the company."

"So you think that Walt didn't choose me?"

"You believe that?" Cambridge laughed again. "For years, the group I work with has been watching Rales and his friends. They would never go away, were always trying to influence the company, always arguing that Walt would want this and Roy would do it this way. We figured one day their voices would grow quiet because they would get too old and just die off . . . but no . . . they came up with this wild story that Walt had a plan. And then you came along.

"Then I came along." Hawk nodded and again noticed how securely Reginald was anchored to the sphere by the ropes.

"I thought we had found the key to the kingdom Rales had given you. That we could have access to all of the plans this group was holding the company hostage with. We couldn't move into the future, because they wouldn't let go of the past. But Kiran Roberts and her friend Jim Masters . . . you remember him?"

Hawk remembered. He had thought that Jim was his only enemy and threat. Then he had found out Kiran was working with him. Together, they'd been trying to steal the key from him. Reginald had finally caught up with them and was able to figure out they were in it together. But now it became clear—he had known that and was working with them.

"I remember, and I remember you giving me time to finish my search." Hawk recalled Reginald telling him to find what he was looking for and be done with it.

"Yes, sadly . . . my group was not able to decipher the clues like you." Cambridge nodded. "You do know your Disney history. So I let you find the key, and I decided to get as close to you as possible. I knew there would come a day when these old Imagineers decided to give you the rest of what they knew . . . and when they did, I would stop you."

"You haven't really stopped me." Hawk became aware of the *whup-whup* of a helicopter approaching.

The velocity of the wind at the top of the sphere had increased tremendously. Hawk saw Reginald struggle against it, relying on the ropes to steady himself. Hawk adjusted his balance to battle the force of the wind striking him, determined to stand his ground as he faced Reginald.

"Sure I have." He defiantly held the box in the air. "Without this, you can't solve anything. No more surprises, no more ghosts from the past steering this company. I don't care if we never find what you are looking for. We win."

A sideways gust buffeted them. Both men suddenly shifted their weight to counter the force of the air blasting across the top of Spaceship Earth. Hawk glanced back and saw the helicopter approaching and knew it would be hovering above them at any moment. If this was Reginald's plan for escape, he would have to act fast, and it would have to be now. If he didn't, the rotors of the helicopter might blow him off the top of the sphere.

A blast of wind nearly knocked Hawk down. Crouching, he steadied himself and glared back toward Cambridge. Adrenaline surged through him, sending every sense into high alert, and a wave of strength shot through his system.

"George and Farren will just find someone else to lead."

"No, I am afraid that they have run out of time as well."

 *Day Five*
Night

THE BELL 407 HELICOPTER STREAKED through the air toward Spaceship Earth. The pilot guided the chopper, its nose dipping as they flew in, high and hot. The Rolls Royce 250-C47B turbine FADEC engine blew them across the sky at speeds in excess of two hundred miles an hour. Instinctively, the pilot cut the speed as he saw the unthinkable sight laid out in front of him.

There were two men standing on top of Spaceship Earth, the global icon of Epcot. The copilot motioned for the pilot to do a flyby. When they realized just who was standing on the top of the world, the copter banked to take a wide perimeter as they turned on the searchlight.

A blinding white floodlight enveloped the two men. Although the bird had flown wide, it had come too close, and turbulence caused by the blades of the chopper was rushing across the top of the sphere, threatening to blow the men from their precarious perch.

From the front of the chopper, both pilot and copilot watched in amazement as the two men squared off as if they were going to fight. Reginald Cambridge and Grayson Hawkes were face-to-face, having a showdown, a hundred eighty feet in the air, silhouetted against a clear Florida sky.

Amazement ignited into horror as Hawk leaped toward Reginald.

 *Day Five*
Night

HAWK KNEW THERE WAS NO MARGIN for error, as he lunged toward Reginald. He trusted that Cambridge was securely anchored to the sphere. If he could get to Reginald and hang on to him, then he would be anchored as well. The wind created by the helicopter as it approached had caused both of them to wobble and struggle to keep their footing. The searchlight, suddenly illuminating and reflecting off the aluminum squares around him, had caused Cambridge to turn his head to avoid the blinding light. It was at that moment Hawk leaped at his opponent.

He aimed toward his midsection. Like a linebacker making a tackle, he lowered his head and dove. He felt Reginald buckle as he hit him. As Cambridge grunted and dropped to his knees, Hawk's momentum caused him to sail around the man's body, landing on the aluminum triangles with a hollow *clunk*. But Hawk held on and was now driving back toward Cambridge, trying to get away from the place where the slope would send him over the edge of the sphere.

He found his footing, and with one hand still gripping Cambridge's harness, reached out for the black box with the other. Both men now gripping the black box, they steadied themselves and regained their footing. The helicopter searchlight danced across the top of the reflective silver dome. Hawk could not wrench the box free from Reginald's grasp.

"Sorry, Reginald." He twisted his body and threw a short punch to the ribcage of the security chief.

Cambridge gasped and let go of the box.

With the box firmly in his grasp, Hawk released his hold on Cambridge and scrambled back toward the open hatch. Cambridge shot out a hand and grabbed his ankle, sending Hawk sprawling face-first into an aluminum triangle of the outer sphere. As he was going down, Hawk tossed the box toward the open hatch and watched it come to rest along the ledge of the opening.

With a firm grip on his ankle, Reginald began to pull him back toward him. If Reginald succeeded in pulling him away from the hatch, and Hawk was not able to grab Reginald for a handhold again, he would easily slide over the edge of the sphere.

Rolling to his back, Hawk unleashed a short kick to Reginald's head. It connected, and Reginald's head snapped back. Releasing Hawk's ankle, he staggered backward. To Hawk's disbelief, Reginald started to slide over the edge of the giant Epcot icon. The momentum from Hawk's kick to Reginald's head had thrust him forward as well, and he was sliding painfully on his back over the triangles.

He felt the anchor ropes Reginald was secured to slide underneath him. Looking toward his feet, Hawk realized with a sickening understanding that they were both going over the edge.

Cambridge fell. Fifteen feet below the point he'd left the sphere, his body jerked to a stop. Cambridge had rigged his climbing harness with enough slack to let him move freely but not enough to allow him to fall to the ground a hundred eighty feet below. Out of breath from the shot to the ribs and the sudden stop, Reginald dangled in the air over the side of the silver dome. He could hear Hawk sliding toward him.

Spinning to his left, Hawk tried to grasp the anchor rope that was holding Reginald. He grabbed it, and it burned his hand as he clamped it with all his strength. Eight feet over the ledge, Hawk tried to catch his breath as he hung on to the rope, hoping it was strong enough to support the weight of two men. Seven feet below him, Reginald looked up, his face slackening as he understood what Hawk was about to do.

Hawk let go of the rope.

The short fall felt like it lasted an eternity until Hawk collided with Reginald. The sudden stop and momentary disorientation dissipated, as he held on to Cambridge with one hand and searched for the rope with the other. Quickly weaving his arm in and out of the rope, Hawk secured himself as he was turned to continue his battle with Cambridge. He didn't have a plan beyond the moment and had not thought about the endgame of this encounter.

But Hawk had trusted Reginald, befriended him, only to discover that Cambridge had used their friendship to try to destroy him. He was angry that Reginald would hurt his friends as well, and his anger drove him to a dangerous edge. Hanging next to Cambridge, the wave of emotion that had propelled him to this moment crystallized in an instant of clarity, and he hesitated. Hawk did not want to hurt Reginald, no matter what he had done. He wanted justice, not vengeance.

Reginald took advantage of the moment and let loose the spool of climbing cable he had carried on his waist. He had come prepared to make a quick escape. Knowing from all the Disney trivia experts that the sphere was one hundred eighty feet tall, he had calculated the shape of the sphere and how much cable he would need to lower himself to the ground. As the cable unfurled, the security chief placed one hand in front of himself and the other behind him at the small of his back.

As Hawk watched Reginald rappel down the side of the dome, he smiled.

Dangling alone on the cable, he knew that Cambridge was gone and would be safe. He had come prepared. It dawned on Hawk that his lack of planning and the flash of anger had put him in a dangerous position. He now had to pull himself back up the climbing rope until the slope of the dome leveled out enough for him to pull himself back to the hatch.

The helicopter kept Hawk focused in the searchlight. The light reflecting off the sphere was blinding and disorienting, and he wondered who was in the hovering chopper and why. If they were enemies, then he was in a bigger mess than just hanging over the edge of Spaceship Earth. If they were there to help him, well, they weren't being very helpful at all. Resisting the urge to look down and watch Cambridge, Hawk pulled himself up the first foot. Wrapping his leg in and around the rope, Hawk now began to climb hand over hand, using his leg as an anchor to keep him from sliding.

The climb was slow, it was painful, and every muscle in his back, arms, and shoulders was on fire. Eventually, he crested the curve of the dome and hauled himself upward by wedging his fingers into the grooves between the custom triangles. An eternity later, he was lying on this stomach next to the hatch at the top of the giant ball. The chopper bathed him in a white light. He rolled over and looked up toward it.

"Hawk, this is Al . . . you OK?" The metallic voice of Al Gann echoed through the night sky from a speaker attached to the helicopter.

Hawk waved to them, indicating he was OK. The sound of the rotors changed, as the whirlybird tilted and veered away from him, leaving him in darkness. He reached over and grabbed the black box by the hatch opening. He stuck it into his pocket, then rolled over and dropped onto the safety of the rickety old scissor lift below.

 *Day Five*
Early Morning

**THE DOOR AT THE BASE OF SPACESHIP EARTH** opened, and Kate emerged with Grayson Hawks supporting himself with an arm across her shoulder. They were accompanied by a security team dressed in blue shirts and white hats. A crowd of security personnel and cast members had gathered at the base of the attraction. The prolonged helicopter hovering had captured the attention of everyone working the park. The sight of two men hanging over the side of the giant space-age ball was one they never would forget.

Juliette and Shep pushed their way through the crowd toward Hawk and Kate. The four embraced in a huddle as everyone looked on.

"Did we get Cambridge?" Hawk asked.

"No," Juliette answered. "He rappelled down the cable and then told the security team you were trapped up there. He told them to go rescue you."

Hawk had wondered why there had been a security detail with Kate when he lowered himself on the scissor lift, but he'd been too tired to ask. He just appreciated the fact that they knew how to get down through the maze of corridors, and he didn't have to stop and figure out the best path to choose.

"After all, he is their boss," Shep added. "How do you feel?"

"Not good." Any muscle that didn't hurt now would be screaming at him by the morning. "How do I look?"

"Better than you feel," Kate answered, winking.

Now the security team, night leads, and managers were gathering around to find out what had been going on. Sensing the need for direction to be given, Juliette pushed into the crowd and began giving instructions to secure the area and get the park ready for the next day. Shep also waded into the blender of activity, allowing Hawk to move off and take a seat on a bench in front of a fountain.

"Hawk?" Kate was looking at him curiously.

"Yes."

"Do you *ever* have a real plan, or do you just kind of make it up as you go?"

"Oh no, Kate." Hawk slowly looked up toward the top of Spaceship Earth. "I always know what I'm doing."

"Would it upset you if asked you something?"

"It depends on what it is, I guess." Hawk looked back at her, understanding she wouldn't have said more if he had told her not to ask. "Go ahead and ask."

"How did you ever pick the top of the giant silver golf ball as the place to hide the pins?"

"I wanted to put them somewhere safe, where no one would find them."

"Then you told the guy who was trying to steal them where they were?"

"Something like that." Hawk shrugged.

"It was a dumb hiding place," she stated flatly.

Shep and Juliette returned, having taken control of the situation without letting anyone know what had really been happening. Hawk and Kate got to their feet. Hawk felt as if he had been run over by a truck loaded with bricks. They slowly made their way back to the main entrance of Epcot. A security guard unlocked the gate and waved them through. Walking out to where the tram would load and unload guests, they came to where Hawk's Mustang was parked askew on the sidewalk.

"Nice parking job, boss." Shep looked quizzically at Hawk.

"I was in a hurry."

"How do you find Reginald Cambridge?" Kate lobbed the question for anyone to answer.

"It will be tough." Hawk snatched it. "He knows the parks just as well as we do, if not better. If he decides to disappear and go underground, he'll be almost impossible to find."

"Let's allow Al and his buddies to take care of that," Juliette added. "I called him when we knew this is where you were headed. I didn't know he was going to arrive by helicopter and nearly blow you off the top."

Hawk agreed that law enforcement could find Reginald, but he knew that any legal action against Reginald would get very murky. There was no way he would ever press charges with the possibility of details about the key to the kingdom or the plan of Walt and Roy ever becoming public. Reginald knew that. The group of people he was working with knew that. They all were keeping secrets, and those secrets granted a certain amount of protection and at the same time meant that the forces trying to control the theme park would continue to wage war. Secrets always cost you something.

The quest for Hawk was to know the players—who was good and who was evil. He had made an error in judgment again. His recklessness was his greatest enemy. Choosing to allow Reginald to have so much knowledge of the inner workings and details of the plan Walt and Roy had put into place had not made him or the Disney Company more secure. It had put it at risk. Hawk was also worried about who else might be involved in this plot. Over the last few days, there had been people with Cambridge every time he had made a move. Who were they? Reginald was now exposed, so he would not likely be showing up again anytime soon. But who were the others?

"We're parked over there." Juliette paused at Hawk's car. "What's the game plan?"

Hawk felt as exhausted as if he were facing the climb up the side of Spaceship Earth all over again.

"There's one more clue to solve. Let's get together for an early lunch tomorrow and see if we can put our heads together and figure it out." Hawk opened the car door for Kate, and she slid into the seat. After closing the door, he moved to the back of the car, where Juliette and Shep stood watching. "Thank you both for being there for me today. I allowed Reginald to . . . um . . ."

"Cause you to doubt who your friends were?" Shep looked angry, then busted into a wide-faced grin.

"Something like that." Hawk lowered his head. "But I knew . . ."

"All things considered, there was enough going on to make things pretty confusing," Juliette reassured him. "But you knew in your heart that Reginald was wrong, that's why you didn't accuse us of trying to steal the key."

"Yes, I knew . . . but Reginald twisted things pretty tightly, and I listened too closely."

"And what about Jonathan?" Juliette asked. "Are you still thinking he might be involved?"

"Nah . . . but I am worried about him." Hawk looked back toward the Epcot entrance. "Nancy managed to cut us all off from one another, and we still haven't found Jonathan. We need to do that."

"We'll drop by his house to see if he's there," Shep offered.

"Thanks. I am going to go home . . . and let's meet off-site . . . at 11:15. Good?"

"We'll be there."

## CHAPTER SIXTY-ONE

*Day Six*
Late Morning

THE CENTRAL FLORIDA GREENWAY LOOPS all the way from Disney into Seminole County. Forty minutes away from the Magic Kingdom, on the opposite side of the Greater Orlando area, is a bustling little community called Winter Springs. When Hawk wanted to go off-site, he meant way off-site. The group was to meet at one of Hawk's favorite off-site stomping grounds, a restaurant that specialized in chicken tenders. He loved the food, the atmosphere, and the name: Huey Magoo's. This small chain of restaurants was owned by a couple of friends who had met in college and decided to chase a dream and go into business together. With a real heart for the community, they had built not just restaurants, but gathering places, and they gave back to the areas their customers lived in. Hawk valued all those things—and the food was great.

Hawk and Kate arrived right on time and found Juliette, Shep, and Jonathan seated at one of the outside tables under an oversized umbrella. Hawk walked over and grabbed Jonathan in a bear hug, relieved to see his friend and thankful that he was fine. Shep had ordered for everyone, and they settled under the gorgeous Florida sky to untangle the web of mystery they were trapped inside.

"I hear you had an exciting couple of days." Jonathan directed this toward Hawk. "I'm sorry I didn't get to talk with you. Nancy called me and told me that after your place had been broken into, we were all in danger, and you wanted us to get out of town, not to take our phones, and—no matter what—not to discuss anything company related for at least two days." He shook his head. "When we got back, I had messages from you, Juliette, and Shep. I'm sorry, Hawk, Nancy made it sound like an emergency. I should have called you to verify."

"It's fine," Hawk reassured him. "We have just had an intense few days."

"Juliette has been telling me. It sounds like it's been more than just intense. But after all, it's you, what else would I expect?"

"It hasn't been too bad . . ." Hawk let this linger.

Everyone hesitated for a moment then exploded in laughter at his understatement. The hostess delivered their baskets of chicken tenders. After making sure that all food and sauces were in place, they said a quick blessing. On the *amen*, everyone dove into the meal. The desire to eat calmed the conversation for a moment, but after the first tender was downed, the chatter came back to life.

"I talked with Al Gann this morning, and there is no sign of Reginald or Nancy. Apparently neither has been back home, and no one at the resort has seen them either," Hawk reported.

"So they've just disappeared?" Juliette asked, as she dipped a chicken tender in Magoo sauce.

"They're staying under the radar," Hawk summarized. "I am guessing they, whoever they are, are trying to figure out what their next play is."

"What do you mean?" Jonathan said, after a sip of sweet tea.

"Well, Cambridge knows I have another clue to figure out . . . but he didn't end up with the collectible pins, so now they have to decide whether they can stop us from figuring it out and finding whatever it is that George Colmes has decided it is time to find."

"So you're going to figure out the clue and solve the puzzle now, right?" Kate had polished off the chicken and was moving into the fries.

"Any luck with the clue?" Shep widened his eyes.

"'*Walt had a dream . . . a dream about tomorrow . . . a vision you can see . . . a vision as it was meant to be . . . a living blueprint where people actually live a life they can't find anyplace else in the world.*' That is the first part of the clue." Hawk had decided he had to once again trust his closest friends to help him.

"Epcot," Jonathan piped in.

"That seems to be the consensus, but Epcot is a big place, and this doesn't give a lot of direction," Hawk replied.

"If not Epcot, then what?" Juliette leaned forward.

"Well, Walt's dream is well documented. But I was thinking that everything I have found in my experience on these quests has had to do with the history of Walt's life. The Epcot that we know and love is not the one he dreamed of. He was going to build a real community, not a theme park."

"That's the living blueprint part . . . right?" Shep asked.

"Exactly. It sounded familiar to me, and I found out that when the clue says, '*A living blueprint where people actually live a life they can't find anyplace else in the world . . . ,*' that is almost exactly how Walt said it in the Florida Project film he made just before he died."

"Help the non-Disney-trivia gal catch up." Kate held up her hand. "The Florida Project film?"

"That's the film made to introduce the big Florida project. You probably have seen cuts of it on television before, but he talks about a real working city of the future.

"Now that Epcot is a theme park and not what Walt wanted to build, his idea is referred to as Progress City," Shep told Kate, as he picked the remnants of chicken from his basket.

"I think the clue is more about Progress City, which was never built. But it was a dream, a dream about tomorrow, a vision as it was meant to be." Hawk thought. "The clue also said, 'A vision you can see. . . .' That's why I was thinking Epcot originally."

The collective thinking caused them all to fall silent once again. Then, as Hawk dipped a fry in ketchup, he paused mid-bite. Using the fry like a baton, he allowed his thoughts to emerge like a symphony.

"The last part of the clue was 'I can see it from here. . . . Go to it. . . . Find that vision. . . . Stick with it,' and that is what is still keeping me stumped." Hawk allowed the refrain to follow again. "'I can see it from here. . . .' It has to be something you can see. 'Go to it. . . .' It has to be someplace to go. 'Stick with it. . . .' I am guessing that has something to do with the pins I've found. I have to stick them on something."

"George said, 'I can see it from here.'" Juliette thought through the options. "Does that mean he could see it? Where was he filming?"

"That has been throwing me the whole time. He was riding on something. It looked so familiar, but the film was too short, and the shots didn't let you see the background very well." Another pieced clunked into place in his brain. "Wait a minute. That's it!"

"Yes?" Jonathan leaned forward.

"I know why it looked so familiar . . . and I know what George was looking at."

"You gonna share with the class?" Kate playfully waved her hand around the table.

"He was riding the People Mover in Tomorrowland. That's why the film would go from light to dark, and I think he was actually sitting in a ride car filming with a camera or his smart phone." Hawk grinned. "That's it—that is why it all looked familiar but I never could nail it down."

"So when he said he could see it from here, he wasn't talking about Epcot." Shep was tracking right alongside Hawk's train of thinking. "He was looking at the Progress City model that you can see from the ride."

"We're looking for the Progress City model?" Kate looked from Shep to Hawk. "But you already know where it is. What about the model is important?"

"That is what we have to go find out." Hawk now knew where the next stop would take him.

The group took a few moments to map out the next steps and how they would make it work. They could position themselves strategically in Tomorrowland after-hours while Hawk took a run at figuring out the rest of the clue. Jonathan suggested that with all that had taken place, they should use a security team. Hawk thought seriously about this. But because of the nature of what they were doing—this layer of secrecy that surrounded the key to the kingdom and this new adventure, and how their trust had already been betrayed—he decided to keep the circle of people involved tight, controlled, and those that could count on one another. They would do this and finish this on their own.

The conversation began to drag, and they made plans to reassemble later that evening. One by one, they got ready to leave. Shep excused himself first, then Juliette, leaving Kate, Jonathan, and Hawk.

Hawk looked at Jonathan. "I am so glad you're OK. And although Nancy did it to divide and conquer, in some ways, your getting the chance to get out of town kept you safe and out of trouble."

"Yes, maybe she did me a favor." Jonathan got to his feet, but his first step was tentative. As he moved, Hawk noticed that he was favoring his ankle or foot.

"You OK? Something wrong with your leg?" Hawk asked.

"My foot, actually. Just twisted it doing something." Jonathan smiled. "I tell you, brother, I am getting old. Hey, by the way, you did re-hide this valuable pin collection, didn't you?"

"I sure did."

"You didn't put it back on top of Spaceship Earth, did you?"

"It is someplace safe, trust me." Hawk smiled.

Jonathan waved and then limped off around the corner. Hawk glanced toward Kate, who had cut her eyes to Hawk and then back to Jonathan's foot. As soon as he disappeared around the corner, she opened her mouth to speak. Hawk slowly raised an index finger to signal her to wait. He stared at the corner where Jonathan had just disappeared, and as if on cue, Jonathan came back around the corner once again.

"Once more, what time to do we meet tonight?" Jonathan asked.

"Midnight." Hawk waved.

Again, Jonathan limped off around the corner. Kate now leaned up in her chair, and once again Hawk waved her off.

"Yes, I saw it." Hawk looked to where Jonathan had been. Every encounter Hawk had been in the last few days, both Jonathan and Cambridge had shown the symptoms of. That was how Cambridge had persuaded him to suspect Jonathan in the first place. Although Hawk wanted to believe he had untangled himself from those he couldn't trust, he once again noticed another connection back to his old friend. Kate had nearly pierced one of their attacker's feet with her heel at the swamp shack. The same foot that Jonathan now seemed to be favoring.

"You don't have to say it, I saw it."

 *Day Seven*
Midnight

**HAWK AND KATE HAD BEEN WALKING** through the Magic Kingdom for well over an hour. Their walk had started on Main Street USA and then carried them on a loop through Adventureland, into Frontierland and Liberty Square, and into Fantasyland. The new look of Fantasyland was still one of the park's latest renovations and had become wildly popular. The new attractions, shops, and dining experiences had made it a place where huge crowds packed every corner during all hours the park was open. As they moved through on this night, in the absence of others, Hawk was able to point out some of the hidden secrets and surprises they had loaded the new area with.

Kate did not know how much input Hawk had into those hidden secrets. This remodel had been the biggest project he had tackled yet in the theme parks, and he had to learn much of what he did in real time. Fortunately, Farren Rales had been available to consult as often as he needed, but Rales had also, on purpose, stayed out the way so Hawk could learn to lead through this unique process. When it had finally opened to rave reviews, Farren had congratulated him and told him he was now ready for even bigger projects.

Glancing at his watch, he saw it was midnight, the time everyone was going to gather in Tomorrowland. The tour for Kate had been to let them move about the park and get a sense whether anyone might be following them. They had not noticed anyone. It also gave Hawk something to do, as he was more than ready to get moving into the plan for the evening. Turning and moving through Cinderella Castle, they picked up their pace. Hawk moved quickly while Kate was still in sightseeing mode, staring at the intricate mosaics on the wall inside the castle.

"Kate, we need to go." He looked at his watch and waved for her to join him. They exited the castle back out into the Central Hub at the end of Main Street USA. Angling down the ramp on the right side of the castle, Kate hurried to catch up with Hawk. She stumbled slightly as she tried to navigate the sloped ramp in her high heels. Losing a shoe a few paces behind, she called out to him, then stopped and went back for her shoe.

Hawk ran back to help her. He was anxious to get started solving this last clue, and he hated to be late. Even though the plan had called for everyone to be in place before Hawk and Kate arrived, he still wanted to get on with this next part of the adventure. He got to her shoe before she did and knelt to pick it up. He turned toward her and lifted her shoe so he could help her put it back on. Kate paused in front of him. A huge, childlike grin spread across her face.

"What is it?" Hawk, on one knee and holding the shoe, looked up at her.

"This is a magical moment, Grayson Hawkes." Kate gazed up at Cinderella Castle.

"A magical mo—what are you talking about?"

"Think about it. I was running down the ramp in front of Cinderella Castle and ran right out of my shoe. And now you're waiting to put my shoe back on my foot. This is like a fairy tale. How many people get to say that has happened to them?" She looked back at him with another playful grin. "I am embracing the moment."

Hawk looked at her, glanced back over his shoulder at the castle, and then back to her again. "Give me your foot please, princess," he said, as he rolled his eyes.

She held out her foot, and he slid the heel back over it. He rose and stood next to her as she gazed back toward the castle again. Waiting for her attention to come back to him, which eventually it did, although it took longer than he had wanted it to, he finally spoke.

"Are you ready to keep moving now?"

She was, and they rushed across the hub and over the bridge into Tomorrowland. Their destination was the Tomorrowland Transit Authority People Mover. The attraction itself was a no-thrills, constantly moving ride that gave you a look from the sky at Tomorrowland and some of the attractions surrounding it. The one-mile-long track provided guests with a ten-minute ride, which, on a hot summer day, was a fairly restful experience. The attraction used to be known as the WEDway People Mover. That all changed back in 1994, when Tomorrowland got a remodel using the theme "The Future that Never Was," because they had found that the future was changing so rapidly that Tomorrowland could never predict it or be ready to showcase it. The result was a name change to the Tomorrowland Transit Authority People Mover.

Juliette was standing in the corner near the entrance to Buzz Lightyear's Space Ranger Spin. This gave her a clear view of the entrance to the attraction, and she could look up and see the overhead ride path as it approached and left this area. On the second level, the People Mover track looped behind Buzz Lightyear's Space Ranger Spin, and this was where the Progress City model was on display. Hawk and Kate looked over toward her as they passed, and Hawk nodded, indicating he had seen her. The two continued toward the escalator that took guests up one level to get on the ride.

Shep was stationed on a bench between the Carousel of Progress and Space Mountain. He also could look up and see the pathway of the attraction overhead with a clear view across the far side of the now-deserted Tomorrowland. Between him and Juliette, they would be able to spot anyone entering the area. The escalator was not running, so Hawk and Kate trudged up the steps. They had planned this as well. Jonathan was at the top, in the load-and-unload area, and would operate the ride if needed. Because they were trying to do this without drawing undue attention, which Hawk found humorous since they were commandeering an attraction, they would run the attraction only if there were a dire reason to. Jonathan was the third line of protection if someone tried to move to stop Hawk, and they would have to get past him to get to the place where the model was on display.

Hawk had needed to do a little research and recon in the afternoon, trying to figure out the best way to get to the model. There were a couple of ways, but the one he had chosen provided the best protection while they got in; by using an unseen service door along the People Mover track, they were less likely to be noticed going in or out. As they reached the top, Jonathan nodded at them and whispered, "All is clear."

Hawk and Kate turned left and walked into the unloading portion of the ride. They were going to walk the line of the track in the opposite direction the ride vehicles would normally move. Since the model was on display near the end of the ride, this was the shortest distance to get there. Following the bend in the track that would take them over the entrance to Buzz Lightyear's Space Ranger Spin, where Juliette was standing, they veered to the right, then over and past the entrance to the Monsters Inc. Laugh Floor Comedy Club, which was now housed in the big Tomorrowland auditorium, then around to the back of both those attractions. As they walked along the People Mover track, Hawk looked over the surrounding area for any unusual or suspicious activity. He saw none, and they turned the corner in the dark tunnel that wound behind the buildings toward their destination.

"The Progress City model was really Walt Disney's dream for what Epcot could be?" Kate asked quietly, as they walked along the smooth concrete pathway. With just enough room to walk side by side, Hawk would reach out with a steadying hand as they entered darker sections of the tunnel between the lights embedded along the ride track.

"Yes, that's simplifying it, but his dream was for an experimental prototype community of tomorrow, or EPCOT. The model is more than that, Kate, it's an important piece of Disney history. It used to be at the Disneyland park years ago as a part of the Carousel of Progress, until sometime in 1973. In that version of the attraction, the final holiday gathering scene offered a glimpse of Progress City off in the distance through the windows behind the audio-animatronic figures. After the show ended, the guests would head up to a second floor, where they could explore the entire sixty-nine-hundred-square-foot model of the city."

"Wow, that's impressive."

"It was an impressive dream." Hawk smiled back at her in the darkness even though he knew she couldn't see it. He used his hand to feel his way along the path until they turned the corner where there would be more light. "The Progress City we have here at Walt Disney World is just a very small portion of that model."

"It would be awesome to see the whole thing."

"I agree." Hawk nodded. "Walt was not afraid to risk it all to accomplish something he believed in."

"Sounds like someone else I know," Kate interrupted. Hawk felt his face grow hot as he blushed in the darkness.

"He really believed he could help solve some of the struggles of people trying to make it in cities across the globe. I don't know if it was right or wrong, but he was chasing a dream that he believed he was supposed to chase. A dream that would make the world a better place and that most thought was impossible. It was just the kind of project that Walt would tackle." Hawk slowed as they approached a corner where light now illuminated their path. The smothering blackness of the tunnel yielded to an area where riders were supposed to peek inside an attraction. He wanted to make sure they were still alone as they stepped back into the light. "After he passed away, there was no one with the vision, drive, and passion for Walt's project. So they build Epcot, which is spectacular, but not what Walt was ultimately trying to do."

"So Progress City was his work in progress . . . so to speak?"

"Exactly."

They rounded the corner to their right and came to the massive glass windows that looked out over Walt Disney's Progress City. His bright and shining future of tomorrow, a glimmering city that contained all the hopes and dreams of what the future could hold. Featuring monorail systems, a huge business center, and massive multi-story high-rises in the center of the city portion, the model, even in this smaller version, was impressive to say the least. Hawk and Kate both pressed up against the glass and looked inside.

"It really is beautiful." Kate scanned the city. "It's a shame he never lived to see it happen."

"Sometimes that's the way dreams work." Hawk glanced to his left, back into the darkened passageway. "It isn't always seeing the dream come true as much as making discoveries along the way to where the dream is taking you that really counts." Hawk motioned for her to remain where she was. "If Walt hadn't been chasing that—" He pointed to the city. "None of what we know today as Walt Disney World ever would have existed."

Hawk now moved alone through the darkness and found the door he was looking for. Completely unseen by passengers on the People Mover, this door had no door knob and was painted to blend into the darkened tunnel. It did have a keyed lock, and Hawk pulled out the kingdom key and slid it inside. He felt it click into place, and with a counterclockwise turn, he felt the mechanism release, and the door opened toward him.

He stepped through it and pulled it closed beside him. Standing on the edge of the Progress City model, he was shielded from view of anyone looking through the window. He glanced up at the catwalks bending in a semi-circle above the window; these contained the lights and wiring used to light up and power the model city. To his left was a stairwell that would carry him to the catwalk. He quickly moved toward it and bounded up the steps to the top.

Hawk walked around the catwalk, looking down at the model city. He stopped in the middle, directly above where he calculated Kate was now standing below him on the other side of the window. He leaned on the rail and was taken again by the beauty of this city, this dream that Walt was chasing. Glancing down, he strained to see if he could spot Kate looking in the window. He couldn't; the angle was too severe. The design was masterful. All the behind-the-scenes pieces needed to make the guest view enjoyable were put into place here just like everywhere throughout the parks.

Hawk surveyed the area around him. He moved methodically to his right and searched for anything that didn't seem to fit. Seeing nothing out of the ordinary, he turned his attention back to the electronics used to light up the area. This display was static; it had been here a long time, and there was no new technology to be found here. Then he noticed a gunmetal-gray box affixed to the railing on the far right of the catwalk.

Moving to stand in front of it, he saw nothing unusual about it. A metal conduit led to the bottom of the box, and Hawk assumed it was a light-control panel of some sort. He crouched, looked at it more carefully, and noticed a keyhole on the bottom of the box. There was no way to see this lock without scanning the box from this angle.

*A living blueprint of the future where people can actually live a life they can't find any place in the world. . . . I can see it from here. . . . Go to it. . . . Find that vision. . . . Stick with it. . . . .* This must be the place. This was Walt's vision, those were Walt's words; George could see the model and had invited Hawk to come to it and find it. He carefully inserted his kingdom key into the lock and turned it.

A clicking noise emanated from the box. Leaving the key in the lock, he pulled back his hands, and the top covering of the box retracted in two distinct pieces. They clicked as they moved, eventually revealing a black control box with an illuminated top panel. Five spaces glowed in the panel, and he immediately knew what the clue meant. The *stick with it* would happen now.

He had concluded that the phrase was a reference to the collectible pins and the play on words was a clever way of letting him know that. The illuminated panel showed him lighted spaces whose outlines matched the classic shapes of the Walt Disney pins he had found along the way. He removed the pin box from his pocket and opened it carefully.

He started at the top left of the panel and inserted Mickey Mouse into place. He moved to the right, where Minnie Mouse had a place designated for her. Below Minnie was a space that outlined Donald Duck. Back to the left, Goofy was put in place. The last collectible pin, fitting into the center space, was Pluto. As he put Pluto into his space, a new light started blinking at the top of the panel. It was a button, an activation switch. He pushed it, and the control panel glowed with a stunning white light. A whirring rose from the model below him.

The model rumbled as though it were coming to life. The floor below him made a grinding noise, and he watched the old fragile display shudder slightly. He expected to see it begin to fall apart, but it did not. Everything looked just as it should. Except the church.

Walt had insisted this house of worship be included in the model. Although he hadn't been vocal about his faith, his children would recall the stories of their dad taking them to church each week, and he had spoken in a very intimate and revealing interview about the importance of faith for him and society. Walt had understood that without faith, there could be no future.

The rumbling was replaced by a rapid series of clicks, and then as Hawk stared over the railing down at the model, the church itself began to lower into the base of the model and disappear. The space where it had been was now nothing but an open hole, a perfect circle about a foot and a half wide. The lighted panel along the rail went dark. Hawk stood there waiting for something else to happen, but nothing else occurred. He studied the opening in the model from where he stood and knew there was only one thing to do.

He made his way back along the catwalk and then descended the stairs to the model itself.

## CHAPTER SIXTY-THREE

*Day Seven*
Early Morning

**KATE YOUNG STOOD WITH HER HANDS PRESSED** against the glass, rising on her toes to get a better angle, to see where the church had gone or what might be in the hole that was now in the model.

To her left, she saw Hawk step tentatively onto the model. He had obviously seen the same thing she had and now was making his way to the opening to investigate. He looked back at her, and she noticed an excitement in his eyes as he was finally closing in on what she knew he believed was the last step toward solving this mystery. He carefully placed his foot on the model, then tested to see whether it would support his weight, then moved another step forward.

His slow and methodical approach was driving her nuts. She tapped her thumbs on the glass as she willed Hawk to move quicker and find out what was there. If he could hear her thumb drumbeat, he did not react. He took his time, reverently traversing this city of the future.

With his back to her, he stood where the miniature church had been. Kate slid to her right, looking for a better vantage point. Stopping, she watched Hawk crouch and then reach down into the opening. He pulled his hand up, but there was nothing in it. She exhaled loudly, the sound echoing in the tunnel, and realized for the first time just how tense she was.

He got down on one knee, similar to the way he had knelt before her in front of the castle, and reached down into the opening again. His arm disappeared into the opening almost to his shoulder before he slowly withdrew it. This time he had something in his hand. Sliding back to her left, she tried to get a clear view of it but could not. She pounded her palm on the window to get his attention.

His head turned, and she motioned for him to show her what he had found. She watched as he turned and held up a book. A thick leather book with parchment pages. Her hands shot out to her sides with her palms up in an effort to ask him silently through the glass if this is what they were looking for. He nodded at her, and she took her hand and wiped it across her brow in exaggerated relief.

Hearing a faint clacking sound behind her, she whirled. A blue ride car rolled inexorably toward her.

Kate slammed herself against the window to keep from getting hit. The back of her head thudded on the glass, as the People Mover car silently grazed past her.

With a heart-sinking realization, she knew the attraction was now running. That was not the plan; Jonathan was not supposed to start the ride, and with a sickening lurch in the pit of her stomach, she feared something had gone wrong. Now that Hawk had found what he had been looking for, all of the pieces of the puzzle were exposed—and were ripe for the taking.

 *Day Seven*
*Early Morning*

HAWK WATCHED IN SHOCK AS KATE PRESSED herself against the window. When she looked toward him, a look of surprise bubbled in her green eyes. Stepping away from the opening, he gently but much more quickly navigated across the model city toward the door he had entered through. Reaching it, he pushed it open, then he ran back toward the viewing area. He could hear Kate yelling at someone but couldn't make out what she was saying. As he rounded the corner and got a clear view of the window, he saw Kate was gone.

Something hard struck him from behind, and he crashed to the concrete pathway. Groggily, he rolled to his left as a blue ride car passed him.

The People Mover ran with very little noise, and he had not heard the car approach. Spaced to operate at safe distances, each ride vehicle offered the luxury of a semiprivate ride along the "Blue Line" of the Tomorrowland Transit Authority. Hawk got back to his feet and glanced behind him to make sure there was not another car close; there was not one there yet, but he knew it would be coming.

The details raced across Hawk's synapses, and he rolled through the situation unfolding around him. Kate was gone, and because she had disappeared so quickly, he had to assume she was now in a ride vehicle. But the ride had not been in operation—and Jonathan stood at the controls.

Hawk had pushed back all his suspicions about his friend, but in a heartbeat, they came roaring back. He had known and trusted Jonathan for years; he wanted to believe that all of the ailments and mysterious absences of the past few days had been orchestrated by someone else. Jonathan had to be his friend. Yet he had turned the ride on. But for what purpose?

Hawk ran out of the tunnel where he could get a clear view of the ride vehicles. Emerging from the darkness of the tunnel, he saw two figures on a ride vehicle; Kate was struggling with a masked man dressed in black. As

Hawk looked on, the ride took a turn, and they fell across the seat. She was too far away for him to be able to help, and he looked from side to side to calculate how to get to her.

His vision exploded with a spectacle of dancing and flashing lights. Bone-jarring pain seared across his shoulders. He lurched forward and felt a powerful tightening over his side as he was lifted up and dumped into a ride vehicle.

He blinked away the flashing lights strobing through his field of vision. Between light blasts, he could see Reginald Cambridge standing over him, breathing heavily, struggling to gather a breath under his aching ribs. Hawk's mind began to rapidly piece together the past few disconnected moments. Reginald had been riding in the passenger car and had hit Hawk across the shoulders and neck. As Hawk fell forward, Reginald had grabbed him and heaved him into the car.

But now Reginald was battle weary from their previous encounters, which gave Hawk an extra moment to catch his breath. Suddenly, Hawk remembered the book he had been carrying. He somehow had held onto it when he had fallen; it lay on the floor of the car, just beyond his reach, as the ride vehicle slipped silently around the curve.

Finding his feet and rising to face Reginald, he noticed at the last moment the punch that was already being thrown his way. The blow landed on the side of his head, and an explosion of stars flew across Hawk's field of vision. Closing his eyes an extra few milliseconds, Hawk bent his knees and ducked down. He clenched a fist and drove it up ramrod straight, aiming at where he believed Cambridge was standing. As he felt the jab connect, he opened his eyes. Reginald's head snapped back, and he fell away from Hawk, back into the seat.

Hawk surged toward Reginald, grabbed two fistfuls of shirt, and jerked him back upright. Driving a knee into his stomach, he heard the air whoosh from Cambridge's lungs. Hawk threw another right hand that crumpled Cambridge back into the seat. As he went down, Hawk looked up to see if he could spot Kate's ride vehicle and figure out a way to help her.

Blinking his eyes and trying to get a clear view of what was happening in front of him, he could see her ride vehicle entering the unloading area, where it would slow down to a snail's pace so passengers could disembark. He saw Jonathan and Shep intercept her car, grab her attacker, and pull him out onto the moving platform. Juliette moved to the ride vehicle to assist Kate, before losing sight of the three of them struggling with the person who had taken Kate from the viewing area.

As Hawk smiled, confident they'd overpower the attacker, the vehicle jerked around a bend, throwing him off balance and over the edge of the blue

JEFF DIXON

ride vehicle. He held on and pulled himself back in, slumping into the seat next to a semiconscious Reginald Cambridge. Hawk shoved him to the edge of the car and they entered the unloading area. Hawk patted him on the knee and laughed.

"Nice try, Reginald. You had to try one more time, didn't you?"

When the doors of the vehicle automatically opened, he saw Shep, Juliette, and Kate rush toward him. Behind them, Jonathan kept an eye on a masked man who lay on the ground, hands bound behind his back. Hawk got to his feet and stepped out onto the moving platform as Shep reached into the car to grab Reginald.

 *Day Seven*
*Early Morning*

**THEY WERE SEATED ON THE CURB** in front of the impressive set of gears that read *Walt Disney's Carousel of Progress*. The security team had arrived along with Al Gann and some of his deputies from the sheriff's department. Hawk flinched as the EMT finished bandaging the cut next to his eye where Cambridge had hit him. Through his other eye, he saw medical personnel wrapping a bandage around Kate's arm where she had sustained a minor wound tangling with her attacker.

The last few minutes had compressed quickly in Hawk's brain. As he had gotten out of the ride car on the People Mover, he had stepped over the masked man on the ground and taken off his mask. Under it was Zeke Reitz, the maintenance worker he had met a few days before. He had snarled at Hawk when the mask was removed and muttered that Hawk was trying to destroy his company. While Hawk's friends had been trying to make sure he and Kate were alright, he had deciphered that Shep had seen some motion above him coming out of the darkened tunnels on the People Mover level from Space Mountain.

Shep knew they had to have been hidden long before he had taken up his station. He had immediately run to the attraction entrance, where he met Juliette, who had seen motion as well. They knew there were at least two people up on the Blue Line with Hawk and Kate but did not know exactly what to do. They decided to start the ride, hoping Hawk and Kate might take that as a sign there was trouble.

After that, things unfolded very quickly, as both the attackers had used the ride start-up to take a quicker way to find Hawk and Kate. Once the friends saw that Kate was in the ride car, they all waited for it to arrive at the unloading platform, where they planned on subduing Zeke, which they did effectively. When Hawk and Cambridge came riding along the track as well, they did the same thing again, and both Zeke Reitz and Reginald Cambridge were arrested. Al had told Hawk they would straighten out exactly what to charge everyone with later.

Kate was now bandaged and seated next to Hawk on the curb. Juliette was talking with Clint, who then made a few notes and walked away, as did the security team and medical team, convinced they had completed their responsibilities. She came over and stood in front of the pair of bandaged warriors sitting on the curb.

"This turned into quite an evening. I know the EMTs said you were fine—are you really?" Juliette looked from one to the other.

"Yes." Hawk touched his eye. "But Reginald is one tough guy. He had a bad set of ribs and still managed to toss me into the People Mover. The guy is a beast."

"Well, I guess he found out tonight that you're more of a beast than he is." Juliette smiled.

"That's me." Hawk probed the cut by his eye a little too hard and winced. "More beast."

"Now, would that make me . . . ?" Kate looked at him.

"Hey, I get it . . . Beauty and the Beast." Shep pointed at them. "Real cute . . . a Disney classic." Then he looked down at the book Hawk had found, which he had been careful to hold on to since he plucked it out of the ride car. He gingerly lifted it from Hawk's hand. "Hawk, do you know what this is?"

"I have no idea." Hawk squinted up at him. "I never got a chance to look at it."

"I'm not sure, but it looks like it's a journal or a handwritten book." Shep flipped through the pages. "And you might or might not believe this, but it was written by none other than Walt Disney himself."

"What?" Hawk reached out for the book and began to examine it.

"I could be wrong." Shep shrugged. "But is sure does look like his hand-writing to me."

"What is he writing about?" Juliette moved to the curb to look at the book, as Hawk flipped the pages.

Shep looked upset at having the book snatched from his hands. "Well, I didn't have time to read it, but it looks to me like there's a lot of information and instruction about how to build Progress City."

"If that's true . . ." Kate leaned in and looked to the book as well.

"Then this is priceless, and . . ." Hawk felt his pulse quicken. "It has details from Walt on how he was going to do the impossible . . . again." He pumped his fist. "I unlocked what never was . . ."

"And protected what is yet to be." Kate finished the thought for him.

Jonathan limped toward them from the entrance of the People Mover, holding something in both hands. Stopping before Hawk, he held out his hands and opened them to reveal five classic character collectable pins and one very old key. He laid them on top of the open book in Hawk's hands.

"I believe those belong to you." Jonathan pointed up to where he had come from. "I figured in all of the confusion, once everyone started snooping around, you had probably left some things back there you didn't want to explain."

Hawk looked at the pins and then back toward Jonathan. "Did you close it up?"

"Sure did. I pulled each pin out of the holding spot and then turned the key. It was actually cool, the church came rising up from nowhere—you know, that would be a great sermon illustration for you if we ever told anyone about this stuff—and then the control box just closed back up." Jonathan paused. "Did I get everything, or do I need to go back?"

"No, I think that is everything . . ." Hawk smiled at his friend. The gnawing doubt about Jonathan once again subsided, as he understood the rationale he had used to start up the attraction. It had been his way of alerting them there was trouble coming. Once Jonathan and Shep had figured out that Cambridge was going to take another shot at Hawk by entering through Space Mountain, they had needed to do something. It may not have been the best plan, but it was an attempt to help. Now he was giving back to Hawk essential pieces of the puzzle he had solved. Perhaps all the misgivings he was struggling with were nothing but coincidence.

"Not so fast." Kate leaned her head playfully on Hawk's shoulder, then straightened back up. "That is not everything. You have to help me figure out how to tell this story . . . because you know, no one will ever believe it. It's just too bizarre. They're going to think we made it up."

"Maybe you should just forget it and not tell it." Hawk closed up the book and placed the pins and key in one hand.

"Wait, that wasn't our deal," Kate argued.

"I know, I know. . . . We'll figure it out." Hawk slowly got to his feet and helped her up. As the group took their first few steps to leave Tomorrowland, Hawk winked toward his friends and said softly, "It's always about the story."

 One Year Later

SEATED AT FARREN'S RESERVED TABLE at Chef Mickey's in the Contemporary, Hawk watched across the empty restaurant as Farren Rales and George Colmes said their good-byes. George had informed them he was going to disappear again, this time into the Florida Keys, and retire for real. Not as a ghost, but as a beach bum. Rales laughed and told him he was becoming the old man and the sea. George knew it was time to go, as he'd fulfilled his most important task as Imagineer and trusted friend to the Disney brothers. He had helped to protect and pass along their dream.

The book that he had been responsible for all of these years had indeed been written by Walt Disney. It contained many of his notes, thoughts, and hopes about the experimental prototype community of tomorrow. He penned his fears alongside his plans for tackling what he knew would be problems and difficulties in making this place a reality. The journal also contained some much more detailed and outlined ideas of what Walt saw as important to remember and implement as he thought about an unknown future. Hawk had read and reread it. Those ideas and dreams, he was now entrusted to keep, hold, and chase.

The year had passed quickly, and once again, Hawk enjoyed his role as chief creative architect for the Disney Company. He was becoming more familiar with how things worked, and his influence rippled throughout the organization. The opposition he had faced in discovering the Disney journal had grown silent over the past twelve months. Reginald and Zeke had both been arrested and were currently spending some time in one of the state penitentiaries.

More troubling to Hawk was that the third accomplice he had faced had never been found; Nancy Alport had just disappeared, and this ever-present group of people who opposed him was still out there—he just didn't know where. Jonathan seemed not to have been involved. Even though Hawk periodically wondered about some of the things that had happened the previous year, Jonathan had stepped right back into being as consistent and constant in his friendship with Hawk and in his role with the rest of the group as he had ever been. The mysterious limp Jonathan had suddenly developed after they had been attacked at the Swamp Shack had bothered him so much that eventually he had asked his friend about it.

Jonathan offered to show him his foot to prove he hadn't been spiked that night. Hawk had laughed and told him it wouldn't be necessary. He didn't believe Jonathan was involved; those doubts had been created by Cambridge, and Hawk wrestled with why he had allowed his security chief to fool him in that way.

With a wave, George was gone, and Hawk got up to move toward his old friend Farren. Stepping up beside him, Hawk patted him on the back as they watched George disappear down an escalator.

"You gonna miss him?" Hawk asked.

"Yes, but I've been missing him since the 1970s. I have gotten used to it." Farren moved to head toward the escalator as well.

The two men followed the same path George had taken. They went down the escalator, walked around to the next, and then went down that moving staircase as well. Silently, they strode through the lobby of the Contemporary and were nearly out the door before Farren spoke again.

"Hawk, so what do you do with the instructions Walt gave you?"

"Funny you should ask. I have a few ideas I'd like to talk with you about," Hawk said. "Can I ask you something?"

"Of course." Farren stopped, as the automatic doors opened into the valet parking area. "What do you want to know?"

"As you have told me the story of the key to the kingdom, you told me there were three Imagineers. You . . . and you had the key itself. Then there is George, who had Walt's personal journal and dream book, and then another . . . who has . . ."

"Is there a question in there?"

"Who is the third Imagineer, and what is that person's role in this key-to-the-kingdom plan?"

"Hey, you!" A bright female voice came from a car whose door had just been pulled open by a valet.

Hawk and Farren turned to see the stunning Kate Young get out of the car and run across the walkway to greet them. She gave Farren a strong hug, then turned to Hawk.

"I was wondering if you were going to be here to greet me." She put both arms around his neck and kissed him.

Hawk and Kate had become an item over the past few months. Since the *Total Access* star had visited a year earlier and helped Hawk on his latest quest, the two had found more and more opportunities to spend time together. They mutually had decided to take it very slow, and did their best to keep their dating relationship from becoming the fodder of celebrity magazines and websites. So far it had gone very well. He wrapped his arm around her waist as he turned back to Farren.

"So, Farren, you were about to answer my question," Hawk stated.

"No, I wasn't." Farren smiled. "What I was about to do was to tell you both to have a good time catching up, and I will see you soon."

With a wink, Farren was gone. They watched him walk away, then turned to make their way toward the Magic Kingdom. Kate was in town for an event she was hosting at the Orange County Convention Center. Normally, it was the kind of thing she never would have considered attending. But lately, she had been agreeing to many more invitations that brought her closer to Central Florida.

Hawk had been finding reasons to fly into New York City more frequently as well. Although neither had mentioned it, they both knew they were starting to get more serious about the way their relationship was heading.

In the days after they had found the Disney journal, the two had fought and almost ended their friendship before it had the chance to begin. They hadn't been able to agree on how Kate was going to tell the story she had uncovered. Eventually, Farren Rales had helped them figure out how to make it work. Kate had written a book.

It was a work of fiction, and she wrote it under a pseudonym, because it was determined that writing it under her real name might be in conflict with her career as an investigative journalist. She had called the book *The Key to the Kingdom*. In it, she had chronicled the tale of Grayson Hawkes as he had been given a magical key that Walt Disney had chosen him to receive. The book, described as factual fiction, had received good reviews.

In an interview, Hawk had been asked about it and said it was just a work of silly fan fiction. He promised he hadn't read it, which he hadn't, and although she had embellished sections of the story, for the most part it was true. It had been an effective way to tell a story that she knew most would not believe. While she was in town, she had warned him that she was going to try to convince Hawk it was time to tell the next chapter of the story.

They paused on the corner, allowing traffic to pass them before they stepped over to the red-brick walkway that would take them to the Magic Kingdom entrance.

"You haven't told me you missed me yet." Kate once again leaned over to give him a kiss.

"I missed you, I promise." He leaned in to kiss her back. Then something caught his eye as they stood on the corner waiting for the traffic to pass and the light to change to red. Pulling away and looking toward a truck that was driving past, he glanced down with a puzzled look toward Kate. "Did you see that?"

"See what?" Kate looked in the direction he was gazing. "That truck?"

"Yes."

"It's just a panel truck. Why?"

"I thought I read something on the side, and it just didn't register quite right with me."

"What did you think you just read?" she asked, looking between him and the truck.

"I thought it said *Specter Cryogenic Labs . . .*"

*Afterword*
There is more treasure in books . . .

WALT DISNEY ONCE SAID, "There is more treasure in books that in all the pirates' loot on Treasure Island and at the bottom of the Spanish Main . . . and best of all, you can enjoy these riches every day of your life."

I am convinced that opening a book is like opening a treasure chest. You aren't always sure what you may find, but there will always be something of value. Perhaps it is something you can learn from; maybe it will be something that will inspire or challenge you; it might even move you emotionally; or, it might just make you smile and be a whole lot of fun. If you are still reading, I hope that as you turned each page, you have found some of those types of treasures hidden among the words, phrases, and paragraphs. I had a great time loading up this treasure chest for you.

This is my second journey with some of the characters in this story. I enjoyed getting to know them a little bit better, and if this is your second trip with them, I hope you did as well. If you somehow missed the first adventure with Grayson Hawkes, then this would be a good place to mention his arrival in the book *The Key to the Kingdom* (hint, hint, hint), but that would probably come across as a shameless plug, and I wouldn't want to do that.

Now, there were some things from the first story that didn't get thrown into this new treasure chest. The villains from the first adventure didn't show up again, there was an amazing audio-animatronic figure that didn't make it, there were some theme park changes that weren't mentioned, and there was a vague reference to something found on an almost magical DVD that somehow didn't get tossed in with the rest. Some of those things would have been nice to find, but I hope the treasure chest was full enough for you anyway.

This book was born in the heart of a huge fan of all things related to Walt Disney. From the theme parks to the motion pictures, I have fond memories of many great days of my life spent in the worlds Walt Disney created. Now to be sure, there is much in this book that is based on very real places that you can go and find for yourself. I hope you will. That is where the phrase *factual fiction* comes from. And if you do, then you can do a little mystery solving of your own, as you unlock a secret you never knew was there or that you find for the first time. In my opinion, that is some of the fun of going to Walt Disney World; there is always something to discover that you never knew was there before.

Sometimes, when I sit down with a book and open the pages, the places it takes me to come alive in my imagination. Walt Disney ignited my imagination as a child, and the places he built continue to ignite my imagination as an adult. I am honored that you took the journey with me. I sure don't take that for granted, and I hope that the time we spent moving through these pages allowed your imagination to kick into high gear, and that you had a little bit of fun.

So what does the future hold for these fictional characters we have met along the way? Ah, that is a good question. What Walt Disney once said about the story of Disneyland comes to mind: "It will never be completed. It will continue to grow as long as there is imagination left in the world." Time will give us that answer, I suppose. But if you do happen to find a treasure chest loaded with Disney secrets and a character they call Hawk inside . . . go ahead and take a look . . . after all, you do have the key.

Jeff Dixon
Writing this note at the Pirates of the Caribbean
The Magic Kingdom, Walt Disney World Resort

## Are You Ready To Unlock the Kingdom?

MOST OF THE QUESTIONS BELOW are answered within the pages of this novel. These are pieces of Disney history, Walt Disney World trivia, theme park stories, and discoveries that you can find on your own adventure to unlock the kingdom Walt Disney created. There are also a few bonus questions tossed in for you to do some additional research. Are you ready for the challenge?

Good luck.

### CHAPTER 1

1) There is a uniquely named souvenir stand on the edge of Adventure-land. What is the name of this stand?

2) *Bonus question (not found in the novel):* Do you know what famous actor it is named after?

### CHAPTER 3

3) What four different rivers do you travel along when riding the Jungle Cruise in the Magic Kingdom?

4) Name two of the boats used in the Jungle Cruise.

### CHAPTER 4

5) Whose influence and love for adventure and exploration served as the inspiration for Frontierland?

### CHAPTER 5

6) Name the former ceremony, featuring a drum and fife corps, that used to take place in Liberty Square in the Magic Kingdom?

7) What makes the Liberty Bell in Walt Disney World one of a kind?

8) What can you find in the Hall of Presidents attraction that can be displayed in only one other place, the Oval Office in the White House?

9) Who was the first president ever to record a message for the Hall of Presidents?

### CHAPTER 7

10) Why are there two lanterns placed in a window in Liberty Square?

## CHAPTER 8

11) What is the name of the ongoing Disney educational program designed for students?

## CHAPTER 11

12) What two words are combined to create the term Imagineering?

13) Who came up with this term?

## CHAPTER 12

14) What connects the Bay Lake Towers with the Contemporary Resort?

## CHAPTER 13

15) Where can you find Moonlight Bay?

16) What do cast members call the door on Moonlight Bay?

## CHAPTER 14

17) What do cast members call the tower in Pirates of the Caribbean?

## CHAPTER 20

18) What two resort hotels were opened along with the Magic Kingdom in 1971?

19) What attraction in the Magic Kingdom was closed and refurbished to create the Adventures of Winnie the Pooh?

## CHAPTER 21

20) What is the name of Walt Disney's aunt?

21) What was her job?

22) What were the names of Walt and Roy Disney's parents?

23) What is the name of the town where Walt Disney's parents were married?

24) What is Walt's cousin's name?

25) What is the last name of Walt's grandparents on his mother's side of the family?

## CHAPTER 23

26) What is the name of the cemetery Walt's grandparents are buried in?

27) What town in Florida is this cemetery in?

28) What is unusual about their grave marker?

## CHAPTER 29

29) In which pavilion at Epcot can you find the attraction Soarin'?

30) What is the flight number for the Soarin' ride?

31) What does the flight number represent?

32) *Bonus question*: At which other Disney theme parks can you find the Soarin' attraction?

33) What two other roles can you find the audio-animatronic model used for Teddy Roosevelt fulfilling in a different attraction?

34) What other role does James Buchanan have in a different attraction?

35) What does Dwight Eisenhower do in Spaceship Earth?

36) What artistic job does Ulysses Grant do in Spaceship Earth?

37) Who hits the golf ball in the film used on the attraction Soarin'?

## CHAPTER 32

38) What is the significance of Engine Co. 71 on the Fire Station in Town Square of the Magic Kingdom?

39) What is the name of the barber shop in the Magic Kingdom?

## CHAPTER 33

40) What is the name of the heavily advertised attraction that was never built in the Magic Kingdom?

41) What did workmen hide behind a wall in a 1981 refurbishment of the Walt Disney Story attraction in the Magic Kingdom?

42) What was the name of the talking owl associated with the above-mentioned attraction that has been lost over the years?

## CHAPTER 35

43) What real town inspired Walt to build Main Street USA?

44) What does the window on Main Street that honors the cast of WDW say?

45) What is the statue of Walt Disney and Mickey Mouse in the Central Park Hub called?

46) What does the quote from Walt Disney on this statue say?

## CHAPTER 37

47) How many hotels inspired the creation of the Hollywood Tower Hotel in Disney's Hollywood Studios?

48) Can you name the hotels from the question above?

49) What is the name of the produce market on Sunset Blvd. in Disney's Hollywood Studios?

50) In what theater did the Walt Disney Classic *Snow White and the Seven Dwarfs* premier?

51) Where can you find that theater in Disney's Hollywood Studios?

52) Who is Mortimer?

53) Where can you find Mortimer and Co. Contractors mentioned in Disney's Hollywood Studios?

54) What electric company building in Disney's Hollywood Studios bears the street number 1928?

55) Where can you find the entrance to Sunset Hills Estates?

56) What year were the Sunset Hills Estates established?

57) What famous Hollywood restaurant opened in 1928?

## CHAPTER 38

58) What year did the famous Chinese Theater in Hollywood really open?

59) How long is the actual track in the Great Movie Ride?

## CHAPTER 39

60) Where can you find the original desk Walt worked at while making the film *Snow White and the Seven Dwarfs*?

## CHAPTER 41

61) What provided the inspiration for the World Showcase at Epcot?

62) In which pavilion can you find the Toy Soldier?

63) Where can you find a window that overlooks the Hundred Acre Wood?

64) On what place in Epcot can you find the words *Otium Cum Dignitate*?

65) What do the words in the question above mean?

## CHAPTER 42

66) Who said, "I get red, white, and blue sometimes"?

67) What type of World War II plane, painted by Imagineer R. Tom Gilleon, is on display in the rotunda at the American Adventure in Epcot?

68) What is the title of the painting that features a teacher and her students in the American Adventure?

69) What two countries bookend the World Showcase at Epcot?

## CHAPTER 46

70) What year did the live action film *The Swiss Family Robinson* hit theaters for the first time?

71) How many steps do you have to navigate to explore the Swiss Family Robinson Treehouse in the Magic Kingdom?

72) What type of tree is the Swiss Family Robinson Treehouse nestled in?

73) What does this name actually mean?

74) How high is the Swiss Family Robinson Treehouse?

## CHAPTER 48

75) What can you find in the Magic Kingdom that is named for Imagineer Roger E. Broggie?

76) What is the name of the mining town in the Big Thunder Mountain Railroad?

## CHAPTER 49

77) Who is the man bailing water at Big Thunder Mountain?

78) What does his name mean?

## CHAPTER 50

79) What is the name of the waterway that surrounds Tom Sawyer's Island at the Magic Kingdom?

80) What is the name of the riverboat that circles the waterway from the question above?

81) Can you name the man you can find at the swamp shack in Alligator Swamp?

82) What is the name of the dog in the boat catching fish at Alligator Swamp?

## CHAPTER 53

83) Who is the fourth Earl of Sandwich?

## CHAPTER 57

84) How many triangular panels are placed on Spaceship Earth in Epcot? (*Note: This number will vary even among Disney archivists, historians, and researchers . . . so in this case, there are a variety of answers besides the number mentioned in the novel.*)

85) What was the restaurant at the top of the Contemporary resort formerly named?

## CHAPTER 59

86) How high is the top of Spaceship Earth at Epcot?

## CHAPTER 61

87) What was the Florida Project film about?

88) Who was the star of the Florida Project film?

89) Where can you see the Progress City model today?

## CHAPTER 62

90) Before it was called the Tomorrowland Transit Authority People Mover, what was the attraction called?

91) The Progress City model was originally on display in what place?

92) The Progress City model was originally displayed in another place as part of another attraction. Can you name that attraction?

## AFTERWORD

93) Where did Walt Disney believe you could find more treasure than on Treasure Island?

## EXTRA . . .

*If you really know your Walt Disney World history, then tackle or research the following questions:*

94) Where did Walt and Roy Disney hold the press conference to officially announce their plans to build Disney World?

95) What was the name of the theater where the Project Florida film premiered?

96) On what date did Walt Disney World officially open to the public?

97) On what date was Walt Disney World officially dedicated?

98) Who did the official dedication of Walt Disney World?

99) On what date did Pirates of the Caribbean open at Walt Disney World?

100) What is significant in Disney history about the date the Pirates attraction opened?

*Now, the questions above are just some of the little tidbits of information about Disney found in the pages of this novel. These pieces of Disney history, fact, and trivia are only part of the story. There is more to discover and always something new to find in a Walt Disney Resort. So have fun, and unlock the kingdom for yourself as you unravel the mysteries of Walt Disney.*

**To discover more, please follow author Jeff Dixon on Twitter @DixonOnDisney and The Key to the Kingdom Series on Facebook: www.facebook.com/KeyToTheKingdomBook.**

**The answers to these trivia questions can be found on the author's website: www.KeyToTheKingdomBook.com.**

The following resources were invaluable in understanding the background, history, operation, and attractions within Walt Disney World.

Canemaker, John. *Walt Disney's Nine Old Men & the Art of Animation*. New York: Hyperion, 2001.

Dunlop, Beth. *Building a Dream: The Art of Disney Architecture*. New York: Disney Editions, 2011.

Emerson, Chad Denver (editor). *Four Decades of Magic: Celebrating the First Forty Years of Disney World*. United States of America: Ayefour Publishing, 2011.

Gabler, Neal. Walt Disney: *Triumph of the American Imagination*. New York: Knopf, 2006.

Gennawy, Sam. *Walt and the Promise of Progress City*. United States of America: Ayefour Publishing, 2011.

Gordan, Bruce and Kurtti, Jeff. *Walt Disney World: Then, Now and Forever*. New York: Disney Editions, 2008.

Green, Katherine and Richard. *The Man Behind the Magic: The Story of Walt Disney*. New York: Viking, 1991.

Hench, John. *Designing Disney: Imagineering and the Art of the Show*. New York: Disney Editions, 2003.

Imagineers. *Walt Disney Imagineering: A Behind the Dreams Look at Making the Magic*. New York: Hyperion, 1996.

Imagineers. *The Imagineering Field Guide to Epcot at Walt Disney World*. New York: Disney Editions, 2006.

Imagineers. *The Imagineering Field Guide to the Magic Kingdom at Walt Disney World*. New York: Disney Editions, 2005.

Kurtti, Jeff. *Imagineering Legends and the Genesis of the Disney Theme Park*. New York: Disney Editions, 2008.

Marling, Karal Ann. *Designing Disney's Theme Parks*. New York: Flammarion, 1997.

Miller, Diane Disney and Martin, Pete. *The Story of Walt Disney*. New York: Holt, 1957.

Mongello, Louis A. *The Walt Disney World Trivia Book*. Branford, CT: The Intrepid Traveler, Vol. 1, 2004; Vol.2, 2006.

Neary, Kevin and Smith, David. *The Ultimate Disney Trivia Book*. New York: Hyperion, 1992.

———. *The Ultimate Disney Trivia Book 2*. New York: Hyperion, 1994.

———. *The Ultimate Disney Trivia Book 3*. New York: Hyperion, 1997.

———. *The Ultimate Disney Trivia Book 4*. New York: Disney Editions, 2000.

Pedersen, R. A. *The Epcot Explorer's Encyclopedia*. Florida, USA: Epcyclopedia Press, 2011.

Peri, Don. *Working with Walt: Interviews with Disney Artists.* Jackson, MS: Univ. Press of Mississippi, 2008.

Ridgeway, Charles. *Spinning Disney's World: Memories of a Magic Kingdom Press Agent.* Branford, CT: Intrepid Traveler, 2007.

Smith, Dave and Clark, Steven. *Disney: The First 100 Years.* New York: Hyperion, 1999; Disney Editions, updated 2002.

——. *The Quotable Walt Disney.* New York: Disney Editions, 2001.

——. *Disney A to Z: the Official Encyclopedia.* New York: Hyperion, 1996; updated 1998, 2006.

Thomas, Bob. *The Art of Animation.* New York: Simon & Schuster, 1958.

——. *Walt Disney: An American Original.* New York: Simon & Schuster, 1976.

——. *Building a Company; Roy O. Disney and the Creation of an Entertainment Empire.* New York: Hyperion, 1998.

Thomas, Frank and Johnston, Ollie. *The Illusion of Life: Disney Animation.* New York: Hyperion, 1995.

Vennes, Susan. *The Hidden Magic of Walt Disney World: Over 600 secrets of the Magic Kingdom, Epcot, Disney's Hollywood Studios, and Animal Kingdom.* Avon, MA: Adams Media, 2009.

Walt Disney Productions. "The EPCOT Film," script by Marty Sklar. The Walt Disney Company, 1996. Available in *Walt Disney Treasures: Tomorrowland* DVD, 2004.

Walt Disney World Explorer CD-ROM. Burbank, CA: Disney Interactive, 1996.

Wright, Alex. *The Imagineering Field Guide to the Magic Kingdom at Walt Disney World.* New York: Disney Editions, 2005.

Yee, Kevin. *101 Things You Never Knew About Walt Disney World.* Second Edition. Orlando, Florida: Ultimate Orlando Press, 2009.

## WEBSITES

These are *a few* of the author's favorite Disney news and fan sites that helped provide information and resources beyond the printed page.

The WDW Radio Show, http://www.wdwradio.com.

Inside the Magic w/ Ricky Brigante, http://www.distantcreations.com.

Jim Hill Media, http://www.jimhillmedia.com.

Theme Parkology: 2719 Hyperion, http://www.2719hyperion.com.

Resort Information, http://www.mouseplanet.com.

DIS, http://www.wdwinfo.com.

Walt Disney World News, http://www.wdwmagic.com.